CU00865094

Starstruck

C. Smith & B. Spackman

Copyright © 2020 Casey Smith and Bridget Spackman

All rights reserved

The characters and events portrayed in this book are fictitious. Any similarity to real persons, living or dead, is coincidental and not intended by the author.

No part of this book may be reproduced, or stored in a retrieval system, or transmitted in any form or by any means, electronic, mechanical, photocopying, recording, or otherwise, without express written permission of the publisher.

ISBN: 978-1-5272-6216-4

For all the people who are opening this book already knowing the story.

The ones who rode the rollercoaster chapter by chapter as we wrote it.

The friends who got excited with us at each twist.

The family who pointed out plot holes and grammatical errors.

And the strangers online whose interest we piqued that Beta read it for us.

We couldn't have done it without you.

Chapter 1

Jonathan

This was always the best and worst part. Every year, the weekend before school started, we'd disappear into the woods. We'd drink, laugh…and confess. The last part was crucial. It was a tradition we'd started back when the world seemed so much smaller. We knew we'd need this closeness to remind ourselves who we were, before the world chewed us up and spat us out. Everyone had a turn. And everyone listened. One by one we'd admit something no one else knew. Mostly it was something that happened the previous year, but some secrets went deeper.

This year finality thickened in the air. Next year we'd have graduated. We could try keeping the tradition intact, college and careers taking precedent. But things would change. There was no avoiding it.

I fixed my gaze on the flames, watching as they curled. My thumb skimmed the neck of my beer bottle, the fierce orange of the fire twisting into a deep red before the color shifted again, electric blue spreading from the base and swallowing the flames before purple tendrils reached to lick the night air.

"Are we boring you?"

I reluctantly dragged my gaze away to look over at Will, his dark eyebrows rising as he watched me. His hulking frame shuffled uncomfortably in the limited space of the camping chair as he stretched himself out, his eyes boring into me as he waited. With a sigh I rolled my eyes, reigning in my powers and locking them down. The rush of magic stilled in my veins, ebbing beneath the surface and waiting for me to release it once again. I ignored the smirk on Will's face as he grabbed another beer, looking at the bonfire roaring in the center of the group as the flames burnt orange once more.

Everyone here knew the big secret. The one that tied us together.

The secret that started when our dad's found themselves in the middle of a superhuman storm when they were barely older than us, the sky twisting in on itself and the heavens screaming back. The way my dad tells it it was like a scene from a movie, darkness engulfing them as lightning split the sky. Until the strike that knocked them all unconscious.

After they woke they noticed a new energy surging within them, their veins pulsing with electricity, darkness fighting to escape their bodies and wreak havoc. The world dropped at their feet, whatever they desired attainable in the blink of an eye. But little by little they learned to control it, to claim a hold over it rather than the other way around.

All but one.

But we don't talk about him.

Our parents soon realized the power wasn't limited to just those in the storm, and the eldest son was born with the gift. A strange sort of voodoo heirloom. But to be honest, I liked them. The ability to conjure or manipulate whatever you desired…Who wouldn't want that?

I cast an anxious glance back to Will, his posture visibly more relaxed as he noted the change in my eyes, the ethereal shine of the powers disappearing and being replaced by my usual green tones. I understood why he wasn't keen on his bag of tricks, why he'd tried to stop using once he'd come of age and reached the peak of his superhuman gift. Why he was always glancing to his brother, David, across the clearing.

"So, who's volunteering to go first?" I arched an eyebrow, sitting back in my chair. Across the flames a set of dark brown eyes looked my way, the amber hues of the fire reflected in her gaze. She started as she saw me look back, a smile playing on her lips as she glanced away quickly. The corner of my mouth twitched into a smirk as I watched her, before drawing my gaze around the group slowly.

"I'll go." A voice submitted.

Ash leaned forward to retrieve the small velvet pouch nestled amongst the rocks by the fire. His blonde head bowed as he weighed the bag in his palm, idly toying with the strings of the bag as he opened it. "I found divorce papers in my dad's office."

The atmosphere in the group stilled, beers pausing on the way to mouths. Alex and Will shot an anxious glance my way before the former patted his best friend on the back, his hand lingering in the gesture.

"How're you doing?" a soft voice murmured from across the circle.

I glanced across at Brooke, watching as she tucked a strand of dark brown hair behind her ear. Her doe eyes were still alight with that amber quality, like the fire itself had nestled there.

Ash met her gaze, shrugging. "I haven't said anything yet. I'm not sure if I should…"

"Try to think positive. I know it looks bad, but...were they signed?"

"No." He considered with a smile, the weight lifting from his tan shoulders as he straightened. "They weren't."

He reached inside the pouch, more relaxed than I'd seen him lately as he pulled out a handful of onyx dust, the grains glittering as they caught the light from the fire. He glanced around anxiously as he cradled the powder in his palm. When we first christened this spot with our confessions lying had been rife, all for the sake of pride. So we'd brought a little magic into the game. Once the dust met the fire it simply burned up with a crackle of sparks if you were honest, but liars would be ousted by the flames, the magic reacting to the heat and turning them a vivid red. Ash took a shallow breath as he tossed the sand, his shoulders relaxing further as it gave a sharp crackle and welcomed the powder, the flames licking the sky unchanged.

Since that first trip no one dared lie again.

Over the course of the hour each of us revealed a sliver of the unseen as we bared our secrets, the sun setting over the lake as darkness began to fall. One secret in particular had us all topping up our beers and raising a toast as Lucas admitted he was finally seeking help and had weekly visits with a shrink. The past year had taken its toll on the youngster of the group, and all of us had taken his cry for help personally.

Other secrets were easier to swallow as a whole; Nathan admitting he'd had his first kiss, or David divulging his newfound love of acting. And some were decidedly more difficult. Alex admitting his long-distance girlfriend didn't want to be exclusive and wanted to keep things as casual as possible. Or my twin sister, Rosie, following that up by saying she and Alex had slept together since. A fact I both wanted to ignore and acknowledge. Rosie hooking up with Lucas had so far been easy to disregard - they kept it to themselves and it didn't affect me. But Alex was in the band. He was an integral part of my future, and I couldn't have this one night stand affecting our friendship.

He avoided my stare as I made a mental note to talk to him before our next practice. Somewhere less public.

The air lightened when Will took his turn. The biggest secret in his life was already out, so he settled with telling us he'd quit the football team. I earned myself a reproachful look from him when I celebrated. I'd never understood his need to play high school football, it just didn't fit with who he was. The only reason he joined was to get out the anger issues he liked to pretend we didn't know about.

But now he could spend more time doing something he actually *wanted* to do. Drumming in the band, for example.

We all knew when it came to the band, I took it extremely seriously. It wasn't just some pastime or hobby. Or even something casual to do with my friends so that we could say we'd tried it. I wanted to play to millions. I wanted our songs to live on and get covered by other artists, simply because they loved a track so much they had to sing along. I wanted to create and keep creating. There was no until for me. No retirement plan or day job I'd considered. But I knew the others had. They loved the band, but they also knew that it was a long shot and might not work out. They had other options, other possibilities they could live with.

Not me.

I wanted to work my way up and keep going. There was no room for an alternative. It didn't help to inspire them that the majority of gigs we got demanded covers, and I abhorred them. It was too much like karaoke. That was the whole point in our name, The Plagiarists. But I'd swallowed my pride on more times than I cared to admit, hopeful that I'd make a connection at one of the dive bars and worm our way into something. So far that optimism hadn't been rewarded. Sure, I could just wave my fingers in the air and magic us into success and fame. But that wasn't what I wanted. We'd either make it the right way or burn out trying. I sincerely hoped it would be the former.

Especially now Will's interests weren't split.

I glanced across to watch the white sparks leaping at the warm night air as he threw his handful of dust, smiling weakly as I looked back to the waiting pouch in his outstretched hand. Great.

I took it from him, weighing the remainder of the dust as I chewed over my words. I didn't have many secrets, and there was only one that I could think of. That I kept thinking of. My eyes rose to meet Brooke's, my smirk dissolving as I saw her staring back nervously. We both knew what she thought I might say. But that felt more like her secret to tell than mine. If she wanted to.

"Okay…" I let out a breath, my gaze still locked on hers. "Mine is that I have a crush."

Her lips parted in surprise as she looked at me curiously, her dark eyes narrowing.

"Is it on yourself?" My sister laughed, raising an eyebrow.

I frowned and peered around the group. Everyone looked skeptical. But, to be fair, this was new to me too. I'd only recently labeled it a crush. It had started with a flirtatious glance, a coy smile…and then a kiss to end all kisses. For years I'd written songs for our band and with each lyric I'd tried to imagine what it would be like to be in love. To physically ache for that person…and like it. To know with utter, terrifying certainty that they owned your heart. That you wanted them to. But it had felt false. For so long I'd scrawled lyrics in a notebook, trying to capture something I'd never even glimpsed. I was a fraud. But ever since that kiss I'd definitely had a taste of something and try as I might to brush it off, I couldn't. With each passing day I'd noticed more about her that had always been there, but I'd overlooked. How I could have seemed unfathomable now. But I had. And I was kicking myself.

"Great reception there, guys." I smirked, rolling my eyes as I grabbed a handful of dust from the pouch. The grains scratched against my palm as I tossed it onto the fire, looking past the luminous white sparks to see Brooke still watching me. Her expression was unreadable as she held my gaze. "I think you're the only one left." I rose from my seat, leaning around the fire to pass her the bag.

She smiled shyly as she outstretched her hand, her fingertips brushing mine and her cheeks flaming as she quickly reclaimed her seat.

She emptied the remainder of the contents into her palm, her manicured nails tracing waves through the sand as she took a breath. "Well...I've had my first kiss too."

My gaze flew to hers, my heartbeat quickening as I watched her. She stared down at the granite dust, weighing it in her hand gently. Colour began to warm her cheeks as all eyes fell on her, her dark waves providing a curtain of privacy.

"You have?" Nathan frowned.

She nodded, still not acknowledging me.

"Who?" Ash asked, raising an eyebrow.

Her eyes finally flickered to meet mine for just a second, her fingertips hovering above the dust as she gave a small shrug. "Some guy."

Some guy?! Really?

"Was it good?" Rosie waggled her eyebrows with a grin.

Brooke blushed further, deliberately avoiding my gaze again as she smiled. "It was."

I sat forward in my chair, raising an eyebrow with a smirk. "I'll bet it was amazing."

She looked up at me, her doe eyes wide. "I won't be kissing him again, so it doesn't matter."

I frowned, wounded. Had I misread the situation completely? Was it really only me that had felt the kiss was the start of something…and not the end.

Brooke threw the dust into the fire as though it had burned her, bowing her head as she sealed the now barren pouch, silence descending on us awkwardly.

"So," Ash grinned, clapping his hands together. "Do we all feel better?"

"I do." Lucas laughed, standing up. "Now let's get drunk!"

I shared the sentiment, catching a fresh beer as Will shared them out, trying and failing to stop looking in Brookes direction. Her body was turned into David's as they chatted, her laugh echoing through the clearing as she playfully nudged him with her knee. I narrowed my eyes at the gesture, reminding myself that they were just friends.

Eventually Rosie and Lucas joined the two of them in conversation, Nathan following shortly after as the band huddled on the opposite side of the fire, talking shop as usual. I sensed the tension that had begun to weave through the four of us, Ash bringing up whether we had anything lined up in the future and Alex asking about what we were doing about college. But my mind was elsewhere, still running over Brookes admission.

After my third cigarette, when I was still no closer to figuring out her intentions, I rose to my feet and tossed down my empty bottle. The guys looked up at me curiously. I had an ace up my sleeve, and I intended to use it. "Who's up for a little game of truth or dare?"

"Obviously." Alex chuckled, rolling his eyes.

The separate groups congregated around the fire once more, the flames less fierce while still stifling in the already humid night. Hands grabbed at fresh drinks, grins eager. I locked eyes with Brooke for the briefest of seconds. Did she know I was hoping someone would call her out on a truth and ask who her mystery first kiss was? If they did would she lie? Or would she tell them about the night we explored the possibility of whatever was between us?

"You first then Taylor." Will grinned, sitting forward again. "Truth or dare."

"Easy. Dare."

He shook his head, smirking as he took a sip of his drink. "Damnit, was hoping for truth." I'm sure he was. I knew I'd opened myself up for questions about my crush too, but as long as Brookes feelings were concealed, mine would remain the same. "Okay, I dare you to jump in the lake. Fully clothed. No magic to dry off."

"And deprive everyone of my nakedness? You're a cruel man."

He grimaced, laughing. "No one wants to see that."

My gaze traveled out to the dark lake a short distance away. The patches of grass and dirt tapered off, the black water still as it reflected the moonlight. In this heat it might even be refreshing.

Casting a glance back around the group, I extinguished my cigarette. Brooke met my eyes shyly, her mouth forming a small smile as she cradled her drink. I tore my gaze away and smirked as I took off at a run, my legs picking up pace as I closed the gap between me and the lake. I kicked off, laughing as I leaped through the air and came crashing into the water. The weight of it dragged me down, my eyes scrunching shut as I swam back to the surface. I shook the dregs from my hair as I broke into the warm night air, the heat smothering compared to the cold depths beneath. I trod water, my arms pushing me to reach land.

I was welcomed back with cheers. Will pressed a cold beer into my hand as I reclaimed my seat, the heat from the fire already drying my sodden clothes.

As the night wound down, the moon moving across the sky as the hour grew later, I avoided every truth I could. I noted with dejection each time Brooke glanced my way that she was doing the same. She knew exactly what was going on.

Instead we watched as our friends admitted which ones in the group they'd ghost, who they thought would be the best kisser or the one most likely to end up in prison. We laughed as Nathan accepted a dare to streak, holding his boxers to cover his modesty as he sprinted between the trees, his inhibitions slipping with every beer he drank. David was dared to let someone send a text to one of his contacts, and Alex cringed as he was forced into drinking half a bottle of whiskey neat, raucous laughter ringing out as he turned and vomited into a bush. My own stomach clenched when Rosie was dared to kiss Nathan, ignoring the way he held her as their lips met.

She beamed at him as she pulled away, her gaze turning to Brooke as she slipped back into her seat. "Truth or dare?"

"Hmm." Brooke grinned, "I think this time I'll say..." Her eyes locked on mine as I sat up, sure that she was about to finally say truth. "Dare."

Or not.

"Okay," Rosie smirked, her eyebrow arching. "I dare you to kiss the most attractive guy here."

Her gaze met mine uncertainly, a pinkish tinge warming her cheeks. Slowly, she stood and placed her drink by her chair. Her head bowed as she smoothed out her top, her chocolate hair falling in loose tendrils. She peered from between them, tucking a few strands behind her ear as she slowly made her way around the circle. My heart began to thump faster. I hoped it didn't show on the outside just how eager I was for her to settle on me.

Her dark eyes assessed me as she walked with deliberation, a smile settling on her lips as she got closer. A smirk warmed my own and I sat up further, placing my beer by my feet. She bit her lip as she continued and stopped before Ash, moving to sit on his knee. My jaw dropped as she reached out to stroke his cheek, her lips coming to crash against his.

He seemed as shocked as I was, but certainly a lot happier. He held her to him as he returned the kiss with a low groan, his hands caressing her. I tore my gaze away, setting my jaw as I tried to tune them out.

After what felt like an eternity they broke apart with breathless laughs. I glanced back as she got back to her feet, her cheeks flushed as she moved towards her chair.

"Well, I'm having a great time." Ash grinned stupidly.

I rolled my eyes, averting them quickly as I noticed Brooke watching me.

"I aim to please." She smiled softly, raising an eyebrow. "So, I'll let you choose how we proceed."

Ash nodded, the grin still etched onto his face. "Truth."

"On a scale of one to ten how glad are you that I kissed you?"

My veins began to burn as though scolded by fresh steam, my heartbeat quickening. I looked down at the dirt by my feet and stood up, conjuring a cigarette. My fingers were beginning to tremble as I placed it between my lips, my eyes closing as I moved back from the circle a few feet.

"I would say a definite nine."

"And what could have made it a ten?"

"A little more privacy." He smirked.

I let out a steady stream of smoke, my eyes still closed as I tried to conceal – and push back – the waves of fire building within me. I felt a sharp stab of pain at my fingertips and opened my eyes, frowning as I realized I'd burned the cigarette down in one swoop. So much so that tiny embers floated up with the smoke. I looked over at Brooke nervously, magically repairing the cigarette before it became too obvious.

Brooke's eyes flickered to meet mine. "Maybe when my brother isn't around to kick your ass."

"Kick my ass?" Ash frowned.

Nathan raised an eyebrow, his gaze serious. "You think I won't?"

Ash fell silent, smiling wanly at the threat. Sometimes it was easy to forget how imposing Nathan could be. He didn't have the powers thanks to his older brother James, and he wasn't as physically intimidating as some of us, but that didn't hold him back from asserting his role as protective big brother. Especially where Brooke was concerned.

"Uh…I think I'm gonna head to bed." Brooke smiled, letting out a small yawn as she placed a hand on Nathan's shoulder with a soft smile. I couldn't tell if it was genuine or she was trying to cool the tension. Her eyes met mine as she stretched, glancing around at the group. "Beauty sleep is beckoning."

Rosie nodded, getting to her feet. "It is getting pretty late."

"Want some company?" Lucas raised an eyebrow.

She looked between him and Brooke, her mouth curving into a smile as Brooke gave a small nod. "Always."

He grinned, offering his arm to her as they headed for a tent without even looking back. I grimaced, glancing toward Brooke just in time to see her disappearing towards her own.

"I advise you against trying to follow her…"

I blanched, looking around at the voice sheepishly. But it hadn't been aimed at me.

Ash laughed as he nodded over to Alex, holding up his hands. "Yeah, I think I'll just bunk with you if that's cool? Keep us both out of trouble."

"You wanna be the big spoon or the little spoon?" Alex teased, the two of them downing their drinks before breaking off.

Will sidled over to me, his gaze uncertain as he looked between Nathan and David. His only remaining choices the brother who shot him suspicious looks or the Italian boy scout who'd make him feel guilty for breathing if he could prove it was a tactic to get at his sister. I didn't envy him. Nor did I especially want either of those options myself.

"I'm crashing with you." He muttered, raising an eyebrow as he finished his drink.

I nodded, watching as Nathan and David headed off to the remaining tent in silence. Will let out a breath as he watched his brother go.

His dark eyes met mine as he took a step towards our home for the night. "You coming?"

I nodded again, dumbly, but my gaze was fixed on a completely different tent. "I'll sort the fire and be right there."

He offered a shrug, disappearing from sight as he slunk to bed. I turned my gaze back to the fire, my eyes altering as the flames threaded through with magic. They gasped and died, tendrils of smoke escaping into the night air. I looked past the orange remnants of the fire, dropping my cigarette to the floor as I took in a measured breath. I knew what I should do. Go and sleep, let this night and its secrets stay in the woods. Let the kiss die here. Hopefully the one between her and Ash with it. But then I'd been trying for months to forget about it. And yet here we were. Dancing around the campfire, uncertain whether it meant something…or nothing. I knew how I felt. But could I live without knowing how she felt? Could I pretend that the voices niggling away at me weren't screaming that she must regret it? Not because the kiss was terrible, because it wasn't. At all. But because it had been with me?

Chapter 2

Brooke

The night air closed in on me as I ducked into the tent I'd claimed as my own, the stifling humidity from the outside only magnifying as I took one last glance at the dying embers of the campfire and zipped myself into the canvas shelter, flicking the switch on the portable lamp I'd stolen from Nathan and illuminating the cozy space. Moisture coated my skin, my clothes sticking to me and my hair dropping from their curls as I took in a suffocating breath and lowered myself onto the sleeping bags I'd previously laid out with Rosie.

Lighting the fire wasn't the smartest idea when it was already so smothering, but it was tradition. And sitting alone I realized it might be the last time we lit it and shared our secrets. The last time we'd tipsily struggle with the zipper on our tents and collapse into giggling heaps. I fixed my eyes on Rosie's empty sleeping bag beside me and grinned.

She'd definitely be leaving our camping trips with a bang.

Kicking off my wedges, I stretched my long tan legs out and rolled my neck from side to side. I felt, and ultimately quashed, the urge to sing. Or yell. Or even laugh. Just to break the silence that settled so oddly around me. Ignoring my loneliness in her absence.

This was just another sign we were growing up.

Rosie and I had been best friends all our lives. We'd grown up together thanks to our parents, and obviously shared a common family secret because of the storm. But that wasn't why Rosie and I were so close. It helped. But there was more to it than being made to spend time together as petulant toddlers.

Rosie was so easy to get along with, and found a reason to smile in every situation. She was carefree and quirky, and...nice! She had something kind to say about everyone. Sure, she could be a little naive, but hell...so was I!

As the only girl in two generations of a big Italian family I was protected. Shielded from suggestive conversations and eager teenage boys. Daddy made sure our friends knew I was off-limits. And in the times he wasn't there Nathan was more than happy to pick up the job.

Which is why my little escapade with Jonathan, and the butterflies I felt whenever I thought about it, were going to remain a secret. Well, that, and the fact that I was certain finding out his sisters best friend had a crush on him was probably going to be the end of our friendship.

Jonathan wasn't the type of boy my family would approve of me bringing home either. He was reckless, arrogant, and *too* charismatic. He charmed everyone, and did it with that signature smirk etched onto his face, his intense green eyes staring into your soul as he wore you down. And before you knew it you were putty in his hands. I'd watched him do it with countless girls. He made you feel like you were the only one he'd ever noticed. The way he spoke to you, his eyes shifting between gazing deeply into yours and flickering to your lips. His fingers gently brushing stray hairs from your face, softly grazing your skin in such a calculated way that it totally made it seem like an accident. The way his body shifted to yours...

They all knew what he was like, that he enjoyed the chase and would move on once he'd gotten his way. And yet they all succumbed.

Just like I would.

I tried to shake him out of my head, dropping back onto the floor and lifting my hips as I wiggled out of my denim shorts. This wasn't the time to get caught up in Jonathan fantasies and what-ifs. I'd had enough Dutch courage to head over there. So instead I stripped down to my underwear, grabbed an old Cosmo I'd stashed away, and tried to ignore the voice in my head that kept muttering that 'bumping' into him barely dressed would push things in my favor. But even with my head still hazy with alcohol it wasn't what I really wanted. I didn't want to lose my virginity as some drunken fumble in the woods after throwing myself at him. No, Jonathan had made his feelings pretty clear after we shared that first kiss. I was inexperienced and he didn't find in me what he sought out in all those other girls. Most likely a casual attitude towards sex and a few notches on their own bedposts.

And so here I was, idly flicking through the top ten fashion disasters in a magazine I'd probably read cover to cover at least once before.

As I turned the page, already bored with the article, my ears pricked up on the crunch of gravel outside. My eyes didn't waver as the zipper slid up and a body shifted into the enclosed space.

I knew she'd forget.

Until fairly recently Rosie had been a member of the virgin club. This time last year we were the majority; now it was just four of us.

To say Lucas had seduced Rosie would make him sound like some kind of deviant, but it wasn't like that. The two of them had a friendship that had blossomed into something *more*, and eventually they'd taken the step all teenagers do. The lines between them blurring, yet ultimately staying in place. But when they needed a more intimate comfort than a cuddle on a rainy day, they had each other.

Which was why I found it so amusing that Lucas didn't have a condom. "There's some in my purse. I knew you guys would forget."

"Forget what?"

The deep voice surprised me, my head shooting up to look at the smirking face of Jonathan Taylor. His eyes swept my body, his eyebrow slowly rising as he caressed every inch of my exposed flesh with his hungry stare.

"Shit. Jonathan..." I dropped the magazine, holding my hands against myself to try and regain some dignity as I flushed red. "What're you doing?" Was I dreaming? Had I fallen asleep reading and my brain was indulging me in the fantasy I was trying to fight off? Or maybe he'd accidentally wandered into the wrong tent.

Oh crap...was I in the wrong one?

He took a quick glance out at the other tents, frowning as he waited a second. He shrugged and pulled the zip halfway, turning his gaze on me once more, this time more serious than amused. "I just wanted to check something..."

"Umm...Okay?"

He lowered himself onto the empty sleeping bag across from me, watching carefully as I moved to sit up, still trying to cover my half-naked body.

He cleared his throat. "Do you regret our kiss?"

No. God no.

"Why would you think that?"

His shoulders rose and fell as he shrugged, not quite meeting my eyes. "I just wanted to make sure. You've been kinda cagey with me tonight."

"I have?"

He nodded, "A little." His lips turned up in a weak smile, but it didn't quite meet his eyes. "I'm not asking you to fawn over me or anything, I just don't want you to regret that it was me."

Oh, I was fawning over him.

I stared down at my hands, resting awkwardly in my lap. "I don't regret it." I dared a glance at him, "Do you?"

I wasn't sure why I was asking. If he didn't regret it that would be great, but what if he did? What if that kiss, that magical kiss, that I thought about every day, was just him taking pity on me? He knew I wouldn't get another boy alone. Even tonight Nathan was around. Did he feel bad because he didn't want me to leave school as a virgin that had never been kissed?

Oh God, he'd still not answered.

The silence was stretching on ominously when his fingers reached out, lifting my chin until my eyes met his. He was smiling mischievously. "Not even a little bit."

"Really?" I whispered, fighting a smile

"How could I?" He moved, sitting beside me. As he shifted the tension jumped several notches, the thick air of the night inescapable as his body brushed against mine. My knee was on fire where his thigh rested against it, my waist tingling as his bare arm brushed my skin.

"I..." I flushed again, falling under the spell of his gaze."I'm not as experienced as your usual type."

His brow furrowed as he looked at me carefully. Could he see how nervous he made me? "You know I don't care about that, right?"

Didn't he? Did he honestly not mind that I was a virgin? That I was naive and inexperienced compared to all those other girls who had willingly surrendered themselves to him...

"I think we both know I'm not the girl you end up with."

"Maybe not." He admitted with a weak smile, "But that doesn't mean it wasn't a hell of a kiss."

"It was. The best I've had."

"As Ash is my only competition that doesn't mean much." There was that Jonathan Taylor smirk again. "But thank you. It was the best I've ever had too."

Now I was definitely blushing. I was the best kiss he'd ever had? Or was that just another line to get to his end goal? Did I care if it was?

Surely I had more self-respect than that.

"Have you..." I met his eyes, unsure why I wanted to take the conversation down this route other than to torture myself further. "Have you kissed the girl you like?" I had an idea who it might be, only one girl fit the picture, but I needed the confirmation.

Jen.

She'd never personally done anything to me, hell, if it wasn't for her I might never have gotten such a crush on Jonathan. Or, I realized with a start, kissed him. But never the less I couldn't bear the idea that he had feelings for her, feelings that stretched beyond their friends with benefits relationship. Especially because on paper she was perfect for him. An Indie chick with an affinity for frequenting gigs and festivals. I'd seen them around Boston together, and to say they often saw each other naked the atmosphere between them was more relaxed than expected.

His fingertips brushed my cheek, all bravado disappearing from his smirk as he assessed me, my body turning into his as I lost my train of thought. "I have..."

"Have you done more with her?" Seriously Brooke, why are you still pushing this?!

"I've wanted to..."

Oh. He'd not...I fought a blush, ignoring the fluttering in my stomach.

It wasn't Jen!

"But?"

"I guess I'm afraid."

"Of?"

I bit my lip, shaking from anticipation. The tension reached an all-new height. I didn't know if it was the alcohol, the humidity, or the enclosed space, but all I could think of was how nothing else mattered but the two of us here, in this tent. And what was about to happen.

I could taste it in the air, the excitement and trepidation as his body moved into mine, our faces inches apart as I responded to his touch, letting him lead me into his warm embrace as his hand grazed my cheek. "Losing her..."

And then his lips brushed mine.

My breath rushed from me, my arms winding around him as I melted into his body, feeling every contour of his abs through the thin fabric of his tee. I didn't care that I was half-naked. I didn't care that anyone could hear us and come and investigate. I didn't even care that by the morning he could regret it all and avoid me. Right now he wanted me, and I wanted him. And that was that. It didn't have to be complicated. We could just stop fighting it and let it happen.

His lips turned into a smirk against the kiss, his fingertips softly stroking my cheek as his other hand wound into my hair, gripping me firmly. His tongue separated my lips, his groan reverberating against my mouth as my own tongue met his. My hands moved down from his shoulders, my fingertips caressing his muscles as they shifted under his band tee.

Could he feel the way my heart sped up when he flexed against me? Or how hazy my head was as I gave myself over to him. I was giddy.

Euphorically so. And when he pulled away I'd be grinning like the Cheshire Cat. And he would have to pull away. Because under no uncertain circumstances was I going to. I would sit here, pressed against him and kissing him until the sun came up if he let me.

But he wouldn't. And all too soon he'd pulled away.

His hands were still holding me, his breathing almost as heavy as mine as he looked at me. There was a glint in his eye that I'd never seen before. It was excited and...guarded. Shy even.

My brain suddenly caught up with me, replaying the conversation we were having right before that kiss. Those few delicious seconds where time slowed. Jonathan was scared of losing her. Of losing the girl he was crushing on.

Was...was that girl...me?

You don't have kisses like that every day. I didn't have much experience with boys, but I felt it in my gut. I just knew. I'd kissed Ash only hours ago, and while it was sweet, and soft and everything I'd been told a kiss would be, it was nothing compared to kissing Jonathan. I doubted it was because Jonathan was a phenomenal kisser, which he was, but because he was kissing me. Because I was kissing him.

It was that first kiss all over again. Only this time there was more desire behind it, more want. More need. It was so much more intense.

"Do you know the effect you have on me?"

Letting out a soft chuckle I ran a finger along his bicep, admiring the bulge of his tensed muscle as he held me. "Probably the same effect I have on most guys?" I arched a dark eyebrow, smiling coyly.

Jonathan brushed a stray hair from my face, his lips tugging into a lazy smirk once more. "One day you'll have an ego to rival mine."

Grinning I shook my head and pressed my lips back against his, enjoying the erratic thump of my heart. "Doubt it." I murmured, "Yours is huge."

The feel of his smirk growing against my lips let me know the innuendo landed. His mouth moving against mine as we kissed once more let me know he appreciated it.

This time we wasted no time testing the water. His tongue met mine almost instantly, my arms tangled around him as I pulled him down, the weight of his body adding to the thrill of finally being able to do what I'd fantasized about. His hands expertly caressed my curves, stroking my side and gripping my hips, pinning me in place. I couldn't deny how excited I was. My body crying out for more. I broke the kiss as I yanked his top over his head, eagerly crushing my lips against his once more as I now felt the heat of our skin touching, my heart hammering as he gripped my thigh, coiling it around him and pressing his hips into mine. And I took back everything I thought earlier.

I was definitely okay with losing my virginity to Jonathan tonight as a fumble in the woods. Actually, I'd be disappointed if we didn't. He meant more to me than just a quick fling. I wasn't cheating myself out of a special night when this could be it. The two of us making love under the stars.

His lips left my mouth, his breath hot on my skin as he pecked at my neck, groaning against my skin as I responded by arching against him. My hands gripped his back, my breathing ragged and my eyes closed as my body came alive in a whole new way. He nipped at my flesh, growling with a smirk as he enjoyed the way my body trembled beneath him.

This was it.

This was definitely it.

Just reach down Brooke, unhook his pants and give him that look. The come to bed eyes. Let him know that you're okay with this. That you want this. Don't leave any room for doubts.

We were too wrapped up in each other to see the heavens light up around us, the clearing illuminating as lightning broke the sky. But we heard the thunder. The deep boom rolling out and jolting us apart.

The moment hung between us, faces flushed as we panted for breath, bodies crushed together, and limbs entangled as we gazed at each other. Lightning flashed again, cracking loudly through the air as it hit the ground somewhere not too far away.

Jonathan let out a breathless chuckle as he rolled off me, laying on his side, his eyes inquisitive as they appraised me. "Are you okay?"

I let out a small laugh, glancing at the roof of the tent as the thunder followed. I hadn't even realized it was raining. "I think I just died a little..." The air between us cooled, my thoughts turning toxic as I watched him glance to the sky. Had he caused the storm to cool things off? Maybe he thought it was what he wanted originally but the more we kissed the more he realized it wasn't. Was it only me that felt like the earth stopped every time his lips met mine?

Almost like Jonathan could read my mind he pulled me against his chest, kissing my forehead and breathing me in. "If you're afraid I could stay? Keep you safe?"

I tried to control my expression as I peered at him. Jonathan knew I loved storms, watching the sky change colors as rain plummeted to earth, drenching everything it touched. As kids I'd take his hand and drag him out into them, the temptation only overshadowed now by his offer. "Would you?" I smiled weakly, stroking his shoulder blade. "I'm not usually afraid, but being in a tent on my own..."

His arms wound tighter around me as he secured me to his chest, his chin resting on my head. "I've got you."

"Thank you." I buried my head into him, kissing the taut skin gently and trying to hide my smile. We both knew I was lying. And we were okay with that. "You know, I uh, I wasn't exactly telling the truth earlier." I breathed him in, my head dizzying at the smell of leather that clung to him. "In truth or dare."

"You weren't?"

I laughed softly, smiling into his chest. "If you think Ash is more attractive than you you're an idiot."

His head shifted from where it was rested on mine, and I didn't need to look at him to know that he was smirking my way once again. "And here you had me doubting."

"You never doubted it. You just thought I was stupid." I replayed the scene in my head, the way he looked at me as I crossed the fire, the way he straightened up and squared his shoulders. It was a low blow on my behalf. But I had to know if he'd react, if he cared if I made a move on someone else.

He chuckled, his lips pressing against my hair as he nuzzled back into me. "A little drunk perhaps. Maybe seeing double and thought you got the right guy."

"I'm still a little drunk. But I definitely got the right guy this time."

I tilted my head to look at him, my heart flipping when he grinned and pressed his lips softly against mine. It wasn't like the previous kisses. It wasn't the nervous first kiss where neither of us knew what the other expected. Neither was it the hot and heavy kiss we'd had only moments before, where months of built-up tension had finally reached crescendo.

This was soft, and tender. The type of kiss when you're exactly where you're meant to be, with who you're meant to be with.

Reluctantly we broke apart, my head resting against his chest as I listened to the soft thump of his heart, stifling a yawn. I wasn't sure if it was because he knew I was sleepy or because inspiration hit him, but he started to hum. A hint of a smile evident on his face he wound the gentle melody around us, his hands stroking my waist as he lulled me into a deep and peaceful slumber.

~~~~~~~

The next morning I woke to the sun glowing outside the tent, laughter echoing as out in the fresh air my friends joked about the night before. But there was one thing they didn't know. Something they'd have questions about soon.

Trying to conceal the huge grin on my face I composed myself, ready to roll and face Jonathan. Would it be awkward between us? Would he rub the back of his neck with that slanted smile as he tried to apologize for our drunken grope?

Or would we just kiss? No words needed. Would he want to take me out? Or tell our friends about what happened? Rather than simply saying he came to see if I was okay during the storm.

I steadied my nerves, eager to claim whatever scraps of time we had left between us as I rolled to face him. Frowning instead when I was met with nothing but an empty space.

He was gone.

Chapter 3

Jonathan

"Look, no one is quitting."

I narrowed my eyes at Ash as he sliced fresh kiwi, his blade cutting with slow deliberation. He had his back to me and was clearly trying to buy time. Trying to find the right way to have this conversation that wouldn't result in a tense stand-off. So far it wasn't exactly working. He was the second behind Will to arrive for midweek band practice at my house and had made a beeline for the kitchen, avoiding my gaze the entire time. I'd left Will in the garage where we played, following Ash without a word. I hadn't even needed to start the conversation either. As soon as he'd noticed my presence he'd quickly busied himself making a smoothie. He'd started by telling me how important this last year of school was and how he really hoped something would happen with the band. I'd let him ramble up until now, keeping my side quiet as I watched him trip over his words. I could hear it in his voice – that he'd rehearsed this in his head over and over. I felt for him. But I felt for me more.

"It's just…" He hazarded a glance over at me, his gaze sheepish as he turned back to the chopping board. "With everything happening at home it would really take the edge off to know it was going somewhere, you know?"

I did know. All too well. I clenched my jaw as I looked away, trying to remain calm. I didn't blame him. I couldn't. The horrible thing was I understood. The band meant more to me than anything, but we weren't exactly taking the world by storm. Hell, we were lucky to get a paid slot playing our own music these days. The trouble was I didn't have a back-up plan. This was it. But Ash…he needed one. His parents had practically bankrupted themselves getting him into Harrison and were counting on him doing something with that. Something I wagered didn't involve touring local bars for spare change. A nagging voice told me I was making it far too difficult for us. My dad owned a chain of hotels – all gorgeous and well suited for a makeshift music video. We could film some stuff and put it on Youtube. It had worked for others, why not us? But I didn't want to do it that way. It felt like cheating. Call me old fashioned, but I'd always imagined being discovered in some bar or local dive and really making it. Being up there with the greats. Not some one-hit-wonder that people tweet about and then move on from.

My gaze rose to look at Ash as he loaded up the blender with his menagerie of fruit. The nagging voice was growing louder with each day that passed, and today it was screaming. If we didn't find some glimmer of success soon there wouldn't even be a band for me to agonize over. Did I really wanna risk screwing us over just for the sake of my pride?

"We'll find something." I nodded, hoping my voice sounded more confident than I felt.

He turned at last and gave a small smile, his gaze almost sympathetic as he reached up to instinctively toy with the beaded necklace around his throat. I narrowed my eyes as I watched him. It was one of those tacky surfer ones you found in a gift shop by the beach, but it meant more to him than that. It once belonged to someone close to him and he never took it off. Worse still, he only toyed with it when he was anxious.

"It's been three years Jonathan. Three years."

I smiled thinly, "And we'll find something. I promise. I even have a paid gig lined up."

"You do?" He raised an eyebrow skeptically.

"Of course." I laughed. "Have a little faith."

Ash forced a wan smile, nodding as he turned to switch on the blender. I winced as the whirring sound filled the room, rolling my eyes as a small surge of energy whipped through my veins.

His eyes flew to the machine as it muted, the colorful fruit still whirring round amidst the blades. "Are you really supposed to use your powers this often?" He raised an eyebrow, running a hand through his blonde hair.

I gave a shrug. "I'm not hurting anybody."

Technically he was right. I wasn't supposed to. Not if you believed the horror stories. But honestly, besides the odd headache it really didn't do any damage. And what was the point of having powers at all if you weren't going to use them?

He rolled his eyes, his shoulders hunching as he peered down at the silent blender. "So, paid huh?"

I nodded slowly, my gaze lowering at my white lie. There was a gig lined up, that part was true. But there was no pay off involved. Not unless I dug into my pockets. I was sincerely hoping he would buy the tall tale though and not ask any more questions. He would get paid, technically. So would the others. So, for the second time, I asked myself what the harm would be?

Sensing the quiet surrounding us, Ash glanced back at me with a questioning look.

"Trust me." I implored, pushing myself back from the counter.

He gave an unconvincing look in return and turned back to the blender, flipping it off. I watched him stare at it for a few moments, frowning slightly as I backed towards the door. "I'll see you out there?"

Ash nodded dumbly, breaking his trance long enough to throw me a genuine smile. "Sure. Be right there."

I kept my eyes trained on him as I left the room, my stomach sinking uncomfortably. Maybe I would have to work some magic after all, if nothing else than to convince the bassist to stick around…I glanced back at the kitchen as the door dividing us closed shut. This particular one lead into a small utility room, separating the garage from the rest of the house. Dad had even soundproofed our practice space for good measure. I looked across at the door leading to the garage, taking in a deep breath. I couldn't let the band crumble. And showing that panic was step one in ensuring it did. I fixed on my trademark smirk and pushed the door open, quickly glancing around the room before settling my gaze on Will. So far it was still just us. I frowned as I headed over to him, "No Alex?"

He gave a small shrug, looking out to the street. "I guess he's running late."

I nodded, trying not to let paranoia creep in. I'd tried to clear the air over the whole Rosie confession when we got back from camping. We'd gone over the expectant conversation any big brother was required to give, with a few light-hearted comments thrown in for good measure. It wouldn't happen again and he knew I still counted him as a close friend. I'd hoped that would be the end of it.

A car approached at a slow pace, pulling to a gentle stop just out of view. I raised an eyebrow, peering slightly to gauge the owner. My shoulders dropped as I recognized the blonde head of hair clambering from the car. Will straightened up beside me, coughing as he glanced around at the sparse garage. A few worktops and stray mismatched chairs made up the furnishings, the band equipment and amps scattered by the back. I raised an eyebrow at him as Rosie entered with her new friend. Her and Brooke had encountered her over the summer and were indoctrinating her into the group slowly but surely. He smiled weakly, shrugging back at me as he ran a hand through his hair. "Allergies?"

"To my sister or the newbie?" I smirked.

"To a subpar lead singer?"

"Brutal." I grinned, glancing back over at the girls. One in particular seemed to be missing. Was she sick?

"You okay there, Romeo?"

My insides jolted as I looked back at him, trying for an easy smile. "Yeah…I'm gonna see if I can retrieve our bassist. He seems to have disappeared on us."

Will nodded slowly, his mouth twitching in amusement. "Sure thing."

I rolled my eyes, casting another look at the girls as I passed by. Rosie raised an eyebrow questioningly as she hoisted herself onto one of the counters, her hair bouncing as she turned back to the redhead. I tore my gaze away as I pushed my way through to the utility room. As I heard the door click softly behind me I took a minute, reaching my hand up to rub at my eyes as I fought off a brewing headache. She was probably just running late too. She never missed a practice. Unless she really was sick? I frowned, opening my eyes to look at the looming door connected to the kitchen. One thing was for sure, without the band there would be no practice. And there was only so long Ash could pretend to busy himself making a smoothie. I took a step towards the glossed wood, frowning slightly as a soft voice floated through the surface to me.

"Ashley."

I took a tentative step closer, my eyes narrowing as I drew a wave of energy to course along my veins. The headache began to pulse with the added strain, but I forced the power to keep rushing out, shaking my head to dismiss the mundane side effect. The door faded before me, the walls with it. I looked through at the kitchen, at them, as the sounds of their voices heightened. They were oblivious, of course. I placed my palm against the wooden pane of the door, smiling wryly as I felt the cool texture against my skin.

"Really?" Ash laughed, turning to face her. "That's cold."

Brooke grinned back at him, arching an eyebrow playfully. "Would you believe me if I apologized?"

"I would not." Ash smirked, tilting his half-finished glass to offer her a sip of his smoothie.

She took the glass with a coy smile, her dark eyes glinting. "Well, that's pretty cold too."

He laughed. "Should we kiss and make up?"

My jaw clench and I looked between them. Maybe he hadn't been so off with me before because of the band. Or maybe not *just* because of the band. What if he secretly liked her too, and why shouldn't he? I couldn't blame the guy for wanting her any more than I could blame him for trying to jump ship.

"One not enough for you?"

"It was a good kiss."

The magic coursing through me begin to boil, my head piercing with the effort to keep calm and, above all, silent. I leaned against the door, my palm flattening against the wood as I closed my eyes. I didn't need to see this, so why was I torturing myself?

"You know, for a minute there I was sure you were gonna pick Jonathan…"

My eyes flew open, shooting up to look at them both.

"Jonathan?" Brooke's voice faltered, the bridge of her nose crinkling as she shook her head with a small laugh. "Why?"

The color rose to her cheeks, her gaze exploring the room as she cradled the smoothie. My insides sank. I'd left our tent before the sun had come up, without so much as a word. I'd intended to talk to her the next morning. To explain. But each time I'd tried she'd averted her gaze and the moment passed. I'd wanted to tell her that it meant something to me. Everything, in fact. That I'd only left before the others could see because I hadn't wanted a repeat of the Alex situation – only worse. If I'd been caught leaving the tent the next morning it wouldn't matter what we said, rumors would fly and assumptions would be made. And while I didn't exactly mind those assumptions, I couldn't do that to her. She deserved so much better than having to delicately explain to our friends that we'd just kissed and slept together. In the literal sense of the word. But with each day that forced itself between us and that conversation, it only left room for doubt. She probably thought I was an ass.

"Just a hunch." Ash shrugged, raising an eyebrow. "But imagine if you had."

"Yeah," she laughed uneasily. "Imagine."

He eyed her carefully, tilting his head to watch her as she moved past him to rinse out her glass. I narrowed my eyes as her chocolate waves fell in the gesture, tumbling down to shield her from his view. From mine. If he reached out to brush it back I might just lose it. I glanced back at the door to the garage, wincing. I couldn't exactly scurry back to Will and claim I couldn't find Ash in my own house. Especially not when he and Brooke sauntered through in five minutes. I began to pace, frowning as I weighed my options. I didn't want to lurk too long and witness something I'd have seared into my memory forever.

"You know, Nathan asked me if he needed to have a talk with you." Brooke smiled wryly, raising an eyebrow.

"Really?" Ash laughed, shaking his head. "And I'm an angel compared to Jonathan." Why did he have to keep bringing me up? Could he tell somehow that I was eavesdropping and thought it would be hilarious - or necessary. Really drive it home that she wasn't interested.

Brooke reached up to tuck her hair behind her ear, turning to lean against the countertop with a grin. "Can you imagine what my parents would say? I don't think Daddy would ever let me set foot in this house again."

"He'd probably send you to a remote convent in Italy." Ash chuckled, elbowing her gently.

"Oh God, don't joke about that." She laughed, rolling her eyes. "Jonathan is definitely his worst nightmare."

"Yeah," Ash nodded, his expression becoming serious as he watched her. "It'd never work…"

My jaw clenched and I turned away, letting out a low sigh as the voices faded just as the door had. That was more than enough. I got the message. Or several mixed messages, anyway. We all knew I wasn't the guy she ended up with, she and I had even said it that night in the tent. I was her 'what if' guy. The dangerous flirtation. Nothing more. The irony of being on the receiving end of that for once didn't escape me. I tried to calm my breathing and allow the magic to dissipate, the dull quiet of the room around me assuring me the trick was over. I opened my eyes and glanced back at the door leading to the kitchen. All was quiet.

My shoulders dropped as I pushed my way back through to the garage. Will stood over by the girls, his drumsticks twirling idly in his hands as he looked between them. I could only imagine the riveting conversation they were immersed in. I frowned as I headed over, nodding in greeting to them. Still no Alex. Some band practice this was shaping up to be. I rolled my eyes and looked around at the abandoned equipment.

"Did you find Ash?" Will asked, glancing behind me.

"Yeah."

His brow furrowed at my short reply. I shook my head, instinctively reaching into my pocket for my cigarettes. My hand came back empty.

"So," The new girl started brightly, "Do you guys play often?"

Not enough, I thought dryly.

Will shrugged, "Every other night of the week. Saturday and Sunday afternoons."

"Wow." She smirked, her gaze settling on mine. "You must be good."

I raised an eyebrow, letting out a soft chuckle. "Stick around and you'll find out"

Will rolled his eyes beside me, shaking his head. "Are there any girls you won't flirt with?"

I had actually been talking about our music.

"Hopefully not me." Rosie pulled a face.

"I dunno…" Will grinned across at her, "You are his twin, after all."

Gross. I looked at him incredulously, laughing despite myself as I glanced across at…Damn, what was her name again?

"Please ignore them." I grinned, "I'm honestly not that bad."

"Having to explain yourself probably means that you are." Will raised an eyebrow.

"It's okay." She smiled coyly, leaning back against the countertop. "I don't mind a little flirtation."

I looked over at Rosie questioningly, laughing as she gave a small shrug. She was some help. I'd known the girl all of two minutes. Whereas normally that might be long enough to casually flirt, she was here at our house as Rosie and Brooke's friend. Essentially off-limits. But then perhaps I was reading a little too much into it. This was new territory. She wasn't…She wasn't Brooke. Somehow with Brooke neither of us could help it. And it was always okay. Until now, I guess.

I winced at the sharp stab of regret in my gut, looking away and tilting my head as a figure sloped into the open garage. "What time do you call this?"

Alex groaned softly, offering a small shrug as he headed over to his keyboard. "Sorry, Dad started on one of his college talks again."

"Now if your other half could make an appearance we might get somewhere," Will added dryly, nodding at the girls as he made for his drum kit.

I glanced over at the door to the utility room, averting my gaze quickly as it opened. "Right on cue," I muttered, unable to watch as Ash and Brooke emerged.

Alex raised an eyebrow at them, mirth in his voice as he flipped switches on his keyboard to bring it to life. "You guys taking advantage of Nathan not being here?"

"A gentleman never tells." Ash laughed, shaking his head as he walked over to his bass.

I was rooted to the spot. There wasn't much distance to travel to get to my mic and guitar, but Brooke was standing firmly in my path. Oblivious. I narrowed my eyes as I looked from her to the mic, judging just how well I could pull off nonchalance without offending her. I felt eyes on me and blinked, looking across at Will. He watched me carefully, his drumsticks poised as he sat astride his stool.

"So what have we missed?" Brooke surveyed the room, her smile faltering slightly as it traveled from me to Ash.

"Jonathan trying to scare our new friend away." Rosie laughed, giving me a gentle shove towards the band equipment.

I looked back at her in irritation.

"Don't worry." Her friend laughed, shaking her head. "We're good."

So good I couldn't for the life of me remember her name. And I could hardly ask at this stage. Rebecca? Renee? It was definitely an R. Unless I was thinking of Rosie. It could be that. I smiled apologetically, tearing my gaze away as I took a tentative step towards Brooke.

"What have you been doing?" She asked, a small smile tugging at her lips. She seemed off. There was no way she could know that I had overheard her talking to Ash. It wasn't possible. I opened my mouth to explain the misunderstanding. To brush it off before this really did become the most torturous band practice my garage had ever witnessed.

"He was flirting. Or trying to." Rosie supplied helpfully.

Nope. That was two for two.

I looked back at Brooke, frowning as I saw a glimmer of hurt on her face. She straightened herself up quickly enough, forcing a laugh as she folded her arms. "You flirt with everyone."

My frown deepened as I looked around the room. I walked towards her as casually as I could muster, color warming my neck as I stopped a few feet from her. She blinked up at me, the bridge of her nose crinkling again. I bowed my head, lowering my voice as quietly as I could to allow us some illusion of privacy. "I do…but I save the real stuff for the few."

"The real stuff?" She arched an eyebrow, her arms still shielding her.

"Yeah. You know…" I looked around at our audience, smiling weakly as Will began drumming lightly. He formed a beat, their gazes drawing over to him as he warmed up. I turned my attention back to Brooke, locking her eyes with mine. "The stolen moments under the stars. That kind of thing."

I suppressed a grin as Ash pitched in, the rhythm picking up. I wasn't sure if he was just following Will's lead, or if he was trying to drown us out.

She stared at me for a long time, her lips drawing into a reluctant smile. "And how many girls have had that so far?"

My grin spread. "Just the one."

Our gazes remained locked for a few sacred seconds as we smiled secretively at one another, the music softly thrumming around us. I don't know why it was so important to me that she knew I cared. Even after overhearing her discussion with Ash only moments ago and slowly, painfully, trying to accept the possibility that I'd imagined her interest…I couldn't bear the idea of her thinking about me that way. Assuming that our fleeting kisses had been some way to pass the time or to try and gain a new move on my roster. She had to know that for me it was something else entirely. Even if that's all she knew.

"I like how I get called out for being late, but Jonathan can just stand around talking."

We both looked over at Alex, broken from our reverie. I narrowed my eyes at him, offering Brooke one last rueful smile before sloping off to my mic stand. She watched me with a faraway look in her eyes, shaking her head as though to brush off a lingering thought. I frowned as I picked up my guitar, tearing my eyes from her as she joined the other girls by the counter. My gaze lowered to the floor by my feet as I strummed the first few chords of one of our songs, not even certain which one I wanted to play until my fingers had decided for me. My eyes closed as the guys slowly brought their instruments into the fold, the melody taking shape.

I missed my timing on a chord and winced, shaking my head as I powered on. I needed to move past this. Past her. I didn't want to…God help me, I didn't want to. But I had to. For all I knew she and Ash were trying to discover their feelings for one another, and I was the good friend on the outside of it trying to get in. Maybe it had meant a lot to me, but maybe I was also allowing my ego to assume it had meant the same to her when in reality…I opened my eyes to look at her, my free hand coming to grasp the mic. In reality I'd been behind it all. All except that conversation between the two of them. She'd told me in the tent that she'd mistakenly chosen Ash to kiss. That I'd been an idiot to think otherwise. But what if it was me she'd mistakenly kissed? I grimaced as I missed the cue for the next verse, coming in late both with vocals and guitar.

I tried instead to wipe her from my mind, at least while I sang. The idea of her secretly wanting another guy was distracting me far too much. I'd written the damn song and it felt foreign on my tongue. I closed my eyes again and tried to focus on the lyrics, my voice catching as images of kissing her immediately came crashing through. I shook them off, my fingers moving between chords as I tried to picture anyone but her. Even some faceless couple would do. Just not…Not us. Please not us.

I opened my eyes and blanched, the color rising to my cheeks as I saw Jen leaning by the entrance to the garage. She looked at me appraisingly, raising an eyebrow with a sympathetic smile. I let out a sigh and dropped the guitar by the mic stand, shaking my head. "Let's call it. We can pick it up again tomorrow."

I glanced back at the guys as I caught one or two eye rolls. This practice had been a washout anyway, from start to finish. I couldn't focus and we were running thin on time. If we had to call in another practice on a day off then that's what we'd have to do. I kind of hoped for less of an audience tomorrow, which was unlike me. I ran a hand through my hair and headed over to Jen, smiling weakly. "Hey, to what do I owe the pleasure?"

"Who says I'm here for you?"

"Wild guess," I smirked.

She let out a laugh, shaking her head. "I had a spare hour before a gig. Figured I'd come and see you guys first."

I really wished she hadn't. Every other night we were good. Better than good. But I'd say that had been our most excruciating performance to date.

"That's a flimsy excuse. You've seen us play loads."

Her mouth curved into an easy smirk. "I thought you might have gotten better."

I couldn't help but laugh. "Ouch." She smiled endearingly, her gaze soft. "So who's this lame band you're gonna see and how did they steal our slot?"

Jen let out a soft groan, laughing. "Some friend of my cousins. I'm not holding out much hope for them."

"Everyone's gotta start somewhere…" I smiled ruefully, raising an eyebrow. "But I expect massive coverage when we hit the big time."

"Are you kidding me? If you hit the big time you'll be giving *me* the exclusives." She grinned.

"If?"

She let out another laugh, rolling her eyes. "Someone needs to check their ego."

"Nope." I smirked, "It's fine."

"You sure you don't want me to massage it for you?"

I felt the mood shift and smiled slightly, glancing across to where Brooke was stood with the girls. The guys had joined them now, and were forming a small cluster. But I could still see her. Of course I could. "I'll get back to you on that…" I murmured softly.

Her blue eyes followed mine, looking over at the group. "Ahhh." She nodded slowly, the coy smile still etched on her lips.

I glanced back at her. "Ahh?"

"You telling me that none of your fan club will do it instead?"

"My sister might not be too keen." I laughed.

"Probably not." She chuckled, nodding over at them. "But the new girl might be."

I frowned as I looked back across the room, shifting my gaze from Brooke to the redhead beside her. She was staring over at us with interest, her smile slight as though working out a tricky problem. "Yeah," I nodded. "Maybe."

My gaze flickered back to Brooke almost instinctively, my heart sinking as I saw her talking to Ash and Alex with a grin. What had she made of my performance? I grimaced, already sure of the answer.

"You okay there Jonathan?"

I glanced up at Jen with a small nod.

She raised an eyebrow as she punched my arm gently. "Just let me know if you have someone else scratching your back, okay?"

I considered her with a smirk, tilting my head. "Jealous?"

"Oh yeah." She laughed, "You're breaking my heart."

My gaze dropped to linger on her lips, my mouth curving into a knowing smile as I felt that old chemistry rekindling. I brought my hand up to brush aside a stray strand of her hair, my fingertips grazing against her skin gently. Jen and I had been so easy together. We'd been less than great loves, but definitely more than friends with benefits. There'd always been an understanding between us. We knew each other. There were no complications or headaches involved. But that had partly been why we hadn't worked. We both needed that lover worth fighting for. That great adventure and epic romance. I hadn't really thought that I might find mine…But these days I was becoming more and more convinced that I had.

"I was gonna ask if you wanted to tag along." Jen began, slowly drawing herself closer to me. "To the gig, I mean. You could get a feel for the bar, maybe try and get your own slot?"

I looked down at her, our faces mere inches apart. "Tempting."

A rustling sound caught my attention. I frowned and looked across just in time to see Brooke grabbing her purse. Her expression was clouded as she glanced back at me, her dark eyes doe-like and guarded. She smiled fleetingly to those around her as she said her goodbyes, her eyes traveling back to mine reproachfully.

"Unless you have a better offer?" Jen prompted, following my gaze with a raised eyebrow.

Brooke shook her head and turned to leave the garage, stopping in her tracks as though considering something. After a moment of deliberation, she spun back on her heel and marched towards Ash, kissing him full on the lips.

My mouth dropped open, my eyes narrowing as I watched. Ash seemed just as stunned, the color flushing his cheeks as he blinked back at her, and then at me.

"Jonathan?"

I finally tore my gaze away, my expression still dark as I looked down at Jen. She looked at me curiously, her eyebrow still raised. I glanced back up in time to see Brooke leaving the garage, Ash hot on her heels. My gaze dropped back to Jen's sheepishly, my smile rueful as I shook my head. "No. No better offers."

Chapter 4

Will

The morning sun was peeking through a crack in my curtains and I groaned in frustration, rolling to bury my face in the pillow. Taking a deep breath, I tried to relax my body and drift back to sleep, but the amount of drinks I'd pounded last night had other ideas. My head was spinning, the room moving on an axis. It seemed like a great idea at the time, the first week of school already over, not that the gang needed an excuse, but that was a good one.

We'd started at the Taylor house, having a few beers after we'd finished our fourth practice that week, and eventually decided to disappear to our usual haunt, The Mill. It was a little outside of town, but it was known for its relaxed atmosphere for carding, meaning if our fake ID's did need checking, no one cared enough to actually question us.

Realizing that sleeping on my stomach was making me feel worse, I rolled onto my back once more, scrunching my eyes against the glare of the sun.

I couldn't win.

Eventually I sighed, raking a hand through my hair before slowly heaving myself to sit and glancing at the clock on my bedside table. 9.17am. This time a week ago I'd still be sleeping soundly, hangover or not.

Well, since I was awake...

I climbed from the bed, my legs slow and unresponsive as I stepped across my scattered clothes, rubbing my temples to try and ease the pressure, surely I had some pain relief somewhere. I headed to my desk, opening the drawer and shoving things aside as I went. It was mainly junk that I might need for school, college brochures making the bulk of it. But eventually I found the small blue packet I was looking for. Dropping two capsules into my hand I tossed the pack away and threw the pills into my mouth, swallowing them dry. Hopefully the headache and nausea would subside soon.

I was just about to close the drawer when a photograph caught my eye, buried beneath a pile of letters. I pulled it out, fingering it delicately as I stared at the object of my affections.

Rosie was standing by the pool in her back garden, her hair blowing in the wind. Her eyes were closed, her head tipped back and her mouth open with laughter. She looked so beautiful.

I remembered taking this. It was my 16th birthday, Mom had bought a new camera to satisfy her need to capture every moment of our lives, and birthdays featured heavily. Even when I made my excuses for band practice Mom had made me promise to take the camera and 'have fun'.

I held the picture firmly, the familiar ache in my chest flaring as I gazed at her, frozen in time. It was strange, realizing the fondness I had for Rosie had turned into a crush. I can't pinpoint when it happened, when the protectiveness over her shifted, when I realized I wanted some reason, *any* reason, to talk to her. But soon enough I found myself agreeing to practice every night, because Rosie was always there, cheering us on.

Glancing around, I released the hold I had on my powers, gasping as they uncoiled from deep within me. Recently, or since I'd turned 18 and got full access to my supernatural gift, I'd found the slightest thought got them acting instinctively. It made me nervous, that they weren't as controllable as I wanted them to be. Sure, it wasn't a bad thing if you really wanted a burger and then you were holding one. But what if I couldn't wrestle them back? What if the next time I had a passing thought about some asshole cutting me off and then...crash.

I didn't want to be like him. Like...

Shaking my head, I tried to wipe those thoughts away. I was only doing the smallest things, getting dressed when I'd overlaid, pulling a few dollars out of thin air when I didn't have my card. Or now, fetching the shoebox I kept hidden at the back of my closet. I heard a rustle as it dislodged itself from beneath my old football jersey, the door creaking as it fought to escape. My hand shot out as the box soared towards me, falling into my arms.

Hoisting myself up on my desk, I lifted the lid and rifled through the contents.

It was like a time capsule, holding everything I'd obtained over the years that made me think of Rosie. Starting with a birthday card she'd made for me when I'd turned 13. I rummaged through the box and found it, smiling.

Have a Baa-rilliant Birthday Will!

The tissue sheep she'd stuck to the front hadn't lasted, now it was just legs and googly eyes with a small white tuft. But it meant something. I'd never had a home-made card before.

I carried on shuffling through the tokens inside, pulling out memories with each item. The pen she'd given me when I'd signed up to the football team, the cinema stub from when I'd take her to some chick-flick.

And then came the embarrassing stuff, the stuff which forced my hand and made me hide the box. Pages of writing. From Post-it-notes to full sheets. Letters. Notes. Doodles. All of them for Rosie. It wasn't a common occurrence to write her letters, but occasionally, when I told myself that things could work out, I'd put pen to paper. I'd tell her I thought she was beautiful, that I could see her eyebrows crease when she saw her reflection, and tell her she didn't see herself how anyone else did. How I did. I'd tell her how she made me nervous, how she made my stomach flip when she smiled, or how my nerves around her made me more reserved. I played my cards close to my chest, but that was because I thought she'd laugh in my face. Or Jonathan would freak out.

I was sure he thought I saw Rosie as a sister too...

Sighing, I closed the box, my powers flaring as I sent it back to the closet. I'd never sent her one. I doubted I ever would.

Jumping from my desk, I looked around my room. Saturday mornings in the summer consisted of a quick breakfast, followed by drumming. I vetoed both things quickly. My stomach couldn't handle food, and the thump in my head meant drumming would be a mistake too. Which meant I'd shower and go out on the bike to clear my head. Hopefully the hangover wouldn't make it an issue. I definitely didn't feel drunk. Or impaired. Just nauseous.

Stretching my limbs out I plodded off to my en-suite, flicking the radio on as I went. And then grimacing as I turned the volume down. Will last night was obviously in the mood to cut loose and didn't care if hungover Will wanted a bit more quiet.

I air drummed along to the song that was playing, kicking off my boxers and climbing into the shower as I went. The hot jets pelted my bare skin, a groan slipping from between my lips as my muscles relaxed in the heat. Summer had made me complacent. It was all fun and games lazing around until noon, getting in a workout and then heading to practice before we hung out. Now I'd got to fit it in around school again. And as Mom kept reminding me - I couldn't slip now. My fate in regards to college might already be sealed, but that didn't mean I should take things easy. If anything she was pushing me harder. Maybe she was worried I'd leave school and decide hitting random bars with the band was the dream. And it was. Except not the bars we were playing now. The ones where people didn't even give us a second glance.

Rolling my neck, I killed the water, grabbing a clean towel from the pile Mom had left me and wrapping it around my waist. My head felt clearer, my joints less achy. Which was a start.

I slipped back into my bedroom and tugged at a fresh pair of boxers from my laundry pile, swiftly pulling them on. I grabbed a beat-up pair of dark jeans and a T-shirt and quickly threw them on too. I was already claustrophobic at being stuck inside, fresh air would do me some good. I slipped on a pair of socks and pulled on my Converse as I headed to my door, reaching for the keys to my bike from the shelf.

My hands clenched around thin air.

I frowned, looking at the wood in betrayal.

My keys were always there.

Or in the bowl, which is what Mom had got it for. Something about me constantly losing my keys.

Dunno where she got that idea from.

I headed from the room, jogging down the stairs. "Mom?"

"In here Willypoo." I cringed at her pet name for me and followed the sound of her voice. She was in the sitting room, her legs draped across Dad's knee as she toyed with his hair, the pair of them watching some program on cars. That was probably Dad's choosing more than hers, but she never minded. I guessed living in this house made her accepting of our love of anything with an engine. She looked up at me as I walked in, smiling softly. "What's up sweetie?"

"Have you seen my keys?" I tried to ignore the smirk and the raised eyebrow she shot my way.

"Lost them again, huh?" Dad asked, laughing and shaking his head, his eyes never leaving the screen.

Mom slapped his thigh, as if she hadn't been silently mocking me only moments before. "Have you checked your room?"

"Yeah, I always put them on my shelf...and I could have sworn I did last night"

"You were pretty drunk though, kid." Dad turned to look at me, smiling proudly, no doubt remembering his own youth and the times he'd crawled home after a night of underage drinking.

They looked at each other, Mom shrugging and offering me a pitying smile. Well they helped loads.

Rolling my eyes, I stalked from the room. Which meant I only had one other person to ask.

David.

I sighed, slowly dragging myself back towards the stairs. Of course, I could always use my powers to find them, save myself the awkward conversation with David and just leave. But that felt ridiculous. And I had to face him at some point.

The two of us had barely spoken in months. I'd tried. But every time I opened my mouth to say something I saw that look in his eyes, the one that told me he wasn't ready. The one that said there was something in me he hated.

It all started with a question. A simple one, which neither of us had ever thought to ask before.

Why did we both have powers?

When Tristan and Leigh gave birth to James they'd realized he'd inherited the superhuman gift, after all it was a huge part of who Tristan was. But Nathan and Brooke were...normal. Nothing tying them to that freak storm. Just Like Lucas' sister Olivia. And Rosie.

So why did both David and I have them?

We brought it up to Dad after spring break earlier this year. His face had dropped, his expression blank as he called Mom through. And then they told us.

It wasn't just the four of them that had been caught up in the storm. Originally they'd had a fifth friend.

Ethan.

Ethan was a year younger, but had slipped himself into the group. Dad had skated over most of the details, preferring not to say anything we didn't need to know. When the storm hit he was only seventeen. He got powers, but they were limited. They came with headaches if you tried anything too big, fainting spells if you carried on. It was a binding, making sure you could handle it before they dropped the world at your feet.

And when Ethan came of age, he couldn't.

It changed everything about him. He became dangerous. At first he'd seemed totally normal, but behind closed doors he was unhinged. It took almost seven years to realize what he was. He had delusions of grandeur, desperate for more...He felt the world owed him something, that the others were holding him back. He had everything he ever wanted at arm's reach, all he had to do was take it, but they wouldn't let him.

In a fit of rage he'd raped my mom, forcing her to his bedroom and beating her into submission before bragging about it. He sent Dad pictures of her, unconscious in his bed, goading them into facing him. I'm not sure what he hoped to achieve taking on four of them, but he scarpered almost as soon as they arrived. And he'd not been seen again. Or at least so far...

For reasons I'll never understand, Mom kept the child he forced within her, and nine months later I was born.

The news was a punch to the gut.

It wasn't as if it changed anything. My mom was still my mom. And my dad, Jett, the man who had raised me, of course he was still my dad.

And yet it changed everything.

I could see it in the sadness on Mom's face that she blamed herself for how I was conceived, as if she knew the pain it would cause me and it was somehow greater than hers. I could see it when Dad held her, stroking her knee, his eyes cast down with a thin smile. Because he blamed himself for her being alone that night. For having no one around when Ethan struck.

I could see it in the way David watched me. A mix of shock, disgust, and fear evident in his stare. He blamed me. He watched our parents hold each other as they relived it, Mom wiping her tears and choking back sobs. And he blamed me. Because if I wasn't here she could move on. But every day she looked at me, and every day she remembered.

The 11 month age gap between me and David was suddenly heartbreaking. Had they immediately tried for their own child when they could? So they could raise their own son and not someone else's?

The week following the revelation I'd been silent.

I'd missed practice. I'd skipped school. I'd hidden away.

Wrapping my head around it seemed impossible. How had she been so brave? How had she kept me, wondering if I'd look like him? And what if...what if I took after him? And I couldn't control my urges like him? Now I'd hit 18 that fear was more real...

Eventually Mom had broken down my wall. She'd listened to my worries and she'd stroked my hair. Then she'd placed both hands on my face and she'd turned me to look at her, and she was honest.

She told me she'd considered abortion. She wasn't sure she was ready for a child at all, never mind one who'd remind her of that night. But then Dad had stepped in, and stepped up. The decision was ultimately hers, and he would stand by her no matter what. But as much as the baby would be half of Ethan, it would also be half of her.

And that's what I had to remember.

That I was hers.

That night I'd re-joined the family for dinner. I was mending. Mom didn't hate me. She didn't see Ethan when she looked at me. Dad didn't despise me because I was a reminder of the guy that had violated his wife. And David...

David wouldn't meet my eye. He wouldn't acknowledge me when I spoke.

And he still didn't.

I took a deep breath as I came face to face with his door, running a hand through my hair. He had to speak to me eventually, even if it was to cuss me out. At least then he'd get it off his chest.

I raised my fist, and knocked.

"Come in." His voice was gruff, I could just about make out a groan and the bedsprings heaving as he shifted. The hangover was obviously kicking his ass too. Maybe I should ask if he wanted to come out on the bike. And Dad. It'd be good for us to have some bonding time...

I popped my head around the door, smiling awkwardly. "Hey..." His gaze turned cold as he realized who it was. "Umm...I was gonna head out on the bike, but I can't find my keys..."

He stared at me.

The silence stretched on between us, the tension reaching all new heights. And just when I thought he was still going to pretend I didn't exist, he spoke. "And you thought I took them?"

"Well, no, but-"

"Because you're used to people just taking what they want."

That stung.

"David, I-"

"No."

"No?"

"No I didn't take your keys." His stare grew dark. Part of me was glad he was finally opening up, speaking to me. The other part, the part that could feel his anger, the part of me I was afraid of, was angry too. He raised an eyebrow. "Maybe no is too hard for you to understand. Your dad had trouble with it too."

My veins began to burn with power, my fists clenching as I tried to calm myself. He didn't mean it, he was angry. And he couldn't attack Ethan so I was here taking his beating.

But he's being such *an asshole! You've never given him reason to think you're anything less than a good guy...*

I ignored the voice in my head, taking a breath. "Can we just drop it?"

David climbed from the bed, raising an eyebrow at me. "How about you make me?"

You could take him easily. It'd be over and done with before he even stepped up.

My powers uncurled further, my knuckles white as I struggled to reign them in as they reacted to the venom in his words. Was this a test? Was he trying to see if I snapped like Ethan? Or maybe he just wanted to fight? Give me a beating to get it out of his system?

"David...we're family. I know..." I sighed, "I know it's completely upended everything, but we have a choice. We can let it get to us, or move past it."

"I will *never* get over having a rapist's son under the same roof."

Yes!

It happened in a second. One minute I was looking at him, his smirk growing as he spat that word at me, the next he was flat on his back. I hadn't moved, my hands still bawled by my sides. But the electricity coursing my veins was evidence enough. The power settled over me like a shield, pulsing around me, clinging to my anger. It was poison, tainting my emotion. It crushed every regret, every worry that this was wrong. And instead it fed on my upset. It fanned the flames of the vicious thoughts locked away at the back of my head.

None of this affects him half as much as you! You're the one who just found out you're only here because some guy decided he couldn't take no for an answer and forced you into existence! How could he even begin to comprehend that you grew from evil, that you're doubting everything you are! And everything you might become...

David rose to his feet, rubbing the back of his head where it had connected with the edge of his wardrobe. He looked satisfied. I'd done exactly what he expected. And now all he had to do was retaliate.

I saw the glint in his eye as his own powers kicked in, his usual dull brown iris brightening and glimmering as he rolled his shoulders. "Get out of my room."

I opened my mouth...

He's all talk...make him regret saying those things! All it would take was one tiny thought and you could close his windpipe...watch him struggle for a few seconds...

Swallowing, I closed my eyes, taking another breath. I needed to calm down. My thoughts were running away with me, my powers beginning to take control. I was just about holding them back, but I was struggling. I was new to this. And I wasn't blind to the realization this is how *he* would've felt.

David stepped towards me again, his powers colliding with my shoulder. "I said get out."

He's gonna regret that...

My hands were trembling. I couldn't hold on...

There was another knockback, my feet stumbling as I was pushed towards the door. "Get out."

Hurt. Him.

Gravity pulled me down as David knocked me flat on my back, a snort of amusement coming from his lips as he turned away.

Don't. Let. Him. Win.

I rose to my feet almost too gracefully, a vicious battle cry filling the room. The fire finally finding release as my powers knocked everything back, a shockwave of energy flying from deep within me. David's body thudded against the wall, his arms and legs frozen as I pinned him in place, his eyes scrunched tight as he gasped for breath. I took a step towards him, my mouth pulling up in a smirk as he struggled to free himself from my hold. But I was too strong. He wouldn't escape if I didn't want him to.

A demonic laugh echoed around the room, and I realized with a start it was coming from me. I reached out and grabbed my brother by the chin, yanking his head to the side.

My head was fuzzy as I tried to stop myself, my powers claiming complete control. I was trapped in my own body, and the more I willed myself to calm down and take over, the more I disconnected from who I actually was.

"Oh little brother." The voice torn from my lips was inhuman. Echoing maliciously in the space between us, the air around us slowly filling with hate and rage. "There's really no wonder *our* parents like me more. You're just *pathetic*!"

David let out a breath, gasping as my powers seized around his throat. "I'm not the one playing in my boyfriend's garage band."

My fist connected with the wall beside his head, a short laugh cutting the air as he flinched away from me. "Whatever I am, you're still *nothing* on me. And that's why you're really angry. Because you've lived in my shadow our whole lives and never matched up, and now something's come to light that's made you think you can finally be better...but instead it's made you realize that even though I'm tainted and might have been unwanted..." I turned his jaw, forcing him to face me. "I'm still better than you."

He finally opened his eyes to look at me, slowly at first, and then they widened in...fear? "Will..." His hands were clenching by his sides as he tried to free his arms. "Your...your eyes..."

I glanced to my reflection in the window.

The muscles in my arms were tensed, bulging with adrenalin.

My face was twisted into an angry snarl.

And my eyes...

...were completely black.

The air was sucked from the room as my powers retreated quickly, David dropping to the floor as I finally regained control. My stomach heaved as my head span. My breathing rapid, my heart hammering and my body slick with sweat.

David shifted to right himself. His hand lifting to rub at his throat as he shakily got to his feet, choking down hungry breaths as his skin burned red.

I'd done that.

My powers had...

I shook my head, I needed to get out of here.

David looked up as I barrelled from the room, calling my name as I forced my way down the stairs. I rushed past our parents as they came to the foot of the staircase, matching frowns on their faces as they tried to question what had happened.

Rushing to the garage I found my bike, throwing my leg over it before I realized I didn't have the keys.

Shit.

I only had two options...

Go back and find my keys. Face my brother and what I'd just done. Or reluctantly use again and get the hell out.

It was a stupid decision, especially after what just happened, but I was too on edge to face anyone in the house. Closing my eyes, I tried to calm the surge of heat in my chest as the magic flowed through me, pressing up roughly against the walls I'd rebuilt to stop it escaping again.

The engine of my bike roared to life and I accelerated, hitting the asphalt of the drive and tearing from the house like a bat out of hell.

The open road gave me space. My mind whirring as I just followed the asphalt, taking each turn whenever I wanted, driving with no end goal. I was weak, stupid to think I'd be any different from *him*. To think I'd be able to control them on my own. They'd fed on my anger, clinging to each thread no matter how hard I tried to bury it. I'd been trapped in my own body, watching as the raw energy of my fury forced itself over David.

And the eyes...

I winced as I remembered the look of fear on my brothers face. He knew what it meant, when your pupil expanded and the soulless void of the magic reflected through them. The energy was bad. It was evil. And it wanted to hurt.

And in that, I had my answer. Try as I might...I couldn't escape my real bloodline.

The wheels of my bike skidded left as I hit the next junction, ignoring the angry blaring of horns as I sped through a red light and narrowly swerved a truck. I was being reckless, and if I hurt anyone I'd have to use my powers, something I didn't want to have to do. But as soon as I'd seen the turn I knew where I needed to go. Call me stupid, but I was a teenager. And hair of the dog might help clear up more than my hangover.

The battered patch of grass beside The Mill was almost empty as I skidded to a halt, jumping off my bike with an easy stride as it clattered to the floor and the engine died. I left it there, laid haphazardly across a grass verge, and walked inside.

As I opened the doors the smell of stale alcohol hit me, my nose wrinkling instinctively. The bar was crowded with overweight men, barely fitting on their seats as they drunk themselves stupid and told stories that scarcely made sense. Barely clothed, aging women, danced by the jukebox. Men wolf-whistling and catcalling at them. A few teenagers I knew from around were playing pool at one of the dilapidated tables by the back wall, laughing and joking.

I kept my head down and walked to the bar, nodding at Mandy, the usual barmaid, as she grabbed a beer from the fridge. She was nice enough, middle-aged, and was probably only working here to keep her only son in a decent education.

She took the ten dollar bill I slipped her and thanked me with another nod as I told her to keep the change. She could keep all my change as long as she kept the drinks coming.

"Will?" I lifted my head half an inch as I heard my name, my face breaking into a grin.

"Rosie-cheeks?" I laughed slightly, turning to face her as she grabbed two beer bottles. The night before hadn't had much of an effect on her, her eyes as bright as always. "What are you doing back here?"

She smiled awkwardly as she took half a step forwards and then paused, glancing back at a table. No doubt weighing up how much I valued our friendship over how protective I could be. Jonathan would kill me if he found out I left her here alone. Something about this place screamed that young females should stick to group outings.

"Uh...I'm just with a friend." Phew. "Do you want to join us?"

I didn't fancy crashing Rosie's girl time, but something about the way she smiled made me think she wanted me to, that she didn't mind me tagging along. And I could never refuse Rosie, so I found myself weaving between tables as I followed her.

Eventually her bouncy blonde head stopped, her body shrinking as she slid into a booth, handing the other beer across the table to a rough masculine hand. The guy stared at me across the table. And I stared back. Rosie completely oblivious. "Will...you know Zak."

Zak wrapped his free arm around Rosie's shoulders, failing to hide a smirk as he slowly lifted the bottle to his lips. "Yeah...we've met. Haven't we Will."

I gulped down half my beer, ignoring Rosie as she shuffled over to make room for me. What the hell was she doing with this asshole?!

Zak was the quarterback for the school football team. And my reason for quitting. Football had never been a great love of mine, but I had the size for it. And I'd be lying if I didn't say I was talented on the field. Once upon a time I could have almost classed Zak as a friend, or a step up from acquaintance at least. We'd played together, for almost two years. Off the field I didn't trust him, he had a habit of thinking he was better than everyone, but on the field...we were quite the team.

That was until I made quarterback after all the ass-kissing he'd done.

Then he was full of 'constructive criticism', trying his best to make passes fail and blame it on me. He was bitter.

The last practice I ever attended he was an insufferable dick, and it continued in the locker room. He just couldn't help himself. But he was all mouth, and when I'd finally had enough he shut up. I thought that was the end of it, until I got up to leave.

The locker room had emptied when he found me, feigning sympathy. He'd heard some of the gang talking, about how David and I were only half-brothers.

He'd laughed.

Of course we were stupid for believing Mom. Everyone knew she was some stupid whore that got knocked up after a one night stand and cried rape. She'd have done anything to keep Dad sweet and make sure she still had a roof over her head.

I'd stood there silently, listening to him lay into my family. And then I tossed my jersey down and walked away.

I'd live with David hating me for my existence. I'd live with my parents knowing I was never wholly theirs. And I'd live with the voices in my head that told me I was on the outside of a family I never belonged in.

But I didn't have to take it from him too.

He was watching me intently now, staring across the table with an amused grin, his fingertips stroking the bare skin of Rosie's shoulder. "We're on a date here. And you're crashing it."

Rosie blushed, averting her gaze from mine and placing a hand over Zak's. "Will could join us though, right?"

"Sure he can." Zak smirked at me, patting the space beside him. "Wouldn't be awkward for him when we start kissing."

Bile rose in my throat and I choked it down. Could this day get *any* worse?! What the hell did she see in him? She was so pure and innocent. And Zak? He didn't even know the word faithful, never mind monogamy.

"We're seeing how things go." Rosie smiled up at me shyly, "That's why we've not told anyone. Please Will...don't tell Jonathan. Let me do it?"

"Yeah Will, don't be that guy." Zak settled back in the seat, his smirk unwavering. "It's hard when someone takes something from you, when you've wanted it yourself for so long." He glanced at Rosie and raised an eyebrow.

I got it loud and clear.

He wasn't interested in her. He'd never shown her any affection before, but he knew I liked her. And this was his way of punishing me.

Rosie turned to look at him, the world slowing as she closed her eyes and leaned in to his body. His arms pulled her closer, his nose brushing hers as he tilted in for the kiss, but his eyes fixed on me, watching for my reaction.

I turned my back on the scene and fled quickly, the second time today that I'd ran rather than face what was happening. I just couldn't do it. Not to her. Would she even believe me if I told her he wasn't interested? That he was just trying to get back at me for something that was mostly out of my control. It would look like I was just jealous.

I downed the rest of the bottle in my hand and tossed it to one side as I met the warm summer air outside. I pulled my bike up, kicking my leg over it and bringing it to life without worrying about using. It purred a few times, and as I hit the asphalt it roared as I pushed it to the limits.

Now more than ever I needed that drink. But this was definitely not the bar I wanted to do it in anymore.

~~~~~

The morning sun was peeking through a crack in my curtains and I groaned in frustration, rolling to bury my face in the pillow. Taking a deep breath, I tried to relax my body and drift back to sleep, but the amount of drinks I'd pounded last night seemed to have other ideas, my head spinning, the room moving on an axis. It seemed like a great idea at the time...

I sat up slowly, rubbing my head as the headache smashed against my temples with unrelenting force. Groaning, I contemplated throwing myself back down into the sheets and forcing myself to sleep again. Visions of the night before started drifting through my head, a half-finished puzzle fixing together as I tried to figure out what had happened.

Slowly it came at me.

The fight with David.

Rosie and Zak.

And then I saw something, and I paused.

Untangling myself from the bed-sheets I crossed the room, stepping over my strewn clothing and ignoring the fact that I'd slept completely naked. There, sitting on my shelf, where they always were, were my keys.

I picked them up slowly, eyeing them as if they were likely to disappear. But yesterday...Yesterday I thought they were there. And they weren't.

Unless...

Had I dreamt the whole thing?

I let out a shocked laugh, shaking my head. Maybe I had. Maybe my subconscious was just fucking with me, forcing me to live out the dark thoughts I kept locked away in the back of my head.

Relief flooded me as I padded back to my bed, dropping the keys on the floor beside a pair of pink panties. Maybe this was why I was always losing them so easily.

I stopped.

Wait. What?

Bending down I reached for the silky magenta fabric, holding the lingerie up with one hand and inspecting it curiously. My head snapped up as I heard the door to my en suite open, my eyes traveling up a pair of long slender legs. My cheeks flushed as I ran my gaze across a naked pelvis and toned stomach before I finally looked into the smiling face of...some girl?

She was beautiful in her own right, light brown hair pulled over one shoulder, her curious brown eyes wide as she watched me. She had a scattering of freckles over her nose, and her lips bore the red staining of a passionate lipstick kiss.

"You gonna sit there all day or are you gonna join me?"

"Umm..."

She laughed, the sound light as it traveled over the sound of the shower. "There's no point being shy now, not after last night."

I blushed as I spotted the used condom wrapper, half-concealed on the floor beside my foot. "We...?" I let the question hang in the air.

"We certainly did." She grinned, raising her hand and beckoning me to the bathroom. "And as soon as you come here we can do it again."

She didn't wait to see if I made a move as she stepped into the steam of the shower, confidence emanating from her as she slipped out of sight.

She knew I would follow her.

I knew I would follow her.

Chapter 5

Rachel

Some people are far too obsessed with happy endings. Boy meets girl, falls in love and off they skip into the sunset. Please. The real world doesn't work like that, and eventually we all discover that truth. Some of us are just faster learners. I'm not a pessimist, I'm a realist. And, some would say, an opportunist. If you wanted something in this life you had to make it happen. You had to find a way.

I stared back at my reflection coolly, my mascara wand poised between my fingertips as I peered into the glass. This was always my favorite part somehow. The private process of adding color and texture to a complexion few would really see, to bare lips and wide eyes. It was art, if you did it right. I liked to take my time and watch as the real me disappeared gradually under the sheer layers and tricks of the trade, another girl entirely emerging from beneath the powder and setting spray. I tilted my face at an angle as I brought the mascara to caress my lashes, my expression steady and sure. The darkness of liner and eye shadow almost drowned out the blue of my eyes, whilst at the same time making them starker. I capped the mascara and set it down in its place by the other tools, neatly maneuvering it to lie in a still line.

My gaze traveled the surface of my dressing table, settling on an old photograph that sat propped up by the objects around it. I smiled at the memory, reaching out to gingerly stroke the image. It had been a lifetime ago. Before we'd all learned some hard lessons. In the picture I was stood in the center of a small huddle, my best friends Tom and Nancy either side. It had been taken on a drizzly summer day. We'd been promised sun, and instead the heavens had opened. But that hadn't stopped us. We were young and desperate to see each other as much as we could before school got in the way. We were squinting against the breeze and rain, hair flying in every direction…but we had the biggest grins on our faces.

I'd always had a soft spot for Tom. He hadn't known, of course. In typical boy fashion he'd been oblivious, overlooking every blush and coy smile. Every attempt to be near him had been read as friendship. It was only when we started back at Leroy that he'd begun to notice. Unfortunately it hadn't been me he'd noticed, but sweet little Nancy. She'd always been mousy and quiet before that, a real wallflower. She hadn't expressed an interest in being anything else. She'd been happy to be background noise. To sit back and let others lead. But evidently over the summer she'd bloomed without even trying. She still looked and acted the same, but whereas before her ashy hair had appeared drab and dull – it now shone. Her smile was bright and her laughter infectious. Better still she had a good heart and could make anyone feel like they were the only person she saw in a crowded room. Tom was falling for her, I could tell. My own heart was being crushed and neither of them even noticed. So I took action.

It hadn't even been hard. I'd bought a burner cell and left some silent calls to Nancy late at night, stolen a few small but noticeable items from her room whenever I could…and then there were the pictures. I'd felt a pang of shame at that part, but it had been more effective than I could ever have hoped so I could only regret it so much. I'd taken them from outside her bedroom window as she changed, making sure to get some money shots in. I'd listened as she told me how she felt watched and afraid, that she'd heard shutter sounds late at night. I'd told her there was nothing to worry about and that everything would be okay. And then I planted it all in Tom's locker.

He vehemently denied it all, of course. But the seed had been planted. She pushed him away, shrinking back into herself until that glorious girl who'd emerged start of term…faded. He fought for her, I'll give him that much. He set about trying to find the real culprit – perhaps to clear his own name more than anything else. But I wasn't stupid. I hadn't left any breadcrumbs. Eventually he'd grown angry at her for not believing him, for throwing away their years of friendship over a cruel prank. He scowled at her in the hallway and yet pined for her all the same. And that was when I concluded the charade. The cherry on top, if you will. The morning after his latest sulky outburst the pictures appeared on every locker and patch of wall, blown up for the world to see. She was mortified and humiliated…and he was arrested.

I sat back on the stool, releasing the photograph to its precarious perch as I examined my make-up. Considering the lengths I'd gone to then, this was a quick mercy. I recognized in Brooke Danes what I'd seen in Nancy that first week back at school. She didn't know it herself, but the world adored her and always would. Guys would always wonder what it would be like to be with her and every girl would always want to be around her just so they could bask in her loveliness. I hadn't transferred to Harrison just so that I could play second fiddle to Nancy part two. Leroy had been good to me, don't get me wrong. But it was hardly the caviar of schools. Harrison on the other hand? That school had the potential to win me some introductions to the right people. The ones who would go on to be remembered. To count for something.

It also had a hefty tuition attached to each semester. One my parents could never afford with their basement jobs. So I'd worked every hour God had sent me at a designer store in the local mall, scavenging each dollar until I could make one year's tuition up. It was unorthodox to switch schools in the last year, almost pointless some would argue. But the last year was what mattered most. I told the Dean there I'd narrowly escaped a stalker at my old school but needed a fresh start. He'd taken pity of me, absorbing every feeble whimper and terrified glance. Yes, I planned to make this year count. I wanted to graduate from the best school in the district, off my own merit. In one sense or another.

After that the world would see me in a better light. Doors would open and I could finally feel like I swam in the right circles. I wouldn't have to borrow the bags or clothes from work, passing them off as my own. I'd be able to get a high flying job and buy the entire store if I wanted to. That was where I'd first encountered Brooke and her shadow. They'd been gathering clothes like the price tags meant nothing. Which they probably didn't. To them. If they knew I worked there, they hadn't let on. Brooke might know, but she was so holier than thou she wouldn't breathe a word for my sake. Rosie on the other hand? She was honestly so ditzy she probably thought the mannequins would ring up her order if she asked them nicely.

I stared back at the girl before me, my mouth curving into a knowing smile as I leaned forward and drew some gloss across my lips. I puckered, stepping back to give myself the once over. My head tilted as I scrutinized my reflection, reaching up to brush my fingertips through my auburn locks. The color glinted in the light like copper, dazzling against the simple black wrap dress I was wearing. I nodded and grabbed some perfume from the dresser, casting another satisfied glance at the old photograph as I dabbed some behind my ears, on my wrists and at my cleavage. Showtime.

The girls had invited me over to the Taylor house for their regular catch up before cheerleading. It was a sweet gesture, sickly almost.

Unfortunately Rosie had run into some car trouble and couldn't make it. Which meant that the stars had aligned to provide me with the perfect opportunity to set Brooke straight before she got carried away and ended up like poor old Nancy. All it would take is some careful timing and the spell would be broken. I slipped on my black heels and hurried down the stairs, waving dismissively as my mom called out something from the sitting room.

I'd seen the way they danced around each other at practice. Hell, we all had. It was nauseating. Brooke had confided in me that during their annual camping trip Jonathan had snuck into her tent in the early hours…and nothing all that exciting had happened. Well, I guess if you were a virginal martyr it was pretty raunchy. But to the rest of us? I rolled my eyes as I got into my car, throwing my cell onto the passenger seat. It was cute how much she was crushing on the guy. And I got it, believe me…she had taste. But he was so not her type it was laughable. He would chew her up and spit her out. If you thought about it, I was doing her a favor. She would forgive me. Maybe even thank me.

I smiled to myself as I guided the car to the Taylor house, glancing at the clock on the dashboard. I was making good time. I reached out to turn on the radio, humming softly to the track as it began midway through. Today was a good day.

Before long the house loomed before me, the driveway clear of cars. I turned off the engine and looked up at it with an odd sense of calm. Soon the band-aid would be off and we could all move on with our lives. I smirked at my reflection in the rearview mirror, tilting it ever so slightly to re-examine my make-up. Perfect. Without a second glance I retrieved the car keys and my cell, tossing them into a small purse I had brought with me.

I stepped from the car and strolled up the driveway, grinning as I saw the closed shutter of the garage door. My gaze traveled to the sitting room as I heard the gentle thrumming of music echoing through the walls. Jonathan was definitely here. I reached out and rapped gently on the door, smoothing down my dress. After a few minutes it opened wide and there he stood. I ran my gaze over him slowly, taking in the mussed hair and weathered jeans. The t-shirt he wore had the markings of some band I'd never heard of and pulled taut in all the right places. My mouth curved into a smile as I admired him.

"Jonathan."

His eyes narrowed as he looked at me. I knew it. I fucking knew it. I smirked, rolling my eyes as I stepped inside. He stepped back with me, frowning as he glanced back at the door.

"It's Rachel." I laughed, raising an eyebrow.

"Yeah...I knew that." He nodded, bringing his hand up to rub at the back of his neck. I chuckled as I watched him squirm, turning my back on him to enter the sitting room. Music blared from the speakers by the TV, the coffee table strewn with scattered sheets and untidy scrawl. I frowned as I took a step closer, peering down at the jumbled mess to see the odd notation. Amidst it all, loosely covered by a sheet of paper with scribbled out words on it, lay a black leather book. The corners were curling from overuse, the first handful of pages crinkled against the stark remainder of the book that sat untouched.

"Rosie's not here."

I straightened up and turned to face him graciously. "I know."

He frowned, moving around me to gather the papers. He wouldn't meet my gaze as he did so, ensuring the black book got swallowed up in the mess. I suppressed a smirk at his secrecy, raising an eyebrow. "Are we alone?"

Jonathan looked up at me bemused, offering a small shrug. "I guess."

I nodded, my expression turning serious as I took a step closer to him. He read the gesture, bringing the stack of papers to his chest as he let out a small cough. "You want a drink or anything while you wait?"

"Sure." I nodded, setting my purse down on the table. "Something strong and delicious."

"Noted." He raised an eyebrow, stalking towards the kitchen.

I let out a sigh as he disappeared, glancing out at the street through the sitting room window. We wouldn't have long before she arrived. Flirtation and subtlety would have to take a back seat. I smirked as I heard the clinking of ice in a glass, reaching down to untie the knot in my dress. With a small shrug it fell to the floor in a graceful heap. I stepped out of it slowly, reaching back to unhook my bra. The silk fabric brushed my fingertips as it too fell to the floor.

"What're you doing?"

A smile tugged at my lips and I glanced at him over my shoulder, raising an eyebrow as I turned my body fully. He stood rooted to the spot, bewilderment visible on his face as he clutched a glass of gin. I watched his eyes as I closed the distance between us, smirking as I saw the color rising to his cheeks. He really was trying to be a good boy. "It's okay, Jonathan." I chuckled, "You can look."

His jaw clenched as he maintained eye contact with me, his green eyes narrowing. "I don't…What're you doing?"

I reached out to take the glass from him, downing the contents greedily. I let out a soft sigh as the liquid went down easily, gently placing the glass back into his palm. "What's standing in your way, Jonathan?" I raised an eyebrow, stepping closer so that my chest pressed lightly against his. I smirked and leaned into him, murmuring against his ear in a gentle purr. "Or should I say who?"

He pulled back as though he'd been slapped, a fresh blush creeping along his skin. "No one…"

"No one huh?" I teased, trailing my fingertips along his bicep. "Then prove it."

Chapter 6

Brooke

I stared into the mirror, my dark eyes curious as they stared back. My expression was blank as I sat there, silently deliberating. The text had come through barely ten minutes ago. Rosie wasn't going to make practice, or at the very least the hour we shared before for smoothies and gossip. Which meant Jonathan would be home. Alone. I wasn't sure why I'd got butterflies at that. It wasn't like I'd just casually drop by to smooch his face and confess that he made my stomach flip.

And then a conversation ran through my head. The one I'd had with Ash a couple of days ago in the Taylors kitchen. I'd tried to bluff past it when he joked he thought I'd kiss Jonathan at camping, but I didn't need to admit it. Ash could read it on my face.

"Jonathan is my dad's worst nightmare."

"It'd never work" Ash smirked, raising an eyebrow.

"And why is that?"

"Because you two will never admit you like each other, for a start."

"We...no, I mean...Jonathan likes a lot of girls."

"Mmm...One in particular I hear."

"I dunno." I was definitely blushing. "Maybe he was lying?"

"Maybe...but why would he do that? And why would he be sneaking out of your tent at 5am?"

That had completely thrown me. Was I stupid to assume no one knew? Sure, Will might have known, after all, he was supposed to be sharing with Jonathan. He'd probably noticed he was alone most of the night. But Ash?!

Groaning I rose to my feet, stepping from my vanity and the contents of my makeup case which I'd upended across the marble surface. I barely wore make up to practice, but since I'd got the text I couldn't help wondering. Planning? Now here I was, pacing in my cheerleading uniform as I scrutinized everything. Was lip-gloss too much? And should I keep my hair down or try and pull it out of the way but in a more *alluring* style?

"Nature called in the early hours and I saw him." Ash smiled at me comfortingly. *"Don't worry. I won't say anything."*

"We...we didn't have sex."

"I believe you. And I mean it, I won't breathe a word. This is between you two".

"You think he really likes me?"

"I think he does. He's different around you."

I'd keep my hair down, loose and wavy. But the outfit needed to go. I needed something more attractive than the outfit he saw his sister wearing four times a week. It needed to be something that told him what I wanted before I'd even opened my mouth. He had to see me and know.

I headed across my room and threw open one of the giant mirrored doors that secured my walk-in wardrobe and all my favorite items. The lights blinkered as I stepped inside, the room almost clinically white, if not for the rows of clothes. Jeans, dresses, shorts. You name it, I had it. In several colors and a range of styles. Clothes were my passion. There was nothing I loved more than picking out an outfit, and wondering what accessories to wear with it.

And shoes.

Shoes made an outfit. The right boots could turn casual jeans and a halter neck into the perfect ensemble for drinks with the girls. Or a pair of Converse with a cocktail dress could take it down a notch into smart-casual.

So now my dilemma started. If I was gonna do this I needed to do it right. I needed to pair the right clothes with the right shoes to make Jonathan see me. Really *see* me. I aimlessly walked up and down, scanning the rails. I could go outside my comfort zone...all black. I had a pair of black leather ankle boots somewhere. And a tight lacy black dress too. I could give my hair some extra volume, maybe with a smoky eye and deep red lips.

But that wouldn't be me. Not really. That would be the girl I thought Jonathan wanted. And I wanted him to want me. Innocent, naive, virginal me.

So that idea went out of the window.

So did the idea of going in my sexiest lingerie.

I didn't want him thinking I was just there for the hook-up. I wanted him to know I wanted it all. The kisses and the snuggles, the bickering and snapping. I wanted the jealousy and the annoying habits and everything in between.

I wanted what my parents had.

I wanted to find my guy. The one who I fell in love with, who I lost my virginity to, and spent the rest of my life growing with. And I wanted, more than anything, for that guy to be Jonathan.

Breezing along the rails my hand touched something soft and white, and I slowly removed it from its place with a smile. It was a simple cocktail dress, a white fitted bodice met a silk band, before the tulle fabric fanned out. It was innocent, and so perfect. The irony of turning up in white wasn't lost on me either.

I quickly changed, grabbing my favorite pair of silver Loubs as I rushed back into my room. The text had been sent over half an hour ago now. I was deliberately wasting time. Because I knew if I did this, if I actually made the move, things could go wrong. And I wasn't ready for that...

My eventful afternoon with Ash sprung into my head once more as I slipped into my Louboutins. Or one part of the afternoon at least. The part with Jen...

It hadn't even started with her. It had started with Rachel.

I was glad I hadn't been around when Jonathan was flirting with her. Or trying as Rosie had said. I was used to seeing how Jonathan was around girls, how they reacted to him, but lately, it was harder. And Rachel was a friend. A new friend at least, and slowly warming to the group, but watching Jonathan flirt with her would be harder. It would be crossing several lines.

And then Jen had walked in. All bright smiles and coy glances. I couldn't hear what they were talking about, but I could see the way she shifted her body into his, the way he smirked and stroked her hair from her face. They were flirting. As if I wasn't standing there as he rubbed yet another conquest in my face. I thought after our night cuddled up in the rain he might have been a bit more tactful with his...relationships. Even if he had been gone by sunrise...which he eventually apologized for?

Which was probably how I'd ended up sharing my second kiss with Ash. And then promptly rushing from the room with him hot on my heels.

"What was that?" Ash raised an eyebrow at me as we paused by my car.

"I dunno. I panicked. Jen walked in and I just-"

"Immediately thought you'd kiss me?"

"Shut up!" I laughed, shoving him playfully. "He's always making me jealous. I guess I wanted to make him feel like that for once. If he even cared."

There was a slight possibility he did, that it bothered him to see me with Ash. Again. But was it because he wanted to be the one I was kissing or because he couldn't believe I'd blatantly pass him over for someone else? Was his ego that big? Maybe it was all bravado so he didn't have to address his feelings...

I paused, sitting at my vanity again. My cell was sitting by my left hand, my car keys by my right. I didn't have any more time. I needed to make the choice. Do I text Rosie and tell her I'll come pick her up...or do I jump in my car and rush round to Jonathan and finally tell him.

Ash nudged me "Get it out in the open."

"I dunno Ash...it could ruin everything."

"Or it could make everything better."

"But...what if I'm imagining it? You know Jonathan. He's a flirt."

Was I imagining it? Had I imagined how he'd looked at me at camping, the way he'd caressed my flesh and crushed me desperately against him?

"He is. And it could blow up in your face. But wouldn't you rather know?" Ash raised an eyebrow at me.

"I don't know! How could I face him again if he rejected me? Or Rosie?!"

"Brooke...do you kinda like him or really like him?" My silence and my cheeks suddenly burning gave him his answer. "That bad, huh? Then you owe it to yourself."

I grabbed my cell, hastily shoving it in my purse, and hooking my car keys around my finger.

Ash was right.

Before I could talk myself out of it, or before I actually paid attention to the negative voice in the back of my head, I rushed from my room, taking the stairs swiftly.

I tried to quieten the clip of my heels on the hardwood, afraid that if my parents saw me they'd make me pause. And a pause meant I could talk myself out of it. I needed to keep going, to focus. By the end of the night I could be so incredibly, blissfully happy.

Or...

No. There was no or. I needed to do this. I couldn't spend any longer watching him sweet-talk other girls, my stomach dropping as he flashed them a smirk and they fell under his spell. At the very least he might not do it in front of me after...

I cast a quick glance at my parents as I slipped from the house, relieved they hadn't noticed my outfit change, completely enveloped in each other. Smiling, I closed the door and rushed to my car, deftly sliding into the driving seat. If I could have a relationship only half as happy as theirs I knew I'd be on the right track. They were definite couple goals. High school sweethearts that had overcome every obstacle thrown at them, because that was what you did, wasn't it? Find someone that you couldn't imagine spending your life without. Someone that stood by and supported you, lifting you when you felt low and fighting your battles with you.

And they had their share of battles.

The storm. Their friend trying to kill them. A child that had inherited his dad's special abilities. You know, normal stuff...

Fighting a nervous smile I brought my car to life, slowly edging down the long drive as I left the safety of my house and worked my way to the Taylors, silently praying that Jonathan hadn't decided to have a last-minute practice. Ash might be an encouraging face, but confessing my feelings in front of the rest of our friends was my idea of hell.

So I was relieved when I pulled up and found an empty drive.

Or, almost empty...

I cast a curious glance at Rachel's car as I killed my own engine. What was she doing here? Maybe she'd arrived before Rosie had text. Rachel wasn't on the squad, being that she was a newbie, but she'd been on her old school's team. So we'd figured it couldn't hurt for her to crash team meets, step in if we needed an extra body, and if she was lucky maybe the rest of the girls would want to initiate her. Originally we'd met her in the mall, casually scrutinizing the latest fashion in one of the designer stores. We'd struck up conversation, finding out she was new to Harrison. So we took her under our wing. And it was nice.

Since Rosie and I were the only girls in the group, we often got roped into whatever the guys wanted to do. Which was fine. Usually. We loved going to practice, and if we wanted to see a horror flick they were always up for it. But as soon as you mentioned shopping, or going for a drink somewhere that wasn't filled with pool tables, they tended to clam up.

Rachel was a nice addition, she'd understand if I asked for a moment alone with Jonathan. I couldn't back down now just because I'd come up against a small blip.

Taking a deep breath, I checked my reflection in my rearview mirror and climbed from the car.

It was now or never.

My heart started hammering as I closed the gap between me and the front door, trying to clear my head from any doubt that might adhere to my nerves.

Just remember Ash's words.

I squared my shoulders with confidence, almost grinning as I opened the door. "Jonathan?" I kicked the door closed behind me, glancing around the open hallway as I listened for any sound of him.

There was a soft thump from the sitting room, a hush, followed by frenzied movements. What the hell was going on?

"We're in here!" Rachel called out. In my excitement I'd forgotten she was here.

I turned to walk towards them, pausing when I saw Jonathan through the open doorway. He was shirtless, tugging his jeans up onto his hips. His belt was unbuckled as he fought to fasten himself up, his eyes narrowed as he looked down at the couch. And the world around me slowed.

No...

No, no, no.

My imagination was running amok. This wasn't how it seemed. There had to be a simple explanation for this. "What's going on?"

Jonathan looked at me as he took a slight step forward. "Nothi-"

"We had sex." Rachel moved into view, smirking as she stepped in front of Jonathan. My stomach churned as bile rose in my throat, my eyes settling on the opened condom wrapper tossed to the floor. "And it was good."

No...

Air rushed out of me. I tried looking past her to Jonathan, hoping I'd see confusion on his face, wondering what she was talking about. But he couldn't look at me. He was staring at the floor. "You..." My voice caught in my throat. I needed him to admit it. "You had sex? With *her*?"

He still couldn't look at me. But his head inclined as he gave a small nod.

My knees threatened to give way beneath me. Nothing could have prepared me for this.

"He did." Rachel was smirking, and I frowned at her reaction. She...she knew Jonathan and I had kissed. I told her after camping. "He wanted a *real* woman. It's best you find out now."

Ouch.

My throat closed as I fought to stop my eyes tearing up. "I..." Was she actually doing this, had I been so naive that not only had I assumed I was more than a midnight fondle with Jonathan, but had invented an entire friendship with Rachel? I'd never felt so stupid. She was right, of course she was right. Why the hell would Jonathan Taylor want me? The virginal friend of his younger sister. I bet they'd sat together after, laughing at how stupid I was for thinking he could ever see me as more than an idiotic teenage girl. I'd not be able to please him the way she could, the way other girls could. I was sloppy, and inexperienced. "Okay." I nodded, dropping my gaze to the floor.

"No, not okay." Jonathan moved around to face Rachel, narrowing his eyes at her. "You can't talk to her like that."

Rachel waved him away, rolling her eyes with a laugh. "Please, I'm doing her a favor."

"You are." I looked up at her, trying to stop my hands from shaking. I didn't want them seeing how much they'd hurt me. "You have." I reluctantly moved my gaze to Jonathan, who still looked uncomfortable, his face drawn, watching me cautiously. "And I'm about to do you one." I tore my eyes from him, settling on Rachel once more. Her smirk grew, another stab of betrayal slicing into my gut. She was ruthless. "He'll fuck you over too. And when he does, you won't have any friends there to comfort you."

"Thanks for the concern, but I'll be fine."

"Brooke..." Jonathan was still watching me.

I couldn't read him. I didn't want to. I was done trying to figure out what his intentions were. I'd made the same stupid mistake as all the girls before me, no doubt I wouldn't be the last. "What?"

He moved around Rachel, stepping towards me. "This isn't...It doesn't mean anything."

Shocking.

Jonathan slept with yet another girl who meant absolutely nothing to him. I almost felt sorry for Rachel. Almost.

"Maybe not to you. But that's no surprise." I couldn't look at him any longer. Of course this meant nothing to him. Just like I meant nothing to him. But this stupid thing meant *everything* to me.

It had taken my hope, and it had crushed it. I felt broken, empty. And *so* ridiculous. How had I believed that I'd be the girl? The one to change him? He wouldn't change for me. He wouldn't change for anyone unless he wanted to. And that wasn't Jonathan.

"I think we're done here." Rachel broke the silence, grabbing her underwear from the floor and shoving it into her purse as she adjusted her dress. She stepped into Jonathan, leaning to kiss him on the cheek and laughing when he recoiled.

I almost laughed too.

He could have ripped her clothes off and ravished her on the floor at my feet and it wouldn't hurt any more than it already had. It was a startling realization, knowing he'd fooled me. That I was just another of his games.

And I could have so easily lost my virginity to him that night.

Thank God for the storm.

"Was this the plan all along?" A tear rolled down my cheek and I cursed myself, quickly brushing it away.

Rachel shrugged, rooting for her keys. "He's...a definite bonus. But not essential." She turned to look at him, appraising him slowly. "Still, who knows? Maybe by the end of the year we'll be Prom King and Queen...and you'll be fetching our drinks."

Jonathan looked up at her, his face pained, almost hopeless. "Just get out." He pleaded.

We ignored him.

This was never about him. Not to Rachel anyway. If I'd shown an interest in Ash it would be him in Jonathan's place. She was evil and calculating, nothing mattered besides her end goal. She wanted me to suffer. But *why*?! Had I been a bad friend? Had I done something to make her hate me? Maybe she'd never liked me at all, just latching on to Rosie and I so she could climb the social ladder at school. But she was mistaken if she thought this was how you did it. Sure, Harrison had cliques, our bullies and our saints. But I tried, throughout my school life, to make sure everyone felt like they had a place, a friend. And that's what we'd done with Rachel. We didn't want her to feel ambushed by a new school, new faces, and a completely new dynamic. We took her in and we included her.

What a mistake that had been.

"Sweetie...when you rock up at school tomorrow no one is going to want to be seen with you." I fought my emotions down and locked them away, I wouldn't give them the satisfaction of watching me crumble. "So the best you're going to get for Prom is turning up with your dad and wearing a dress off last year's sale rack."

Her eyes flashed as she glared at me. She wasn't the only one who could pick up on someone's insecurities. She obviously thought I hadn't noticed she never bought anything when we went shopping. And the funny thing was it didn't matter as much as she thought it did. We didn't care who she wore and how much her wardrobe was worth. We cared about how much her character was worth.

Which evidently wasn't a great deal either.

She advanced towards me, raising an eyebrow as she flashed me a malicious smirk. "You may play innocent but there's dirt under those manicured nails. And I'll find it." She glanced back at Jonathan as she shoved past me. "I hope you enjoyed the show."

And with that she was gone.

Sorrow washed over me, my throat tightening as we stood in her absence, both silent, waiting for the other to speak. But I didn't want him to. I didn't want to hear whatever he wanted to say, because he'd assume with a few words and a careful grin I'd forget. But I couldn't. I didn't want to hear excuses and promises. I didn't want to hear that it was a mistake and he didn't mean it.

Because he had.

Because if I'd meant *anything* to him at all she never would have been an option.

A ragged sob left my mouth before I could hold it back, my eyes squeezing closed as I tried to fight back the tears, my lip trembling. It was happening. It was overcoming me and I was going to cry. I was going to break right here.

"Brooke..." His fingertips were soft on my shoulder, alighting all those happy moments we'd shared. My first kiss...the frenzied make-out...the snuggling. The way he'd held me through the storm, humming softly into my neck and stroking my arms. He'd made me feel so secure. So wanted.

And now it was all tainted. Ruined.

Because I saw through all those moments. I'd taken my rose-tinted glasses off and I saw everything clearly. I was nothing but a pawn.

I recoiled from his touch, disgusted to have the hands that had just held Rachel now on me, moving to leave. "Don't." I held the front door open, turning to face him but unable to actually look at him. I couldn't. "Can you do me a favor?"

"Anything." He stepped forward, hopeful as he looked across at me.

I met his eyes. I wanted to see this. I needed to. "Stay away from me. I just...I don't know if we can be friends anymore."

The hope died in his eyes, his mouth dropping open. "What?"

"Did I stutter?"

His head bowed to the floor as he shook his head.

With that I walked from the house, climbing into my car to make my escape. I was on autopilot, still fighting my feelings until I was somewhere safe. Somewhere away from him and the scene I'd just walked out on. Somewhere I could just try and forget.

I slammed my foot on the accelerator as the perfect place came to mind. It was stupid, and reckless, but safe. Somewhere I could break, away from my friends and family and their curious stares, but a place they'd be in a flash if I needed them.

Jays.

My parent's bar. Unlike most of the bars we frequented for drinks Jays was classy. Mom made sure of that. The inside was well lit and warm. Families sitting around eating, watching screens dotted around the walls.

The stage against the back wall, reserved for family entertainment, was usually used by kids as they chased each other around. And Mom loved it. It brought a smile to her face whenever she saw a family enjoying themselves together.

As I headed inside I noticed tonight was no different. The hustle and bustle of the evening rush keeping most of the staff busy, so no one batted an eye as I slipped behind the bar, grabbing a bottle and disappearing to a booth away from everyone. I opened the drink taking a breath before I gulped at it, wincing as the sharp taste hit my throat. And then the burn spread to the rest of me, and my walls finally began to crumble. I stifled a sob, sinking deeper into the booth and taking another shot. I'd keep drinking. I'd drink the whole bottle if I had to, until I was completely numb to what had happened, until I could barely recall the whole affair.

Jonathan...half naked...their bodies glistening...

Shot.

Her head rolling back as she moaned his name...digging her fingernails into his back...

Shot.

I grabbed my cell, quickly scrolling to my conversation with Ash. I paused. Screw it. I tapped out a quick text and hit send.

It blew up in my face. Oh well x

With that I turned it off. I didn't need to speak to him, I couldn't bear to go into it, or lie and tell him I was fine. I didn't need concerned messages from my family if he told them. I just needed to be left alone.

"Well well Miss Danes...fancy seeing you here."

I looked up into the face of Zak Warner, the school Quarterback. I'd definitely need a few more drinks to get through this. I lifted the bottle to my lips, my head starting to fog as I gulped at the sharp clear liquid. If Jonathan was known for his reputation with the ladies, how he was the bad boy everyone wanted to change, Zak was known for how awful he was. He was sexist and selfish. And any girl that had been with him would agree. And yet, he always found himself several more.

I gave him a cold look, "What do you want?"

He took that as an invitation to join me, sliding into the booth and immediately placing his hand on my inner thigh. "You looked like you could use some company." He shifted closer, his hand sliding further up. "Drinking alone..."

I was frozen as I looked at him, feeling his fingertips creep higher. He knew I was a virgin. Everyone knew I was a virgin. And yet...he didn't care. He didn't mind that I was inexperienced and probably clumsy. It didn't bother him that he'd be taking something from me, because it made him feel like *he* was worth something.

"I could keep you company. Turn that frown upside down." His other hand wound around me, his lips moving against my ear as he breathed me in. "Or we could...head somewhere else? Away from prying eyes? And you could tell me what's wrong?"

He didn't care about that. Of course he didn't. All he saw was a broken girl, sat alone and clutching a bottle of vodka as she cried. He'd hit the jackpot.

I could slap him, shove him away and run into the night. But something inside me didn't want to.

I wanted this. I wanted to go to his car, and let him undress me. I wanted him to kiss me and touch me, I wanted him to take me in his back seat, and rip my virginity from me as he did. And then maybe with that gone, I could finally be taken seriously. I wouldn't be the idiot virgin anymore. I'd be a woman.

And I wouldn't be overlooked again.

"Just shut up." I raised an eyebrow at him, taking one last mouthful of vodka before offering him the half-empty bottle. "I'm not an idiot Zak, I know what you want. I want it too. So let's just get to your car and get it over with."

He took the bottle and placed it down on the table, laughing and shaking his head as he stood up. "I thought you'd be harder than that." He offered me his hand and yanked me to my feet as I took it, his grin wide. He eagerly pulled me along behind him, glancing around to make sure I was still ready and willing.

And I was. I was a big girl and I knew what I wanted. Him. Right now. No questions. No small talk.

Once outside Zak slammed me against his car door, his lips crashing down on mine as he pinned me against his chest. It was nothing like the curious kiss I'd shared with Ash, or...

No. Don't think about him.

I yanked open the door behind me, almost laughing as I toppled into the driver's seat and Zak landing eagerly on top of me. His hands were blindly groping at my dress, yanking it up around my hips as his kisses became more breathless and sloppy. I took a breather as he pulled away, his eyes lustful as he caressed the length of my legs with his gaze, starting from my exposed thighs. He placed his hands down on them, tugging them apart as he slowly made his way north, skimming my skin as he reached for my underwear.

A distant vibrating caught his attention and he paused, glancing to the dash where he'd stuffed his cell. Whoever was calling didn't warrant him answering, before it rang off he'd lifted my hips, inching his fingers into the silk of my underwear and slowly sliding them down. He reached the bottom of my thighs, just about to sweep them from my body when his cell vibrated again. Someone really wanted his attention.

"Who is it?" Maybe his parents wondered where he was, or one of his football buddies wanted to meet up.

"Just my girlfriend." He rolled his eyes in annoyance, reaching to shut off his cell.

And I froze.

His girlfriend.

He had a girlfriend.

No.

I couldn't.

With a start, I realized where I was and what I was doing. The alcohol immediately wearing off as I pushed him away from me. I had to get away. This wasn't right.

I felt sick.

I ignored his yells as I stumbled into the cool evening air and away from him. He was pissed. I could hear it in his tone. But I didn't care, he could be pissed, because I wasn't *that* girl, and I couldn't *be* that girl.

Choking down air my throat closed up, my chest burning as the last few hours slammed into me again, making me face the sobering reality. To admit what a complete mess I'd almost made. That wasn't me. The promiscuous girl who had sex to hide from emotion.

I wasn't Jonathan.

A sob broke the air as I stumbled back towards the bar, the tears starting to fall. Hot, wet, messy tears. They were unrelenting, each drip searing into me as I cried over a boy I'd never truly had. Because he'd made me doubt myself and what I stood for. Because he'd made me feel like I was less than worth his time. Because he'd made me think that losing my virginity would make me happy.

But I wasn't happy. And I wouldn't be. I'd hold onto my virginity and I'd give it to the man I loved. The one I'd spend my life with. Because *he* would be worth it.

And the realization it wouldn't be Jonathan made me choke.

But at least it wouldn't be Zak either.

I heard the roar of his engine as he sped away, leaving me leaning against the building in a drunken stupor, defeated and alone. My tears became heavier, the brick cutting into my palms as I fought to remain upright, the physical ache of my heart being broken stinging more. Replaying the moment I walked in, the panicked look on Jonathans face as he desperately tried to cover what had happened. If I hadn't walked in would he have told me? Or would he have forced Rachel to keep quiet until he could coerce me into having sex with him? And I would have.

My tears continued to fall. Silent black rivers marking my skin.

I wasn't sure how long I'd stood there, half propped against the wall, my broken cries turning into breathless whimpers, when a pair of strong, tan arms wrapped around me, pulling me easily against a familiar body.

I glanced up through my tears.

Nathan.

Chapter 7

Rosie

My hands gripped the porcelain rim of the sink as I hunched over it, my knuckles white as I stared down into the black expanse of the drain. A clear drop fell onto the pristine surface, trickling down sluggishly. I brushed at the track on my cheek, my breathing measured as the weight in my stomach dissipated. The worst was over.

My grip relaxed as I focused on the trail the teardrop had taken, my throat burning with an acrid taste. I wouldn't have long before they'd miss me. Before they'd start asking questions. My eyes closed as I swallowed painfully, opening again to stare at the edge of the mirror before me. Shame surged again as I drew my gaze higher, just barely glancing at the blonde girl before me. She stared back with contempt, her blue eyes alert as they traveled across every flyaway hair and blemish. I tore my eyes from her, dragging my bag across the counter to find my breath spray. My hand tightened around it as I released a burst down my throat, wincing as my stomach lurched. I shook my head to dismiss the instinct, straightening up with a haggard breath. I threw the spray back into my bag, glancing at my reflection once again as I placed the strap on my shoulder. My fingers gripped the leather, my nails digging into it as I scrutinized the girl staring back. I shook my head again and looked down, my feet marching me to the exit.

My footsteps echoed across the polished wood as I strode back to the drama studio, casting a furtive glance around me for any witnesses. The corridor remained empty, the only sound the distant chatter from inside the studio itself. I pulled on the heavy door and slipped inside, blinking as the dimness engulfed me. A stage flanked the back of the vast room, a handful of students stood in small clusters atop it. My gaze ran across the sea of plush chairs, stopping as they landed on a familiar face. Or the back of one, anyway. I scurried down the aisle to reach his row, my pace slowing as he turned to acknowledge me.

"What'd I miss?"

David moved along the row to free up a seat for me, gesturing with a rolled-up sheet to the stage before us. "They're just running through some exercises to wind down."

I nodded, my hand coming out to grip the back of the vacant seat as the blood rushed to my head. I closed my eyes for a moment, my fingertips tracing the velvet fabric as I steadied myself.

"You okay?"

My eyes flew open to meet his, a blush warming my cheeks as I nodded with a limp smile.

His gaze grew curious as he studied me, his hand outstretching. I ignored the offering, slipping into the seat gingerly. "Honestly. I'm fine."

He arched an eyebrow at me, sinking into his seat as he glanced down. A small bottle of ice-cold water appeared in the hand he'd proffered to me, his eyebrow raised as he held it out. "Take it."

I rolled my eyes, "I'm fine-"

"Take it." He repeated, his voice becoming stern.

I eyed the bottle warily, my stomach sinking as I took it. His gaze stayed on me as I cradled the cool plastic, a weary smile playing on my lips as I gently unscrewed the cap and took a small sip. I fought a wince as the liquid hit my throat, my insides protesting. Satisfied, he sat back and looked over at the stage. I watched him carefully, replacing the cap and slipping the bottle into my bag. "What's that?" I gestured to the paper in his hand.

He blinked, frowning down at it. "It's just a list of parts for the end of year performance. Figured I'd look over it…"

I smiled wryly, raising an eyebrow at him. "You're really serious about this, huh?"

David let out a small sigh and nodded, glancing back at me bashfully. "Kinda."

"I think it's great."

"You do?"

"Yeah." I grinned, "You're going after something you enjoy. What's not great about that?"

"I guess."

"So uh…" I hesitated, peering at him. "What does Will think to it all?"

"Nice segue." He smirked, raising an eyebrow.

Ah. I sat back, defeated. "Sorry. I was trying to be subtle."

David turned to look at me fully, amusement etched on his face.

"What? I can be subtle."

He let out a laugh, gesturing to my shirt. "Sure you can."

I followed his gaze and grinned despite myself. A large animated black sheep adorned my chest, thick-rimmed sunglasses and a party blower completing the design.

"Well…since we're on the topic now…" I began coyly.

"Can we not be?"

I watched as he looked down at the rolled-up paper, his jaw clenching as his expression darkened.

"He's still your brother, David," I said in a small voice, thankful for the dim lighting.

He didn't answer, his gaze fixated on the scroll. I looked back up at the stage area, the silence dwarfing us. A handful of girls were stood to the right, grins adorning their faces as they spoke in hushed tones. I frowned slightly as a couple glanced our way, their smiles widening as they let out a chorus of giggles.

"Ignore them," David muttered beside me.

Colour flooded my cheeks and I sank deeper into my seat, paranoia filling my senses as they continued to whisper.

"They'll be bored once there's fresh gossip." He insisted, his dark eyebrow arching.

They couldn't have found out about Alex? There was no way. He wouldn't have breathed a word. Still, I squirmed under their mocking glances. I knew what everyone thought about me. I was essentially a stereotype. The dumb blonde cheerleader who opened her legs up to anyone willing to pay her a compliment or two. Except I didn't. I'd only ever been with Lucas and Alex before now. Not that it mattered. Once people decided something about you, it tended to stick. But, God, if they did somehow know about Alex…what would he say? Would he be mad? My stomach heaved again and I placed a hand over my mouth.

"You sure you're okay?" David frowned, his shoulders hunching as he peered at me.

I nodded, not trusting myself to speak.

"It's not a big deal. Half of it's probably made up anyway."

My eyes narrowed, my fingertips moving from my lips timidly. "What's the rumor?"

"Jonathan and Rachel." He shrugged. "She's telling everyone how he fell for her and couldn't resist."

"Resist?"

David sighed, shaking his head. "They slept together."

"When?" I blurted, looking at him incredulously.

"Last night I guess."

"But…" I shook my head, my mouth agape.

David let out a soft chuckle and nodded. "Yeah, I know."

A loud trilling sound chimed out, the bodies around the room gathering their bags and jackets wordlessly. I pulled mine onto my shoulder and stood carefully, determined to avoid another suspicious look from David. He stood with me, his hands hovering by his sides as he watched my movements. I slipped into the aisle, glancing back at him gratefully as we milled out of the studio into the main lobby. This building stood separate to the rest of the school, an elegant gravel path guiding from the stone steps of the theatre. Lush green lawns broke up the distance, scattered trees providing minimal shade. I blinked against the stark light of the day as we emerged at the top of the steps, my eyes narrowing as I spotted a familiar redhead walking along the path ahead.

"Excuse me," I muttered, gripping my bag to my side as I marched across. I had no idea what I was going to say, only that I had to say something. I knew what Jonathan could be like, he had a way of enchanting girls without even realizing he was doing it. Normally I kept out of it. But…she was a friend. A new friend who clearly thought there was more to their tryst than he did.

My pace slowed as I approached the small gathering of girls, my fingernails digging into the bag strap gently. This would not be a fun conversation. They turned to look at me, amused smiles adorning their faces. Thankfully none of them had been in the drama studio just now. Rachel emerged from their cluster, raising an eyebrow with an easy smirk. "Can we help you?"

I frowned, my cheeks warming as I glanced from her to the fresh audience. "Uh…"

"Use your words, Rosie." She grinned, a soft wave of laughter chorusing around us.

"I heard about you and Jonathan."

She waited a moment, her eyebrow arching again. "And?"

"And…" I hesitated, biting my lip. "I just wanted to check that you knew what you were doing. We're friends after all."

A smirk spread across her face, her gaze even. "We're not friends."

"What?" I frowned.

"You want me to draw a picture? Would that be simple enough to penetrate those thick roots of yours?" She grinned, taking a step towards me. "We're not friends. Never were."

I eyed her warily, lowing my voice to a murmur as I felt redness flooding my cheeks. "Why are you saying that?"

Rachel laughed, the sound cutting through the air between us. "You gonna cry?"

A thousand retorts span through my mind, each one angrier and more cutting than the last. But my mouth remained closed, set into a sad grimace as I stared back at her. Nothing I said now would make a difference. She'd shown her true colors. I shook my head, my gaze steely as I shoved past her to move along the path leading to the main building. As I did so I felt the air leaving my body, the gravel before me blurring as my head went light. I fought to keep my steps straight, my body walking with determination until I could be sure I was out of sight.

As I strode into the main building the gentle trickling of students around me grew into a stream. I looked around uncertainly as my feet slowed, my gaze searching for any friendly faces. I let out a small sigh of relief as I spotted a brunette at the end of the hallway, her head bowed as she crammed some books into her locker. Brooke. As I took another step forward a pair of muscular arms wound around me. I span with a yelp, my eyes wide as I turned to face my attacker. Or, as it turned out, my boyfriend.

"Zak."

His mouth lifted into a lazy smirk, his dark eyes boring down on me as he maintained his hold. "You were expecting someone else?"

"No." I laughed, shaking my head. I brought my palm out to rest against his chest gently, taking a small step back. "You just caught me off guard."

"My apologies." He chuckled, raising an eyebrow. "You joining us for lunch?"

The color drained from my face, my mouth setting into a cheerful smile as I nodded dumbly. "Sure. Only…" I glanced back at Brooke as she stared dolefully into her locker. "I just wanna check on something first. I'll catch you up?"

His brown eyes followed my gaze, a small smirk playing on his lips as he nodded. "I'll save you a seat."

I smiled brightly again, taking another tentative step back. The last I'd heard we were still keeping 'us' a secret. Although I guess since our encounter with Will the other night that ship might've sailed. Not that Will would be spreading the word, but it made it seem sordid to keep up the charade when one of my closest friends already knew. I felt a pang in the pit of my stomach as I realized my best friend still didn't. Perhaps Zak wouldn't mind if we were out in the open about it now? He was hardly playing it cool.

His eyes settled on mine briefly, before slowly traveling down along my body. My cheeks flushed as his hands released their hold, his fingertips brushing against the fabric of my top. "Cute."

He raised an eyebrow, his touch hovering near the animated sheep design. I smiled shyly, reaching up to gently grasp his hand. His dark eyes warmed as he raised our clasped hands, kissing the back of mine softly. My cheeks warmed again and I slowly pulled away, my mouth twitching into a grin as I turned to make my way to Brooke. Before I'd even gone a few steps he grabbed at me, tugging me back into him with force. I let out a gasp as I collided into his chest, his lips crashing down onto mine. My eyes closed as I returned the kiss, my palms resting on his arms gingerly. His tongue pushed its way into my mouth, a low guttural groan escaping his lips as he gripped me to him. After a few moments I gently pushed him back, laughing breathlessly as I looked up at him. That certainly answered my question about us being a secret. His dark eyes stared into mine, his mouth twitching into a languid smirk as he stepped back. "Don't keep me waiting."

I blinked, nodding stupidly as he strode past me to the dining room. His words weighed heavily in his wake, my stomach churning as I debated whether I'd already kept him waiting too long. I hadn't exactly done the whole boyfriend thing before. This was all new to me. And it wasn't as though my reputation didn't precede me – rightly or wrongly so. Could he be getting bored already? I shook my head to clear my thoughts, blanching as I looked back to where Brooke was now headed toward the dining room. Crap.

I scurried over to her, hurrying to keep up with her pace. "Hey!"

"Hey." She smiled softly, her head still bowed as she walked.

"How're you doing?"

She paused, turning to look at me suspiciously. "Fine. Why?"

I glanced around, lowering my voice to a murmur. "I heard about Jonathan and Rachel."

"Oh." Her face paled. "Yeah, I know. Typical Jonathan, right?"

"I don't like it." I let out a sigh, darting another look around the slowly emptying hallway. "I feel like she just befriended us to get at him like some crazed fan or something. Plus, she's been really horrible since…I mean, I know he's not exactly innocent but-"

Brooke's bottom lip began to tremble, her head bowing as a tear escaped. I frowned as she tried to quickly swat it away, her cheeks flushing as another one followed suit. I placed an arm around her shoulders and swiftly steered her into the nearest available classroom, closing the door behind us. She let out a sob as we moved into the private space, her gaze still boring into the floor determinedly. I released the blinds on the window of the door, turning to look at her tentatively. "Brooke. Are you okay?"

She shook her head slowly, her mouth grim as she wiped at her cheeks. "I'm such an idiot!"

I frowned at her. "No, you're not. What happened?"

"Your asshole of a brother happened." She laughed bitterly, her voice wavering.

Ah. I had a feeling I knew where this was headed, but I really hoped I was wrong. Not because it wouldn't be perfect, but because he might have already messed it up. "What did he do?"

"What didn't he do?" She scoffed, moving to collapse into one of the chairs. I followed her silently, sinking into one across the aisle. "He broke my heart…" She finally submitted, her gaze lowering shyly to the desk before her.

I opened my mouth to speak, my insides sinking for her. Nothing I could think to say sounded right. So, I said nothing. Instead I simply reached across to place my hand over hers, squeezing gently.

She lifted her doe eyes to mine with a small smile. "He made me feel so special. Like I was the only girl he'd ever needed."

I nodded slowly, tracing my thumb across her skin delicately. He could do this to girls, but this was different. Brooke and my brother had always had this…chemistry. I'd glimpsed it for years, but figured they'd address it when the time was right. I hadn't envisaged that it would end like this.

"Brooke." I began gently. "Did you…did you two?"

She shook her head with a sad smile. "No. Thank God. But I wanted to…" Her eyes met mine, fresh tears brimming in them. "I would have."

"How long have you liked him?" I breathed, placing my other hand around hers so they were engulfed.

"Since our first kiss. *My* first kiss."

Realization dawned, my eyes widening as I stared back at her. "Your secret guy?"

Brooke nodded slowly. "It was when you were ill."

"Wow. I had no idea."

She let out a soft chuckle, her palm turning in mine gently. "There's a lot you don't know. Like how he stayed in my tent at camping. And how we almost…" Her eyebrows rose suggestively.

"Wow," I repeated dumbly, glancing away. "So, wait…did he lead you on?"

Her shoulders rose in a weak shrug, her bottom lip quivering slightly. "I feel like such a loser. He…I thought I was the girl he spoke about. He was so charming. I've seen him pull all of the tricks out of the bag before but..." Another tear rolled down across her cheek, the droplet landing on the fabric of her sleeve. "I was stupid enough to think it meant something when he did it to me."

I narrowed my eyes, reaching down to drag my chair along the floor to get closer to hers.

"You're not stupid. Not at all." Truth be told, I'd considered whether she might be the girl he'd confessed to having a crush on too. It had made sense. It still did, oddly. "I'm so sorry, Brooke." I frowned, pulling her into a hug. She leaned into me gently, her hands raising to return the embrace. A horrible thought struck me, my expression darkening as I pulled back to look at her. "Did Rachel know?"

She bit her lip as it began to tremble again, nodding.

"I'm going to kill her."

"If it helps, she didn't do it to get to Jonathan." Brooke smiled wryly. "She did it to get to me."

"You?" I frowned, shaking my head. "But why?"

"I have *no* idea." She shrugged, laughing bitterly. Her mouth set into a grimace as she glanced away. "I walked in and caught them. She said Jonathan was just an added bonus."

"Oh my God." I breathed, my blood running cold as a wave of shame flooded through me. She'd set it all up to ensure Brooke would find them. She'd purposely set out to hurt her. And I'd enabled it with my 'car trouble'. I averted my gaze, bile rising in my throat as I fought to hide the guilt that was no doubt etched onto my face. My car had been working fine. It was me that had crashed. I'd taken it too far and passed out on the way back from the mall. I'd just barely been able to pull over before the world became a blur, my head spinning as I sent the last text I could manage before sleep claimed me. It was my fault Rachel had been able to do this to my best friend. I prayed she'd never find out.

"I was going to tell him how I felt," Brooke admitted ruefully, her fingertips toying with the cuff of her sleeve.

"I don't know what to say," I mumbled, grimacing. "I wish I could make it better."

Her knee nudged mine gently, a small smile playing on her lips. "Not hating me for keeping it all a secret helps."

"As if I could ever hate you. Besides, we all have our secrets."

"We do." Her expression became serious. "And I'm glad you mentioned it actually."

My insides jolted as I met her gaze. "Oh?"

She looked down at my clasped hands and took them in her own, our roles reversing. "Is everything okay with you? You've been acting pretty off lately."

"I have?"

"Yeah. You've been…absent? Like sometimes you're not really paying attention. Or you'll find excuses not to do things."

My stomach turned to lead as I stared back at her, my skin ashen as I chewed over my response. "I'm fine." I offered with a soft smile, grimacing inwardly as the very same words I'd said to David echoed around me once again. "I uh...I have actually been keeping a secret. But we've only just figured out what we are." She waited patiently, cradling my hands. "Zak and I are dating."

"Zak?" Her face fell, her hands relinquishing their hold slightly. "As in Zak Warner?"

I nodded slowly, raising an eyebrow. "Yeah. He asked me out the first week of school." I frowned as she looked away. "I was going to tell you, honest. Please don't be mad."

"I'm not mad. I'm worried." Brooke met my gaze evenly, her voice firm. "Rosie, Zak's not a good guy."

I pulled my hands from hers, flinching slightly. "What?"

"He's just a bit of a sleaze...I mean, you've heard the rumors?"

"I have. But he likes me. And he treats me well."

"I just want what's best for you." Her gaze softened, her lips forming a concerned smile. "Do you really think that's Zak?"

I stood up, looking anywhere but at her. My cheeks flushed crimson as I pondered her question honestly. He was the first guy to have ever wanted me for more than one night...or a few. He wanted to take me out on dates and hold my hand. Have others know he liked me. Besides, I couldn't hold his reputation against him. I knew what it was like to have one formed around you without much in the way of evidence. And so far he had been really sweet to me. Attentive. Caring. I brought my gaze to hers, nodding. "I do."

She stood up with a weary smile. "Then I'll support you."

"You will?"

"Of course I will."

I pulled her into a warm hug, burrowing my face into her shoulder with a wan smile. "Thank you." Her hands rubbed at my back gently, her perfume lingering around us as she pulled away. Just knowing that much lifted some of the weight that had settled in my gut. It meant a lot that she'd be there whatever happened. It was my duty to do the same for her, especially owing to my part in it. "So, I think I know step one in fixing your broken heart." I began brightly, reaching out to brush her cheek.

"You do?"

I nodded seriously. "Me and you are having a good old-fashioned sleepover tonight. At yours. We can have a pamper."

Her lips twitched into a grin, "I'd like that."

"Good." I beamed, snaking through the aisle towards the door. I hesitated, turning to look back at her. "You're worth a thousand of her, Brooke. He'll realize that soon enough."

She gave a small shrug, her smile fading. "She gave him exactly what he wanted. He realized it wouldn't work like that with me."

"And it shouldn't."

"I know." She let out a sigh, "I guess eventually I'll realize what a blessing it was."

"You will. You've come out of this with dignity." I smiled, raising an eyebrow. "You should be proud of who you are."

She stared back at me quietly, her expression softening. "Thank you."

I nodded, gesturing to the classroom door. "You ready to face them?"

"I'm ready to pretend they don't exist." She raised an eyebrow, linking her arm through mine.

I pulled her into my side as we ambled through the door into the now deserted hallway. Already a flurry of thoughts span through my mind, and in turn my stomach was beginning to ache dully with the pressure of it all. Zak would understand me sitting with Brooke today. I'd find a way to make it up to him, to make sure that he knew I cared. That I was all in. I didn't want to lose him before we'd even started. And the sleepover would be fun, and was definitely needed. By both of us. I'd just have to hope that I could avoid any more questions or uncomfortable encounters. I could nibble something and then fill up with water, bloat myself out until the time came to cleanse my system. It would be fine.

It had been so far.

Chapter 8

Alex

An excited wave began to sweep the room as the clock ticked closer to freedom, to the end of another school day and the sixteen hours until we were back. I glanced to our English Professor, completely oblivious to the chatter, as he droned on about the effects of Shakespeare on modern language.

I slumped back in my chair, running a hand through my hair as my cell vibrated on the desk. A quick glance to the left let me know what was waiting.

Jonathan.

He raised an eyebrow as I made a show of dragging my cell towards me, already knowing what it would say.

Practice in an hour. New material.

Well that was obvious.

I nodded, smiling awkwardly for his benefit but knowing he wasn't buying it all the same. He didn't care, turning his back as he shoved his cell away and muttered something to Will. I tried to catch Ash's eye as we simultaneously began to pack our things away, but he was oblivious.

Things with the band had been tense lately. Scratch that, things with everyone had been tense lately. And I was sat in the middle without a clue what was going on.

It had started with Will and David, then Jonathan had avoided directly talking to Ash. And now the girls had abandoned us. Sitting apart from us in class and avoiding us altogether outside of them. I glanced to the left once more, watching Jonathan pull out a battered packet of cigarettes as the bell rang. His eyes were drawn across the room as Rosie and Brooke stood, neither of them looking our way as they joined the throng of bodies that edged towards the door.

I pretended not to see his shoulders slump.

"I might be a bit late." I smiled awkwardly as Jonathan turned to face me, an eyebrow raising slowly. He'd recently come to the conclusion that he was the only one that cared about the band. And it might have been true in some sense, but in so many others he was wrong. Not that I was doing a great job at changing his mind.

"How late? I really want to try and get this song smoothed out."

"I promised Melissa I'd drop her at the mall. Josh has football. So literally ten minutes?"

He nodded, glancing past me at Ash. "You okay for it?"

Ash turned back to look at us, already sneaking towards the door. "Huh? Oh, yeah..." He smiled awkwardly, "I was just..." He didn't need to finish his sentence. We all saw his gaze flick to Rosie and Brooke.

Jonathan didn't respond, simply nodding as he turned back to Will. I waited a second, deliberating whether to hang back with the surly drummer and the moody lead singer, or follow the cocker spaniel of the band.

I chose Ash.

Weaving around the desks I hurried to catch him as he slipped through the door, "Hey...everything okay?"

Ash smiled weakly, his head bowed as he watched his sneakers hit the wood floor. "Yeah, just feeling the pressure."

"School? Or home?" I deliberately kept the band off that list.

He shrunk into himself, groaning. "Both? My parents have gone from screaming at each other to whispering. And shutting up whenever I'm around."

"Maybe they're trying not to drag you into it?"

He sighed, shaking his head as we pushed through the main doors of the school and out to an almost empty parking lot. "I don't think so. They've never been so secretive before."

I nodded, unsure what to say. Ash had been my best friend for the better part of my life, we'd been there for each other through almost everything. So I knew how strained things were with his parents. I'd been at his house when the shouting started, deliberately turning the TV to maximum volume in a desperate attempt to drown them out. Or the radio. Eventually the arguments had stopped bothering him. He'd grown so accustomed to the constant yelling that it was just background noise, and completely out of the norm when he didn't go home to it.

And with the divorce papers still weighing on his shoulders it was easy to see why this new development had added to his stress.

His hand reached up to his throat, gently rolling the beads of his necklace between his fingers. "I should probably get home and grab my bass. See you soon?"

"Yeah, sure." I clapped him on the back as he turned to walk to his truck. It was weird praying he'd walk into the house to see his parents yelling at each other again.

Watching him drive away I unlocked my own car and tossed my things into the backseat, climbing in and starting the engine. I'd try extra hard at practice later, keep a hold on things and stop them spiraling. Maybe then Jonathan wouldn't feel like we were looking for an escape clause. And maybe things would become less tense.

That was a lot of maybes. And for a guy that had no idea what was going on I wasn't sure where that would get me. But sitting in the school's parking lot would only manage one thing, I'd be even later to practice and Jonathan would have someone new to be mad at.

So I got my ass, and the car, in gear and drove from the school, heading home.

Pulling onto the street in front of the quaint white house I called home I noticed two things. One, Melissa was already on the front step. And Two, Josh wasn't at football. His car occupying the spot on the driveway.

"I've been trying to call you." Melissa skipped over as I climbed out, raising her cell as proof. "Josh isn't at football."

"I noticed." I peeked at my cell and saw Melissa *had* called me. A whole thirty seconds ago. I wrapped my arm around my little sister as we walked back up the path, Josh leaning by the doorframe and eating an apple. "Hey." I nodded in greeting.

He nodded back, his mouth full as he grunted his reply. To look at the two of us you'd be forgiven for thinking we weren't actually related. Where he was well built with wide shoulders and a shaved head, I was dark-haired and tall, probably my only advantage when we used to fight.

And then there was Melissa.

She was the youngest; protected by her two big brothers. And rightly so. She had a cheeky grin and a smart mouth, her blue eyes toeing the line between innocent and mischievous. She had us wrapped around her little finger and she knew just how to keep it that way.

Not that we minded. It was nice to have someone to look out for, especially when things could have gone so differently for us.

I don't remember much of our early life, whether I'd regressed any bad memories or I was just too young, I didn't know. But Josh did. Not that he'd ever tell me much more than the scraps I did remember. He saw it as protecting me, which I couldn't blame him for, in his situation I'd probably do the same.

But it didn't make it any easier to try and face a past I knew so little about. Especially when it had a hold over my future.

See, Josh and I weren't American. Yes, we'd spent all our lives here, we lived here and had a family here. But our birth parents, who weren't the parents we knew, or even the parents I'd ever known at all...they weren't from the USA.

Our father was a professor originally, working at one of the most prestigious schools in London. He loved music, sports, and classic cars. Our mother a classical music teacher, her tutoring stretching from the violin and the cello, to her personal favorite, the piano. Which was where I'd found my love in music.

From the photographs I'd found and the brief conversations with Josh I knew they'd fallen in love young, moving quickly from one stage to the next. And then our father got the opportunity of a lifetime. A job offer here, in Boston. A chance he would've been stupid to miss. An opportunity that could've changed my entire life if he'd rejected it.

But of course, he couldn't. He was ambitious, determined, and it was everything he'd worked for. So they'd packed up and moved across the ocean, unaware that they were bringing a third person.

Josh had been born within six months of them moving, and I'd followed almost three years later. They were happy. They had a perfect little family in their perfect little house. And things were good.

Their home was full of love. Laughter. *Music*. I didn't remember much but I remembered the music. Our mother was always playing, she'd sit by the piano and sing, laughing as we danced and played. Whenever I remembered it an odd calmness embraced me, a familiar old blanket wrapping around my shoulders. It was a comfort I hadn't realized I'd needed, but one I'd be naive to ignore. I didn't know them, but these people, the ones I fought to remember and Josh struggled to forget, had given me life. They'd given me meaning and passion. How could I give up on their memory?

I was four when they died.

Old enough to remember their faces and their unconditional love. Too young to remember who they were. Or the night we'd been taken from the only home we'd known and forced into the system. Josh said I'd cried a lot at first, always clinging to him and asking when Mommy was coming home. How could he even begin to comfort me when he was still just a kid? How could he promise me everything was going to be okay when his life had been upended too?

But he had. He'd been my armor, the reason I didn't remember being passed from home to home, retreating further into myself. It's the reason I never pressed him for more. He'd been strong enough to get us through it, and if he didn't want to relive it I wouldn't make him. I owed him that much.

Luckily Melissa's parents had come across us within the first two years. They'd had trouble conceiving Melissa, and was told it'd be almost impossible again. So they'd decided to adopt. I don't think their intention was to adopt two children already older than their firstborn, but something happened, something swayed their decision.

And almost twelve years later here we were.

I knew I couldn't dwell on the past, couldn't live there. After all, I might not have this life if things were different. I might not be in Harrison, there might be no band, or at least I might not be in it.

There wouldn't have been Friday night gaming marathons, or Sunday morning walks through the Common. There'd have been no little sister swinging off my arm and demanding I drive her places. And how could I trade that for a family I never knew?

Turning to Melissa I pressed a gentle kiss to her hair, laughing as she elbowed me in the gut. I still wouldn't change it. "So what were you calling for?"

"Oh, yeah." She grinned, moving to stand by Josh. "Since he's not got football Dad says Josh has to take me, so you can get to practice."

I paused, waiting for Josh to protest, waiting for Melissa to say she was joking. "He...he did?"

I loved my dad, our dad, but hearing he was encouraging practice made me anxious. It wasn't that he hated my passion for music, or wanted me to choose a different path, he knew how much it meant to me. He actively encouraged me to practice. He bought my sheet music, he listened to me play. And he was the one who bought the grand piano that sat so proudly in what would've been the dining room. Had the piano not been so *grand*.

No, Dad's issue was that he thought I was wasting my talents. He wanted me to pursue it through college, head down the classical route. He knew how music affected me, how it was the first thing I leaned on when emotions ran high. There was a song for everything. On any instrument. And I could play several. Piano. Violin. Guitar. If I wanted I could make the entire band redundant.

Except maybe Jonathan.

I could play his guitar like a pro but I couldn't sing to save my life.

And I definitely didn't have the charisma to be the front-man.

Josh rolled his eyes with a smirk, tossing the apple core into the garden. "I don't mind. I need to go get some sneakers so I was heading there anyway."

"You sure? I already told the guys I'd be late."

"Yeah, don't sweat it." He thumped me playfully on the arm. "Just don't forget to point the groupies my way when you hit it big."

Shaking my head, I took a step backward with a laugh. "I'm not gonna ask twice."

Melissa grinned brightly, "Give Jonathan my love."

I ignored that, raising my hand as I waved goodbye. That was definitely one downside to having a younger sister. I wouldn't mind her crushing on a guy her own age. Hell, she could have a crush on Will and I'd be okay with it. But having a crush on Jonathan made me feel uneasy. He wasn't a bad guy exactly, he was just more of a free spirit in the relationship department than I cared to expose my sister to.

Sliding back into my car I realized just how much of a hypocrite I sounded. Had I not had to explain myself to Jonathan after camping about my night with Rosie? He'd been pissed off. His protective side over Rosie very rarely came out. She usually batted him away, his opinions were irrelevant when he was such a...player?

I thought back to that night as I pulled from the house, running a hand through my hair. I'd been in a low mood at the time, having spent practice wondering what I'd done to mess up the first relationship I'd ever had. Chelsea had called me that afternoon, she explained she wasn't having doubts, but we were young and miles apart. She didn't mind keeping in touch, visiting and hooking up, but she also wanted to be free when I wasn't around. And she hoped I'd want that too.

I'd agreed. I didn't see a choice in the matter in all honesty. Protesting would've only left me in the same situation. Except I wouldn't get to enjoy her company when she was in the state. But awkwardness coiled in my gut whenever I thought about it. I wasn't that guy, and it wasn't the relationship I wanted.

After we'd wrapped up practice we'd decided to have drinks, as teenagers often do, which had led to a more intimate situation between Rosie and I. We were in her room, I'd snuck off and was deliberating calling Chelsea and ending the whole thing. I wasn't cut out for the type of lifestyle where I'd casually sleep around and pretend I was in a relationship after. Of course Rosie made it her mission to pick me up and dust me off. She'd stopped me calling Chels, she'd taken my cell and tossed it away. She'd promised me that if anyone was going to regret the situation it would be Chelsea, and one day she'd kick herself.

 It helped. And soon enough we were kissing. Which then led to other things. It was a perfect night, and I meant it when I said I didn't regret it. But I also meant it when I said it'd never happen again. Rosie wasn't *my* girl. We both knew that.

I never did call Chels when I'd sobered up. I was still anxious about the entire thing, thinking about her being with other guys and assuming I was okay with it. Texting her didn't seem like the mature way to deal with it, but every time she called I found an excuse not to answer. Because deep down I wasn't ready to give up on her yet.

She was my first girlfriend, my first summer romance, and my first time. Call me a hopeless romantic but maybe one day we'd find our way along this path and back into something more serious.

A guy could hope at least.

As I turned onto the Taylors street I saw a familiar convertible coming towards me. Away from the direction I assumed they'd be heading. Brooke slowed to a stop as we met, smiling across at me as I wound down my window to speak to her and Rosie."Hey...you guys skipping tonight?"

Rosie cast a nervous glance at Brooke, almost too quick for me to notice, but I had. Her smile was more forced than I was used to, pretending everything was okay. Whether that was for my benefit or Brookes I didn't know. "Yeah. We're off shopping."

"Can never have too many shoes." Brooke laughed softly, turning back to the road.

I nodded, the knot in my stomach tightening. Rosie and Brooke never missed practice. They were our biggest fans, and I probably wasn't the only one who played better when they were around. Everything just came so easily when you had the encouraging faces of your best friends grinning and cheering you on. They did more for our confidence than Jonathan and his constant criticisms anyway.

"It'll be weird." I tried for a smile, raising my eyebrows at the two of them. "Not having you there."

"Aww, we'll miss you too." Rosie laughed, sliding her shades down over her eyes.

Brooke muttered something and Rosie turned to look at her, smiling softly and nodding.

"We should go anyway." The blonde turned back to me, "My brother will be waiting for you."

I nodded dumbly, waving a beat too late and watching as the car disappeared around the corner.

And then it hit me. Why things were so tense with everyone.

The rumors had started a couple of days ago. Rachel had slept with Jonathan. Actually from what I could gather they weren't rumors. Jonathan hadn't denied it, and Rachel was eager to share the story. I guess she thought it was a way to get recognition? After all, even if people were talking bad about you they were talking about you. She was out to make an impression.

And then Rosie and Brooke had dropped her as a friend...the two of them avoiding practice and the band.

I slammed my hand down on the steering wheel, running a hand through my hair. Stupid, stupid, Alex! It all seemed so obvious now. He was mad at *me.* Well, maybe not just me, but he could hardly take it out on Rosie. It was such a double standard, hell, I couldn't blame the guy for being pissed. Rosie had slept with me, and Lucas, and Jonathan had to be okay with it, because we looked out for her, and we cared. But we were friends. And it was a very fine line to walk and not mess up.

And then Jonathan had tried walking it. He'd slept with Rachel and everything had hit the fan. Rosie was annoyed at him for ruining a blossoming friendship.

And he was annoyed at me because I'd done the same.

Shit. Shit. Shit.

I took a breath, looking up at the house as it loomed in the distance. I wouldn't bring it up. I wouldn't make things more awkward. But what I would do is play my god damn hardest. I'd prove to Jonathan that this band meant everything, that his friendship meant everything.

And then maybe, just maybe, the rest would fall into place.

Chapter 9

Ash

I stared up at the house, the backpack hanging from my shoulder as the minutes ticked by. I'd have to go in eventually. Another minute and the neighbors would be twitching at their drapes to see what the young hoodlum was up to. Well, hoodlum might be a bit of an overshot. Still, I was beginning to look suspicious. I sighed and threw a glance back at my jeep, fighting the temptation to get back in and keep driving. Yes, there were bigger problems than mine. I wasn't some kid. I knew people fell out of love and families broke up. I just never figured it would happen to mine.

I looked back at the house and bowed my head, sloping towards the front door. My feet stopped before it, my hand hesitating by the handle as I braced myself for the shouting on the other side. For the heated voices and harsh words, and then as they became aware of their son in the room…the silence. I took in a measured breath and pushed down on the handle, the door giving way gently. I paused on the threshold timidly, frowning as the soft sound of conversation drifted over from the next room. Had divorce actually made them amicable?

I stepped into the living room, my tread careful as I peered around at the empty space. An archway led into the dining room to my left, and from there the voices emerged. Soft, warm voices. The kind I hadn't heard in years. I stopped in my tracks, hiding behind the wall so I could listen in.

"Do you think we should tell him?"

I frowned down at my shoes as I heard the calm clarity in Mom's voice. She sounded almost…happy?

"Not yet. In time." Dad answered, his own voice reassuring and tender.

So that was it. They were divorcing each other. And, after years of cutting comments and tense looks, they were happy. They were actually happy…apart. My stomach sank, my heart heavy as I pushed back from the wall and marched towards the basement door.

"Ash?"

I ignored her calling after me, my footsteps quick as I reached the top of the stairs leading to the basement. I shut the door, sliding the deadbolt into place. My bag dropped to hang by my side as I stepped back. I knew it was selfish to be angry that they were ending things. If it made them happy, I should be happy...But they hadn't always fought. They hadn't always snapped and glared at each other. They'd loved each other fiercely once. I could remember it, perhaps more vividly than they could. It was my fault it had come to this. And that wasn't just me throwing a little pity party. They'd sent me to a school that they couldn't possibly afford. One they thought would do great things for me. One that would create prospects and opportunities. Dad had worked so many hours to foot the bills he was practically a ghost in our house. Mom had grown lonely, and then resentful. But then she'd feel so much guilt over it she'd end up crying into a glass of wine. I'd witnessed it first-hand. It never changed. The tears only became quieter and the glass fuller.

Of course, it hadn't helped that my aunt had moved away around the same time. But no-one blamed her. Least of all me. I brought my fingers up to touch the beads around my throat, my eyes closing at the memory. After what happened I think we all wanted to leave. But they'd plowed on. For me. And what did they get in return? A broken marriage and a son who was playing bass for loose change with his friends. I honestly had no idea what I wanted to do with my life. I had my part-time job as a lifeguard down at the beach, but that was all.

My head fell back and I let out a breath, opening my eyes to the door opposite. I had to get out of here. The entire house was closing in on me and only one place would help take the weight off. The one place I could go and just feel free. I turned and hurried down the steps leading into the basement – into my room. The entire bottom level had been converted into a private space just for me. Another costly addition. But I wasn't going to lie, it really helped to have a whole other floor to escape to when stuff got heated. I had a kitchenette and a small bathroom, a bed that flanked the back wall, and a makeshift sitting room. I had all I needed. A TV, console, and a chair to sink into. For the past few weeks that had very nearly overtaken the beach as my favorite place. I'd been playing a horror game I must've played a thousand times, hunting for trophies. To be honest I was replaying the game for more than that.

I'd begun messaging someone from across the sea online, another teenager looking to lose themselves in a creepy and otherworldly environment. They'd helped hunt down the more evasive collectibles and had provided a welcome distraction. More than that, they'd gotten me talking. I'd opened up about the screaming matches, my role in it all, and generally whatever else I'd been holding in. Because I knew I'd never meet them. And they'd never have cause to spill what I'd said. Not that there was much to spill. I'd been honest about how I felt to anyone who asked. It was just easier to talk to a stranger. He'd talked through some of his stuff too. Shared the load. We met up most nights on the console, talking through our days while we battled grotesque creatures and searched for hidden relics.

I felt kinda bad though. Last night it clicked that he lived in England, which meant that each time we met online it'd be the early hours on his end. I'd finally suggested he look me up on Facebook instead. It wouldn't be hard. My parents had given me the worst possible middle name to ensure I'd be ridiculed by friends and foes alike. But, in their defense, it made it easier to locate me on the web. So, at some point over the next few days Ashley Stanley Horne could expect a friend request from RickiP02. Whoever that turned out to be.

I tore my gaze from the console with a weak smile, catching sight of my bass resting in the corner of the room. So far Jonathan hadn't called an "emergency" practice today. So far. The day was still young. We had the gig tomorrow that Jonathan promised would allay any fears of the band heading down the drain. I wanted to believe him. I did. I believed he'd fight for the band, that it meant everything to him. But I just wasn't sure the universe had received that message. I also wasn't sure how much of my involvement in the whole Brooke/Rachel fiasco he knew about. I'd been trying to help. I genuinely thought he liked her. That she was the mystery girl. All the signs pointed that way. To be honest, I still stood by that. I knew Jonathan, perhaps better than he'd give me credit for. He was proud and definitely egotistic. But he was also different around Brooke. He cared what she thought about him. If you asked me, which not many people did (and Brooke certainly wouldn't anymore), he'd sabotaged it. He was, ultimately, a chicken when it came to being vulnerable. This would've been his biggest risk and biggest payoff.

And now, thanks to me, Brooke had been the victim. If I hadn't tried to push she might've just ignored her crush and moved on over time. She wouldn't have been in the crossfire. She hadn't exactly spoken to me since either. She hadn't avoided me, or even been angry or cruel about it. She'd just shrunk away.

A soft rapping noise broke my reverie, the sound echoing down the stairs. I narrowed my eyes, tearing my gaze from the instrument as I stalked into the kitchenette. I couldn't bear it if they started treating me with kid gloves. Already I received soft glances and weak smiles. With divorce on the horizon they might even ask me about my feelings. I wasn't sure they wanted to know how I really felt about it, because the minute they asked I'd be honest. I wouldn't be able to stop myself. It'd all come out and they wouldn't be able to handle it.

So instead I was gonna take the mature approach and avoid the situation altogether.

I ignored the gentle but persistent knocking, retrieving a six-pack of soda from the fridge. I needed to get out and fast. I'd have to cut through the living room to reach freedom, but if I was clever I might just make it without much contact. God, that sounded awful. The sinking feeling in my gut reminded me that what I was doing was not only cowardly, but cruel. I looked up the looming steps to the basement door, grimacing as I began my ascent. I could only avoid the conversation for so long, and no matter how much time I put between it and myself it'd still suck. Still, I wasn't ready to hear it yet. I wasn't ready to see the sympathy in their eyes as they realized that I'd be the only one grieving the marriage. I wasn't sure I'd ever be ready. As I reached the top of the stairs I took in a measured breath, my hand reaching out to grasp the door handle.

I edged it open, peering through the gap to see if the coast was clear. It was. I slipped into the barren room, glancing around at the seemingly deserted house. They'd be somewhere, discussing what they could do to make it easier. I wanted to tell them it was okay. That I'd get over it and adjust…But I couldn't. Because it wasn't okay. Not by a long shot.

I set my jaw and strode out, my gaze fixed ahead as I sought out my jeep. I tossed my backpack inside and went around to the trunk, placing the cans in a cooler box. In less than thirty minutes I'd be on the warm sand, the crashing of waves replacing the foggy thoughts flooding my mind. I pulled out my cell as I got behind the wheel, texting Alex to meet me when he was done. He'd gone to Nathan's for a study session, one of a handful they did just for kicks. Both were insanely clever, so it was a safe assumption this counted as a fun Friday night for them.

I drove in silence to the beach, just wanting serenity. As soon as I'd been able to I'd trained to be a lifeguard here, taking whatever shifts I could around school and practice. It was my second home. I slipped into the back seat after parking up and made use of the black-out windows, tugging down my bottoms awkwardly and doing a quick swap into some swimming shorts. I tugged my top off and bundled it with my discarded jeans, grabbing a spare towel from the trunk. I always kept a few things handy in the jeep, just in case some decent waves appeared at short notice.

I released the surfboard and held it under my arm, grabbing the cooler box with my free hand. My footsteps quickened the closer I got to the sand, a smile playing on my lips as I stared out at the rolling waves ahead. It'd been far too long since I'd felt the cold rush of a crest beneath my body. I missed it sorely.

I found a spot and dropped everything, scrutinizing the waves as they rolled in. As I leaned down to hook my ankle up to the surfboard leash an old memory surfaced, my blood running cold. I shook my head to free it, grabbing the board before I changed my mind. I couldn't help but grin as I felt the cool, wet sand sinking beneath my tread. The water met me, sending shivers through my body as it enveloped me inch by inch. My grin remained as I waded deeper, scanning the horizon to determine the point of the coming waves. I gripped my board to my chest and waited, the adrenaline coursing through my veins as I counted the seconds ticking by.

As one approached I turned my back on it and pressed against the board, my arms paddling against the surf rhythmically. I felt the swell beneath me, lifting into a crouch as the wave took shape. My arms outstretched to give me balance, my feet planted against the board as I twisted and turned to peter out the crest. Air rushed past me as I maneuvered the folds of water to remain upright, my hair lifting on the breeze. There was no feeling like it. A delirious mixture of freedom and danger. I'd learned long ago to respect the water. And I'd learned the hard way. Water splashed against my ankles as I crouched down to meet the board, my hands gripping it as I moved to lay on my stomach to paddle back to shore.

The sun beat down on me as I strode across the sand, a wry smile on my face as I tilted my head back to embrace the heat. For this time of year it was rare, but welcome. I buried the end of my board, crouching to remove the leash from my ankle. With a small smile I fanned out the towel and flopped onto it, letting out a sigh as I closed my eyes to the bright sky. My smile grew as I put my hands behind my head, my skin warming under the afternoon sun.

I frowned as a shadow fell across me, opening my eyes. A pair of smirking faces looked back, the brightness of the day turning them into dark silhouettes. I brought a hand round to shield my eyes, propping myself up using my elbow.

"Don't strain yourself." Nathan grinned.

Alex let out a small laugh, arching an eyebrow. "Topping up your tan?"

I rolled my eyes, smiling despite myself as I sat up. "Took you guys long enough. Sorry to interrupt your date."

They exchanged an amused look, Alex shaking his head as he sat down beside me. "You're just jealous we didn't want you there."

"Oh yeah." I laughed. "So jealous."

"I can hear the hurt in your voice," Nathan smirked as he gracefully sat down, brushing the grains of sand from his hands.

"Look," Alex grinned, "You can see the tears building."

"Remind me why I invited you guys?"

"You'd be miserable if we weren't here," Alex said simply.

I knew a part of him was continuing the joke, but I also sensed an element of truth it. He knew without me having to say anything whether things were rough at home. He knew when to be there. I smiled lazily at him, giving a small nod. "So, how're you guys doing anyway?" I peered around to address them both, raising an eyebrow at Nathan. "How's Brooke?"

Nathan looked away, his expression sober as he set his jaw.

"Brooke?" Alex frowned.

"Yeah." I raised an eyebrow, lowering my voice. "Jonathan screwed her over."

"She's fine," Nathan said flatly.

"Wait, what?" Alex looked between us, "Brooke and Jonathan? Since when?"

My shoulders sagged. "Since…Well, I don't know exactly. She liked him, they kissed. Then Rachel happened."

Alex winced, bowing his head. "Awkward." He frowned as a thought occurred to him, looking up at Nathan. "Is that why they're avoiding us?"

Nathan sighed, his gaze softening as he relented. "She just needs space. It's nothing against you guys."

"I didn't even know she liked him." Alex shrugged, shaking his head.

"Can we stop talking about him?" Nathan rolled his eyes, the hardness returning to his voice.

I exchanged a look with Alex, smiling weakly. A tense blanket of silence fell over us, the crashing of waves now all the more appreciated.

"Sorry man," Alex muttered, peering across at him. "If it helps I thought she liked Ash."

I blanched. "You did?"

"Yeah." He shrugged. "Why else would she keep kissing you?"

I slowly lifted my gaze to Nathan's, his dark blue eyes fixed on mine.

"Uh...Innocent kisses." I offered, smiling meekly.

I found myself wishing, not for the first time, that I had some of those handy powers the others possessed. I'd make it so that lovesick teenagers didn't play mind games and just got together so that my life would be easier. I glanced across at them both, curious as to whether they wondered about the otherworldly gifts they weren't privy to. I guessed for Nathan it was worse. Alex and I had had no clue about any of it before the gang spilled the beans. We were blissfully ignorant of magical storms and weird party tricks.

"Brooke was trying to make him jealous." I submitted.

Nathan looked at me steadily, his voice dubious. "By kissing you?"

I narrowed my eyes as Alex suppressed a laugh. "Yes. By kissing me."

Alex smirked, shaking his head. "Just so I know I'm all caught up. Brooke likes Jonathan. They kissed. Then she kissed you to make him jealous, so he slept with Rachel…to make her jealous?" He frowned again, rolling his eyes. "Honestly. I don't even know why I pretend we can have normal lives."

"She was gonna tell him how she felt too, right before." I smiled bitterly. "I pushed her into telling him."

"It's not your fault."

I looked up at Nathan in surprise.

He shrugged weakly, "You thought you were helping."

I hoped Brooke believed that too. I'd tried to help. I really thought I *was* helping.

"How're you handling all this, Nathan?" Alex raised an eyebrow at him.

"I'm not his biggest fan." He offered, chewing over his words. "I just hope he stops messing her around now."

"By backing off or taking things further?" Alex asked.

"By giving her space to realize he's not God's gift to women."

"It'll be okay." Alex reached out to clap him on the back. "Jonathan will be scared of going near her now it's out. Your family are terrifying."

Nathan laughed, the mood considerably lightened. "We're not that bad."

"Yes, you are," I smirked.

Alex grinned. "I genuinely thought your dad was in the mafia when I first met him."

Nathan raised an eyebrow as he looked between us. "Seriously? Way to stereotype guys."

"Well." Alex laughed. "I know who's side I'm taking in all this. Sorry, Jonathan."

"You think he'll be all angsty tomorrow night?" I asked.

"Were you not paying attention to the 'new material'?" Alex groaned, rolling his eyes.

I nodded, my shoulders sagging. The only thing more annoying than a smug Jonathan was a morose one. We'd never hear the end of it.

"You girls done gossiping about Jonathan Taylor?" Nathan asked dryly.

I laughed, cocking my head. "Alright…I *have* been meaning to ask you about this mystery kisser of yours."

He froze. Nathan had never been easy to read. At the start of summer I'd experienced my first glimpse behind the curtain. Rather unexpectedly, might I add. We'd been at a party round Jonathan and Rosie's house, the hour late and the drinks running dry. I'd found him laid out on a sun lounger by the pool, a half-empty bottle of whiskey in his hand.

Without expecting much, I'd asked if he was okay. A simple enough question that I presumed would merit a simple enough answer. But that's not what I got. I got the real Nathan. He told me how he was scared. Of falling short on his grades, of disappointing his family, of never meeting his dream girl and living happily ever after. In short, he was afraid of failing. Something I guess every teenager felt at some point. I tried to tell him it wouldn't matter, that his folks would always be proud of him. And that he'd find her, whoever she was, someday. He'd scoffed at that. He knew he was burying himself in his studies. That he was missing out on the real world and the people in it, because he was trying desperately to secure a future. I remember feeling at a loss for words. Unsure how I could convince him that he had nothing to worry about. He was doing just fine.

That's when he said it. He felt like he belonged to a family of heroes. His dad defended those without hope and his brother put his life at risk for people who would never even know his name. It didn't help that they both had actual magical abilities either. Nathan was afraid he was the weak link. He told me the only superpower he had was his brain, and he was just trying to make use of it. He wanted to be a hero somehow too. To matter. Of course, I told him vehemently that he did. Absolutely he mattered. He'd gone quiet then, the barrier he built returning brick by brick. Sensing my window was closing, I'd leaned over so the others couldn't hear and told him in the most authoritative voice I could muster that he should find his own happiness. Seek it out and take the risk. If he wanted a great romance to remind him that he existed beyond books and tests, find a girl and lay a kiss on her. I was 90% sure he wouldn't be rejected anyway - he had the trademark look of a Danes. I wasn't sure I'd gotten through to him. Not until his confession around the campfire.

"Yeah, Nathan," Alex smirked, sitting back onto his elbows. "Tell Ash all about her."

He frowned, looking between us uneasily. "Why are you guys being weird?"

Alex chuckled, relenting. "I saw her coming out of your house when I got there."

I raised an eyebrow at Nathan, grinning.

"It's not like that." The color rushed to his cheeks. "She's a friend."

"A close friend?"

"A friend who was your first kiss..."

Nathan rolled his eyes, ignoring us both as he gazed out at the horizon. The blush was still evident as he shrugged, a small smile playing on his lips. "Okay, Jess and I are good friends. And we did kiss. But that's all there is to it."

"No more kissing then?" Alex pressed with a grin.

"No more kissing."

I raised an eyebrow at Alex. There was definitely more to that story, but we wouldn't get any details unless Nathan was willing to divulge them. Alex shrugged in response, chuckling as he pulled his cell out of his pocket. I looked away pointedly, curious as to whether Chelsea was messaging him about how great it was for them to be casual. Great for her, sure. But Alex? He needed more. After everything he'd gone through with his family, stability was paramount. He needed someone to choose him. To stick by his side and be there. I'd thought that Chelsea would be that for him. It turned out I was wrong.

But I was done meddling. I was definitely, absolutely done meddling.

I sighed and reached over to the bundled clothes peeking out of my backpack, digging my cell out for the distraction. The small light on the screen blinkered up at me, my curiosity growing as I unlocked it and read the notification.

Someone had sent a friend request. A beautiful, blonde someone. She was about my age judging from the picture, her wavy hair falling in gorgeous tendrils as she beamed at the camera. I instantly accepted, scrolling through to read her profile. She lived in the United Kingdom, loved horror films, and was called Ricki. My body stiffened as I read and re-read her name, my head bowed as I cradled my cell.

No way. No fucking way.

"Who's that?" Alex frowned, raising an eyebrow.

My heartbeat quickened as I stared at her picture, a smile forming on my lips. "Ricki."

Chapter 10

Jonathan

I'd pulled it off. Just about. I brought the cigarette to my lips and took in a steady stream of smoke, holding it a moment before releasing the plume. The grey tendrils floated into the night air, disappearing as they rose higher. I followed their trail, watching until all that remained were the stars above. I permitted myself to gaze at them for longer than I should have, my insides clenching painfully as I cradled the cigarette between my fingers. We had a gig. It was paid. And better yet, we were playing our own songs. All three boxes were ticked. I'd sweet-talked the owner of a bar we'd frequented a few times, convincing him that we warranted a paycheck. Tony had submitted, after a few grumbles and attempts to weasel around the issue. So, I'd saved the band for another night. I should wear a goddamn cape.

There was only one, albeit monumental, obstacle that stood between me and a good performance tonight. And she was standing inside with my sister, pretending I didn't exist. I brought the cigarette to my lips again, wincing at the memory of the last time she'd spoken to me. I could still hear the hurt in her voice, the way it had broken. I knew Rachel had been a bad idea, but I'd no idea how bad. I didn't know it would result in this. I mean, we definitely had a thing. An unnamed, unaddressed, and extremely undeniable thing. But I'd heard her loud and clear that day at practice. She didn't see a future with me beyond flirtation. And that was fine. Really. Sort of.

The point was she never would have chosen me and now…now she definitely wouldn't. The nails were firmly in that coffin. But her reaction had been so…visceral. So raw. There had to have been more than just embarrassment at the situation, more than just jealousy. Or was that me getting carried away? I had a tendency to do that. I took in another drag as I considered, not for the first time, the words that had been said that night. Not just by Brooke, but by Rachel too. She had been vile. Incredibly vile. And personal. I shook my head, frowning as I let out the smoke between my pursed lips.

The door to my right swung open with a bang, the sound reverberating into the night air. I stepped back from the wall with a start, relaxing as I saw a bulky form storm outside, his breathing ragged as he looked left and right. Raising an eyebrow, I let out a short cough. He spun to face me, his hand coming up to rub at his jaw nervously. "There you are."

"Tony." I nodded, flicking the ash from my cigarette.

His face softened, his eyes darting back to the bar. "Uh…Listen, kid."

"No," I said firmly, straightening up and crushing the cigarette against the wall. "Whatever you're about to say, don't."

He opened his mouth to speak, the frown marring his features as he took a tentative step closer.

"No," I repeated, narrowing my eyes. "We had a deal."

"We still do." Tony held his hands up in surrender. "But-"

I let out a bitter laugh, rolling my eyes as I glanced away. "But."

He waited a moment, his expression weak as he slowly lowered his hand, "You gotta understand, kid. It's packed in there."

"So?" I raised an eyebrow. "That's a good thing."

"It is." He agreed. "It also means I can't risk the place becoming a mausoleum if no one can sing along to the band."

I gestured back at the building. "What if they're here for us? You even consider that?"

He scoffed before the thought could catch up, his eyes widening as he realized the sound had escaped. He coughed to cover it, looking down at his feet. I shook my head and stared at him, my jaw setting.

"You can still play, and I'll still pay you guys. Fair is fair. But uh…no original stuff, okay?"

I fought the urge to throw it back in his face, the frustration flooding my veins and spitting into anger. I closed my eyes and steadied my breathing, nodding slowly. It wouldn't do any good. Not at this stage. The band was set up, the crowd had arrived…The options were largely limited.

I grimaced as he made his way back inside, shaking my head. The guys were going to kill me. They were actually going to kill me. I opened my eyes and let out the breath I'd been holding, uncurling my fists by my side. Well, at least the nerves I'd felt surrounding the gig had now been replaced with dread. That was something. I raised my face to allow the cool night air to cloak my skin, smiling wryly as I turned to look at the door leading to the bar. I would have to face the music, as it were, sooner or later. I pulled open the heavy door, weaving through the staggered crowd to reach the stage at the back. I didn't even bother to look up as I did, certain I wouldn't want to remember any of the faces here tonight. Certain they wouldn't remember me.

The guys were already in position, their grins widening in anticipation as they exchanged glances. I moved towards the mic stand and dragged it to my level. I couldn't tell them. If I did we'd look like a joke. My eyes flickered up to the faces before us, smiling weakly as I saw my sister. She beamed back, nodding her support. My lip curled as I saw the guy standing next to her, his dark eyes glinting as he draped an arm around her shoulders. Zak Warner. I rolled my eyes and lowered my gaze, shaking my head as the lights dimmed. I just had to get through it, maybe even have some fun – or pretend to, at least. Once it was over I could drown myself in copious amounts of beer.

Gripping the mic, I kept my gaze to the ground and thought as loudly as I could. I looked back at Will, taking the deeply etched frown on his face as a sign that he had gotten the message. I moved my gaze over Ash, and then Alex. They looked back in confusion, nodding dumbly as they glanced down at their instruments. *Follow my lead.* That was all I'd given them. All I could given the time constraint. I hoped that was enough. I closed my eyes again and took up my guitar, resting the strap around my neck as I found the chords. I began to play softly, my insides squirming as I counted down the seconds until the guys caught on to the fact that this wasn't our song.

"I used to be a lunatic from the gracious days…" I began softly, opening my eyes to glance to either side of me. Alex narrowed his eyes as he began to play, shaking his head. "I used to feel woebegone and so restless nights." The bass kicked in, the drums echoing in softly. They knew. I opened my eyes to the beaming crowd, faltering as I spotted her. Brooke met my gaze, her doe eyes fixed on mine as she cradled her drink. "My aching heart would bleed for you to see…"

Her resolve broke, her eyes lowering as the song began to take shape. I frowned as David moved to stand beside her, his expression unreadable. She glanced up at him gratefully, raising her glass to sip from her straw. A loud sound echoed from my right, the bass humming as Ash raised an eyebrow at me. Shit. I smiled weakly and continued singing, tearing my gaze from her to…anywhere else. It worked. Kind of. It wasn't my best performance. But at least the band hadn't left me hanging acapella. They played through the rest of that song, and the one after that, and the one after that. Until, mercifully, the set was done. The crowd cheered and clapped, a couple humming along to some of their favorites as the lights rose just a fraction. I lowered my guitar to the ground carefully and leaped from the stage, forcing my way to the bar. The bartender looked up at me and nodded in understanding, uncapping a beer and sliding it across. I grasped the cold glass in my palm, hunching my shoulders as I bowed my head.

A loud, irritated cough sounded out behind me, a set of shadows falling across the bar. I grimaced, taking a deep breath before turning to face them. "Great set, guys." I tried cautiously, my gaze traveling between them. "You played really well…"

"Yeah." Will nodded, arching an eyebrow. "We're experts at covers now."

"I could play *Livin' on a Prayer* in my sleep," Alex muttered.

My smile wavered as I took in their grave expressions, the air cooling as they stared back. I glanced back at the bar, trying to determine how many beers it would take to win back their confidence. If I could. At last my eyes fell on Ash, my stomach sinking as I saw the look on his face. It was past anger and frustration, it was weariness. I dropped my gaze, taking a consolatory sip of my drink.

"Dude." Will let out a sigh, shaking his head. "What happened?"

"Tony changed his mind last minute." I submitted. "Honestly. If it helps, we still get paid."

They exchanged unconvinced looks, their silence serving as an answer.

"I'd rather we played our own songs…" Will offered softly.

"Me too." Alex nodded.

Ash's expression clouded as he averted his gaze.

"And you think I don't?" I laughed weakly, rubbing at my temple. "Look, the next gig we'll only do our own material. I swear."

The weight of another loaded promise hung between us, the desperation evident in their wan smiles as they tried to convince themselves to believe me. Again. We just needed a break. For someone to take a chance and trust that we knew what we were doing. We were good. Better than good. But so far that was the world's best-kept secret.

Will was the first to break the silence. "Get the beers in and we might consider forgiving you."

My shoulders relaxed as I turned back to the bar, holding up three fingers to the bartender. The beers slid across the counter towards us, the condensation leaving a clear trail on the wood. I passed Ash and Alex theirs first, smiling as they nodded in thanks and moved back to weave into the crowd. I peered to see the path they'd taken, my insides forming lead as I saw her. Of course. Luckily, she hadn't seen me yet. I knew that because she was still smiling, albeit weakly. Her gaze was fixed on Rosie as they talked, Zak standing by my sister's side. He looked bored, his hand dropping from Rosie's shoulder as she stepped forward to greet the guys.

Will reached past me to grab his beer, raising an eyebrow as he took a sip.

"So," I began idly, relaxing my stance as I cradled my drink. "How're things with you and Chloe?"

His expression was unreadable as his gaze followed mine. He shrugged as he watched them, before turning his back on them completely. "We're having fun."

I nodded. I'd seen him sneaking around with her at school, but so far all I'd gotten in the way of an explanation was that they were casual. Which made absolutely no sense. I didn't really know the girl. She could definitely be into casual stuff. But Will? This was an even weirder stretch than Alex.

"So I take it she won't get an invitation to meet your mom anytime soon?"

Will scoffed, shaking his head as he took a sip of his beer. "Not likely."

I watched him, draining my beer before placing it on the bar. I didn't want him to think I was raining on his parade, especially as I was hardly one to talk, but I hoped he knew what he was doing. And why he was doing it. For as long as I'd known Will he'd never been interested in anything other than the real thing with a girl. He'd been holding out for it. I knew that without him even voicing it. So this was…Unsettling.

I glanced across at Brooke again, my stomach dropping. Lucas had finally joined the party, Rosie leaving Zak's side to greet him with a warm hug. That hadn't caused my insides to jar. That was fine. Lucas could gladly have my blessing over Zak. No, it was what happened next that unsettled me. It lasted only a second. Barely that. But I'd seen it. As Rosie left his side, Zak reached across and brushed back a stray lock of Brooke's hair, his fingertips grazing her earlobe. I frowned as I watched her look away and sink into the crowd. Zak grinned smugly as he leaned closer to Rosie, murmuring in her ear. And then he left too.

"Everything okay?" Will asked beside me, his body shifting as he sought out whatever had jolted me. He wouldn't find it. The moment had escaped, and so had they.

"Yeah." I nodded dumbly, pulling my cigarettes from my pocket in gesture, "I'm uh…just gonna grab some fresh air."

I ignored him as he rolled his eyes and returned to his drink, my attention fixed on the door to the back lot where this night had begun. It was probably nothing. Brooke knew better than to go near that cretin. And, I hoped, he knew better than to flirt with my sister's best friend. Still, he'd definitely tried something. I'd seen it clear as day. I needed answers. I needed Brooke to tell me I'd imagined it. That my sister was dating a guy who treated her right. That he hadn't tried it on with the girl that I…the girl that I liked.

I shook my head and forced my way through the crowd of bodies, letting out a breath as the night air hit me. I took another step and allowed the door to shut softly in my wake, my eyes taking in the deserted lot spanning the back of the bar. I hadn't really thought it would be that easy. She was probably holed up in the ladies' room, taking cover until the coast was clear. From him and, I guess, from me. I took out a cigarette and propped it between my lips, shaking my head as I cupped the end. I cast a furtive glance around the still night before my powers flickered to life, the tip of the cigarette burning softly. I eyed the end of it as it blossomed into a fierce orange, taking in a slow drag.

"Brooke. Anyone would think you were avoiding me…"

I frowned at the deep voice, looking up at the barren space.

"I am." Came the familiar voice. "Now if you don't mind-"

My hands dropped to my sides as I heard her gasp sharply, my gaze searching as I gingerly wandered forward a few steps.

He snorted cruelly, his voice taking on an edge. "You weren't saying that the other night, were you? When you were begging me to have sex with you."

My blood ran cold, the cigarette dangling from between my lips as I peered around at any shadow that could be hiding them. They were definitely here. And she was definitely not safe. I dropped my cigarette to the floor, crushing it under my shoe as I strode towards an almost invisible alleyway. It eventually led onto the street, Brooke trying to evade him by making a clean break for a cab. He'd been too fast. Too forceful. He had her backed into the wall, leering down at her as he held her to the spot. I frowned as I watched her gingerly rub at her wrist, her gaze downcast as a faint red mark began to emerge on her skin.

"It was a mistake…" She said quietly.

I walked towards them, agonizingly aware of how each step seemed to last an eternity.

Zak's laughter rang out, his grin widening as he looked down at her. "You weren't saying that then. What's changed?"

Her eyes shot up to him incredulously, her voice rising despite its tremble. "My best friend! Your *girlfriend*!"

The powers in my blood began to surge, liquid venom coursing through my veins as I closed the distance. I was trying to calm down. Really, I was. But I could feel it. The need to destroy him. To remove him. Just like that. I shook my head as I pushed down the more menacing thoughts, aware that Brooke was there too. I didn't want to lose control and hurt her in the crossfire.

"Rosie?" Zak scoffed, his fingers coming up to trail along her bare throat. They landed gently at the apex of her collarbone, hovering there as he pressed himself closer. "She's a good girl. But she's not as good as you…"

My gaze flickered to Brooke in time to see her wince and shrink back. She had nowhere to go. And he knew that. He knew she'd said no. He also knew he was dating my sister. Rage was bubbling under my flesh and I set my jaw, striding towards him. I yanked him back from her roughly, spinning him to collide with my fist.

He stumbled back and landed against the wall, sputtering in shock as I dragged him to his feet by the scruff of his shirt. Electricity sparked from my knuckles as I hit him again. And again. Singe marks flared on his skin where my punches landed. He sank back to the floor, spitting blood onto the cold stone. I took a step back, for his sake more than my own. I was breathing heavily, my fists uncurling and flexing as I peered down at him.

His lip was twisted into a nasty snarl, his expression still smug. "The fuck you playing at?"

My gaze traveled from him to Brooke slowly. She stared back at me open-mouthed, goose-bumps prickling her arms as she took a tentative step towards me.

I narrowed my eyes at him, my voice low and measured. "You leave Brooke alone. And you leave my sister alone. Got it?"

He glared back up at me, a smirk tugging at his lips as he hoisted himself to his feet using the wall. He brought his hand out to massage his jaw gingerly, laughing as he looked back at Brooke. She averted her gaze, moving to stand behind me. I was glad of that at least. She still trusted me. Even if she did think I was a jerk. Zak took a step towards me, the glint in his eye returning.

I narrowed my eyes as he pushed past me and headed back inside the bar. I turned slowly to look at Brooke. The guy had a nerve. I would give him that. He was going to brazenly walk back to my sister and explain away his bruises as...what? Her brother bullying him?

I shook my head, the magic still coursing through my veins at an alarming rate. The air thrummed around me as the gentle shiver in Brooke's breathing hitched. I looked up at her, my gaze softening as I took in her small frame, her eyes downcast as she cradled her arms around her body. I wanted to wrap my arms around her. To hold her tightly and warm her, to make her feel safe. I wanted her to know that I cared. That I always would. But I was as frozen as her, my nerves shot as I considered the fact that she might not want me to.

That she might never want me to.

Chapter 11

Brooke

I was still shaking.

Hot, salty tears were building behind my eyelids as I drew in a ragged breath, my heart was in my throat, hammering loudly.

I'd never been so scared, staring at Zak as he backed me against the wall, completely powerless as he towered over me. He was so arrogant. So confident I'd want to sleep with him that he couldn't acknowledge that I'd changed my mind. He just couldn't comprehend my drunken yes had rapidly turned into a sober and terrified no. That the idea of willingly going near him made my skin crawl.

I still couldn't believe I'd almost given him my virginity.

And kept quiet about it. Slapping on a smile as I watched him with his hands all over Rosie. His eyes all over me.

There was that shame again.

I'd tried. I really had.

I'd found the words on the tip of my tongue when Rosie told me about their blossoming relationship.

Zak is a complete douche. He kissed me. We were going to his car. We were going to have sex...he was going to cheat on you with your best friend! What kind of boyfriend does that?!

But I'd glanced up and seen the look on her face. She was almost bouncing, eyes shining with the promise of a new relationship. Her cheeks flushed, her voice lilted and girlish. She liked him.

I'd watched her face fall as I tried to voice my concerns. She pulled away.

And I knew.

She'd stay with Zak regardless. I'd just be the jealous friend who'd been knocked back by the guy she liked and wanted everyone else to be miserable too. Maybe Rosie wouldn't be so harsh, but I would. And Zak would enjoy turning her against me if he could.

The longer I kept quiet the longer he would.

And hopefully now Jonathan would too.

I still hadn't looked his way. But I sensed him looking, fists clenching, jaw set. The raw heat of his anger was engulfing me, and I knew if I braved his gaze his eyes would shimmer as he fought to control his powers. Could I ask him to keep quiet?

Would he?

Rosie was his twin after all.

"Are you okay?" He broke the silence, his voice was low, soft. He was trying not to intimidate me. Was it obvious how shaken up I was? He scoffed as I nodded. Clearly it was. "Brooke...are you really?"

I nodded again, still unable to look at him. Ever since Rachel I'd avoided him. I didn't sit with him at lunch. I didn't joke with him in the hallway. Hell, I'd even skipped practice and supporting my other friends because he was there. I couldn't trust myself around him, even now, standing three feet away the tension settled over me.

Coming here was a mistake. I'd known from the moment I'd promised Ash that I'd regret it. And I did. Not because I was standing here with Jonathan, trying to desperately ignore the urge to kiss him one last time. No, that I could handle. Albeit it was harder when he was standing so close and I could smell the familiar mix of his cologne, leather, and cigarettes blowing towards me on the breeze.

The regret was now firmly settled with Zak. And how much of an awful friend I was being. Rosie deserved better.

"Brooke?" Jonathan encouraged.

I nodded. I still couldn't look at him. I couldn't face the confusion and shame in his expression. "Th-thank you."

"What was that about?"

I opened my mouth to speak before my brain fully engaged. How could I explain this? This entire thing had been a car crash from beginning to end. And what about Jonathan's part in it? Sure, he wasn't in the spotlight, but he still had a cameo. My mouth closed, burning my eyes into the floor. "Nothing. Just Zak being Zak."

Hopefully he'd buy that. Zak had a reputation for being on the sleazy side. But I wasn't sure how much of our exchange he'd heard, or if he just saw the anxiety in my posture and the way I avoided his stare.

"Did he..." He cleared his throat, "Did he hurt you? Before? He...said something."

My cheeks burnt with shame at the weight of his gaze, the power of his words. Oh, he'd heard alright. Every sordid word that fell from Zak's mouth as he'd pinned me to the wall, his hips crushing mine. I swallowed the bile that crawled up my throat, wincing as it burned. "Just drop it." I moved to brush past him, "It's nothing."

He moved with me, blocking my path while still maintaining the space between us. He was trying to honour what I'd asked, to keep away from me. Maybe he did care.

"Brooke...It's not nothing." He sighed, this time closing the gap as he moved. "If he's done something you need to tell me."

"I don't need to tell you anything! He. Didn't. Do. Anything!" I snapped, lifting my head to glare at him.

And I was stunned into silence.

Meeting his eyes, all the fear, all the anger and resentment I'd been harbouring, just disappeared. I felt secure. Even though I was still standing in a dimly lit alleyway, alone with a teenage guy, I felt safe. I *was* safe. No matter what happened between us, I could trust Jonathan to keep me out of harm's way.

The way he was looking at me spoke louder than words. He was worried. His eyebrows were pulled together, his mouth turned down. He wasn't stood as rigidly as he'd been before. The anger and tension had disappeared from his shoulders, replaced by worry and frustration. Worry because he could still see the fear in my eyes, frustration because I wouldn't tell him why Zak had been advancing on me alone in the dark.

I took a moment, closing my eyes to shut out the intensity of his stare. "He didn't do anything...because I did."

"What do you mean?"

Jesus, was I really going to tell him? Was I going to open myself up and share the one thing I'd ever been ashamed of? "I just...I didn't want to be a virgin anymore."

Yes. Yes I was.

The gap between us closed significantly as Jonathan moved again, his hand reaching to brush away my tears before he stopped, dropping it to his side. "You're worth so much more than him."

And didn't I know it.

Instead I shrugged, wiping my cheeks briskly. "Don't worry. I'm still a virgin."

"What made you want to lose your virginity to him? Of all people..."

And there was the million dollar question. The one I knew he'd eventually get to. Could he honestly not connect the dots? Or was he after the ego boost of hearing me say it? Whatever it was I was done. If I had to spell it out for him I would. Then maybe I could close the door on this whole humiliating thing and move on.

My stare was steady as I looked at him. I could do this. I could ignore my heart as I met his eyes, I could pretend my fingers didn't twitch to brush the stubble on his jaw. I could force the memory of his lips on mine from my head. I could do this.

"You did."

"Me?"

"Well...you and Rachel." I scoffed indignantly at her name, of all the people he could have used to get to me it had to be her? "I just...didn't handle it so well." Understatement of the year there, Brooke. You got absolutely wasted and almost let some creep take something you'd been proud to hold onto. And then been carried home by your brother and had to explain why he'd found you drunk and crying in the parking lot. Not that I'd had the balls to tell him about Zak. Only about Jonathan.

Jonathan groaned, running a hand through his mop of brown hair. "Rachel meant nothing. It was a huge mistake."

"It doesn't matter what it was." I shook my head as the images swarmed me again. Rachel's smug face as she chewed me up. Jonathan realising his dirty little secret was already out. "I was coming to tell you." I let out a mocking laugh, realising just how stupid I'd been. I really had fell for every line he'd fed me.

"To tell me? To tell me what?"

"To tell you that..." I bit my lip as I looked at him, suddenly shy. He had to know I liked him as more than a friend. As more than my best friends older brother. I'd kissed him numerous times. And the kiss at camping was something else! I'd poured everything in me into it. I'd made sure I'd made an impression. Had he really not got a clue?! "To tell you that I liked you. And that I...I wanted you to..."

I stopped, flames engulfing my face. I didn't need to go any further. It was painfully obvious what I was trying to say. To both of us.

Jonathans mouth dropped open, his eyes widening in surprise. "You...like me?" Surely he wasn't that good an actor?

"How could you not know?"

"Well...you kept kissing Ash for a start. And then..." This time it was Jonathan that was nervously fidgeting. His fingers tapped against his thigh where I could see the swell of his cigarette packet crammed inside. "I heard you guys talking. About how I was the type of guy you couldn't take home."

Oh.

He'd heard all that. But then...how had he not heard Ash goading me into telling him? Unless he had...

I was getting another headache trying to second guess every move he made. Every word that slipped so skilfully from his tongue had me figuring out every way around it. It was exhausting. But I didn't trust him anymore. I wasn't stupid enough to believe everything he said, so instead I tried to figure out what angle he was working.

Jonathan was still looking at me. I sighed, ignoring my cell as it rang persistently from inside my clutch. "I said that because Daddy wouldn't like it. Not me." I raised an eyebrow his way, "And for your information I kept kissing Ash because I was sick of being the girl you want when there's no one else to entertain you."

A frown marred his perfect features as he began to stutter some apology or another. I didn't care. I ignored his pleas for me to look at him, for me to listen to whatever he had to say, instead I busied myself with my clutch, retrieving my cell. I knew I was being unfair to him. We'd had almost eighteen years of friendship behind us. We'd been through so much that it was hard to see him deliberately trying to hurt me. But then again I wasn't going to let him accidentally keep hurting me because of a misplaced crush either.

Jonathan and I just didn't have the same core values. He did as he pleased, flirting, kissing and screwing his way through the school. And maybe I'd read too much into things after our first kiss, after the following kisses.

Jonathans eyes were searching as he stepped forward, his hand reaching up to my cheek, only this time he didn't move away.

I did.

I could be friends with him. I could enjoy his success with the band and listen to them play. I could probably handle seeing him with other girls eventually, the ache in my chest not nearly as debilitating as it had been with Rachel. I could probably watch him be happy and fall in love in due time.

But what I couldn't do is let my guard down.

I couldn't trust myself to not read into everything he did. Every look, every smirk, every touch would make me think he saw me in a different way. I'd open all those wounds up again if I started to believe in him. In us.

I jumped as my cell rang again, looking down at the screen as Nathans name flashed at me incessantly. He was probably nervous about me being in a bar again, a bar with Jonathan none the less, and was calling to check on me.

I'd promised him I'd stay with Rosie and share a cab home. He'd not been happy to let me leave without him, but I was sure if he'd tagged along it would have been Jonathan than took a beating. I'd tried to keep them apart as best I could. I could see the murderous look in his eyes as soon as Jonathan made an appearance or someone brought him up.

So the least I could do was answer the call and let him know I was fine. That he could stop worrying and I'd be home soon. I'd deliberately leave out the part about Zak. I'd not be able to stop Nathan kicking *his* ass even if I wanted to.

I held a finger up to Jonathan as he started to speak again, sliding my thumb across my cell as I picked up the call. "Hey, Nath..."

"Brooke, finally!" He let out a laugh, oddly excited. His voice had taken a light raspy tone, rather than the stoic coolness I was expecting. "You need to get home right now."

The line crackled in my ear, the rest of his words drowned out as I heard laughter in the background. Everyone sounded thrilled. What the hell was I missing?

"Nathan?" I asked, brushing past Jonathan as I made my way from the alley. "I didn't hear you. Is everything okay?"

"Everything is great. You- " He laughed again as he was cut off, a brief shuffle of movement from the other end.

"Brooke?" That was a different voice.

That was a painfully familiar voice, one I hadn't heard in weeks. It couldn't be? I thought he was still on tour. He was supposed to be stationed in Syria for the remainder of the year at least.

But it was. I could hear it in the background as my parents celebrated, as Nathan laughed, enjoying my stunned silence.

James was home.

Chapter 12

Rosie

I t didn't mean anything. It didn't have to mean anything unless I let it. I stared down at the phone in my palm, my fingers stroking the edges idly as I watched the messages piling up. I'd stopped myself at the third, determined not to be *that* girlfriend. But the blue ticks stared up at me tauntingly, each minute that stretched out becoming longer and more painful. He'd read them. So why hadn't he replied?

I frowned at the screen as it began to fade, the colors dulling. My thumb swept out to light it up on reflex, my insides sinking with shame as I read and re-read every word I'd typed out hours ago. Had I said something wrong? Annoyed him? I hated that I cared so much. But then was it so bad that I did? We were a couple after all, and we'd only recently…cemented that. I'd wanted to make it right. To make it mean something. So we'd waited. But since then…Since then he'd been acting off.

I shook my head, my eyes scrunching shut as I gripped my cell tightly. I was obsessing over whether or not a guy had messaged me back. Over whether I was enough for him. Or if I was in fact too much. And the worst part was that I really did care. I didn't want to. I wanted so desperately to be that strong, independent woman that felt secure enough to just love herself. But that just wasn't me. I wasn't sure it ever would be. How could I expect him to want me when I didn't even…I shook my head again to clear the thought, my eyes opening slowly.

A brunette stared back at me in the thin sliver provided to her by the mirror in my locker, a wan smile on her face as she tilted her head at me. I turned to face her, slipping the cell into my pants pocket as I shut the locker. My fingers traced the faint outline bulging against the fabric, already itching to retrieve it. I forcefully withdrew my hand and smiled slightly.

I hadn't seen Brooke much since the gig, settling for hurried phone calls and sporadic texts. If I didn't know better I'd have been concerned after her disappearing act following the show, but luckily my darling brother had provided an explanation of sorts. I wasn't sure how much he knew, or how he even knew anything at all considering he'd kept a careful distance since the Rachel fiasco, but it seemed to check out. Her big brother had come home unexpectedly. I couldn't blame her for rushing to him. James had always carried a natural air of authority, even when we'd been younger. He had his head screwed on. He could take care of himself. But although his special abilities certainly gave him an edge, he was still ultimately human. More than that he was family. I'd have felt that same panic if Jonathan had been the one to join the army and ship out. And not just because he was reckless and attracted trouble.

Still, Brooke didn't approve of Zak. She'd said so, to her credit. She'd also said that she'd stand by me, and she was. But she retreated inside herself a little when his name was mentioned, biting her tongue and removing herself from the conversation. I suppose I didn't blame her for that either. I just hoped she wasn't going to retreat too much. That her absence this weekend had been more to do with her brother coming home than with avoiding me.

Brooke stared at me cautiously, the corners of her mouth twitching into a shy smile as she glanced up and down the hallway. Was she looking for him? Ensuring the coast was clear so she wouldn't have to pretend she didn't think he was a jackass?

I opened my mouth to speak at the same time she did, grinning as we both stumbled over our apologies.

"You first." She laughed.

I smiling wryly as I opened my mouth to begin again. I wanted to say how I'd missed her. Not because I hadn't really seen her – we weren't joined at the hip and that was fine – but because I could feel her pulling back from me. I could tell something unspoken sat between us and it was beginning to fester. I didn't want to lose her, especially not over a guy. Instead, I said nothing. Because before I could a pair of arms encircled us both, drawing us into him as Lucas led us along the hallway.

"Well aren't I the luckiest guy in school right now?" He cast us both an affectionate look.

"Such a charmer." I teased.

"He's not wrong though." Brooke grinned, leaning around him to look at me.

"There's a first for everything." He let out a laugh, cocking an eyebrow.

I grinned up at him, my body automatically sinking into his side as we walked. I'd missed Lucas. He hadn't voiced his thoughts on Zak, and he hadn't been pulling away – he knew better than that– but the dynamic had changed. I wasn't sure if Zak was the jealous type, but any guy could get a little green-eyed over his girlfriend still hanging around with someone she'd slept with just short of a month ago. The strange thing was I didn't think he *was* jealous of Lucas, or threatened or…anything, really.

It was Will he had the problem with.

I knew they'd never been best buddies, but there was this animosity between them that prickled the air. Even I'd noticed how Zak changed around Will, how he'd hold me a little closer or kiss me a little longer. He'd never been like that around Lucas – and as far as I was aware he didn't know about my rendezvous with Alex – but with Will it was different. Which was odd because…well, we'd never even kissed, let alone anything more. Will didn't even see me that way. He was a perfect gentleman and we were very much…platonic. I smiled wryly as I pictured him, as I'd done over the years. There was no shame in admitting it. He was very attractive. But it'd never come to anything.

Lucas on the other hand I did have a history with. A very public one. It was no secret and neither of us were ashamed. We'd always been close, until one day we were very close. I loved him. Not in a romantic way, but I did. He made me laugh and feel better about myself. I'd walk the hallway at school in army boots and a neon tutu, a ripped band t-shirt held together with pins, or sometimes even a Hello Kitty dress with fishnet tights. I'd receive perplexed looks and hear whispered comments. I didn't mind, for the most part. But now and then, on a bad day, I'd let those comments seep in. I wanted to be liked, I could admit that. But I also wanted to be me. And for me, clothes were about having fun as much as anything else.

One of the things I loved about Lucas was that he was honest to the point of being blunt. It never ceased to make me laugh, especially when he wasn't aware of how blunt he'd been. So, on those days when I felt detached and low I'd ask him how I looked. He'd give me the once over, smile, and say I looked like a five-year-old given free rein in a department store around Halloween. He'd then pull me into his arms and tell me I made it work, and that I was beautiful. It wasn't hard to see why I'd fallen into kissing him. And why I now missed his company, more than his body.

I looked up at him, "How're you doing, anyway?"

"Same as always." He shrugged, the corner of his mouth tugging into a knowing smile. "Therapy is going well, if that's what you're getting at."

"Was I that obvious?"

He grinned, raising an eyebrow. "A little."

"Nothing wrong with checking in." Brooke scolded playfully, "We care about you."

"We do." I nodded.

He let out a laugh. "I'm fine. Seriously." His gaze softened as he smiled down at me, his voice lowering. "You know you'd be the first to know if I was going down that path again."

I held his gaze for a moment, smiling timidly. "Promise?"

He kissed my forehead gently, his hand slinking from around Brooke to hover before me. "Promise."

I stared as he extended his little finger, tucking in all the rest. My hand reached up to link our pinkies together, a grin forming on my face as I nestled into his side once more.

"I always look like the third wheel with you two," Brooke smirked, raising an eyebrow. "Where's David when you need him?"

"Sorry" I let out a small laugh. "And how is Brooke?"

She smiled back at me. "I'm good."

"Good." I grinned, raising my head to peer up at Lucas. "And Olivia?"

Lucas chuckled at the mention of her name. "Same little hurricane she always is. Mom's getting her into ballet to try and chill her out. Personally, I think she'd be better off with kickboxing."

"Nothing wrong with an energetic ballerina." I countered. Olivia was Lucas's little sister and at the tender age of five was still discovering how much fun it was to keep grown-ups on their toes. She was definitely a force to be reckoned with, but she was also incredibly adorable. She also, much to Lucas's chagrin, had a massive crush on a certain dark-haired drummer. The girl had good taste.

He laughed. "She doesn't have it in her to be dainty. I'm sure Mom was hoping she'd come out and automatically love dresses and girly stuff." Francesca Campbell was stunning, and ran a model agency in town. She always looked like she'd just stepped off a runway, so the idea of her trying to play dress-up with her little girl wasn't hard to picture. "Instead she just wants to wrestle." He continued.

"Once upon a time so did Rosie," Brooke smirked, arching her eyebrow at us.

Heat rose to my cheeks and I glanced away. "So," I cleared my throat, "How's James? It must be nice having him back."

She grinned at me playfully, taking the hint. "It's amazing. Today was the first time in ages that he's woke me up with coffee and a bagel." Her smile turned wistful. "I've missed our morning tradition."

"I'll bet. You guys are so cute. Jonathan never brings me bagels." Her face turned ashen as she averted her gaze, a sudden quiet choking our trio as his name hung in the air. I winced, looking at Lucas for assistance. He offered a small shrug. Great.

I let out a sigh as we ambled along, lifting my gaze along the hallway before us as a flash of color caught my eye. Zak. A smile tugged at my mouth as I raised a hand to wave at him, our eyes locking as he turned casually to glance back. His dark eyes stayed on mine, his expression unreadable as he watched me. My hand wavered in the air, the smile faltering on my face. He rolled his eyes, smirking as he turned back to his friends and headed into the cafeteria. My hand fell limply to my side and I glanced at Lucas and Brooke to see if they'd witnessed our exchange.

Neither met my gaze as we kept pace. I couldn't be sure if that was for my benefit or if they really hadn't seen. I hoped for the latter.

I pulled my cell from my pants pocket, frowning as I lit up the screen to view our messages. Still no replies.

"Hey man."

I blinked stupidly as I collided with dark fabric, the solid build beneath it steadying me in my tracks. My cheeks flushed with embarrassment as I peered up at Will, smiling despite myself as the heat radiated from his grasp on my arms. My own hands, one of which was still cradling my cell phone, were raised up against his chest. He lowered his hands carefully, smiling lopsidedly as he took a step back.

Lucas smirked beside me, raising an eyebrow. I looked fleetingly from him to Brooke, my cheeks reddening further as they both stared back in amusement. "Uh…hey." I smiled shyly at Will, hastily burying my phone back in my pocket. "Are you joining us for lunch?"

"Hey." His expression faltered as his gaze landed on Brooke. "Uh. Maybe."

I offered Brooke a small smile as I connected the dots. Things were still divided when it came to the gang, but it was getting less strained at least. Give it a few more weeks and we might even witness Brooke and Jonathan teasing each other like they used to. Maybe.

"You sitting with the band?" Lucas guessed.

Will paused, letting out a breath as he nodded. "Probably."

"We could walk in together though?" I tried, my cheeks warming as his dark gaze fell back on mine.

He smiled, his mouth opening a fraction, about to speak. A pair of tanned, manicured hands appeared from behind him, snaking across the ridges in his torso.

"Hey, hot stuff." She purred, inching around him to take my place.

My insides twisted as his gaze warmed, the smile on his lips curving into a playful smirk. I averted my eyes bashfully, the heat in my cheeks now belonging to another emotion altogether. I'd never seen Will like that, so flirtatious and confident. I wasn't prepared for just how much it got to me seeing another girl pawing at him. Which brought about the next layer of redness – shame. Shame because I had no right whatsoever to have an opinion on who he could touch and who could touch him back. We were friends. I didn't own him, and if he was happy then I should embrace his new love interest. Welcome her.

Besides, I really shouldn't even permit these stolen glances at him when I was seeing Zak. I was beginning to feel greedy – and I was starting to question whether those rumors about me were in fact dead on. Perhaps I was that girl that liked to be passed around. Perhaps that's all I ever would be. My gaze lowered as a thought crept in…perhaps that was why Zak had become so distant since we'd had sex. He'd thought I was better than I am. That I was worth something more. Maybe he'd woken up to reality and now wanted an out.

"You know my friends? Rosie, Brooke and Lucas." Will gestured with his free hand, his other holding her close to him.

I forced myself to look up, a faint smile warming my lips as I nodded. "Chloe right?"

"The one and only." She grinned.

Jonathan mentioned seeing Will around with this girl a few times now. Her name had stuck in my mind. And now I had a face to attach to it. A beautiful, happy face.

"It's nice to finally meet you." Brooke offered with a smile.

"So how did you guys get together?" I blurted. Brooke looked across at me questioningly, shaking her head.

"Uh…" Will laughed, rubbing the back of his neck. "Do you wanna tell them?"

"Is that because you can't remember?" Chloe teased.

"Maybe."

Lucas let out a low whistle as he looked between them, chuckling. "You're making me look good here, Will."

"It was clearly a night to remember." Chloe laughed, leaning up to lightly kiss along his earlobe. "The morning after wasn't half bad either."

Her words stabbed my stomach and I looked away. It was only a blip. A confusing situation with Zak combined with seeing Will in a new light. Nothing more than that.

"Well, that I remembered…"

I winced as I heard him growl the words, my gaze trained on the floor as they began to kiss.

"You're spending far too much time with Jonathan." Brooke raised an eyebrow, her tone teasing.

Will and Lucas laughed, oblivious to my inner ache as we resumed our trek to the cafeteria. I shook the jealousy free, or as much as I could while they remained entangled.

The familiar din of chatter filled the space as we arrived, a heady mixture of different smells floating around, each one turning my stomach. My gaze searched the room for friendly faces. Jonathan was at a table near the back, Alex beside him as they pored over some sheets. Will nodded to Chloe in their direction. "Save us a seat?"

"Yes, sir." She saluted him as she backed away.

I watched as she confidently sat down opposite my brother, glancing back over coyly. My gaze moved back over to Will, my stomach knotting as he watched her.

"I see David," Lucas announced, kissing my cheek. He raised an eyebrow as he wove around Brooke and Will. "You joining us when you have food?"

"Uh...sure." I smiled weakly, glancing around the room to make out where Zak had gotten to. If he was mad I should really talk to him. In a way that made it impossible to ignore me with stagnant blue ticks.

"So," Will cleared his throat. "You two okay?" His gaze settled on mine, his eyes darkening. "I miss you at practice."

"You do?" I fought to suppress a smile.

"Of course. It's not the same without you." His cheeks tinged ever so slightly as he looked back at Brooke, clearing his throat again. "Both of you."

I exchanged a glance with Brooke, grinning. "We miss you too-"

"Guess who."

I frowned as Will disappeared, a pair of hands covering my eyes. I raised my fingertips to them, gently teasing them loose as I turned to face their owner. "Hey." I smiled slightly, taking him in. He didn't seem mad. The opposite in fact. I glanced around to seek out Brooke, watching her disappear towards David and Lucas. I looked back at Zak as he reached out to stroke my arm. "You must've just missed us in the hall."

"Huh?" Zak frowned, his nose crinkling. "Oh. Nah, I saw you with Lucas and Brooke. I figured you'd catch me up."

Oh.

"And now look." Zak raised an eyebrow, smirking as he moved to drape his arm around my shoulders. "You're all alone with Will."

I met Will's gaze and blushed at the implication. "Yeah, Will and I were just saying how we don't get to see much of each other anymore."

"That's what happens when you get into relationships."

"Not exactly." Will narrowed his eyes. "Most people don't mind their partners spending time with other people."

I frowned, peering up at Zak. "You don't mind, do you?" It was the question I'd been plaguing myself with most of the day.

"Depends which friend." He shrugged, "Don't want my girl hanging with a load of guys now, do I?"

My blush deepened. So he did mind. "It's not like that…"

"Sure." He scoffed.

Will looked between us for a long moment, letting out a sigh as he rubbed the back of his neck. "I should go. Chloe will be wondering what's keeping me." His gaze lifted to mine in question. "See you around, Rosie-Cheeks?"

I grinned. His pet name for me was painfully appropriate. It was as though all I did was blush, especially today.

Zak watched him slope off towards their table, a slow smirk forming on his face. Cold air hit my skin as he removed his arm, the warmth gone from his eyes as he turned to face me. "You sitting with us?"

"Oh." I faltered, glancing across to where Lucas was animatedly talking with David and Brooke. "Of course." I swallowed, forcing a smile. He was definitely punishing me for something. And whatever it was, I was sure I deserved it. If it made him feel better then I would sit with him and his friends.

"Hurry up and get your food then." He rolled his eyes. "Grab me a burger while you're at it."

I blanched, reaching out to gingerly stroke his hand. "You're not upset with me, are you?"

"Why?" He frowned, his gaze traveling to look down at our hands curiously.

"Well, I…" I smiled weakly, shaking my head. "Never mind. So, you're not mad?"

He pulled his hand back, shaking his head. "Nah, we're good."

I watched as he turned to go back to his table, retrieving his cell from his jacket pocket. His mouth curved into a grin as he darted his thumb across the screen, replying to a message. I turned to queue for the hot food, digging out my own phone. The blue ticks stared up at me, his online icon flashing cruelly. I tossed the cell into my bag instead, casting my eyes downward as I moved along the line. I placed a burger on my tray for Zak, wincing as I took in the sheen of grease coating the bun. My fingertips traced along the edge of the tray as I moved in a trance, forcing myself to notice the way the sauce on the burger trickled out. I gulped, already acutely aware of the budding sensation flooding from the pit of my stomach.

I glanced up at the cashier as I got to the front, grabbing at a handful of candy bars flanking her till. She frowned at me as she totted up the total. "You hungry, sweetie?"

I smiled weakly as I looked back down at the small stash before me. "Something like that."

Chapter 13

Nathan

I could sense the passion and urgency in her voice, the sound of it rising as she found her argument amidst the clutter of mishandled evidence and coerced statements. She was young, only a little older than James, but she was good. I could hear her potential with every syllable she uttered. So why was I rewinding it to the same part, for the third time in five minutes?

I couldn't focus. Her words came through loud and clear, but all I could think about was how long I had left. My right hand twitched to turn the cell in my palm, the time lighting up. I could probably wait another twenty minutes. That should allow enough time to do the exchange properly. Discreetly.

I turned my cell back down to rest against my thigh, my eyes scanning the length of the Charles River. Fall was creeping into Boston like a shadow, the leaves warming and curling with each passing day. I glanced at the overbearing tree to my left, the gnarled limbs twisting as they reached out for the path in front. Usually the route was a favorite for couples and joggers, the odd cyclist…but as a brisk chill began to approach the crowds had thinned. I wasn't complaining. I liked to have my spot as peaceful as possible when it came to down time – which these days involved courtroom memoirs and a mystery read.

My gaze traveling back to the open backpack on the bench beside me, the corner of my latest literary tryst peeking out. I smiled as I stared down at the innocent object, a thin sliver of paper just visible along the edges of the book. The note lay neatly folded, pressed firmly in place.

"Oh my God baby brother, what are you doing?"

I frowned, sitting up as I sought out the owner of the voice.

"It's a Sunday morning Nathan, the day of rest. Or fun. Or…anything but monotonous anecdotes about dumb criminals who got caught."

I brought my hand up to remove one of my earphones, hovering it by my ear as I peered around. The voice remained in my left ear, the familiar drawl of my brother echoing back from the device. I replaced the earphone and rolled my eyes, settling back onto the bench.

"Come on, do something spontaneous. I dare you."

I turned the cell over and held down the power, smiling as the screen went dark. Silence swathed me generously, the gentle sounds of the world around me emerging one by one.

"You think that'll stop me?" I could hear the mirth in James' voice as he let out a laugh, "Unless you really seize the day kiddo I'm gonna sing you the complete works of Disney. Starting with Frozen."

I pulled a face and yanked the earphones out completely, tossing them into my backpack, along with my cell. As my fingertips brushed the paperback I hesitated, drawing it out an inch or two. *Give it another fifteen minutes and you can go*, I coaxed myself. *Be patient.*

I didn't want to set off too soon and…And what? Blow my cover? What if she already knew? It was a possibility. Still, it was better to err on the side of caution. Keep things as they had been. They were good - we had a system going and it worked. It was nice. Why risk interrupting it?

"I'm sure it can't have been that bad…"

"Can we just drop it? It really, *really* was."

I looked up at the voices, my jaw setting as I saw them idly walking along the path. Jonathan. Of course he'd be here to ruin my day. Were he and my brother teaming up or something? I drew the bag shut and narrowed my eyes, watching as he took a drag on his cigarette. The smoke plumed from his mouth as he shook his head, his expression sullen.

"Fine." The brunette by his side rolled her eyes at him playfully. "But I think you're being a tad overdramatic."

He arched an eyebrow, the cigarette dangling from his lips as his mouth lifted into an easy smirk. "Me? Never."

I draped the backpack over my shoulder as I stood, my hand gripping the fabric as I watched them. I'd seen them hanging around at school, enough to know that she was in the friend category – an upgrade from his usual conquests. She must feel so honored.

They stopped on the path, their heads bowed as they exchanged wry remarks. My anger building as I hovered there, my mind flooding with images of my sister's wounded expression the night I found her. The night he broke her heart. It'd taken Ash texting me for someone to be there for her, to hold her and remind her that she was worth something. Even if she didn't believe me. He hadn't even had the guts to apologize. He probably thought there was nothing in it. Perfectly innocent behavior. A victimless crime.

But to go around flirting with girls and leading them on…it was cruel. More than cruel. It was wrong. Especially when that girl was a friend. How would he like it if Lucas had done that to Rosie?

I closed my eyes as I felt my free hand forming a fist, shaking my head to clear the thoughts. I'd promised Brooke I wouldn't interfere. That I wouldn't do the overprotective brother routine…but the more I thought about it, about her wondering why she hadn't been enough, about the tear tracks on her cheeks, about how unsettled she was after the gig last weekend…The more I just wanted to pummel him. If he was any other guy I would have. As would James and Dad. So, what, he was allowed to treat

Brooke like this because we all hung out? Because it might make things awkward? No. Screw that.

My eyes opened to stare at them, my heartbeat quickening as the burgeoning rage bubbled within me. Brooke might get mad at first, but in the long run she'd understand. Appreciate it, even.

It was all the convincing I needed.

My bag dropped to the floor with a thud, my eyes narrowing as I strode towards them with clenched fists. With each step time slowed, allowing me to enjoy each second as Jonathan turned in bewilderment, the cigarette still dangling from his lips. His eyes widened as he realized what was about to happen, deftly removing the lit cigarette and tossing it. His friend glanced between us, her mouth dropping as she took a tentative step back. My mouth tugged into a sly smile as I closed the gap and raised my fist. The punch landed beautifully.

He stumbled back, rubbing his jaw as he looked up to meet my gaze. "What the hell, Nathan?"

I swung my other fist, sending him flying back onto the ground. I stared down at him, hesitating a moment before grabbing him by the collar to hit him again. And again. His hands outstretched to push me back as he tried to argue his defense. But I knew there wouldn't be an opportunity like this again. To just lay into him without our friends intervening. I had to make the most of it.

His friend beat her fists against my back to draw me off him, her voice rising as she tugged at the back of my shirt. He allowed a few more punches to land before his hand came out to grab my fist, his fingers closing around it tightly. I blanched, frowning as I caught his eye. The green began to glint as he held my fist, his jaw set as my hand began to warm with a current of hot sparks. I winced, struggling to pull it free.

"That's enough." He raised an eyebrow, waiting a beat before releasing me.

I stepped back, nodding dumbly as I massaged my hand. His eyes returned to normal as he looked around, his expression guarded as he slowly sat up.

"Jonathan-" She began.

"I'm fine." He cut in. He turned his head to the ground and spat blood, before looking back at her. "Honestly." He said in a softer voice, "Nathan and I need to talk. I'll catch up with you tomorrow, Jen."

She frowned, hesitating as she slowly drew her gaze to mine. I looked away as I flexed my hand.

Jen eyed me warily, "If you're sure…"

"I am."

Her gaze turned to his, concern etched on her face as she nodded slowly. She cast one last glance at me before turning and walking the way they'd come, her cell already out of her back pocket.

"Feel better?" Jonathan raised an eyebrow, getting to his feet.

I stared at him evenly, my jaw setting. No. In fact, if anything, I felt worse. I'd imagined beating him up would've left me feeling invigorated. Righteous. Like some good guy in an old novel who defended those who needed saving. Instead I felt stupid. A sentiment I rarely experienced, and wasn't keen on. He was still watching me, waiting for an answer. I couldn't find one. I was too preoccupied with trying to work out how many people had witnessed me assaulting Jonathan, and whether or not I regretted the act – or just how public it'd been.

"This is about Brooke, isn't it?" He raised an eyebrow, wiping the blood from his lip.

I didn't answer.

His gaze lowered as he nodded, letting out a sigh. "Look, I got to her as fast as I could. Really."

I frowned at him. What did that mean?

"I get you're mad, and I get why. But I couldn't have known this would happen." He shrugged, shaking his head.

"Are you actually being serious?" I narrowed my eyes. "How could you *not* have known this would happen? It's what you do."

"What? No it's not."

"Please." I laughed, "This has Jonathan Taylor written all over it."

"Wait..." He frowned slightly, tilting his head. "What're you talking about?"

"You messing with my sister's feelings, giving her mixed messages and leading her on."

He paused, his expression softening. "Oh."

"Oh?" I raised an eyebrow. "That all you can say?"

"I thought..."

"You thought?"

He shook his head, running a hand through his hair.

I smiled bitterly, "My point exactly. You don't think. You just act."

Jonathan's mouth curled into a wry smile as he glanced my way, shaking his head again.

"What?" I narrowed my eyes. "You have something you want to say, say it."

He didn't bite.

"Come on, Taylor. Suddenly you've gone shy? What is it I said that amused you so much?"

His green eyes rose to meet mine, the trace of a smirk still evident on his lips. "Let's just say you could do with taking a leaf out of my book."

I scoffed. "Seriously? Your ego knows no bounds."

"This isn't about ego. It's about not being so terrified that things won't pan out that you actually take a chance. Live a little."

"And to hell with everyone else, right?"

His expression clouded, faint bruises creeping up beneath his skin. "I never meant to hurt Brooke."

"No, but you did."

He hesitated, chewing over his response. "That's between us. No offense Nathan, I get the whole overprotective brother act...really, I do. But this has nothing to do with you. Or anyone else."

"Stay away from her."

"Yeah," he smiled weakly. "I'm trying. It's not as easy as you think."

"Well try harder."

He stared at me evenly, the silence thickening between us. I was the first to break it. "You say that you care about her..."

"I do-"

"Good. So prove it. Let her move on. Because we both know it won't end well for her. And if you honestly give a rat's ass about her happiness...You'll stop. Stop the flirting, the meaningful looks, the inside jokes. Just stop."

Jonathan looked at me, his expression guarded as he absorbed my words. His gaze fell to the floor for a moment, before flickering back to mine in what almost looked like defeat. "Okay."

"Okay?" I frowned.

He nodded slowly. "You're right. I know you're right...I just wish you weren't."

I smiled weakly, that awful bad guy feeling sinking into my gut once more. "Thank you."

He gave a small shrug, his eyes lowering to look at my right hand. I followed his gaze and the awful sensation grew as we watched the bruises on my knuckles take shape. This was not my proudest moment.

"I can make them disappear." He offered, his face still unreadable. "If you like."

I hesitated, contemplating his offer. Brooke would kill me if she put two and two together. I'd thought of that and reasoned she'd get over it. But the more I stared down at the ugly patterns against my knuckles, the more I wished they weren't there at all. Jonathan was wrong. I *had* done something without thinking about the consequences, and it didn't feel great.

"No." I shook my head finally. "I'm fine."

He nodded, running a hand through his hair. "Nathan, I know I act impulsively. That I'm reckless and stupid...but you really should try it. Just a little."

I looked up at him.

"But just a little." He repeated, raising an eyebrow. "I know it's doesn't seem logical, but sometimes good things happen when you take a risk."

I wanted to apologize and remind him that I didn't normally do this. It wasn't me. But he knew that. And, to really drive home that guilt, he understood why I'd done it.

"I'm gonna..." He gestured back up the path, smiling weakly. I nodded, still unable to verbalize how I felt, watching as he turned and walked away, getting out a fresh cigarette as he did. There was a strong possibility that the entire school would know about this come tomorrow morning, but I was certain it wouldn't come from him.

I rolled my eyes and turned, slinking over to grab my abandoned bag. As I drew it over my shoulder, I looked around at the Charles River, desperately trying to reclaim the sense of serenity and excitement I'd felt not long ago. It was time to head to the bookstore, to do the one thing I'd been looking forward to doing today. I couldn't allow what had happened to linger and taint the rest of the day.

I bowed my head as I set off in the opposite direction, my brow furrowed as I concentrated on the cool breeze and everyday noises – imploring them to remove any residue of the Nathan Danes that had just beaten up a friend in broad daylight. To allow the kind, patient, intelligent guy that existed to emerge again. That was the guy I wanted her to see. To know.

I looked up meekly as my feet slowed to a stop, the Barnes and Noble looming. I'd first seen her a month and a half ago, in this very building. I went there almost every day, out of habit more than anything. Ever since I was a kid mom would take us to the bookstore when Dad had a big case notching up his stress levels. She'd let us choose whatever we desired and sometimes I would test that generosity – landing myself with the reproachful look only a mother can give. Over the years the trips had of course dwindled, but I always came back.

It was my haven.

And in that haven I'd glimpsed her.

I could still recall the exact moment I'd seen her, the exact moment I knew. Sure, there were plenty of pretty girls in Boston. But she wasn't just pretty. She was…unique. Beautifully unique. I'd been an hour deep into my search for the right book to match my mood. I couldn't decide whether I wanted to solve a complex crime or dive into a bizarre horror story that might – just might – keep me glancing into the dark recesses of my room. And during this search, this agonizing ordeal of pinpointing something that you just knew *had* to jump out at you…she did. I'd glanced up, and my heart stopped.

And so I'd done the closest thing to flirting I'd ever attempted. I'd bought her a book. And neatly folded within that book I'd written a note. Nothing too corny. I hoped. I'd hazarded a nickname for her – and told her in simple terms that I thought she was enchanting. That I wanted to start something. An exchange for old souls. I was crudely aware that she might've found the gesture hilarious or pathetic – or, indeed, both. But somehow, she'd been charmed. My Mouse had tucked a book aside in return, securing it behind the front counter with a note slipped inside the sleeve. She'd called me her Romeo.

Since then we'd gone around and around, leaving books for one another that thinly veiled who we were. What inspired or entertained us. A little window into the soul I desperately wanted her to see. I glanced around at the shelves as I walked to the front desk, my heartbeat picking up as I searched for her. The coast was clear. I'd probably missed her whilst my fist was having a conversation with Jonathan's face. I frowned as I unzipped my backpack to retrieve her book, catching sight of the bruises on my knuckles. Or the absence of them. My frown deepened as I scrutinized my hand, taking in the unmarred skin.

Jonathan.

I let out a low sigh as I approached the desk, gently lowering the book onto the counter. The clerk looked up at me with a smile as I gingerly slid it across to her, my fingertips hovering on the edge of the cover. She raised an eyebrow, her smile warming as she teased it from my grip. "Good morning, Nathan."

"Hey, Clarissa." I nodded, casting another furtive glance around. "Is uh…Is there anything for me?"

"I'm sorry, no." She shook her head, delicately tying a reserved tag around the book. I watched as she placed it beneath the counter, her blue eyes twinkling as her gaze traveled past me to a far corner of the store. "Not yet."

I frowned, turning to scan the bookshelves. A glimpse of onyx hair caught my eye, her head bowed as she inspected the book in her hand. I nodded slowly, my heart rate quickening as I stared after her. Each time we'd done this I'd managed to slip by. To know she hadn't seen me. I wasn't sure why I was so afraid of that. Only that I was.

I cast a weak smile back at the clerk, pushing myself back from the counter. There was still time to make a quick exit. I could hide out in a nearby store until she'd gone and then come back to collect my book. The exchange between two mysterious strangers would survive for another day…no bubbles burst. My gaze flickered back across to her as I hurried along the aisle towards the door, drawing my bag over my shoulder as I bowed my head. As the door grew closer I felt my pace slow, my trembling insides forming steel as I stopped altogether. I allowed myself a minute before slowly looking up at her. She was still poring over the contents of the book, a small crease forming over the bridge of her nose as she judged her find. She hadn't seen me. I could just go. Right now.

I drew my gaze towards the door, then back at her.

No.

I could hear the voices of Jonathan and James echoing in my mind. Their insistence that I seize the day and take a risk drumming against my temples like a maddening march. I hated to admit it, even to myself, but they were right. I was playing it safe when it came to her. I hesitated a second longer, drawing out the opportunity to chicken out.

My jaw set as I turned from the door, my hand gripping the strap of my backpack as I strode over. Her petite frame was dwarfed by the towering shelves, a small smile playing on her lips as she mouthed a passage from the book to herself silently. I felt myself grin, my pulse relaxing as I watched her. She was adorable.

Speak, I reminded myself. Don't be that guy that stands and stares at women he doesn't know.

"See anything good?" I ventured, hoping my voice didn't betray my nerves.

Her dark eyes flashed to mine in surprise, a faint blush warming her cheeks as she gently placed the book back on the shelf. "Oh. Uh…" She smiled shyly, her hand staying against the spine. "Maybe."

"I'm sure you'll find something amazing" I smiled, raising an eyebrow. "You always do."

Her gaze held mine for a moment, the tinge in her cheeks deepening. "It's…It's you?"

I couldn't work out whether she sounded happy or disappointed. I hadn't really planned for either.

"Surprise."

I watched as she glanced away, her brow furrowing as though trying to unravel a complex riddle. The ghost of a smile played on her lips as she looked back up at me, reaching up to tuck a strand of dark hair behind her ear.

"I wondered if you'd be interested in grabbing a coffee sometime." I smiled, secretly impressed at how level and calm I sounded. Confident, even. "We could talk properly?"

"I'd like that."

"You would?" I grinned.

"Yes." She laughed, raising an eyebrow. "Just…let me buy your next book first?"

My entire body both relaxed and electrified simultaneously. This was actually happening. I nodded dumbly, fighting to suppress the beam as it stretched across my face. "Sure. I have yours behind the counter."

She grinned, her eyebrow arching again as I hovered beside her. "Are you going to watch me or can I surprise you?"

I let out a laugh, holding my hands up in apology. "I'll meet you outside?"

She nodded, smiling as she secretively glanced around at the shelves. I smirked as I watched her desperately try to not give the game away, the blush forming on her cheeks each time I caught her eye. I held my hands up again with a grin as she shot me a playful glare, turning and walking from the store.

As soon as the cool air hit me I let out the breath I'd been holding, running both hands through my hair. That was probably the bravest thing I'd done to date. And I'd do it all again to see that smile light up her face. To be the reason behind it.

The door trilled behind me, the light scent of her perfume greeting me as I turned to meet her. She looked up at me timidly, cradling a store bag to her chest. I looked at it questioningly, raising an eyebrow as she opened the top and reached inside. Her expression was unreadable as she passed me the book, her fingertips lightly grazing mine. My gaze flickered to hers as I took it in my hands, my mouth tugging into a grin as I traced the title. *Romeo and Juliet.*

"Great minds think alike, I guess."

She let out a small laugh as she retrieved the same copy from her bag. "I guess so. We obviously have great taste."

I paused as I appraised her. "I know I do."

She met my gaze, her cheeks turning a deep shade of pink. Her dark hair fell into her face as she bowed her head, her lips curving into a coy smile.

I grinned, clearing my throat as we began walking towards the nearest coffee shop. Her fingers reached up to draw back the strands that had fallen, tucking them gently behind her ear. I resisted the urge to assist her, my fingertips tracing the cover of the novel in my hand instead.

So far, so good.

Chapter 14

Brooke

Tick. Tick.Tick.

The sound of the clock was echoing around the room, each second dragging as the hands barely shifted. The fact I'd been staring at it for the best part of an hour didn't help either. Stretching out I decided to remedy that, taking a quick glance around.

Everyone in class had their heads bowed, pens in hand as they drew, or sketched, or in my case aimlessly doodled, on whatever canvas they'd chosen. Art had always seemed like an easy class, only now I wasn't so sure that assumption was correct. Over the years I'd become a pro at drawing out a silhouette, fashioning clothes around it before I made the image a reality on my mannequin. So how hard could drawing fruit be?

Turns out very.

Miss Walker, the most stereotypical art teacher I'd ever encountered, would purse her lips as she got to my work. Her usual smile replaced by a dull glance and a brisk nod. I don't think it was that she didn't like my work, though she never said otherwise, she just didn't see *me* in it.

Though I also wasn't sure what else she was expecting. I didn't know what she needed from my work, what expression she was craving that I'd failed to give her.

The minute hand on the clock moved marginally. One step closer to freedom.

I glanced back to my sketch, deciding to spend the rest of class idly finishing it off. But it wasn't there, my eyes widening as I realized my rough doodle had been replaced while I was distracted. My fingers reached to brush the new paper, a smile tugging the corner of my lips.

A brunette grinned up at me, her hair bouncing in waves, one of her chocolate eyes closed in a wink. A skin-tight bodysuit clung to her curves dangerously, accentuating her buxom chest, a hand curled around a baseball bat. One of her legs was bent at the knee, the heel of her thigh-high boot resting on the chest of a dark-haired guy, who was staring up at her with a mix of adoration and complete awe. Beneath the drawing was a line, written in quick scrawl.

Brooke just keeps batting them away

I grinned as I turned to my right, finding the curious brown eyes of Matt Cooper staring back at me. A pink tinge creeping up his neck as he shifted in his seat, waiting for me to speak.

Was he nervous?

Matt and I had known each other almost the entirety of high school, the two of us friendly, without actually crossing the line into friendship. We'd worked on group projects, we'd made small talk, but that was it. Maybe this was his way of pushing the boundaries to see if he could break through?

"You drew this?"

The blush creeping across his olive skin retreated as I spoke, his lips turning up in an easy smile. "Is that okay?"

I glanced back down at the way he'd drawn me, the way he'd drawn *us*. "What would you do if I said no?"

He laughed, running a hand through his soft brown hair. "Probably sit here awkwardly for the next ten minutes and then run like Forrest."

I let out a small laugh of my own, turning back to the sketch and finding new details.

The pencil drawn in Matt's hand that touched the tip of my boot, the sketch of him drawing the copy of me. His other hand clutched around my boot to pull me down on him. I could even see the smattering of freckles I had across my collarbone.

"It's amazing," I whispered breathlessly.

"I had a great model to work with."

My head whipped around, my eyes meeting his as we both blushed at his words. Was he flirting? Did...did he *like* me? It was safe to say when it came to guys I was fairly naive. Had Matt been giving off signs and I'd overlooked them? And what if he was flirting? What then?

"Oh. Thank you." Great start, Brooke.

He fidgeted with the sketch pad, smiling softly. "You're welcome."

"Can I keep it?"

His grin grew, pleased that I wanted it. "Of course."

"Thanks..."

We smiled uncomfortably at each other as I tucked the drawing into my own book. Conversation reaching a standstill, the tension settling awkwardly. A voice in the back of my head was telling me to push it, to engage him again to see if he was interested. And if I was wondering if he was interested, did that mean I was too?

Screw it.

I wasn't going to make the same mistakes twice. I wouldn't sit around and wait, trying to read into his cryptic behavior, wondering if he liked me or if he was just naturally charming, while he moved his attention elsewhere.

"Why me?"

Matt looked taken aback that I'd spoken again. "Oh. Uh..." He smiled slightly in my direction, his cheeks warming. "Well, I think you're beautiful."

I guess that answered my question. Sort of. "You do?"

"I always have."

I paused. "How long is always?"

"You've always been beautiful." He shrugged, as if that admission was an obvious one. "I guess I started to notice about a year ago."

My stomach flipped.

Was this what other teenage girls felt when guys made moves? Was this how it was supposed to be? Just so simple. He'd not lied or bluffed his way out of it. He'd just looked me in the eyes and admitted he thought I was beautiful. "How come you've never told me before?"

"I wasn't sure you'd be interested. Or available."

Was I interested?

I bit my lip, giving him a slow once over, seeing him properly for the first time. Before I'd only ever looked at him as a friendly face, now I was looking for something deeper. Something more. He was definitely attractive, in an effortless way. He didn't dress himself up to attract the opposite sex, he didn't have that signature air of bravado around him that clung to most guys. What you saw was exactly what you got.

And I was surprised to find I liked it.

His lips parted as he grinned at me. He knew what I was doing, but he didn't show off. There was no flexing as my eyes roamed across his physique. No cocky smirk as I admired his jaw.

His dark eyes locked on mine as I finally looked up, my own smile tugging at my lips. "You're very attractive," I confessed.

"Thank you."

"And...I'm single."

"Yeah. But..." His eyebrow raised slowly.

"But?"

He weighed his words, tapping his pencil on the desk. "Well, honestly, I kinda thought you and Jonathan Taylor had a thing."

I flinched at his name, looking down at my hands. How had I been so transparent about my feelings for Jonathan while he had no idea?! And yet half the school did. Matt had picked up on it.

Rachel certainly had.

"No...we..." I tapped the table anxiously, watching the tips of my manicure drum against the wood. There was no we. The potential Jonathan and Brooke boat had sailed, and quickly become a shipwreck. We were too different, wanted totally different things. Which was okay. He was allowed to want to be single. To sleep around.

But that wasn't me. I wanted stability, long term commitment. You could call me young, a hopeless romantic. You could laugh at me for wanting that fairytale ending and the prince charming. But there was so much more to me than that. I wanted to build a fashion empire. I wanted the world at my feet. And I'll be damned if I wouldn't have a loving husband and children surrounding me while I do that. It was the Italian in me.

But Jonathan...Jonathan *wasn't* that guy. He was the reckless fling of my teenage years. Or he could have been.

Sighing I looked back at Matt. "No, we're not."

He smiled warmly, raising an eyebrow. "His mistake."

"So everyone keeps telling me."

The air between us stilled again. Tension filling the space. It was the effect I was used to Jonathan having on me, the anxiety and the confusion. But why should he ruin something he had no business being a part of?! Why was I letting him have so much power over me and...whatever *this* was?

I'd vowed that I'd get over this teenage infatuation with him. I was closing that door and I wasn't looking back.

"Well I like you." Matt drew my attention back to him, his cheeks starting to flame again. "And I'd like to take you out some time. If you want."

The question didn't surprise me, at least not now, possibility sparking between us. It was fresh and new, completely unknown.

So why was I tense?

If I'd been enjoying the flirting, enjoying a guy being interested in me, not the chase, or the fact he could be my first, why were my palms clamming up?

I knew why, obviously. I'd be stupid to not understand my own body. I was panicked. I didn't have a great track record with guys, or at least the only two I'd ever made a move on. Jonathan had beaten my heart, and Zak had messed with my mind. The baggage I'd already begun to drag around would be dumped between me and a potential partner, especially now. After...

I shuddered.

I didn't want to think about that night after the gig. I didn't want to think about Zak. Or that he was *still* dating my best friend while I kept my mouth shut.

Then again...so far so had Jonathan.

Matt cleared his throat, his eyebrow rising, the question still hanging in the air between us.

I opened my mouth to speak, still unsure what was going to tumble out.

Luckily I never got that far.

I released the breath I'd been holding as the bell echoed around the school, signaling the start of lunch. I dragged my gaze from Matt's as I scooped up my sketchbook and hooked my purse over my forearm, pretending I hadn't seen his face drop.

"Saved by the bell?" He bundled up his own things, throwing me a forced smile.

I was being stupid. Matt was a decent guy. A *good* guy. I'd never seen him drunkenly groping girls in dark corners at parties, or charming them from their underwear with a silver tongue. He was the type of guy to offer you his jacket on a cold night, to watch you walk to your door safely, even though it's only three feet from where you were kissing goodbye.

He was the type of guy you'd feel comfortable taking home to your parents.

I smirked as I rose to my feet, nudging him playfully. "Join me for lunch?"

"Yeah, sure thing."

Matt lifted my books easily, adding them to his own as we slipped from the room and ambled into the hallway, heading towards the cafeteria.

As we followed the crowd through to the semi-packed lunch hall I noticed our usual table was empty. Or at least the table that I'd dragged half of the group towards after the fall out with Jonathan.

I knew from a conversation with Nathan last night that he was going to be spending extra time in the library. He'd finally met a girl who was as nerdy as him, and the two of them were planning on pouring over more college prospects without distraction.

A quick scan of the room alerted me to Rosie's presence, Zak by her side at the Jocks table. But there was no David, and no Lucas.

David had been there from the start, joining me at a new table while people whispered and stared. To be fair he was relieved to be away from Will. My heart ached when I saw the confusion behind his eyes as he looked at his older brother. I could only imagine what was running through his head. They were both hurting, but sooner or later they'd find that bond between them again, they'd be okay. But for now, they needed space.

And with Rosie and David choosing me, Lucas was only ever going to be a few steps behind.

So where were the two of them now?!

"You know..." Matt slipped our books down onto the table as we stopped, looking at me with a shy smirk. "You still haven't answered my question."

Ah.

That.

I shook my head slowly with a laugh, looking at him from beneath my lashes. "Maybe."

He fake stumbled backward, clutching at his chest with a laugh. "Ouch."

I couldn't help laughing along with him, trying to pinpoint the fluttering in my stomach as I playfully jabbed him in the ribs. "I didn't say no."

"Ah, but you didn't say yes. I'm mortally wounded."

I toyed with a strand of my hair, pouting playfully. "How can I make it up to you?"

"Hmm..." He stepped towards me, his soft brown eyes sparkling mischievously as his head dipped towards mine, his hand reaching out to stroke my cheek, tilting my chin towards him. "Buy me a large banana milkshake and I'll consider it."

I flushed, my heart pounding in the limited space between us. "Look at you breaking the rules."

"I'm a feminist." He grinned, his nose almost touching mine now.

"Anything else?" I bit my lip. I couldn't help myself. We'd stepped up our game. Flirting had come so naturally the moment he'd taken that step closer. But internally I was beating myself. I wasn't an easy girl. I was sixteen when I'd had my first kiss. I was still a virgin. So why did I feel like a whore for considering Matt with everything I'd been through with Jonathan. And the disastrous encounters with Zak.

"Just the milkshake." His eyes closed momentarily as his nose brushed gently against the side of mine. "And a yes." Our faces were inches apart as the intimacy between us flared, and then he winked.

He was determined to get this date out of me.

Giving him my own wink in return I took a step away and broke the moment, cool air and the babble of chatter washing over us once more. I didn't say anything as I grabbed my purse, Matt sliding onto a seat as I headed to fetch a milkshake.

A large banana milkshake.

And a date?

As I joined the queue of students I took a breath, trying to calm my heart and my head. Hoping for once they'd just stop fighting each other and get along. I was ashamed to admit I was still pining for Jonathan. I missed the flirting and the teasing, the way he always made me blush. I missed feeling nervous around him, like he knew what I was thinking without me even opening my mouth.

And then there he was.

I'd looked up, turning to look back towards Matt, and instead found myself looking at Jonathan. His head was bowed towards the almost empty table, dark tendrils falling over his forehead. I couldn't see his face, couldn't see his expression. But a familiar figure was sat beside him, her posture relaxed as she rested her hand over his.

Jen.

Her mouth was moving quickly as she spoke, leaning closer. He nodded. His hand turned beneath hers, encasing her slender fingers in his.

There was that stab of jealousy.

I don't know how she did it, how she could be so happy enjoying his body but nothing else, knowing when other girls took his fancy he'd move on. Either she was way more into him than I thought, and had convinced herself that he'd always come back, or she was just as nonchalant as he was about the whole thing. I'd never seen her with other guys. But maybe she wasn't as obvious about it.

Jens free hand rose, brushing the hair from his face at the same time he lifted his head. His eyes automatically meeting mine.

I inhaled sharply.

Not because he'd caught me looking, or even because it was the usual reaction whenever he looked at me, but because his face, his perfectly flawless face, was beaten. The skin under his right eye was a deep purple, yellow undertones stretching out beneath it. His bottom lip was split, a thick red line creasing the pink skin.

He maintained eye contact with me as Jen continued to talk. What the hell had happened? Had he hit on the wrong girl and an older brother had put a stop to it? Or maybe Jonathans arrogant attitude had gotten him into trouble after one drink too many.

An uneasy thought struck, and I bit down on my lip as I broke his gaze, turning away regretfully. Zak had done this. It made sense, guilt eating away at me. If I'd not gotten myself into another stupid situation with that complete asshole Jonathan wouldn't have had to step in. He wouldn't have punched him. And Zak wouldn't have retaliated.

Although I didn't believe for one second he'd acted alone. Zak probably wasn't even there at all. He'd have got his goons to do it for him. Save face with Rosie.

Smiling thinly, I paid for Matt's milkshake, taking a deep breath as I grabbed two straws and tried to steady my nerves. The least I could do was go over and apologize. Face him and my faults at once.

You can do this...

Just go over, ask if he's okay. Say sorry. It doesn't have to be any more difficult. There doesn't have to be mind games. You can rebuild what you had before, maybe not exactly as it was, but definitely better than this. Anything is better than our group ripped down the middle.

I lifted my chin as I turned. It would be a minor detour on the way back to Matt, but he wouldn't notice. His head was low as he sketched, smiling at whatever he was creating.

Jonathan had returned his attention to Jen as soon as I'd broken the moment earlier, his head now bobbing as he nodded to whatever she was saying.

It was now or never.

My feet moved automatically, pulling me towards him and closing the gap.

There were two tables separating us when he finally looked up. Confusion clouded his features momentarily, his hand lifting to run through his mess of hair.

Only one table between us now. I took a breath, trying to keep my expression neutral. Back straight. Shoulders squared. Exuding confidence.

Almost there.

Jonathan's features shifted as he looked up into my face.

Three foot away.

His eyes were cool.

I opened my mouth...

...And he turned away.

I felt the wind rush out of me as he shifted his posture, my cheeks burning as humiliation crept up my spine. That was my answer. Jonathan didn't want to speak to me, let alone even acknowledge my presence.

Had I deserved that? After all he was the one who'd hit Zak. I'd never asked him to, I hadn't made him do it. But maybe he didn't see it that way. Maybe to him it was a way to make things up to me, and having his ass handed to him had tipped the scales in his favor...

My face burned even hotter as I walked back to Matt, Rachel sat at the next table watching me with a smirk spread across her smug face, her new friends whispering and laughing behind their hands. They would be absolutely loving this, watching as the naive little virgin crashed and burned with the guy everyone knew she had the hots for. No doubt Rachel would use it in her favor and spread some rumor around the school. I grit my teeth, swallowing down my shame at being a laughing stock once more. I was done with this whole fucking thing. If Jonathan and I couldn't even be friends now, then so be it. I was trying.

I *had* tried.

I took a deep breath, turning away from Rachel and carrying on across the floor to Matt, faking whatever scraps of confidence I could find.

He looked up as I drew closer, his pencil dropping into the spine of his book. His lips parting as he shot me a soft smile, before frowning as he caught the tense expression on my face. He pulled my seat out for me and cleared space for our milkshake with an almost effortless movement, sliding his hand over mine and giving it a gentle squeeze as I lowered myself onto the chair. He hadn't seen the way Jonathan had given me the cold shoulder, nor had he watched as Rachel and her gang of bitches had sat and laughed, but I knew he could see through the fake smile I'd slipped into place.

I knew that I didn't have to pretend it was okay with him. He wouldn't care, and he wouldn't judge. And he didn't. He sat patiently and he listened to me talk for over an hour. About my misplaced crush on Jonathan and how awkward things had become, about how Daddy and Nathan scared off any guy that had shown the faintest interest in me, and all about how James had recently returned home.

Matt was particularly interested in the last part, asking questions about when James had joined and when he'd shipped off. He'd sat back and grinned as I'd become more animated, sharing stories of how James would call and write as often as he could, remembering the immediate rush of love whenever we met him from the airport, taking in his girlfriend Elle as one of the family, and how it felt like I had a sister now because we'd shared the bond of missing him. I told him about how happy I'd been to go home last week and find him there waiting for me with open arms, the happy tears I'd cried at learning he was home for good, and the suspicion and sadness I'd buried within me at wondering why he'd been given the all-clear to return home permanently. I wasn't dumb, James wouldn't go AWOL, and I knew how much joining up had meant to him, he wouldn't walk away so easily. Which could only mean something had happened.

Something bad. But just like I told myself, I now told Matt the same, he was here, and that was all that mattered.

I'd realized as we'd gotten to the bottom of our milkshake glass, chairs scraping as people began moving to their next class, what Matt had been doing. He'd seen the glimmer of hope, of happiness, in my expression when I'd brought up James, and he'd run with it. He'd taken my mind off Rachel. Off Zak and Jonathan. And he'd made me laugh.

And as we were walking to the door he'd stopped and asked me one last time if I wanted that date. Even after everything I'd told him about my family being protective and about Jonathan, he still liked me, he still wanted to enjoy my company.

He said there was no pressure, that I could say no.

But I didn't.

Because he'd learned so much about me already, and I wanted to know more about him. I wanted to know what he liked, what his ambitions were, and what he imagined his future like. Hell, I wanted to know the small stuff too. What his favorite colour was and if he preferred hot or cold drinks.

And as we walked the halls, Matt slipping his hand into mine, I felt something inside me shift.

My head and my heart finally found the same page.

Chapter 15

Rosie

I delicately drew the lace taut, my gaze flickering uneasily to the slender slope of my leg as I tied my sneaker. My eyes narrowed at the sight of it, my fingertips tracing the imperfect shape with slow precision. As I sat up I hazarded a glance around, careful not to stare as I scrutinized the near-perfect array of bodies scattered around. Locker rooms turned even the most confident woman into a wreck. It was a setting designed to make you feel uncomfortable, exposed…judged. I'd never really given it much thought before. That's not to say I hadn't been victim to the odd blush or tactile change. Of course I had. But I'd never felt like this before. I knew it was in my head. But all I could think as I sat in my cheerleader outfit, my skirt flared around the top of my thighs, was that everyone was laughing at me. That they were sneering and casting comment.

I looked down at the thick folds of the jacket covering my arms, gingerly closing it to shield my chest and stomach. It was Zak's, so the school colors matched enough that I figured I'd get away with keeping it on. At least for practice. I'd have to figure the rest out later.

"You ready?"

I looked up at Brooke, offering a small nod. "Almost. I'll meet you out there."

"I'll save you a spot."

I waited as she turned with the crowd to filter into the gymnasium, glancing around furtively before getting to my feet. I opened my locker, my gaze scanning the room one last time. It had emptied, save for a few stragglers near the door. But they were too preoccupied gossiping to notice. Shielding myself from view, I dragged my sports bag along the metal surface. My heartbeat quickened as I gingerly pulled at the zip, burrowing my hand inside to search for it. I smiled as my fingers closed around the plastic bottle, casting another look around the empty benches as I opened the safety cap. I tilted the bottle, two caplets falling into my open palm. I let out a small sigh as I tipped my head back and swallowed them, wincing as they went down.

They would help. They *were* helping. A little boost to my energy levels, just to keep me going. This new crash diet had really knocked me and honestly I felt like I hadn't slept for days. It was just a matter of adjusting though. Give it a bit more time and I would be doing backflips again. Only this time with less cargo.

I replaced the bottle and zipped up the bag, taking a step back as I closed the locker door. My sneakers echoed in the empty room as I traced the route to the gymnasium, hugging Zak's jacket around me as I shoved against the heavy doors. I grimaced as the stark lights of the gym hit me, the sharp sound of sneakers squeaking against polished wood assaulting my ears. I took a step back as my senses adjusted, my eyes beginning to sting. Hopefully my vitamins would kick in soon.

After steadying myself a moment, I reluctantly opened my eyes to the brightly lit room. I grinned in relief as I spotted Brooke in a corner, sat on the wooden floor with her legs stretched out before her. She sat up, smiling as she waved me over. I bowed my head as I headed across, praying our captain hadn't witnessed my tardiness. The last thing I needed was to be made an example of. I joined her on the floor, smiling weakly as I watched her gracefully lean to grasp her toes. My gaze turned to my own podgy legs, the smile dying on my lips as I straightened them out and attempted the same warm-up stretches I'd done a thousand times before. My stomach clenched as I lowered to meet my knees, my arms outstretched. I winced, drawing myself back as the unmistakable urge to wretch took hold. I drew in shallow breaths as I commanded the nausea to pass, my hand trembling as I rested it against the floor.

"Are you okay?"

I looked up at Brooke with a small nod. "Yeah, my own fault for eating right before practice."

She stared at me, unconvinced. "You sure?"

"Absolutely." I nodded again, forcing a bright smile. One I hoped would satiate her. I felt her gaze still on me and raised an eyebrow, smirking slightly. "How're things with you?"

She let out a small laugh, rolling her eyes. "Lucas was right. You suck at subtlety."

"I prefer to think of it as ballsy."

"Things are good." She grinned, the hint of a blush forming on her cheeks. "How're things with you? Still all loved up?"

I glanced down at the jacket dwarfing my frame, tugging the fabric closer. "Yeah, we're fine."

At least, I thought we were. He'd been blowing hot and cold more than usual this week. One minute he couldn't keep his hands off me and the next…it was as if I didn't exist. It'd taken all my strength not to open that can. If he was losing interest, I wasn't sure I was ready to know. It felt safer to savor the moments when he did look at me as a boyfriend might, and forget the rest. It probably hadn't helped that my brother had laid into him after the gig. For reasons I was still unclear of, save for the assumption he was just being…Jonathan.

"You excited for tomorrow?" I raised an eyebrow, attempting a tactile change of subject.

"Yeah." She grinned, her head bowing as she leaned down to meet her toes again. "A little nervous. First date and all."

I watched her for a moment, smiling as I tried to work out how someone like Brooke could possibly be nervous for a date. She was the epitome of the beautiful girl next door. Any guy would be lucky to take her out, and they would all know it too. "I think it'll be amazing." I grinned, "He seems like a nice guy."

She let out a laugh as she turned to me, her arms still outstretched. "He's probably the nicest guy I've ever met."

I grinned as she trailed off, a wistful look overtaking her features.

"Oh God, am I gushing?" Brooke laughed as she sat upright.

"I would definitely say you're in gush territory."

I let out a laugh as she buried her face in her hands. It was nice to see a guy having this effect on her, instead of making her feel insecure and uncertain. Not that I was naming any names but…my brother had hardly given her a warm welcome into the world of romance. Still, she was happy now and the group had just about edged out of the uncomfortable zone. Perhaps in a few weeks we'd all be sitting together at lunch again.

"Okay girls, enough chatter."

Brooke and I looked up at Heather, our cheer captain, as she clapped her hands to demand attention.

"We all warmed up? Good." I blanched as I glanced down at my body, a guilty hue crawling along my cheeks. She continued without waiting for a response, her honey-colored hair dancing as she turned on her heel to address the length of the gymnasium. "We're gonna start off easy today before we jump into the routine. So get in position for a few basket tosses and we'll take it from there."

I watched as Brooke elegantly got to her feet, letting out a small sigh as I followed suit. The bright lights danced for a moment as I readjusted, a sharp pain shooting into my side. My gaze shot to her in alarm as I rubbed at the spot through the thick fabric of Zak's jacket. Clusters of the squad grouped into teams, a guy and girl wandering over to us. I smiled in greeting as I recognized Finn, one of the bulkier guys in school. He'd always been really kind and didn't take himself seriously, so it was rare any comments were made about his role on the squad. Although whether that was down to his good nature or the sheer muscle mass, I couldn't be sure. My smile faltered as I looked past him to the girl, recognition dawning as I took in her cruel smirk. She'd been there to snarl beside Rachel when the news of her and Jonathan had emerged.

Her gaze settled on me, the corner of her mouth tilting in satisfaction. "You going on top Rosie? If we can lift you."

"Easier to lift Rosie than the weight of you and that failed boob job." Brooke arched an eyebrow, folding her arms.

Finn laughed, unsuccessfully attempting to disguise it as a cough. He turned his head, grinning as he got into position as the spot. I smiled weakly as Brooke and my biggest fan squared up, drawing their arms into a neat cross. I'd hoped to sit this one out, so to speak. Perhaps take up Finn's position at the back. Out of sight and, if I could help it, out of mind. No such luck. I looked from Brooke's sweet, encouraging smile to the bored disdainful expression opposite her. I could've sworn before now this girl and I'd been...not friends exactly, but certainly not this.

Okay, time to step up. No biggie. Just because I wasn't feeling my best didn't mean this would be a disaster. It was just practice. Not a big game with the floodlights hitting you. No crowd. Just...a room full of people who would be able to tell if you did it wrong.

I let out a sigh, limbering up my arms and legs gingerly. My hands rested lightly on their shoulders as I placed my foot in the space provided, hoisting myself up. As the air whipped past me my grip tightened on them, a blush warming my cheeks as I steadied myself.

The girl lowered her arms a fraction, yelping dramatically. My head span as the unstable hoist shifted beneath me. She let out a laugh as she saw my panicked expression, rolling her eyes. "Relax, I've got you. Although you might wanna lay off the doughnuts."

Brooke glared at her, digging her nails into her clasped arms.

She let out a sharp gasp, narrowing her eyes. "It was a joke, jeez."

"Funny."

I smiled wanly at Brooke, my grip softening as I stood to my full height. Not the most encouraging start. My gaze rose to look ahead as I felt them raise and lower their hold, the room lifting up and down as though I was in an elevator with no door. I swallowed as I felt the momentum peak and the time to jump arrive. My side stabbed painfully as I soared into the air, my head becoming lighter the higher I went. I tried desperately to focus on the position of my limbs, the outcome I wanted for the landing. But I couldn't focus. Because as my body began to fall back to the ground, the last strands of consciousness were plucked away and darkness engulfed me.

I winced as hardwood and warm bodies collided with me, the latter breaking my fall. My eyes opened, stinging as the lights broke through once again. I turned and crawled, my arms nearly giving way as I found a space away from everyone.

"What happened?" An agitated voice asked loudly, a palm coming out to my forehead.

"Lardo here toppled us like skittles."

I grimaced, attempting to open my eyes again. It was less stark the second time around, the voices less like drums. The girl was actually the farthest from our little huddle, her head bowed in embarrassment. I hazarded a guess she hadn't stuck around to catch me when I fell. Finn sat beside me, concern etched on his face as he supported my back. Heather crouched before me, her palm on my head. And to my other side, Brooke. A faint bruise on her calf from where she'd hit the floor. I smiled weakly, mortified.

"I'm fine." I murmured, ushering away Heather's hand.

None of them looked convinced.

"Honestly." I let out a small laugh, "I just got a little dizzy."

Heather arched an eyebrow at me skeptically. "Can you stand?"

"Yep."

She stood up slowly, her eyes guarded as she waited. My hands flattened against the wooden floor as I curled my legs into my body, rising to my full height. A sharp gasp escaped as I straightened up, my foot stumbling back to regain my footing. Brooke shot up to grab my arm, her grip firm but gentle.

"See?" I forced a bright smile, "Good as new."

"Rosie…" Heather shook her head. "I'm sorry, but I can't let you finish practice like this."

"But…I'm fine," I said in a small voice, my gaze darting between them. "I swear."

"You're pale, clammy and you almost collapsed. It's not just for your sake. You could've hurt Brooke, Yasmin, or even Finn. I'm sorry." Heather raised an eyebrow. "Go home. Rest. And we'll see where we stand next practice."

That didn't exactly fill me with optimism.

"Am I okay to take her home? I don't want her driving."

I looked up at Brooke.

"Of course." Heather nodded, casting me a sympathetic look before turning on her heels and commanding the others quit gawking. My cheeks burned as Yasmin eyed me, shaking her head. Finn was last to leave us, a frown marring his features as he stood up and gave me one last once over. I hugged the jacket to my body as we turned and shuffled from the gymnasium, my head bowed.

As we entered the locker room Brooke ushered me onto a vacant bench, offering me a smile as she opened first her own locker and then mine, pulling our bags free.

"I feel like such an idiot." I looked up at her, "I'll be fine in no time."

She paused, lowering the bags onto the bench. "Heather's just worried. *I'm* worried."

"There's no need."

"But I am."

I peered up at her, watching as she moved to sit beside me. "There's something going on. I know it." Her gaze softened, her voice gentle. "You don't have to tell me but...I'm not stupid, Rosie. Don't lie to me either. Just promise me it's not serious."

I held her gaze, my smile slight as I nodded. "I promise."

"Good." She reached over to squeeze my hand, standing abruptly. "Then let's get you home."

With an air of maternal determination Brooke grabbed both bags and slung them onto her shoulder, turning back to face me. I desperately didn't want to lie to her. It wasn't serious. Now and then I got a little neglectful and took it too far. I could appreciate that. But on the whole I had it in hand. So, why did I feel guilt weighing heavily in the pit of my stomach? I hazarded a glance at her as we walked the hallway, her pace slowing to match mine.

"Hey, you two. Heading home already?"

We both faltered as we looked up at the familiar voice. David glanced between us, a scroll of paper loosely wound in his hand. He tapped it against his leg distractedly as he met us.

Brooke held me to her side protectively. "Rosie's not well..."

"You're not?" He frowned.

"I'm fine. Really."

"She's playing the hero. She went dizzy at practice." Her eyebrow arched in my direction. "And now she's going home to rest."

He glanced around the deserted hallway, his gaze hovering on the doors to the auditorium. As he looked back at us, he tightened the scroll and buried it in his pocket. "I'll zap you guys there if you want? Saves the car journey."

Brooke smirked, "So I can walk back for my car?"

"Don't worry, I'll deliver it like a good valet." He teased.

"Thank you." She smiled, "Cutest valet I've ever seen."

He raised an eyebrow, his mouth curving into a grin. "Oh yeah?"

I raised an eyebrow as I looked between them, coughing.

"Sorry..." David laughed, reaching up to rub the back of his neck.

Brooke looked up at him with a shy smile, clearing her throat. "So, would you mind dropping my car home?"

"Yes, miss." He grinned with a salute.

She laughed, rolling her eyes as he stepped closer. He met her gaze for a moment, smiling as he cast one last glance around the hallway before placing one hand on her shoulder and the other on mine. I closed my eyes to prepare for what was about to come. On a good day it could turn your stomach. On a day like today? I grimaced, holding onto Brooke as the air whipped around us. In a split second we arrived in my bedroom, my eyes slowly opening to take in the familiar surroundings. I let out a shallow breath as I loosened my grip on Brooke's arm, smiling weakly at their concerned expressions. David moved back from us, conjuring a tall glass of water and setting it down.

"You want me to run you a bath or anything?" Brooke asked softly.

I shook my head, moving to sit on the bed. "I'm good." I looked between them, the sinking sensation I'd felt before gradually returning. So far I'd kept Brooke from practice and David from the play. He'd taken the leap after all. My shoulders sank with guilt. "You guys can head off. Maybe grab a movie?"

Brooke frowned, glancing at David warily. "I dunno."

"My mom should be back soon. Really, it's okay." I arched an eyebrow, taking a small sip of the water to prove my point. "Go."

"We could check in on you later..." David mused, tilting his head as he looked at me. "If you're really sure?"

"Positive."

Brooke watched me for a moment, frowning as David slipped his hand into hers. "Text me if you need anything."

"I will." I smiled, nodding as they both disappeared from sight. A slight gust followed in their wake, lifting the curls of my hair gently. I let out the breath I'd been holding, my gaze slowly rising to look at the offending glass of water. My throat tightened as I watched the bubbles burst in the bottom. My eyes closed to block it out, my mouth parting to take in another measured breath. I had to get out of there. Get some air, or…A smile tugged at my lips, my eyes opening as the thought occurred to me.

Zak.

We'd already arranged to meet later, after practice was due to finish. But surely he wouldn't mind me showing up early? He might even be touched. We could cuddle up and watch something on TV. Have some quality us time.

The smile still playing on my lips, I drew myself to my feet and took a hesitant step towards the door. The room stayed upright. A definite improvement. My mouth stretched into a grin as I grabbed my car keys and ambled from the room, reaching out to steady myself using the doorframe and walls. Just in case. I drew in a shallow breath as I looked down at the looming stairs, biting my lip. A part of me wished I'd just asked David to drop me at Zak's, but then even if that thought had arrived sooner…I wasn't sure how he'd feel about that. My hand gripped the banister as I slowly made my way downstairs, listening for signs of life. Nothing but the gentle hum from the garage as Jonathan worked on another song. I hurried to the front door, quietly slipping through it. Driving wasn't my wisest move, but how else would I make it there? If I took it nice and steady, blasted the air con…I would be fine.

I mentally thanked David for being such a prompt valet as I unlocked my car, sinking into the driver's seat. The cold air bathed me as the engine purred into life, my skin erupting in goosebumps.

Luckily it wasn't a long journey to Zak's house and in what felt like no time at all I was rolling the car to a gentle stop just outside. I stopped the engine and sat back in my seat, laughing slightly as I glanced down to see my fingers trembling. That was either adrenaline or the pills finally kicking in. Either way, I'd made it. Now I could relax. I released my seat belt and stepped out of the car, smiling as I glanced at Zak's car on the drive. As I neared the door, my heartbeat began to pick up speed. What if he was busy, or got annoyed at me just showing up?

I frowned back at my car sat idle, shaking my head as I turned and rapped on the door. No second-guessing. Not anymore. It was becoming exhausting. I narrowed my eyes as a low hum of music pulsed through the door, leaning closer. He was probably holed up in his room playing games or something. I tried again, louder this time.

Nothing.

Tentatively, I reached out to grasp the door handle and gave a gentle push. The door edged back quietly, the music from upstairs becoming louder as I stepped inside. This, he would definitely be pissed about. Breaking and entering…not exactly a great feature in a girlfriend.

I shook my head, gripping his jacket around me as I edged to the bottom of the stairs. "Zak?"

No answer.

Again.

My hand gripped the banister as I started the climb, my heart pounding louder with each step. The music reverberated through his bedroom door as I approached it, the tempo echoing my insides. I outstretched my hand, wrapping my fingers around the doorknob gingerly. The song dropped its volume for a second to lead into the chorus, the unmistakable sound of a woman moaning disrupting the snippet of silence. I held my breath, my hand frozen as I inched closer. A voice inside me implored me to step back. To leave. But I couldn't move. I could practically hear my own heartbeat hammering away, desperate to save itself from what lay in store.

Another moan, louder this time.

Go, the voice screamed at me. *You don't need to hear this…and you definitely don't need to see it.* But that was it. I did. I knew what was happening on the other side of that door. Lying to myself wouldn't make it any less true. It'd only mean that I'd have to smile sweetly at Zak and pretend everything was fine, when inside I was picturing it all. Torturing myself. I closed my eyes, steeling myself. Before I could turn back or, worse still, stand there longer, I forced the door open.

And there it was.

My heart breaking.

I stared at his bare back rising and falling as he lay on top of her, muffled groans emerging amidst the loud music. My chest tightened as I watched them, my feet stepping back against the doorframe. My desire to discover them was now replaced by a desperation to leave. But although my body was inching away, my eyes couldn't stray from the wrenching image before me.

She saw me first.

Her hand tapped at his shoulder, her moans dying in her throat as she tried to get his attention. I took another step back, my foot colliding with the open door. It rocked back, a thud echoing in the room. He froze, slowly and reluctantly turning to look back at me. I stared at him open-mouthed, rooted to the spot. My chest tightened as I drew my eyes from his to the woman lying beneath him.

Chloe glanced between us uncertainly, her cheeks tinged pink.

Chloe?!

Will's Chloe.

I frowned, shaking my head as I tried to piece it together. None of it made sense. Or at least, some parts didn't. My limbs finally woke up upon seeing her face, my legs forcing me from the room. I flew down the stairs, my head growing lighter again. I had to get out of there. Go somewhere, anywhere, he wasn't. I could faintly hear him behind me as I fled, panic evident in his hurried movements and raised voice. He was calling out for me to stop. To listen to him. But my body knew better. My brain switched off as I stumbled from the house, gasping as I took in lungfuls of air. I got halfway down the drive before my eyes welled up, my hand digging into my jacket for the car keys. I stopped short. His jacket pocket, I reminded myself.

Not mine.

Never mine.

"Rosie, Jesus! Would you give me a second?"

I withdrew my hand to wipe away a stray tear as it escaped down my cheek. Taking in a measured breath, I slowly turned to face him. His dark eyes searched mine as he stood opposite me, nothing but a pillow covering his modesty.

"Why?" I breathed, urging my lip to keep from trembling.

"Shit, I dunno…" He shrugged, his brow knitting as he chewed over his answer. "I guess I have a bigger sex drive than you."

Oh.

I watched him for a moment, trying not to allow that worm inside my head. But it was too late. Just like that I understood. I trusted what he said, even now. I hadn't been enough.

His dark eyes narrowed as he looked at me, his head tilting. "So uh…are we okay?"

"I don't…" I frowned, shaking my head. "I need to think."

He nodded, "I get that. It's a big ask. I know I'd not be comfortable with you and other guys…"

"Zak." I looked up at him, swallowing. "Just answer me one thing. Are you sorry?"

"Of course."

"You are?" I smiled slightly, angry at myself for how hopeful that made me feel.

"Yeah." He shrugged. "You didn't need to see that. I should've checked the lock."

My insides burnt as I stared back at him. That was all he had to say. That was all I was worth. My body saved me yet again, my feet dragging me to my car. My hands shook as I retrieved the key, opening the door and slinking into the driver's seat with as much dignity as I could muster. It wasn't much. I daren't look out the window to see if he was still there. To see if he would come to his senses and rush over to me, beg me not to leave. But I knew as I heard the thud of the front door closing that he'd gone back to her.

Just like that.

I pulled my seat belt on and started the engine, my fingers trembling. I couldn't go home. Not after this. Not yet anyway. Which only really left me with one place I could turn to. Brooke might still be out, just like I'd insisted, but if she was home she'd know what to say, what to do, to make it hurt a little less.

Another tear escaped as I drove the long private stretch to Danes Estate, my jaw setting as I fought to keep back the flood. I didn't want to start crying, because then I would have to tell myself to stop. And I wasn't sure that I'd be able to.

The gates rose before me, leading to their circle drive. I glanced over at the intercom, pressing my finger over the call button. It buzzed loudly, a light flashing.

"Hello?"

My body relaxed at the sound of her voice.

"Brooke, can you let me in?" I paused, catching sight of my reflection in the rear-view mirror. "Is David still with you?"

"Rosie?" I could hear the frown in her voice. "Uh, yeah. Hang on."

The intercom buzzed loudly, the gates slowly drawing open to allow me along the drive. My car slowed to a stop by the house, the engine dying quietly. I removed my seat belt, taking in a shallow breath as I stalled for time. I needed to tell her, to talk to her…but I also knew that the moment I did, it'd be real. It'd be out in the open and I could never take it back.

I slowly clambered from the car and made my way to the front door. It was already ajar, Brooke and David standing on the threshold and peering out in concern.

"Rosie?" She frowned, stepping towards me. "Are you okay?"

David's gaze softened as he stared at me, before glancing between us. "I'll uh…I'll catch up with you later."

I nodded at him gratefully as he slipped past, my gaze dropping to the floor.

Brooke's arm came around my shoulders, her head bowing into mine as she gently guided me inside and shut the door. "What's happened?"

I looked up at her, my throat becoming strangled as a sob tried to claw its way out. I gasped as I swallowed it, my eyes brimming.

Her gaze moved past me to the living room, her voice lowering. "Let's go to my room."

Following her gaze, my heart sank more. James was sat on the sofa, his girlfriend Elle laid out with her head on his lap. They were deep in conversation, his fingertips gently stroking her hair. Not the loving picture I needed to see.

I let her usher me upstairs, my insides dulling as I replayed the last half hour over and over in my mind. Soon she would know. And it'd be over. The make-believe vision of our high school romance would be destroyed. The door clicked behind her, her touch gentle as she guided me to the bed and set me down.

"Rosie." She murmured, crouching down before me. "You're starting to really worry me."

"I saw Zak with Chloe."

She frowned. "What?"

I smiled bitterly, brushing away a rebellious tear. "I saw him having sex with Chloe. Will's Chloe."

"Oh. Oh, God." She gaped, her hand moving to shield her mouth. "Rosie, I'm so sorry…Is there anything I can do?"

I narrowed my eyes as I tasted the words on my tongue. Will's Chloe. His girlfriend. A spark of anger ignited in my chest. Zak cheating on me…As much as it hurt, I understood it. I didn't want to. But I did. The fire in my chest grew as I shook my head, images of Will and Chloe kissing in the hallway at school flooding my mind. They had looked happy. She had made him look that happy. So how on Earth could she do this to him? He was the kindest, sweetest guy that ever existed. And he'd chosen her. She should be thanking her lucky stars, not risking whatever they had for…For my boyfriend.

"Rosie?" Brooke prompted, frowning.

I looked up at her, stunned as the anger inside me built. It felt more comforting than sadness. "Chloe. His fucking girlfriend…"

She smiled uneasily, "Would it be less horrible if it were someone else?"

"I…I don't know. Maybe." I shook my head. "I mean, don't yell at me for this but…I can see why he'd cheat on me. But why would she cheat on Will?"

"Jesus, Rosie. Stop." Brooke stood up, her dark eyes narrowing as she stared down at me. "Will is my friend too, but he's not here and he doesn't know. Let's focus on you."

"You're right." I murmured. "He doesn't know. Should I be the one to tell him? What if-"

"Rosie!"

I blanched, looking up at her.

"What about you?" She raised an eyebrow, crossing her arms.

Right. Me. My shoulders sank as I gave a small shrug, smiling weakly. "I don't know. I'm not sure how I feel. We didn't really get a chance to talk it over."

"You spoke to him?" She frowned, her arms dropping by her sides. "You didn't just kick him in the balls?"

"No. Should I have?" I frowned, looking back down at the cuffs of his jacket around my wrists. "I…I told him I had to think."

"What is there to think about?"

My insides ached as I shook my head. "It was just a one-time thing. He regrets it."

"No, he doesn't."

I peered up at her, swallowing slowly.

"He'll do it again, Rosie. Has he even apologized? Does he feel bad at all?"

"Well, I didn't really give him a chance to explain…"

"What's to explain?" She exclaimed, her eyes wide. "He's a dick!"

"He's my boyfriend."

Her gaze darkened as she looked down at me, shaking her head. "Please don't make excuses for him. It wasn't a one-off…He's just…He's the worst kind of guy."

"He's not-"

"He is! He's an asshole and he doesn't give a shit about you. He never has."

I flinched, frowning as she began to pace.

Her breath caught, her expression turning into a grimace as she glanced back at me. "We…we were going to have sex."

My heart stopped as her words hit me. "What?"

Her gaze settled on mine, her eyes brimming as she shook her head again. "It was the night I caught Jonathan with Rachel. I was really drunk and he hit on me. I…I didn't want to be so stupid and innocent anymore and he…he wanted me."

I brought my hand up to my mouth as a sob choked me, my fingers trembling from the effort.

"You tried calling him. Twice. While we were… in his car." I felt her eyes on me, the desperation and guilt evident in her voice. "He ignored it. But the minute he told me he had a girlfriend I got the hell out of there."

"Oh, God." I breathed, my tears finally falling.

"That's not all…"

It wasn't? I wasn't sure I could take much more.

"At the gig, when he rushed you out…"

I nodded slowly, bringing my gaze to hers.

"You know how he got roughed up?"

"Yeah," I said hesitantly. Zak had fed me some story about my brother trying to scare him away. He'd told me how he had taken the punches for us. To prove himself.

"Jonathan did that." Brooke nodded slowly, wiping her cheeks. "Zak got handsy with me outside. He…he had me pinned in the alley." She looked down, her expression darkening. "Jonathan overheard us and dragged him off."

My head span as I relayed what she'd said. The marks on his face, the way she avoided him. It…It made sense. I gulped, wincing.

She hurried over, falling into a crouch before me. "We wanted to tell you. Honestly we did…"

"He did that?" I breathed, looking up at her.

She nodded, looking down at the floor.

"I'm so sorry."

Her eyes shot up to mine in surprise. "What?"

"I bet you hate me…" I smiled bitterly.

She must've been so terrified. So sick with guilt and shame. And she couldn't even tell me, her best friend. If I'd been enough for Zak perhaps he wouldn't have strayed at all. He would've taken my calls that night and saw she got home safely. Instead of trying to take advantage of the situation. Of her. I felt sick. First her and soon Will. My inadequacy was spreading like a sickness, hurting those around me.

"No one hates you Rosie. No one. Especially not me."

I smiled weakly as I looked down at my hands, watching hers close around mine.

"We hate *him*."

Her words weighed like an anchor, my insides aching as they absorbed the finality of it.

"Rosie?"

I peered at her, already sensing what she was about to say, but dreading it all the same.

"You are going to end it, right?"

Chapter 16

Brooke

A dull beep pierced the veil of my dreams, cutting through my alternate life and washing it away with every incessant ring of my alarm. My eyes were heavy as I prised them open, wincing against the sun streaming through the gap in the curtains as I reached blindly to kill the noise. With a satisfied moan I snuggled back into the pillow, pulling the comforter tighter around me. Eager for sleep to claim me, I closed my eyes...

There was that noise again!

This time I sat up, groaning in frustration as I slid my finger across the screen to turn the alarm off altogether. How had time gone so quick?! The digits on screen blinked indignantly, my body slow to shake off the lethargy that gripped me as I tried figuring out why it was so late. And why I'd set an alarm.

Rosie.

I looked at the pillow beside me, seeing her blonde hair fanned around her like a halo. Her chest rising and falling as she slept. I hoped after yesterday she was enjoying peaceful dreams. Dreams of meadows. And sheep. With no asshole boyfriends. But I knew all too well how hard reality could be to escape from.

I gently stroked a stray curl of hair from her face, smiling as her soft pink lips twitched into a half-smile, before slipping into a mask of peaceful slumber once more. I stared at her for a moment longer, admiring everything in her that she saw as a flaw. Her porcelain skin. Her pink cheeks. The cute button nose that crinkled when she laughed. But the longer I looked the more I noticed things I hadn't before, things I should have. The purple shadows under her eyes. The dry cracked lips. The limpness of her usual bouncy mane.

Anger swelled inside me.

I'd been pulling away from her since *that* night. Anywhere she was Zak was never far behind, and being within touching distance of him set fear in my gut. Like the coward I am I'd kept quiet, watching as he paraded around with her. When all along he'd been causing her pain too. I could see the physical signs of the stress. And looking back I'd seen them all along. The way she'd smile with anxiety in her eyes.

How dare he make her feel like she'd never be enough.

Maybe now she could move on? She could take some time and build herself back up, find a guy who worshipped her, rather than expecting her to bow down. And she deserved that. She deserved to have someone lift her higher, Zak wasn't that guy.

Leaning down I kissed her forehead before I untangled myself from the bed delicately. I needed to shower and start getting ready. And Rosie needed to rest. There was no way I was going to wake her.

I tiptoed across the floor, slipping into the en-suite and turning on the shower before slipping from my underwear and climbing in. Tilting my head back I let out a moan as the hot jets massaged my flesh, relaxing my tensed muscles and invigorating me. When Rosie had turned up so suddenly last night I saw in her eyes that something had happened. I just hoped she knew what a blessing this was. But that wouldn't come immediately. She was still debating breaking up with him at all. She saw herself as a failure, like this was somehow her fault, that she'd made him do the things he'd done.

Maybe the reality of what Zak had done to me, what he and Chloe had done to Will, would keep her on the right path. Her love for us would outshine any superficial feelings she might have once had for Zak. I had faith in her, even if her faith in herself had been misplaced.

I lathered myself up and thought about other events from last night, the happier moments. The movies and ice cream. Giggling into our pillows as we reminisced about the time we'd forced Lucas and David to come for manicures. Lazing on our backs, staring at the ceiling and holding hands beneath the duvet as we made the same promise we always had. That no matter what, we had each other.

Sighing, I finished rinsing off, watching the last of the soap swirl itself into the drain. Was I a bad friend for deserting her? For going on a date when Rosie's relationship had just crumbled? I stood there a second longer, deliberating, enjoying the feel of the warm spray before I reluctantly turned off the jets. A shiver of cold ran up my spine and I quickly grabbed one of the plush Egyptian cotton towels that was hanging on the rail, wrapping it around my slender frame as I stepped carefully from the shower and onto the tiled floor.

Wiping the condensation from the mirror I stared through the steam at my reflection. Last night I'd mentioned canceling and Rosie had vehemently denied my request, going so far as to stop talking whenever I brought it up. She was always going to be the same selfless Rosie I'd grown to love.

Now it was my turn.

Matt wouldn't mind if I called a rain check. Rosie and I could have some retail therapy. Go to the salon and do something different with our hair. Or head to a restaurant and order the most extravagant desserts. I could take her mind off things. We could have the date we both needed.

Smiling at my reflection I nodded. It was decided!

I moved across the floor, cautious to avoid the small pools where water had slid from my body, and back into my bedroom. I grinned as I crossed the threshold hearing the familiar thump of a bushy golden tail wagging by the foot of my bed.

Sammy.

His little black nose lifted in my direction, his tail thudding harder as he saw me slinking closer. The big bundle of fluff had been part of our family for most of my teenage years. We'd always wanted a pet, it was the only thing missing from our otherwise perfect lives. But Daddy had been firm, which I wasn't used to. His arguments against a dog had been reasonable. He and Mom worked. James, Nathan, and I were at school. The poor little pup would be left home alone.

But then things changed.

James had left school and joined the army, and Mom had convinced Dad that a pet would brighten things up. And so this tiny Golden Lab had fallen into my arms and taken over my heart.

So it wasn't surprising to see him lounging across the floor waiting for me.

I grinned as I headed over, rubbing the soft spot behind his ear. "Is Rosie in your bed, buddy?" He let out a soft sigh and I almost laughed. We were both used to getting our own way.

"What time is it?"

I jumped at the noise, looking at the figure sitting up groggily in my bed. Her hair was sticking up oddly around her head, the tired bruising under her eyes more evident.

Hugging the towel closer I checked my cell, grabbing myself some fresh underwear from the drawer as I did. "It's almost twelve."

"At night?!"

"No." I chuckled, moving to sit on the edge of the bed. "Midday twelve."

"Oh." Her arms stretched out as she yawned, her back arching before she flopped back down into the safety of my bed. "What time is your date?"

I paused, watching her shuffle to the middle, one blue eye peering at me curiously. "Matt said he'd be here at two...but look, I've been thinking..."

She groaned, rolling onto her back. "No, Brooke."

"There's still time for me to cancel. We could do something?"

"The only thing I'll be doing is sleeping. And you should go out and date one of the nice guys."

I opened my mouth to argue and was met with a Rosie Taylor scowl. They weren't particularly threatening, and to most people aired on the side of cute, but I knew she only pulled them out when she meant business. This topic wasn't up for discussion any longer.

She was going to sleep, and I was going on my date with Matt.

Her face relaxed into a smile when she realized she'd won, her foot nudging me from beneath the folds. "We can gossip about the date when you're back. Now leave."

Laughing I shook my head and rose to my feet, holding my underwear closer. "Of course, Sleeping Beauty."

I glanced at her one last time before I crossed the room to my vanity, eying the clothes Rosie and I had picked out last night. Along with us talking shoes and accessories we'd emptied my cosmetics across the floor and gone through everything.

No detail left to chance. We'd even checked the weather forecast, windy with a slight chance of rain. So I'd be putting my hair up in a casual bun, leaving enough loose hairs to frame my face, but not leave me windswept. My make-up would be subtle, but noticeable. And rather than a dress, I'd be wearing my favorite pair of skin-tight jeans with my Jimmy Choo platform ankle boots. I'd even let Rosie talk me into pulling my leather jacket from retirement.

I dared a glance back to the bed, grinning at Rosie spread out across it. I couldn't get ready here. The hairdryer alone would wake her again. And if she was going to be stubborn about me keeping my date the very least I could do was let her sleep. So instead of sitting at my vanity I bundled everything into my arms and edged from the room, careful to hold it open for Sammy as he hurried after me.

I kicked open the nearest available door, opening up one of the many spare rooms we had, and shuffled awkwardly before dumping everything onto the light blue bedspread of the empty room. The house had previously belonged to my Grandparents, and needed an abundance of rooms for the immediate and extended family when they came over to visit from Bologna. Especially when they all came at once.

I sighed as I dropped my towel, rooting around in the pile I'd upended on the bed in search of my underwear. I slipped it on easily, standing to my full height and frowning as something caught my attention from the corner of my eye.

It was a painting. Though not a particularly amazing painting. It was a scenic beach watercolor, the sun setting while a boat bobbed lazily near the shore. My parents had returned home with it after one of their annual vacations alone. Originally it had hung above the bed, but...

I took a nervous step forwards, my skin alight with the memory of that night as I reached forward to lift it from the wall. How had I been so distracted? Finding myself in this room and knowing what happened, hidden between these four walls. On the very bed where my belongings now sat.

Propping the picture against the bed frame I took a breath, the dull thud of my heartbeat in my ears. And then I looked up, the evidence still there, as clear as the day he'd done it. Four letters burned into the wall, scorched into the house like it was seared into my heart. I reached out a finger, tracing the deep grooves of the lettering.

J.T & B.D

I dropped onto the bed, biting my lip as the memory of that night rushed at me from a box I'd tried to close so many times...

It was the beginning of the year, late January. Daddy was working yet another high profile case, he'd been getting home later into the night, sometimes only hours before he was due to be back out. Mom was trying to keep things as light as she could, but we could all feel the absence around us whenever Daddy worked too hard. Not least because if things got particularly tough he'd find solace in the bottom of a whiskey bottle. Not that he had a problem with alcohol, he just found it difficult to shrug work off at the door, drink occasionally took the edge off.

This was one of those cases.

And with James away in the army our home suddenly didn't feel so friendly. Nathan and I kept as busy as we could, he buried his nose in school, and I tried to distract myself with fashion. So it was a small mercy when Rosie was quarantined with a nasty flu strain and Jonathan had moved in for the week.

I gulped, dragging my eyes to the floor and shuffling further onto the bed. How was it, that after everything, even the memory of the way he held me broke my reservations. I could feel it in the way my heartbeat quickened, my breathing more shallow. Closing my eyes I counted to four as I inhaled, six on the exhale. I was going on a date with Matt.

I couldn't let Jonathan in again, even the memory of him.

Of *us*.

I pulled the towel back around my body, just in case anyone walked in, and reached for the hairdryer, hoping the noise would drown out my thoughts. But I was unwilling, my emotions rewinding to the beginning of our story.

As I got ready I found myself drowning deeper in the memory. Reliving that night, watching a younger version of myself parade around the room with Jonathan, laughing and joking. Because we did. Before. We hadn't always had intense chemistry, electricity sparking whenever we sat too close or our eyes met across the room. Before that night we were just two very good friends...

I smiled, remembering the casual way Jonathan leaned against the wall in front of me, playing with the flame of his lighter. I'd watched for a moment, admiring the purple hue that had slowly shifted into a royal blue, tossing him ideas of pillow fights and ice cream. After all, it's what I'd have done with Rosie.

"Are you trying to burn my house down?" I'd laughed, settling myself down on his bed and raising an eyebrow.

He'd met my stare, my breath catching as I noticed for the first time how dazzling his eyes were when he used. The color of his iris magnified, a bounty of emeralds shining back at me, refracting the light. He smirked, his hand moving from his body as he held the lighter up, enjoying my intake of breath as the wall caught fire. It burned white with heat, spitting embers as the flame ate away at the wallpaper. He'd enjoyed my panicked reaction a moment longer before the flame was smothered by his powers, his initials forever burned into the house.

I'd jumped up, eager to feel the welts he'd made, desperate to have my initials burned there with his. It felt right. Like we'd want a permanent reminder of the time we'd spent together alone.

The rest of the evening had passed in a blur, yet I remembered every detail. I could easily recall the pizza he conjured, I remembered the lights dimming as the TV flickered to life, my favorite film automatically playing.

I remembered my surprise at realizing he knew what my favorite film was.

It was about half-way through that I'd caught Jonathan looking at me. He'd been sat with his back against the head of the bed, his legs stretched out. His hand had been idly toying with my hair as I'd laid curled in his lap, my head on his chest. I'd chanced a glance at him, surprised to find he'd done the same. I couldn't quite read his expression, his eyes guarded yet alert, flicking between my eyes and my lips.

Tension built between us as I turned in his lap, his free hand drawing me closer as his other tangled in my hair, holding me against him.

And then his lips were on mine.

The world dropped from beneath me as I tasted him, my body alive with anticipation as I'd responded so willingly to him. I'd blushed as a soft moan was ripped from my lips, wrapping my arms around him, eager to feel every inch of his body, his own groan bringing me to the edge. We were a tangle of limbs as we made out, his tongue skillfully slipping into my mouth and meeting mine in a frenzied dance as we breathed each other in, losing ourselves in the moment, in the others embrace, as we slipped deeper into the kiss.

My body was on autopilot as I arched against him, gasping in surprise as he broke away, his soft lips darting kisses along my neck to my ear before he'd growled my name. Everything inside me had clenched with excitement, every fiber in my body begging for him. I'd never experienced anything like it. I was still only sixteen, I was inexperienced with relationships, I'd chosen to focus on school. Boyfriends and hooking up were ·so juvenile to me, when to others they'd seemed so much more important, more mature. But we had our whole lives to find the one and fall in love.

Yet as Jonathan's lips had met mine again I'd felt everything flip. *This* was what teenagers were chasing down, the rush of adrenaline when someone poured themselves into you with something as simple as a kiss.

I'd been so sure in that moment that he was the one. I'd felt weightless, but like gravity was holding me to Jonathan. I'd been tied to him. I'd had my first kiss and with it I'd given him my heart.

The rest of that night had faded into the haze, my skin tingling as I became hyper-aware of how close he was without touching me.

I'd eventually drifted off, curled up in his lap. Where I'd dreamt about him holding me that little bit tighter and kissing me once more. But if the next morning, and the following months, had taught me anything, it was that Jonathan had no intention of kissing me again.

Until camping...

I could still feel his lips on mine, his hands on my waist and his breath on my neck. But now I also felt the empty hollow in my chest at my first heartbreak. I'd believed that Jonathan had felt all the things I had, that he'd shared the sentiment that they were more than kisses. But maybe that was because he was my first...Jonathan was already a pro. With a handful of girls tucked under his belt.

My next kiss could feel the same, it could feel better.

And it would definitely be with Matt.

Butterflies fluttered in my stomach as a knock echoed through the house. And I grinned to myself as I took a steadying breath, this was a good sign. I'd spent so long focusing on Jonathan that I'd barely thought about Matt, and how *he* made me feel. And now I didn't have time.

I pulled on my clothes and slipped my feet into my boots, grabbing my cell from the bed before I gave myself a quick once over in the mirror. My cheeks were already flushing with nerves, the heat sweeping up the back of my neck as I tucked a loose strand of hair away.

You can do this Brooke.

I cast one last glance at the letters burned into the wall as I grasped the painting.

It was time to move on.

I lifted it easily back onto the wall, not bothering to straighten it before I turned away. Jonathan had shown his true colors. Not once, but twice. Twice he'd made a move on me and then pretended it hadn't happened. Twice he'd been alone with me and almost seduced me. Twice he'd dropped me almost immediately after. As soon as I wasn't the only choice he had anymore. And now he'd decided I didn't exist at all. So why was I still giving him the time of day?

Instead I focused on the way I felt when I was with Matt.

Closing my eyes, I imagined how his lips would feel on mine, his hands stroking my waist. He could make me feel so much better than Jonathan ever had if I gave him the chance.

Grinning I glanced behind me one last time at that room, at the painting hung haphazardly on the wall, at the space where I'd started to fall for Jonathan. And then I closed the door, locking the memory in there.

Chapter 17

Jonathan

I stared idly at the open magazine, toying with the corner of the page. Grainy images of lead guitarists on stage, heads bowed to the crowd, filled the paper, broken apart by sporadic blocks of text. I recognized them easily enough. Fresh faces that had made it. Worn ones that had survived it. I wasn't sure which I envied most. The younger ones looked energetic, passionate and raw. They gripped their instruments as though they might disintegrate, teeth bared as they played. But the older ones carried a distinguished, worldly air that you couldn't buy. You had to earn it. They cradled their instruments, their expressions an odd mixture of anguish and devotion. They loved music, and it loved them.

I let out a sigh as I dug out my cell to glance at the time. Twenty minutes late. By this point we'd be onto our third song, at least. We'd be warmed up, caught up, and playing. The air would be filled with the beats of Will's drums, the melodic sound of Alex's keyboard, and the deep thrum of Ash's bass. And weaving through all of that would be me and my guitar. Heaven.

Except none of that was happening. Instead, I was sitting on a brand-new couch courtesy of my extra special abilities, with my feet propped on the coffee table I got to match. Poring over music magazines that weren't holding my interest like they used to. I was getting agitated. I needed to play. I sat forward, tossing the magazine onto the stack on the table. I had conjured it in a foolish attempt to remedy things. To improve them. I glanced at the counters behind me, my shoulders sinking as I pictured Brooke and Rosie perched on them, their legs kicking in time to the music. I'd taken for granted when they'd come and listen to us play. Even their presence made a difference. I knew that now.

But the counter also reminded me of a certain redhead who'd stormed into our lives and destroyed everything. I'd hoped the new couch area might draw the girls back. But they didn't even know it existed, because they hadn't been here since.

The gentle rumble of a car pulling up jolted me, an irritated half-smile tugging at my lips as I stood and turned to face the newcomer.

"About time…"

I frowned as I saw Rosie's car come to a stop, my gaze traveling the length of the road by our house as I made my way over. Where the hell were they?

She sat behind the wheel for a moment, unaware of my presence. She stared straight ahead, hands limply grasping the steering wheel. I frowned, tilting my head to peer at her through the window. Still oblivious, her gaze lowered a fraction to focus on the taut leather. I quickly walked around to the passenger side, slipping in beside her. A melancholy tune assaulted my ears, the soft tones of a heartbroken woman filling the space with anguish.

Jesus.

I raised an eyebrow at her, taking in the hunched shoulders and sunken eyes. She'd spent the majority of the weekend at Brooke's house, having some quality girl time I assumed. Could they have fought? It didn't seem like them, but then…Her lip trembled as she slowly withdrew her hands from the wheel, her wounded gaze betraying the feeble smile she attempted for my benefit.

"Rosie." I began cautiously, turning in the seat to face her fully.

She shook her head quickly, her smile cracking as she fought another tremble.

Shit.

I leaned across and pulled her into my arms, my hold on her tightening as she physically began to shake, strangled sobs interrupting the music. My hands stroked her back in small measured circles, my eyes glinting as I shut the song off. She sank into my arms as she cried, her face buried in my shoulder as the silence settled around us. After a few agonizing minutes she gave a small sniffle and pulled back, her hand coming up to wipe her cheeks hurriedly. I frowned, conjuring her a tissue and offering it feebly.

She gave a small laugh, shaking her head weakly. "I'm sorry."

"Don't be." I shook my head.

There was no way Brooke would let her leave like this. Even if they had fought, for her to be this upset…It couldn't be Brooke behind it. It just couldn't. But then who'd done this to her? I had someone in mind who fit the bill. Someone who could hurt a girl and not give a damn. I just hoped for his sake it wasn't-

"It's Zak." She finally submitted.

Of course.

"He…" Her breath caught in her throat, her gaze dropping to her hands as she wrung them together. "I caught him with another girl."

I looked away, turning my focus onto the road as I took in a slow breath. I had to stay calm. I could beat him up tomorrow, today she needed me. I glanced back at her, placing my hand over hers. "He's an idiot, Rosie."

She smiled ruefully, giving a small nod.

"Hey." I lifted her face to look at mine. "I'm serious."

Her eyes began to brim, but she nodded more resolutely this time. Her gaze clouded as she turned my hand over in hers, "Brooke told me. About what he did. Or tried to do."

Oh.

My jaw set as I recalled that night behind the bar. How small Brooke had looked. How frightened.

"She told me that was why you hit him." She smiled slightly, meeting my gaze. "Thank you."

I nodded, unsure how to respond. It hardly felt like I'd earned much thanks. I'd still kept my mouth shut about what kind of guy Zak was. I'd allowed him to go on hurting her.

"We should go back inside." She cleared her throat, hastily wiping her damp cheeks. "I'm meeting Brooke and I should clean myself up first."

"You are?"

"Yeah." She nodded with a small smile. "Matt wanted to take her out for some breakfast, but the only way she would allow it was if she could come to my rescue right after. Best friend duty."

"I could run you a bath? Bubbles, salts... I'll even throw in a few ducks."

"Ducks?" She laughed, raising an eyebrow.

"Yeah." I grinned, "Colourful, quacking ducks."

"You realize I'm not five, right?"

"Okay, no ducks." I shrugged, smirking as I caught the look of disappointment on her face.

She smiled slightly, "Maybe just a couple."

I nodded, reaching across to ruffle her hair gently. She laughed and edged back, batting my hand away as she got out the car. I took in a measured breath and did the same, walking along beside her to the open garage door.

"No practice today?"

"Uh…" I hesitated, casting another furtive look around. "Just running late."

She raised an eyebrow. "And you're not tearing them a new one? Who are you and what have you done with my brother?"

"Ha. Ha." I rolled my eyes as she headed inside. My eyes glinted again as I filled the tub in her en suite, ducks and all. She'd be okay. I'd make sure of it.

"Hey…"

I turned to look behind me, smirking as the guys slowly entered the garage. "Finally."

Will smiled slightly, glancing first at Alex and then at Ash. "Sorry man…"

I raised an eyebrow, shaking my head. "No time for excuses. We're already behind."

"Uh…We need to talk."

I stopped short, frowning back at Will. I closed the distance between us and clamped my hand on his shoulder seriously, lowering my voice. "Are you breaking up with me?"

He shrugged my hand off and rolled his eyes, reaching up to rub the back of his neck. "This is kinda serious."

I wasn't sure I could handle any more heavy topics. But there was obviously something in the air.

"Okay." Alex measured his words. "It's about the band-"

"We're not trying to issue an ultimatum or anything." Ash blurted, the color rising in his cheeks.

I frowned at him, waiting for the but.

Ash let out a weary sigh, running a hand through his hair as he avoided my gaze. "It's just that...We put a lot of hours in on new songs, for no one to hear them."

There it was. Or as good as, anyway. I turned to look at Will as he took the baton.

"You know I've always been on your side-"

But...

"But it's getting harder to juggle everything now."

I raised an eyebrow at Alex. "You agree?"

He offered a small shrug. "I love the band. But I can't rely on this as a career if it's not going anywhere..."

Three for three.

I sighed and looked down at the floor, unfolding my arms. I couldn't say this was a surprise. I'd seen the signs for weeks. We all had. But I'd hoped we'd come through it. We'd enjoyed playing and creating together for years. And that'd been fine. That'd always be fine for me. But not them. This was the proverbial elephant in the room and it was past time we addressed it.

"We're not saying we wanna walk away." Will stepped forward, his voice level as though reading my thoughts. "Just that we could ease off the pedal?"

I nodded slowly, coaxing myself into trying to reach a compromise. Whatever that meant. The worst thing I could do at that moment would be to bite back. I had to pick my battles if I wanted to keep the band together. "So," I hesitated, looking at them all in turn. "Less practice?"

They exchanged glances before Ash nodded. "It'd help."

"We don't mind keeping it on as a hobby. But it's a bigger priority than it needs to be right now." Will shrugged.

Did he just call the band a hobby?!

I took in a measured breath, smiling bitterly. "What if I got us some more gigs?"

Another pause.

I raised an eyebrow as they all looked to one another, trying to determine who would handle this one.

"I'd like to say that would be enough, but…I'm not sure it is," Ash mumbled.

"It'd kind of add to the workload." Will nodded feebly.

"Workload?"

So now the past time of playing in the band had transformed into a task. An obligation. My fingers tapped my jeans pocket, itching for a cigarette.

Alex smiled slightly. "School. Exams…College."

"Girlfriends. The gym. Our social lives." Will added.

I tried to chew over my words. I was getting angry, but I knew their reasons. I understood them. I just didn't like them. "I didn't realise it was becoming such a chore," I muttered sullenly.

"It's not!" Alex frowned, stepping forward. "You know I love music as much as you. But I can't justify spending more time on the band and not having a secure job. You know?"

I did know.

"The band will always be a priority," Will said levelly, his tone serious. "It just needs to share the limelight."

Resistance, it appeared, was futile. I was outnumbered and out-argued. Still, it didn't sound like the band was over. Just…less of a pursuit and more of a…I winced inwardly. I couldn't bring myself to use the 'h' word. But I had to grasp the straws as they fell. It wasn't done. There was that.

"It will make it mean more." Will tried softly, forcing a wan smile onto his face. "The times we do play. We'll be…"

"More into it." Alex finished, frowning as Will shot him a dark look.

Ash laughed slightly, the sound breaking the tension. "What he means is that we'll be more rested and can perform better."

"Yeah." Will agreed, "Without the pressure of perfecting everything all the time, we'll feel more at ease."

Alex nodded. "It'll be like the old days. When we did it for fun."

I raised an eyebrow, biting my tongue. I didn't like a single thing they'd said. Nor did I agree with it. Time away from practice wouldn't make us sound better. It'd make us rusty.

I glanced up to their waiting faces, their expressions wary.

"Sure." I submitted.

Will nodded and moved to stand beside me, clapping me on the back with a forced smile. I was convincing no one.

"How about we definitely agree to every Sunday afternoon?" He raised an eyebrow, his hand staying by my shoulder.

"Once a week?" My eyes shot up incredulously, all attempts at bravado completely disappearing. "That's it?"

"Uh." Will looked back at the guys, slowly withdrawing his grasp. "We're open to suggestions."

I nodded, folding my arms. I definitely had a suggestion or two.

"Three times a week?"

They stared back.

"The weekend ones are mostly okay with me." Alex said hesitantly, "It's the ones in the week that I'm having issues with."

"Twice a week," I replied firmly, raising an eyebrow. "Three times if we have a gig."

Will opened his mouth, faltering before finally nodding his assent. "Okay…that's fair."

It was more than fair. But I wasn't about to correct him.

"So, we're good?" He smiled weakly, glancing between us all.

"Of course."

They looked at me uncertainly, a fresh air of awkwardness cloaking the room. I attempted a small smile, unfurling my arms in an attempt to detonate the tense atmosphere. Whatever happened, they were my closest friends. Band or not. I just had to remember that. Today had been a washout. Not a single instrument played or lyric sung. But at least we were being amicable. Mature. I'd get more gigs and secure my three practices. We'd get back on form and they'd remember how good we could be. It wasn't out of reach. Just playing hard to get.

"I uh…I should head home." Ash said sheepishly.

Will nodded, glancing at me warily. "Yeah. I'm supposed to meet Chloe…"

"Go." I forced my smile to lift a little more. "Really. I'll catch up with you guys tomorrow."

"You sure?" Will hesitated.

I nodded, my gaze flickering to Alex. "It's fine. Honestly." They exchanged the same uncertain look, not accustomed to a reasonable front-man. I chuckled, opening my palms out in gesture to usher them off. "Before I change my mind."

Will laughed, nodding. "I'll heed that warning."

"Me too." Ash grinned.

I watched as they all turned back down the drive, bowing my head. Not a great day.

"Hey, Brooke."

My gaze shot up, my insides jolting as I saw her.

Perhaps I spoke too soon.

She smiled at the guys warmly, offering a small wave as they met her along the main path to the house. "Hey, guys. You all finished?"

Ash glanced back at me, his smile slight. "Yeah. You meeting Rosie?"

"Yeah." She grinned. "I'm taking her out for a girly afternoon."

"You should take Ash along. He needs his hair doing." Will smirked, reaching across to mess it up.

Ash leaped back, laughing as he fought him off. I watched them for a moment, before looking at her. To really look in what felt like forever. I'd honestly tried to keep my distance like Nathan had asked. But each second was proving to be agony, with each glimpse of her a bittersweet hit. I craved her, as ridiculous as that sounded. My pulse picked up speed and my skin electrified as my body became aware of just how close she was. Which wasn't nearly close enough.

"Rosie's in the bath." I declared stupidly.

Brooke's gaze met mine, her dark eyes unreadable. "I know. She said she'd be down soon."

"We should uh…" Ash allowed his sentence to trail off, looking between Alex and Will.

"Go? Yeah." Alex laughed as he headed off.

I watched the others follow, slowly drawing my gaze back to Brooke. I frowned as I caught her staring, her expression still guarded as she ran her eyes along the length of me steadily. Somehow I didn't think she was flirting. A soft pink tinged her cheeks as her eyes finished on mine, her arms folding as she turned and strode towards the front door. I glanced back at the open garage door, magically closing it and following her. Was she really that adamant to avoid me?

I caught the door before it shut, stopping short as I found her halted in the hallway. She appeared rooted to the spot, her head lowered as she turned to meet me. She unfurled her arms and shook her head. Her gaze fell on the open doorway to the side of us, her voice hardening. "I'm gonna wait in the kitchen."

I followed her gaze, my insides sinking. The doorway opened out into the living room, the offending couch staring back at me spitefully. It didn't matter that I'd magically changed it at least three times. It still felt dirty. And I hadn't been near it since. So I couldn't exactly blame her for giving the room a wide berth. As for Rachel, I'd heard her more than seen her. A small blessing. Except for the fact that everything I'd heard was vile and untrue. I hoped over time she'd tire of using the fabricated summer romance she was telling everyone we had, and would move on. Whether that was with some other poor schmuck or with another school entirely, I wasn't fussy.

I sloped after Brooke into the kitchen, smiling wryly as I watched her delicately seat herself on a stool by the counter. Her hair bounced in the gesture, the light casting golden flecks amidst the soft chocolate waves. She looked up at me questioningly, her expression cool. My smile faltered as I ran a hand through my hair, clearing my throat.

"So uh…how're things?"

She raised an eyebrow. "Fine. You?"

Ouch. Okay, awkward encounter number three was go. I could do this. Seeing her in this setting beat not seeing her at all. Even I wasn't going to be dumb enough to not savor it.

"Rosie told me…"

"Told you what?"

"About Zak." I rested my hands on the island counter between us. "Well, kind of. She didn't say who she caught him with though."

"Oh…" Her gaze softened. "Yeah. I…I told her about my stuff too."

I watched her skin pale as she averted her gaze, her eyes darkening with the memory. I'd give anything to take them away.

"Yeah." I leaned across the counter. "She told me that too. Are you guys okay?"

She finally looked up to meet my eyes. "I think it helped?"

"I think so too." I agreed, keeping her gaze.

I fought the instinct to place my hands around hers, or to cup her chin and kiss her lightly. She stared back at me shyly, her lips parting. I frowned, leaning closer still. When she didn't back away, I reached my hands towards hers a fraction. Testing the water.

"Hey!"

I blanched, looking at the dark-haired guy suddenly standing between us. He smiled, oblivious.

"Sorry for the rude entrance, your dad let me in." He turned to Brooke, his smile widening. "You forgot your cell."

"Thank you!" She grinned, hopping from the stool gracefully. Her mouth curved teasingly as she took it from him, holding it in the air between them. "Did you steal this so you could see me again?"

"Damn." He smirked, "You caught me."

I stood back from the counter, setting my jaw as I took in the display. He enveloped her in his arms, holding her to him as he brought his lips to hers softly. I grimaced, tearing my gaze away. It was nauseating. Painful, even. Not least because it was with him, and not me. An equally irritated, spiteful voice reminded me that it could have been. She had admitted herself that she liked me. Wanted me. Or at least, she used to. Before I went and wrecked everything. I rolled my eyes as they continued, my eyes boring into the floor by my feet.

"I'll call you later?"

"I look forward to it." I heard the smile in her voice, my insides clenching.

"See you, Jonathan." He nodded, smiling back at Brooke as he headed for the door.

I grunted in response, watching him leave. Brooke was staring after him too, a small smile playing on her lip

"He seems nice."

Her dark eyes flickered to mine, her eyebrow arching. "He is."

We held each other's gaze a moment before I broke it off with a small sigh. He did seem nice. Annoyingly nice. I ran a hand through my hair, trying to shake off my attitude. I'd promised Nathan that I'd behave. For her. She deserved the good guy. And he was nothing if not the good guy. But then what did that make me? Surely I wasn't foul enough to fall alongside Zak?

"Jen is nice too."

I frowned at her, perplexed. "Uh. She is?"

Her eyes drew themselves from mine, an odd sense of sadness flickering across her expression. It was gone in an instant, but it'd been there. What did Jen have to do with anything? We were friends…Nothing more. Not lately, anyway.

"All set?" A bright voice chirped from the doorway.

We both turned to look at Rosie as she sank inside her sweater, the soft fabric melting into folds. She smiled at us, her doleful eyes the only indication that everything wasn't right with her world.

"Of course." Brooke nodded, heading out into the hallway with her.

I followed slowly, my eyes fixed on the gentle bob of Brooke's hair as it moved in time with her steps. I ached to touch it. To touch her. I let out a shallow breath as she turned to face me questioningly, glancing back at Rosie.

I smiled as my sister ducked into my arms for a hug, rubbing her back gently. "Have fun."

She peered up at me, nodding slowly. "We will."

I released her, hazarding a glance at Brooke as she opened the door and stepped outside. Rosie followed her down the path to her car, her steps quickening to keep up.

Look back, I beckoned. *Just look back. Just once.*

I cradled the door as I watched her get to the car, her head bowed. She hesitated, her eyes flickering to mine for an instant. I felt my mouth tug into a smile as she looked back down, sinking into the passenger seat. I took a step back, my smile transforming into a lazy grin.

She looked back.

I turned my back on the door as it shut, still grinning, and came face to face with my dad. "How long have you been stood there?" I narrowed my eyes.

"Long enough." He smirked.

I rolled my eyes, crossing the distance between us. "You didn't see a thing."

"No, course not." He chuckled, shaking his head.

I rolled my eyes and took the stairs two at a time, barrelling into my bedroom with earnest. I scanned the room determinedly, grabbing my hoodie from the bed and pulling it on. I moved towards the desk in the corner, my eyes glinting as I pressed my fingertips again the top drawer. It gave a gentle click and released, revealing a worn black notebook and a collection of pens. I took the notebook out gingerly, my fingertips tracing the star hand-drawn on the corner of the book. It was slowly filling up, but there was still some room left. I buried it in the pocket of my hoodie, tucking a pen in beside it, and turned to grab my acoustic guitar from by the wardrobe. Casting one furtive glance around the room, I nodded to myself and allowed my eyes to glint once more. The room gradually dissipated around me, the walls stripping away to reveal the bandstand in Boston Common.

I slipped down to sit on the concrete base, peering up at the entrance to the bandstand. It was my secret hiding spot. My place to go and write, to be inspired…to remember.

Our first kiss hadn't been entirely spontaneous.

A few months before it happened, we'd all been here together. The height of summer basking us as we hung out around the steps. I'd been sat with this very notebook in my palm as I tried in vain to summon the words to match a melody I'd had in my brain for days. The others had been occupying themselves, playing games, and laughing about nonsensical things. But Brooke…She was sat not far from me, drawing one of her designs and humming.

Humming my song.

I'd recognized the nameless tune right away. I'd been humming it myself all week, trying desperately to make something of it. And here she was, lending her soft melodic voice to it. I'd never heard it sound so good. So right. It was then I realized it was her song. They all were. I'd watched her doe eyes searching her paper, grasping her pen as she mused over her sketch. I had, for the first time, become aware of the different tones in her hair, the fullness of her lips, and the beauty of her voice. And in that moment, as my own pen touched my paper and words began to take shape, I wondered how I'd never noticed those things before.

And then the rain had come.

A light spattering. Nothing disastrous. But the gang had flocked up onto the bandstand to stay dry, laughing and shrieking. Brooke...she'd smiled up at the sky and closed her eyes. She'd welcomed the rain.

I'd felt something click into place that day, and each day since. From that moment I couldn't help but see her as she truly was. The inspiration behind my lyrics. She'd been there all along. The reason. My reason. And so, a few months afterward, I'd found myself alone with her and I'd kissed her. Because each song I'd written and each melody I'd hummed, had told me to. I glanced down and pulled the notebook free, tracing the star once more.

They always would.

Chapter 18

Will

I took a breath, staring at the fluorescent lighting above me as I lay back on the weight bench. Today had been another awkward day at school. Jonathan was still smarting over the band's latest hiccup, no matter how much he protested it was fine. Half our friends were still avoiding us, only now they had extra company thanks to the Danes bringing along their dates. And now Rosie was avoiding me too. I'd seen her with Brooke. I'd seen her with Lucas. I'd seen her with Jonathan. Yet every time I'd appeared she'd made her excuses. I was still trying to work out what I'd done.

Lifting weights would remedy that. At the very least it would tire me out so I'd stop thinking. I gripped the bar firmly, testing my hold as I took another steadying breath, keeping my gaze on the ceiling as I exhaled. I was taking my time, or more accurately, I was deliberately wasting it. Working out was a lifeline, it helped me deal with my pent up anger, especially now I'd walked away from football. But life was never that smooth. And whereas before David would join me in our home gym, now there was nothing but an empty space.

Weights had never been David's thing, but he'd been a damn good spotter. And without him my options were slim to none. Either I didn't work out. Or I kept my powers ready to go just in case I overshot my abilities and tried killing myself.

So here I was, pushing my luck and hoping I could fight my powers back into their box if I needed to. Only now I was left alone to my thoughts, forcing myself to work harder.

So I added extra weight for the band issues. Which had gotten significantly bigger.

More for the tension brewing between David and me.

Another lot for senior year stress and college worries.

And remembering camping, before things had gotten so awkward and everything had fallen apart, that had pushed me over the edge.

Hopefully the more weight I added to my bench press, the less it would weigh on me.

I grit my teeth, tensing as I lifted the bar from its hold, grunting as my muscles strained under the tension. With a guttural roar I lifted my arms, my adrenaline levels peaking as I held the weight, almost grinning. I heaved a sigh as I lowered them once more, the weights sliding back into place on the bench before I straightened myself, shifting to sit up and taking pause when I realized I wasn't alone.

Dad was standing in the doorway, grinning as he leaned against the frame. To look at the two of us you'd be forgiven for thinking we were biologically related, especially since he still looked fairly young for his age. And acted like a teenager half the time too.

He took a step into the room, running a hand through his shoulder-length brown hair and sweeping it from his face, something I was sure he'd perfected. "How much was the lift?"

I hunched forward from my position, grabbing the back of my now damp T-shirt as I yanked it over my head. "Just over 120kg"

"That the most you've lifted?"

I shrugged weakly, already mentally downplaying his pride. Before the revelation of my real father I'd enjoyed the praise of my parents, basking in the congratulatory hugs at my almost perfect grades and ribbing David at falling short. Only now it felt wrong. Whereas before it was a friendly rivalry, now it felt like I was deliberately out to prove I was better.

The son they didn't plan, didn't want, trying to constantly overshadow the one they conceived together.

Dad nodded, his mouth pulling into a tight smile. "David not here to spot you?"

I sighed, shaking my head.

He crossed the space between us, clapping his hand against my shoulder as he forced his smile to look less fake. "He'll come round eventually."

Pulling my gaze from his I nodded. I didn't need to tell him how much I hoped that was true, how I'd wake up wondering if this was the day David would finally try and bridge the space between us. My parents felt it too. Dad especially. It was hard for him watching us avoid each other, when all he'd ever wanted was to feel like he'd fathered us both. And sure, it didn't take blood to make a family, but we sure as hell kept reminding him I wasn't his.

"Thanks." I stood up, smiling weakly as I used my balled up T-shirt to mop my brow before tossing it into the hamper by the door, watching as Dad glanced to the wall behind me, the noise of David's TV blaring through the wall. I followed his gaze, smiling weakly. "I think he's hitting the books."

Dad let out a short laugh, grinning at me as he shook his head. "Better than repeatedly hitting drums." His eyebrow raised in my direction.

Now it was my turn to laugh. "Touché."

My parents had bought me my drum kit just before I hit ten, partly to stop me asking, mostly to stop Jonathan asking. Even as a kid he'd wanted to play. In the early days it was a lot of making noise, but eventually we'd realized we were good. Later Ash and Alex had joined and we'd gone from good to pretty damn great. And while my parents cracked jokes about the noise, they were glad I'd found something to distract me.

Even if things were strained now.

I couldn't blame Jonathan for having tunnel vision, for having a goal and wanting to see it through, but lately practice hadn't been what it used to be. There was no Brooke and Rosie. Ash was preoccupied with his parents. Alex had his nose buried in college brochures. Even Jonathan didn't seem *into* it anymore. He wanted to carry on, to perfect every song and nail every solo, but something had changed, that spark inside him had...dimmed.

"I came to tell you that you had a visitor anyway." Dad broke the silence, smiling weakly.

"I do?"

He nodded, smirking slightly.

Ah...Chloe.

He stood to one side as I moved for the door, laughing as he began to follow me downstairs. "Young love."

I fought a blush. No one's idea of fun was being embarrassed by their parents. "Shut up." I laughed, jogging down the last few stairs and turning left for the kitchen.

Dad moved to the front door. "I'm going to pick your Mom up from Francesca's anyway. I promised her dinner and cocktails tonight so you guys are alone. And Will?"I paused, glancing back over my shoulder at him. "Don't forget to wrap up."

I cringed again. "Jesus, Dad!"

Laughing he tossed me a fresh tank-top, the glimmer of magic dying in his eyes as I caught it. "You're still shirtless. What did you think I meant?"

I shook my head with a laugh, hoping Chloe hadn't heard our little exchange. "Enjoy dinner."

"Enjoy your friend."

Before I could throw him another stare he laughed, the front door clicking into place as he disappeared from the house. It wasn't unusual for Dad to treat Mom, mostly he tried to keep the romance alive with spontaneous flowers or jewelry. But in the last few weeks he'd been taking her out for dinner at least once a week, looking for excuses to leave me with David.

Or just get away from the tension.

I headed into the kitchen to find Chloe, grinning when the first thing I saw was her legs, rocking back and forth as she perched on the counter. Her grin lit up her face when she saw me, her eyes gliding appreciatively up and down my half-naked form. If working out felt good before, it felt better knowing the effect it had on the opposite sex. I moved to stand between her legs, letting out a breathless chuckle as her hands wound around me. "I *was* gonna get a drink."

Her hands slipped to my lower back, pulling me closer as she scooted forward, her legs coiling around mine. "You work up a thirst?"

I nodded, fighting the smirk as her body inched into mine.

She briefly glanced down to my left hand, the top Dad had conjured still balled there. "You planning on wrapping up?"

I groaned, rolling my eyes as I fought a grin. "You heard that?"

"I did." She laughed softly, "And if you don't mind I'd prefer you didn't."

Her legs squeezed tighter around me, her body pressed against mine as she pulled me into a long, slow kiss. My hands shifted to her waist, holding her desperately as I returned the kiss, my fingers finding the soft flesh of her hips underneath the hem of her shorts.

Her mouth turned up into a grin against my lips as she pressed her chest against mine, moaning softly into the kiss. "Take me upstairs"

I broke the kiss, momentarily stunned.

Her eyebrow arched as she stroked a finger down the center of my torso, licking her lower lip as her eyes dropped to watch as it brushed the hair at my navel. Her hips ground into mine, my hands dragging her into my arms as she wrapped herself around me.

It didn't matter that David was home and was going to hear everything. Chloe was what I needed right now. She was the only distraction that wiped the slate clean in my head, so that all I could think about was which part of her I was going to kiss next.

My hand slipped to caress the curve of her spine, grabbing her ass with a groan as my lips moved to her neck, nipping at her skin and enjoying the whimper that met my ears in response. I pressed her against the fridge, pinning her in place with my body as I began to tug at her top, frowning when I heard a faint knocking. Chloe's hands worked their way to my neck as I moved to pull back, demanding more attention.

Grinning I trailed kisses down her bare shoulder, edging her bra strap to one side as she arched against me gratefully.

There was another knock. Louder than the first.

Frowning I glanced behind me. "Was that the door?"

Chloe shrugged, her lips grazing my jaw before her breath was warm in my ear. "I didn't hear a thing."

This time whoever was knocking was more persistent, their open palm slapping against the glass. Angry footsteps barrelled down the stairs,

David casting the pair of us an annoyed glance as he yanked open the front door. "I'll get it then."

I groaned internally, rolling my eyes as I reluctantly lowered Chloe back to the floor and threw her an apologetic smile. "It's probably for him anyway." I murmured, leaving one last kiss on Chloe's forehead.

I turned to tug her from the room and stopped short.

Rosie was standing in the kitchen doorway, her eyes darting around the room, taking in my bare chest, our flushed cheeks, and Chloe's top hanging off her slim frame. Her gaze was mostly passive, but when she saw our clasped hands anger and hurt flashed across her face.

I smiled awkwardly at Rosie, blushing further. "Hey Rosie-cheeks."

She smiled shyly, her hands wringing together. "Hey...Could I talk to you?" I opened my mouth, stopping short when she cast Chloe a cold stare. "Alone."

"Is that really necessary?" Chloe stepped forward, tugging her clothes back into place, and narrowing her eyes.

Rosie ignored her, tilting her chin in my direction. "Will?"

"Me?" I frowned. What did Rosie need me for? Especially after giving me a wide berth all day.

"Please. It's important."

I caught David's eye as he stood behind her. "Uh..." I broke his stare, squeezing Chloe's hand to get her attention. "Do you mind?"

Chloe didn't turn to address me, instead moving to rest against my chest and pulling my arm around herself as she stared at Rosie. "I'd like to stay."

I looked at the brunette nestled against me. "Okay..." I met Rosie's soft blue eyes, smiling weakly. "Is that okay?"

"Mind if I stick around?" David stepped forward to join our group, glancing between us all slowly.

Oh, now he wanted to spend time with me.

He read the silence, three pairs of eyes looking at him coldly, turning with a sigh to traipse back to his room.

I waited a moment, straining my ears to listen for the dull thud of his bedroom door closing. Once I was satisfied I looked back at Rosie, frowning at the dull pallor of her complexion, watching as she played with a loose thread falling from the sleeve of her hoodie. "So...What can I help you with?"

"Umm...Have you guys..." She looked between Chloe and me nervously and I fought the urge to go over and wrap her in my arms. Her gaze eventually settled on Chloe, her throat cracking as she spoke. "Does he know?"

Chloe stared back coldly.

Rosie's eyebrows raised into her hairline, her hands crossing in front of her as she stared right back.

And I was stood on the outskirts, not privy to what was bubbling between the two girls. The clock ticked ominously, stretching the silence as I waited for someone to speak.

Obviously that person would be me.

"What am I missing?" I untangled my arm from Chloe, turning her to face me. "Do I know what?"

"Nothing." She smiled, reaching out to stroke my forearm. "She's got the wrong end of the stick."

"No I haven't!" Rosie exploded, taking a step forward.

Groaning I leaned back against the fridge in exasperation as the two of them turned to face each other, Chloe nuzzling into the crook of my arm once more. "Can someone just spit it out!"

Rosie's posture relaxed, shaking her head at Chloe. "Fine...you had your chance." Her eyes flitted to me, holding my gaze before she looked at her hands. "Will, I...I caught Chloe and Zak in bed together."

The room definitely stilled at that.

My arm tensed around Chloe, my body stiffening as Rosie's words echoed loudly at me in the silence of the room. Zak. And Chloe. They'd...

"I'm sorry Will." Rosie took half a step forward, her hand reaching for me before she paused, realizing Chloe was still relaxed against me. "Are you okay?"

I looked up at the blonde, my gut clenching with hurt as I took in her solemn expression. My arm dropped from around Chloe as I sidestepped her, moving to Rosie. "Are...are *you* okay?"

"I'm better." She shrugged, reaching out to take my hand and stroking it with her thumb. "It happened a few days ago, but I wanted to give Chloe the chance to tell you herself."

I looked down at her hand in mine, my shoulders sinking. "Chloe and I...have an understanding."

"You do?"

"Neither of us wanted to be in a relationship. This is a casual thing..." I glanced back to Chloe. "She's free to have sex with whoever she wants."

It had never been the way I wanted to start a relationship, casually hooking up with a girl who was also sleeping with other guys, but after that first night something in me had snapped. And it was hardly the greatest opener for a serious relationship, I still couldn't remember how we'd met, or how long we'd been talking before I brought her back to the house. But what I did remember was the way my heart ached when I saw Rosie and Zak. I remembered the way I'd felt like such a hopeless sack. And right then I'd wanted to get it out of my system.

The next morning Chloe and I both agreed we didn't want to be tied to each other. While I was happy to have her climb into my bed and erase my stress, I didn't want to make moves on another girl, I didn't want to complicate my life, making all the same mistakes Jonathan did. One casual hook up was more than enough.

Rosie shrank back, her mouth opening as she tried to form words, her hand trying to pull from mine as she blushed, Chloe grinning triumphantly. Awkwardness was radiating from her as she tried to take herself from the conversation. I yanked her closer on instinct, trying to ignore the excited thump of my heart as she rested her hand on my bare chest to steady herself.

"She can still have sex with whoever she wants." I smiled thinly across at Chloe. "Except me."

"What the hell?" Chloe raised an eyebrow, her hand on her hip.

"Zak? Really?!"

Rosie flinched in my arms and I stroked her hair to soothe her, Chloe rolling her eyes at the pair of us. "What's the big deal? We're casual."

"Zak and Rosie weren't!" Anger rose in my throat, my free hand clenching as I steadied my breathing. I didn't need to explode now. "Shit, Chloe, you could have slept with David and I wouldn't have cared. Zak was out of bounds."

"They seemed pretty casual on Zak's side." Her eyes rested on Rosie as she smirked. "I didn't think they were serious."

"Don't start making excuses now."

"Why are you so upset?! It wasn't a big deal."

But it was a big deal. Looking down at Rosie as she nestled against me it was obvious. They'd hurt her. They'd completely stomped on her first relationship, breaking her trust in Zak, and probably herself too. And that hurt me. Not just because Zak had took his revenge out on me and Rosie had gotten in the crossfire, not just because she'd spent days hurting for me as well as herself, but because all I'd ever wanted was to give her a million reasons to smile. And all they'd wanted to do was watch as she cried.

My free hand cupped Rosie's chin and I tilted her face to mine, stroking the single tear track that ran down her pale cheek. "Is it a big deal to you?"

Her cheeks flushed as she opened her mouth. "I..." Another tear slipped out before she nodded.

I released my grip on her face, wrapping my arms back around her and ignoring how perfectly she fit against me. Now wasn't the time to get carried away. "So it's a big deal to me."

Chloe raised an eyebrow, staring coldly. "Wow." She gazed between us, her cheeks coloring with annoyance. "I guess I'll leave you two lovebirds alone."

The irony. The girl who'd been so eager to jump into bed with other guys was jealous of me hugging another girl. I rolled my eyes at her. "Goodbye Chloe."

She stared at me, waiting for me to back down and tell her I was overreacting. But there was no space for negotiation. She'd hurt one of my closest friends. So she had to go. She rolled her eyes with a huff as she realized I wasn't shifting, pushing past us as she stomped from the house, slamming the door as she went.

Rosie and I stayed locked together, her head rested against my chest. I was such a masochist, enjoying the moment, my lips twitching to fight the smile as I closed my eyes and told myself I was just being a friend, I was just comforting her.

"Are you sure you're okay?" Rosie's voice was soft, muffled against my chest.

I smiled weakly, looking at her. This moment spoke more about Rosie than anything, even though Zak had cheated, and she knew about my arrangement with Chloe, she was still more worried about me. It explained why she'd been avoiding me all day too. God knows my reactions could be temperamental.

"I'm fine." It technically wasn't a lie. In regards to this whole debacle I *was* fine. I'd never given enough of myself to Chloe for her to hurt me. But I *was* hurting for my friend. I stroked her cheek softly as she turned to look up at me, "How're you? I mean...shit, it can't have been nice walking in on them."

"It wasn't." Her eyes clouded with the threat of fresh tears. "But I'm getting there."

"Are you guys...over?"

Rosie stepped back, her arms slipping from around me before she took my hand once more. "Almost. He's been calling and texting...I've not answered. But now you know I'm breaking things off."

That was something at least. "I'm sorry for all this Rosie-cheeks."

"You shouldn't be apologizing."

"I kinda should." I sighed, running a hand through my hair as I reluctantly stepped away from her, "This isn't what I expected to happen."

Her nose wrinkled as she looked at me, tilting her head with confusion. "What do you mean?"

No. This wasn't a conversation we were going to have. Not now. Not ever. How could I tell her that the only reason Zak wanted to date her in the first place was to piss me off? That he and Chloe hooking up was another attempt. How the hell could I stand here and say her first relationship was nothing but a game. She'd be crushed. And I wasn't going to be the reason behind that.

I sighed as I pulled her back into my embrace, my eyes automatically closing as I breathed her in. No, I'd save her that heartbreak. I pressed my lips gently against her forehead, fighting down the jump to my heart. "It doesn't matter."

She stayed in my arms a moment longer, but all too soon she pulled away, glancing to the front door sadly. "I should go..." Her hands flittered to her hair as she tucked a strand behind her ear, glancing at me shyly. "Call me if you need to talk."

"You too. You know where I am."

I followed her to the door, pulling it open and standing aside as she slipped out into the autumn air. I opened my mouth to speak, to say goodbye, as she turned back to me. We both grinned stupidly at the other, our cheeks reddening. And then she leaned up on her tiptoes, my eyes closing as she pressed her lips to my cheek.

Every nerve ending in my body woke, the touch of her puckered lips against my skin still warm even after she pulled away. "Bye, Will..."

I lifted my hand to wave, still dazed as I watched her climb into her car and drive away. Once she was gone I stepped into the house and closed the door, leaning my head back against it as I ran a hand through my hair. I shouldn't be enjoying her failed relationship, or mine, but I couldn't lie to myself. She still had a pretty big hold over me.

"Did you really just let her go?"

I glanced up at the voice, David standing on the stairs and watching me curiously. His lips turned up in an awkward smile as he took a step closer. Blinking I rubbed the back of my neck, knowing exactly what David meant, but too surprised to actually respond.

After all this time, he was finally talking to me.

Chapter 19

Rosie

I t was never supposed to be this way. To end like this. I wasn't naïve. Not every relationship had a happy ending. Movies sugar-coated things until they were sickly sweet, because real life didn't work that way. But that didn't mean I wasn't disappointed. I'd never expected him to be chivalrous, to bestow grand gestures upon me, or to gush about his feelings. But I'd expected him to be honest. To care. I felt sick at the thought of it. Knowing he didn't. That he never had.

Worse still, it wasn't just me he'd hurt. *That* I could've handled. Maybe not with my dignity intact, but still. I could've excused away his cheating, his lies…the gut-wrenching memory of seeing him with her. But there was no way I could've blotted out the vision of him hurting my best friend. Of scaring her. Of relishing it.

I let out a low sigh as I turned the napkin over in my hand. I had to do this. For her if not me. Although, there was the smallest sliver of myself in there too. I didn't deserve this. My opinion of what I did deserve wasn't that high, it was true. But I didn't deserve this. And if I carried on and pretended what he did was okay, he'd do it again. And again. And each time my heart would break a little more until there was nothing left. I had to do this. There was no other way.

"Hey babe."

My blood ran cold as I heard his voice, my fingertips pausing against the creases of the napkin. The table shifted as he sat down opposite me, setting down his cell. He leaned back, his expression bored as he looked around at the small café.

"Hey Zak." I murmured quietly, placing down the napkin on the curve of my saucer.

His mouth twitched into a familiar smirk, his dark eyes creasing as his gaze ran over me. A cold wave flooded my body.

"Finally come to your senses?"

I swallowed, gingerly placing my hands in my lap. My fingertips wrung around each other. The last thing I needed was to give him a reason to pounce on how uneasy I was. He eyed me as I hesitated, the smirk still resting on his lips.

"Yeah." I nodded, lifting my head to meet his gaze. "I have."

"Good." He grinned, casting his gaze around the room once more. His eyes settled on a nearby waitress, hovering before reluctantly drawing themselves back to meet mine. "So, I figured we'd head back to mine and watch a movie?"

The glint in his eyes suggested he had little intention of us doing that, his mouth curving as the suggestion landed. I forced myself to keep staring at him, my hands now tightly clasped as my pulse quickened. Not with fear or nerves, but with anger. Not only did he assume all was forgiven, he had the gall to invite me into his bed. That bed.

"Zak." I began, tearing my hands apart and placing them delicately on my lap. "It's over."

His dark eyes narrowed, the atmosphere shifting as he sat forward. "What?"

"It's over," I repeated, holding his gaze. "We're over."

His lips curved into an amused grin, his eyebrow slowly lifting. "You're joking."

"No." I shook my head. "I deserve better. And…so do you."

I jolted with surprise as those last few words left my mouth, my gaze lowering as I realized I actually meant them. He deserved to be with someone he wanted above others. Someone that meant something. I wasn't her. I wasn't sure any girl would be for a while. But that didn't mean he wouldn't find her. Perhaps if he did, he wouldn't cheat or lie.

His laughter brought me back into the room, his smirk returning as he sat back in his seat.

I eyed him warily. "Why are you laughing?"

"Because you're cute."

"Cute?"

"Yeah." He nodded, his expression darkening as he leaned across the table. "You actually think you can do better than me?"

I opened my mouth to reply, frowning. The truth was no, I didn't. Zak wasn't all bad. He could be funny and attentive. When he wanted. He could also be cruel and neglectful, as I'd discovered. I deserved to be without him, but I wasn't sure that I *did* deserve someone else. I couldn't help but hear that small voice gnawing away at me, whispering that it was my fault. That I'd unwittingly cause another guy to do the same.

"Rosie, babe. Come on. I'm the quarterback…who's better than me?"

I winced at the certainty in his voice. The smugness. And so I presented the only argument I had.

"Someone who won't cheat on me…"

He rolled his eyes, sitting back. "Jeez, are you still on that?"

"Yes." I frowned. "Zak, it hurt."

"Would it help if I said sorry?"

I stared at him, taking in the slouched demeanor and tired gaze. He didn't care. Even now. I swallowed, shaking my head. "Not if you don't mean it. And I don't think you do."

"Then pretend I do."

My eyes flew up to his, my stomach clenching as his words landed. I reminded myself again and again that I wasn't enough for him, that he wanted better. And in my lowest moments, that he *deserved* better. I told myself he didn't really care about me or how I felt. And still, when it came from his lips, I was surprised. It was a guttural punch and, winded, I pushed back from the table.

"No." I murmured, more to myself than him. My hands trembled as I planted them on the tablecloth and rose to my feet. His eyes stayed on mine as I leaned down to retrieve a bag, placing it before him. "We're done here."

A frown marred his features as he stood up to peer at the contents, his eyes narrowing as he saw his jacket.

"You're making a *big* mistake."

I shook my head slowly, pushing the bag towards him. "I don't think I am..."

He paused a moment, before moving around the table to stand facing me. His dark eyes glinted as he stepped closer, a smirk tugging at his mouth. "I'd think about that if I were you."

I blanched, instinctively stepping back. "I...I have."

"Really?" He laughed. "Because I'm pretty sure when word gets around school about you having a casual fling with *another* guy...you'll regret it."

I smiled weakly, dropping my gaze. "I thought you'd say something like that."

"Know what else I'm gonna say?"

My fingertips grazed the table as I took another step back, his body moving to fill the space. I peered up at him, shaking my head slowly. His gaze ran along the length of me, his smirk growing as he slowly trailed his hand along my arm, snaking higher until it reached my neck. His head tilted as he grazed my skin lightly, his mouth curving into a sly grin. I flinched away from him, gasping as he regained his grip deftly. His grin widened as he held me there, inching closer to ensure that I heard every word. "That the only reason I took pity on you was because I knew it would get to Will."

"Will?"

What did Will have to do with anything? Why…Why would it irritate Will if Zak and I were together? I knew they had history, but we were just friends. We'd never had any…moments. Any snatches of time where his hand had grazed mine or our gazes had locked. Nothing to create that grey area. I bit my lip as I thought of the last few times I'd encountered him, the butterflies he'd created. And then another thought occurred to me. This could be another ploy of Zak's. A way to mess with my head. A last laugh over the ashes of our relationship. Because if Will really did only see me as a friend, or worse a sister by proxy, then me reading into every second glance and intimate gesture would ruin things.

I peered up at Zak, imploring a simple and honest answer. "Is that true?"

He smirked in satisfaction. "Maybe."

I let out the breath I'd been holding, wounded. *There* was my grey area. Was Zak finally being honest, or was it all just another joke? My insides ached as I stared back at him, trying to find the guy that had first won me over. The side that was kind and flirtatious. But as I looked into his eyes all I found was the guy who'd hurt me and found it funny. Who valued his ego above my feelings. I became acutely aware of his hand still grasping the side of my neck, his thumb tracing small circles by the base of my ear. With my heart hammering I drew up my hand and brought it against the side of his face with a loud slap.

The café around us quietened as he stepped back, his skin tingeing pink from the assault. His expression hardened. I blanched as he charged the short distance between us, his eyes narrowed. He grabbed the bag from the table, his lips inches from mine as he paused. His breath was hot on my mouth as he towered over me, his sneer returning. "Tell Brooke I said hey."

My gaze flickered up to his, my lips trembling as he pushed back and stormed from the café, the door clattering behind him. To anyone else it looked like a bad break up. The kind of everyday car crash you try to avoid gawping at, but still can't resist glancing to. Those glances burned into me as I stood rooted to the spot. No doubt wondering who'd dumped who, what he'd done to deserve his slap...and whether I warranted one in return. My limbs moved slowly, leading me in his wake towards the door. Once outside I looked around hastily, my heartbeat still erratic as I walked the short distance to my car. I got behind the wheel and let out a breath, laughing shakily. These days all I did in my car was experience traumatic after-effects.

I put the car in gear and pulled away, my fingers tapping erratically against the steering wheel as I drove. The adrenaline was slowing with every minute that passed, my insides settling the further I got from the scene of the crime. It was done. It was quite possibly the briefest relationship known to man, but I'd made it through. And it wasn't full of regrets. Not entirely. And so, as I drew the car to a stop at the base of our drive, I relished in a smidgen of pride. I'd broken it off, not him. My terms. It felt good. The one thing he'd granted me after the entire debacle.

I got out of the car and made my way to the house. Tomorrow at school I'd probably feel worse. I trusted that he'd spread vicious rumors around, and they'd lap it up. The days and weeks that followed would hardly be a walk in the park, I wagered. But today I'd enjoy the silence. To appreciate that I'd been there not just for Brooke and Will, but for myself.

"Rosie?"

I froze, turning to look into the living room. My mom peered up at me from the armchair as she muted the TV. I beamed, slipping inside to join her. With all her long shifts and odd hours it felt like an eon since I'd seen her. I missed her. But if she was home that meant a few days off. The timing was impeccable.

"You okay?" She smiled, standing up.

I nodded, drawing my arms around my waist. "I am."

Her smile warmed, her eyebrow arching. "That all I get?"

"Sorry mom. It's been a weird few days, I guess."

She looked at me expectantly.

I let out a low sigh. They'd find out eventually, better it come from me. "I caught Zak cheating. I ended things. Just now actually."

"Oh." She frowned, moving towards me. "Are you okay?"

"I am."

Her eyes clouded as she peered at me, unconvinced.

"I wasn't. I was hurt. I guess I still am, but I did the right thing and we just...weren't going to work."

She nodded, a frown still marring her features.

I let out a small laugh, witnessing doctor mode in my mom. A side glimpsed when Jonathan and I had been younger and more reckless. It usually came accompanied by scrapes and bandages, followed by hot chocolate and hugs. Today I suspected she was working up to the latter.

"Honestly, mom. I'm okay."

"Hmm." She finally answered, smiling weakly as she nodded to the kitchen. "If you like we could have a girly night? Make a batch of cookies and watch some films. Your dad won't mind." She glanced back at the living room. "He may even join us."

"Maybe later? I wanna wash the experience off me first."

"Okay. Take your time."

"Thanks mom." I pulled her into a hug, nestling into her shoulder. My eyes closed at the familiar scent. As I pulled back the cold air replaced it, the warmth of her embrace fading as I dragged myself up to my room. It really did sound like a perfect evening. A remedy to the colossal afternoon. But I hadn't been lying. I needed to cleanse myself of the last remnant of being Zak's…anything.

I headed into my room with my head bowed, tugging off my hoodie and tossing it onto the floor as I padded through to the en suite. Without looking up I turned on the shower, the hot jets shooting down against the tiles. Steam rose around me as I pulled off my remaining clothes, my gaze avoiding the obtrusively large mirror above the sink.

I stepped under the water, tipping back my head and closing my eyes as the torrent coursed along my scalp. My blonde waves tumbled into flooded tendrils, my skin prickling. Sighing I leaned back against the tiles, opening my eyes slowly as the jets rained down onto my skin. I didn't want to look down. To see my body. Feeling it was bad enough, being a part of it worse still. I wanted to take myself back. To be in the moment where I liked myself. Felt proud and certain. It'd only been a glimpse, but I'd felt it.

I closed my eyes again and shook my head to clear the thoughts seeping in. But it was no good, the moment had passed. And it had taken that girl with it. I let out another low sigh and turned the shower off, stepping out onto the mat gingerly. Staring ahead, I drew a towel around my body and secured it, padding back through to the bedroom.

I lifted my gaze to the bed, frowning as I saw a shoebox sitting there. I walked over curiously, casting a suspicious look around the room. The box stared up at me ominously. There was no note, no address. Nothing. Glancing around once more, I moved to sit on the mattress and pulled it onto my lap, my fingertips gently teasing at the corners. It lifted away easily, revealing an inside packed to the brim. Folded sheets of paper lined the base, a plethora of objects scattered over them. I frowned and reached inside, retrieving an old homemade card with remnants of glitter and tissue still clinging to the surface. My fingertips cradled the edges of it as I set it down beside me, peering at the other treasures. A loose pen rolled around the box as I tilted it on my lap, scrutinizing a length of yellow ribbon as it coursed among a sea of post-it notes and photographs. I took one of them out, my frown deepening as I stared at the younger version of myself, her beam bright as she attempted a half-hearted pose. Her gaze was warm and inviting to the camera. Or the person behind it.

I placed the photo to one side, my breath catching as my eyes fell on a ticket stub. My fingers grazed it lightly, tracing the title of the movie as a faint smile greeted my lips. It had been some truly cheesy film where the trailer was full of longing looks between the main couple, the music dramatic. It'd made no qualms about the fact it was a tearjerker. It was guaranteed. I'd wanted desperately to watch it and, although she'd put up a fight, Brooke agreed to go. The tickets were booked, the snacks mentally picked out, and the waterproof mascara firmly in place. And then she'd had to cancel. She was sick. So, I'd resigned myself to waiting until it was on blu-ray and I'd headed back inside. Just as Will was leaving.

My brother had been beside him, talking shop, and had heard the whole thing. Obviously it was a font of amusement for him because he'd proceeded to volunteer Will to be my chaperone. Will shifted in embarrassment, no doubt working up to the rejection. But he'd said yes, to both our surprise. He drove us, bought snacks, and appeared suitably uncomfortable during the soppier scenes. It had almost felt like a date. I'd had to remind myself that it wasn't several times. Still…I'd remembered that night for a long time. It meant a lot to me. I guess I hadn't been alone in that. My frown returned as I replaced the ticket stub to retrieve one of the letters lining the bottom.

I could place his handwriting immediately, my fingertips tracing the scrawl as my breath caught. I unfolded the paper and devoured every line, drinking them in hungrily. I read and re-read each line until I had them memorized, moving onto the next letter. And the one beneath that. There was a good handful of varying shapes and sizes. Some on neat lined paper and some on whatever scrap he had to hand. Some seemed paced out and mulled over, but then others were passionate outbursts. It was like being given a glimpse into his heart and mind all at once. My mouth dropped open as I read them all again, my gaze darting from the sheets I gripped to the photographs and other oddments.

Will.

He liked me.

My pulse quickened as I lowered the papers back into the shoebox, placing it on the mattress. My hands cradled themselves by the knot of my towel as I paced my room, shaking my head as his words echoed. The voice I hated sprang up as though summoned, demanding to know why on Earth he would like me. Why someone like that, like him, would be remotely interested. My heart ached as I thought about how much he *did* want me. The things he'd written. I chose to ignore that pestering voice, to believe his instead.

My towel dropped to the floor as I marched to my dresser, tugging free whatever clothes I could find. I had to act fast. To do, rather than think. Because sooner or later that horrible doubt would creep back in like rot. My fingers shook as I pulled on a pair of jeans and a bright top, yanking the cast-off hoodie over it. My hair still hung limp around my shoulders, as I slipped on some sneakers and cast a quick glance in the mirror. My skin was ashen, dark rings under my eyes. The neck of my hoodie was already damp from my hair, which itself stuck out in odd directions. I looked a mess.

But if I stayed to pick out an outfit, to neaten my hair or paste a layer of make-up on…I'd chicken out. I'd convince myself that the box was a practical joke. A cruel one orchestrated by Zak to drive that wedge I'd feared before. I ran down the stairs, shouting to Mom that I'd forgotten something important. Something that just couldn't wait. Technically, it wasn't a lie. I half-heard her reply as I raced from the house, diving behind the wheel of my car and speeding away. My fingertips danced against the leather once more, only this time the adrenaline that coursed through my system felt warm. Happy. Not cautiously optimistic or relieved.

Just…happy.

My tires screeched as I pulled up outside his house, slamming the car door behind me. I caught sight of his motorbike, my hands beginning to tremble with each step closer to the door. I rapped on the wood, wincing as the sound echoed back to me. After a few moments of silence the door opened to reveal Mr. Anderson.

His eyebrow raised in amusement as he folded his arms, a smile warming his features. "Hey! Which one of my sons is in trouble?"

My cheeks began to redden as I averted my gaze, forcing the grin from my lips. "Hey Jett. Is Will home?"

"In his room." He stepped to one side as he gestured at the stairs. "Probably being all angsty on his drum kit."

I walked over the threshold, peering up the stairs nervously. My hands wrung together as I considered how close he was. And how real this was.

"You want a drink or anything?" Jett asked, his eyebrow arching again.

I shook my head dumbly, swallowing as I dragged myself a few steps farther. I grasped the banister, hazarding a glance back at him. He smiled and gave a small salute, closing the front door before heading back into the kitchen. I held onto the banister as I made my way upstairs, taking in shallow breaths as I commanded myself to be brave. To get to him. Everything else was just…static.

As I reached the top and worked my way across the landing to his bedroom an awful feeling of déjà vu attacked my senses. I was cast back to another landing and another closed door. Beyond which my heart was shattered. I stared ahead mutely, my skin prickling as I stepped forward. The guy who waited on the other side of this door would never break my heart, I was sure of it. More than that…he'd never want to. He cared about me. I raised my hand and knocked, my insides quaking with anticipation.

Another pause.

The door swung back, a naked torso greeting me. My mouth dropped open as I stared at the tanned flesh, beads of sweat forming on the ridges of his muscles. I dragged my gaze higher and closed my mouth, meeting his curious gaze. The sweat betrayed the fact that he'd been practicing. My entire body froze. I wasn't sure what to say. I wanted him to know that I cared about him too. That I ached for him. And not just physically, but with everything underneath that. I was his.

I took a step closer, my gaze still trained on his. His eyes narrowed uncertainly, tiny golden flecks lighting up the mahogany as he considered me. I stopped before him, reaching up to lightly place my hand on his chest. Right by his heart. He swallowed, leaning down an inch as I tilted my head back. His dark eyes searched mine one last time, before he brought his lips to meet mine in a gentle kiss. I gasped and urged closer, my mouth trembling as though kissing a boy for the very first time. It was tender and sacred, something I'd never experienced.

I pulled back as we broke the kiss, gazing into his eyes questioningly. A wondrous smile tugged at his mouth as he pulled me into his body, holding me tightly and crashing his lips against mine once more. I felt the longing in his kiss, a soft moan escaping as I wrapped my arms around his neck and returned it with everything I had.

I grinned against his lips and stroked the hair at the base of his neck, pressing myself into him with a whimper. The warmth of his hands cradled me, his heat traveling as his grasp slid underneath my hoodie to caress my lower back. And to my surprise, I didn't stop him. I didn't flinch or pull away. My skin cried out for him. My mouth curved into a grin as he broke the embrace, his breathing short and quick. His dark eyes found mine, a smile playing on his lips.

"Wow." I breathed, letting out a soft giggle.

He grinned, lowering his mouth to mine in a soft kiss. He held his lips inches away, murmuring in wonder. "I can't believe I kissed you…"

"I can't believe you haven't until now."

His cheeks warmed as a blush reached them, his gaze turning bashful. "I didn't think you'd want to."

I frowned, reaching up to stroke his cheek tenderly. "I think you're incredible."

"You do?"

I nodded seriously, my voice a low murmur. "I really do."

His grin returned, his dark eyes dancing. "Rosie?"

"Yes?"

"You wanna go out with me sometime?"

This time it was my turn to blush. Every part of me lit up, sparks ricocheting as his words landed. "You mean that?"

He nodded, his lips grazing my forehead gently. "I really do."

Chapter 20

David

"You never really understand a person until you consider things from his point of view – until you climb in his skin and walk around in it."

I curled the corner of the page between my fingertips, my lips parting to murmur the words. They still sounded foreign on my tongue, but their meaning weighed heavy. I'd been trying, really trying, to make amends with Will lately. To try and remedy the tension wedged between us. Wedged between us by me, in fact. I remembered a raw anger, a hatred, towards him. It had gotten under my skin, twisting every fond memory into something alien. I'd known even then it was misplaced. That it wasn't Will I was upset with. That the real villain was long gone. No, my brother just had the misfortune of being the closest thing to him. The catalyst I could direct my fury towards.

I'd resented every snide look on my face, every cutting remark and cold stare. I'd become the bad guy and yet I couldn't stop myself. I'd wanted to, desperately. I'd tried to swallow those words and contort my scowl into a smile, but it'd been no good. I'd been an awful brother. I wasn't sure what the light bulb moment had been. Whether it was the words of Harper Lee resonating with me through the worn pages of a high school play, or the expression of sheer anguish on Will's face as he witnessed the girl he was crushing on be used and cast aside. Either way, it'd been a wake-up call.

I had to be there for him.

I *wanted* to be.

And so I had been.

For the first time in a long while I'd reached out and talked to him like a brother. He'd been skeptical at first. I couldn't blame him. But after a while I think he finally trusted me. Trusted my advice. That I cared.

Still, as much as Will wanted to pretend the whole saga had never happened...I couldn't. I could barely look at him, knowing how I'd treated him. Giving him a gentle push towards his dream girl was the very least I could do in penance. Besides, judging by the glimpses I'd seen into how Zak had treated Rosie, I'd been doing them *both* a favor. She'd been looking tired and worn for a while now, her usual spark not there. I was certain that given a few weeks with the right guy she'd bounce back. And Will was definitely the right guy.

He didn't think so. Not that I'd helped matters. But even I could see during those dark moments where my sight of him had been clouded he was a good guy. He wasn't...him. He could *never* be him. Still, Will couldn't swallow that pill. He was bound to question himself. They shared DNA. He'd probably re-examined every outburst he'd had, every misuse of powers, and put them down to genes. Will was one of the nicest guys around, an actual gentleman. There was no doubt he was as far from being that guy as possible, DNA or not. But I understood. I could see the flicker in his eye when his voice rose, that shadow that crossed his face when his fists clenched because he was about to lose it.

And yes, I'd seen something that...I wasn't sure how to process. How to address. And so I hadn't. He'd seen it too. But we were the only witnesses and it would stay that way. The last thing he needed was to feel watched and ostracised. His eyes could turn magenta for all I cared. He was still Will and he was still my brother.

My fingertips cradled the edge of the page as I mulled over the ominous figure that now lurked in the background of our family tree. I wanted to cast him aside completely. Pretend the whole revelation had never happened. But then I suppose we all did. Still, a morbid, curious part of me itched to know if he was still out there. Our Intel on him was bare, which I understood. He was hardly gonna be the topic of choice at the family BBQ. But we did know that he was their friend, and then he turned. Became a monster. Committed unspeakable acts and ditched town. I wasn't sure whether knowing what had come of him would comfort me or not. At best, he might have overindulged on the dark magic he was so fond of and tapped out in some alleyway. Dying alone, his outsides finally mirroring his wretched soul. Or he could have finally gotten caught and be wasting away in a maximum-security prison somewhere.

Option B sounded less comforting, but ultimately it was much less likely. No prison would hold him. He'd probably allow himself to be caught, just so he could break himself out again, taking out everyone that got in his way. That option carried a lot of innocent bystanders being slaughtered and opened the unsettling possibility for Option C. My least favorite. That he was still out there. Doing God knows what to God knows who. Getting away with it, over and over.

The worst part about Option C was that we didn't know what he looked like. The confession from mom and dad hadn't exactly involved getting out the old yearbook and taking a jog down memory lane. It'd been more like a sprint. He could be tall, short, fat, thin…He could have even changed his appearance.

I glanced around the quietly mulling coffee shop, my brow furrowed.

He could be anyone.

I shivered involuntarily and looked back down at the book. No, it was probably for the best we did bury our heads – as unhealthy as that sounded. If we allowed ourselves to go down that road we'd only end up paranoid and broken. And then he'd win. I cleared my throat and sat up straighter, my gaze running over that same line. For what was probably the hundredth time. The words just floated off the pages, escaping my brain entirely. It was a welcome distraction from…him. So I needed to focus and work on my drawl. Without taking it too far. I didn't want to caricature the character. To make it look like I was doing a cheap imitation of Gregory Peck. I wanted to pay homage to him, of course, but I wanted to do the role justice. To make the audience care not just about the story and what it meant, but the characters too. I wanted them to believe in them. To look at the stage and see past the lighting and props. To see Atticus, instead of David.

In order to achieve that it'd help if I could actually retain a line or two. I let out a sigh and dropped the book onto the table, reaching out for my coffee. I brought it to my lips and faltered, peering down into the dregs at the bottom.

Well, that wouldn't do.

If I was going to push through my family trauma and revise a few pages I'd need copious amounts of caffeine.

I set the cup back down and glanced around at the neighboring tables, my fingers hovering by the porcelain. It would be so easy to just magically refill it with the beverage of my choice. No queuing, no waiting, and no paying. It was that last snag which stopped me. The majority of the staff were students and got the bulk of their pay from tips. Tips that were housed in a jar on the counter. I sat back with a resigned sigh and grabbed the cup, slipping from my hidden nook at the back of the coffee shop. It never tasted the same anyway.

I glanced back at the abandoned table, my backpack slumped on the polished wood beside the barely thumbed book. I'd been coming in that often it was safe there while I dashed to the counter. My gaze fell across the tables flanking it, their owners typing away with heads bowed. A tall stack of textbooks weighed down the tables, nestled beside the laptops precariously. I turned back around, continuing my pursuit of the dark stuff. I should probably berate myself for focusing on the arts as a newfound passion when I could be focusing on my studies instead. But if acting didn't work out I wouldn't be headed to college in any case. I'd be working with my dad in the garage, fixing up cars and bikes.

And that suited me just fine.

The soft sound of laughter greeted me as I rounded the corner, my mouth tugging into a grin. I stopped short and took in the sight. Something that had been all too rare lately. Brooke Danes, smiling because of a guy. I'd heard about her dating someone called Matt, but this was the first time I'd seen them for myself. I raised an eyebrow as I watched for their body language, my head tilting. I recognized him from around school, he'd always seemed nice from the little I knew. Kept himself out of the headlines. Now he was stood beside her before the coffee counter, smiles on their faces as they shared a private joke. They looked cute. Angst free.

I edged closer, empty cup in hand as I came to quietly stand behind them in the queue.

"So, what's the one thing you've always wanted to try from the menu, but never have?"

She looked up at him with a wicked grin, her tone teasing. "You do realize I'm Italian, right?"

I suppressed a smirk.

Matt raised an eyebrow, his grin matching hers. "Earl Grey then?"

She let out a soft laugh, shaking her head as they took a step forward together.

"Mind if I cut in?"

Brooke turned to face me, her brown eyes lighting up. My smile stretched wider as she enveloped me in a hug, my arms coming around her. I caught the scent of her perfume as she nestled into me, closing my eyes for a second. As she pulled away I caught Matt staring at us, his expression curious.

I laughed uneasily, rubbing the back of my neck. "Hey. You guys okay?"

"Yeah." She beamed, stepping back to stand beside him. "Just figured we'd come for a caffeine fix. I'm guessing you had the same idea?"

I followed her gaze to my empty coffee cup, nodding with a smile.

"Late night?" She smirked, raising an eyebrow.

"Mind out of the gutter." I chuckled, shaking my head. "Nothing like that."

"First time for everything."

Matt looked between us, reaching out to take the cup from my hand. "I'll get the drinks in. Let you guys catch up."

I smiled slightly at him, an odd sensation of guilt creeping along my spine. God only knew where it was coming from, but I felt it all the same. Was I third-wheeling, cutting into some inappropriate territory by sidelining him from the conversation on his own date? I'd only meant to say hey. Be friendly. But I'd caught that flicker of suspicion on his face as we'd hugged. An intimate hug, sure. But nothing sinister. Nothing for him to lose sleep over.

Brooke leaned into him, kissing his cheek in thanks. "I'll have my usual please."

He nodded, casting another quick glance in my direction before turning back to the counter.

I watched after him, gently steering Brooke to one side. "So, I hear he got the Danes seal of approval?"

She looked back over at Matt with a grin, nodding as she appraised him. "Daddy said he was as much of a gentleman as he could wish for me."

"High praise from the big guy."

She laughed as she turned back to face me, her dark eyes glinting playfully. "He still watches us like a hawk."

I grinned. "As he should."

She fake gasped, tilting her head in amusement. "Are you implying that I'm not to be trusted?"

"I'm implying that he's right not to trust horny guys around a girl as cute as you." I countered.

Her cheeks warmed as my words landed, her voice lowering to a murmur as she shoved my arm gently. "Not all guys are like you."

"Shame."

Brooke smiled, peering up at me. "Isn't it just?"

Now it was my turn to blush. I met her smile as we stared at each other, the air decidedly tense as silence slipped between us. What was I doing? This definitely felt like dangerous ground, even by our standards. We hugged, we shared intimate moments and yes, we flirted. But not like this. Our flirtation was playful. Innocent banter.

"So," I coughed. "You like him, huh?"

Brooke bit her lip, nodding. "I do. He's a good guy."

"He is." I agreed, stepping back a fraction as he began making his way over.

"Are my ears burning?" He raised an eyebrow with a grin, holding out a cup.

I took it from him, smiling slightly as I glanced down at the wisps of steam rising from the coffee. My gaze traveled from it to their take-out cups, sat within a cardboard tray for two.

"What gave it away?" Brooke grinned, nestling into his side as she took her coffee from the holder.

"All good I hope." He chuckled, kissing her cheek gently. His eyes slowly rose to meet mine, his smile faltering. "Will David be joining us?

"Nah." I smiled evenly, "I wouldn't want to intrude."

We stared at each other levelly for a moment, another loaded silence encroaching the space. I tried to soften my expression, to remember that Matt *was* a good guy. He'd done nothing wrong, so why was I acting as though he had?

Brooke pulled a face as she sipped her drink, peering up at him. "Did they remember the hazelnut?"

He frowned, looking back at the counter. "I'm not sure…"

"It's okay." She smiled between us. "I'll be right back."

Matt opened his mouth to stop her, closing it helplessly as he watched her escape from his side. He let out a small sigh as he turned back to face me, smiling wanly.

"So, you and Brooke huh?"

He nodded. "Yeah. Me and Brooke."

"I'm guessing her dad gave you the lecture?"

"Yeah." He nodded again, offering a small smile. "He did."

"So I don't need to remind you if you hurt her your body won't ever be found?"

"Wow." He let out a laugh, his eyebrow arching. "That's dark."

I'd been aiming at playful. Perhaps my tone had been off. Still, the more I thought about it, the more I was happy with the statement. I was protective over her. And he might be a good guy. He probably was one of the few at Harrison I *did* trust with her. But that didn't mean he wouldn't hurt her. A gentle reminder of the support system she had in place couldn't hurt.

I raised an eyebrow at him, slowly drawing my cup to my mouth and taking a sip.

"Okay." His expression became curious again. "I get it."

I nodded as I took another sip. I tried to remind myself I was only doing what Nathan would. That I was looking out for her by setting a precedent to the new guy. He probably understood that too. Except...I felt uneasy. As though a bigger part of me knew I wasn't being entirely honest about the situation. Sure, I was giving him the stare off for her benefit, but it wasn't just that. I *did* trust him not to mess her around. I should be trying to find common ground with him, to make him feel welcome.

Instead, I was warranting suspicion.

From him and me both.

"I think they poured in half the bottle this time." Brooke laughed, falling in beside him again.

We both turned to look at her, relief showing on our faces as we let out small laughs. I raised an eyebrow at her as I tried in vain to rescue the atmosphere one more time. "Take it steady or you'll be bouncing around like Rosie."

"I'm a pro at it now." She grinned, taking a sip as though to prove her point.

I glanced across at Matt to gauge him. To see whether my first impression had stuck or if there might still be room to convince him that I wasn't a total dick. His hand slipped around Brooke's, his head bowed to hers.

"Well, I should let you guys get back to your date." I smiled, watching for his reaction.

His gaze slowly rose to mine as he smiled thinly. "Thanks."

I guess that answered my question.

"We still on for the movies tomorrow?" Brooke smiled up at me, her lips puckering to blow into the small gap on the lid.

"Uh." I paused, letting out a weak laugh as I averted my gaze. "Of course. Wouldn't miss it."

"Great." She grinned, turning to face Matt. "We should probably head out. We promised we'd take Sammy for a walk."

He nodded, his shoulders relaxing in what I assumed was relief. "Absolutely."

"Have fun." I smiled, lifting my cup as they headed out. I waited a beat to see if she'd glance back, guilt flooding me as he did instead. His expression was still unreadable, but his gaze held that same suspicion I'd felt moments before. He opened the door for her as he stared back, a frown marring his features as he tore his eyes away and walked beside her down the street. I turned and walked slowly back to the hidden nook of the coffee shop, my own brow fraught as I tried to reconcile just what'd happened.

I'd been acting like…Like I was jealous. Which made absolutely no sense because Brooke and I were friends. Good friends. We'd never so much as kissed. So why was I reading into the moments where she'd leaned into me, her cheeks tingeing as she blushed? Why was I watching her lips pucker and imagining what they'd taste like? Why was I wishing it were us on the date, and not them?

I groaned as I slumped into my chair, setting the cup down on the table. The why was pretty obvious. Because suddenly she was unavailable. She wasn't my best friend that I went to the movies with, playful banter flying between us. Now she'd become a woman that I saw through the eyes of the guy she was dating. A beautiful, intelligent woman who was…happy. She was happy with Matt. Because perhaps he'd always seen her that way. He hadn't needed it to be revealed to him.

He had simply seen her.

The trouble was, now so did I.

Chapter 21

Will

Has something ever happened that's made you step back, almost pause, as you weigh up whether it's really happening? Where you wake up and automatically the world seems brighter? That's how things are now, ever since Rosie and I finally kissed!

My stomach had clenched with nerves as I'd stroked her cheek, searching her eyes to see if this was why she'd turned up. But the moment our lips met everything had fallen away until there was only her, and the way she felt against me. It had been so natural to cross the line from friends into more, and that was strange at first, as if we'd both expected nervous laughter and awkward silences.

What *had* been awkward was sneaking around.

The stealth texts sent under our friend's noses, or the quick kisses we stole between classes. Keeping my hands off her in front of them was practically impossible, already on one occasion I'd found myself reaching for her hand, only to stretch out my arms awkwardly when I saw Lucas glance our way. If she was any other girl I wouldn't have minded them seeing. But she was Rosie. She wasn't just any girl to begin with.

She was *the* girl.

And we'd decided that we couldn't go public without getting the blessing of our friends. Or one friend at least...

Funnily enough we'd also come to the agreement that I'd be the one to broach the topic with Jonathan, though I'd no recollection of agreeing to it, rather just nodding when Rosie suggested tonight after school. So like the man I am I'd spent all day avoiding him, distracted and trying to figure out how to get his blessing without pissing him off. The first step would be getting him in a good mood. And while I knew of a few things that would get him grinning, I definitely wasn't willing to do them.

But then I'd had an epiphany. Or at least realized the most obvious solution. It had taken all afternoon to convince Ash and Alex to agree to practice and cancel their original plans. When I'd mentioned us coming over for a spontaneous rehearsal Jonathan had slapped me on the shoulder with the first genuine smile I'd seen in days and I knew I'd made the right choice.

Only now as I stood on the Taylors driveway, checking my cell as the minutes ticked on I was getting nervous again. I could hear the thrum of Jonathan's guitar from the open garage as he waited, the noise traveling easily as the world around me stilled with my growing anxiety. Ash and Alex had promised they'd be here and ready to practice by 6pm, and I'd really hoped we could turn up together, a joint force. Maybe then Jonathan wouldn't feel like we were looking for an escape clause. And if the band was a sure thing maybe he'd be less likely to have an issue with me dating Rosie.

I was trying not to think of what would happen if Jonathan didn't want us together, but the longer I waited the more the thoughts began to gnaw away. It somehow felt right that for every good thing there was always bad right around the corner. Jonathan forbidding me from dating his sister was the perfect thing to come along and pop my bubble. But what would I do? What *could* I do if he refused us? I'd only just learned what it was like to hold Rosie, to kiss her soft, pink lips. Trying to imagine letting her go so soon was unbearable. But did that mean I'd choose her over Jonathan? The idea of walking away from our friendship, from the band, was just as painful. He'd been there for me through everything, hadn't looked at me like I was a different, more dangerous, person when he'd found out about Ethan. I trusted him with things I didn't trust my family with.

I ran a hand through my hair, turning to look behind me as I heard the crunch of tires easing up the drive. They were here. The peaceful bliss that ignorance brought was running out and time was slipping away. Soon enough Jonathan would know. Which meant soon...so would I.

I stepped towards Ash's jeep as he killed the engine, flashing the two of them a weak smile as they climbed from the vehicle, their eyes burning into me, clearly still pissed. Part of me couldn't blame them, after all, I'd taken their side when things had got tough. We all loved the band, but Jonathan's ambition was wearing us down more than usual, especially when he was on *our* case to perfect everything...but it was always *him* screwing up.

I wanted to thank them for turning up, for helping me, but they had no idea they were doing this for me. For Rosie. They thought I'd just been listening to Jonathan whine about missing two practices already and I was tired of it. I was going to let them keep thinking that too, the less people that knew before Jonathan the better. I didn't expect it to work in my favor exactly, but to know he was our main priority had to count for something, right?

"I could be surfing right now." Ash broke the tense silence as we slipped into an easy stride towards the garage, raising an eyebrow at me. I ignored him, or tried to. I didn't need to feel guilty about dragging him away from his first love so that I could break the news about mine. Guilt at screwing one of my friends over was enough. But when he opened his mouth to speak again I shot him a look, smiling thinly when he held his hands up and closed his mouth.

As we headed into the garage Jonathans hand dropped from his guitar, the note he'd been strumming dying as his mouth pulled into an easy smirk. "Welcome back."

"What can I say?" I laughed, clapping him on the shoulder. "We missed you." I shot Ash and Alex another look.

Play along. Fake it if you have to, but for fucks sake don't screw this up.

"Thought you might." Jonathan laughed, clearly not feeling the tension from the other half of the band. If I had to use my powers to take the edge off and make the atmosphere more relaxed I would, but toying with people's emotions was a step too close to what *he* would do...

Alex cleared his throat, stepping over to the spare keyboard he used when we practiced in the garage. "So are we working on the old stuff or the new?" He cracked his fingers, holding down a note and looking up at Jonathan.

"Well as much as you girls complain, I wanna run through the new stuff."

I winced inwardly at the comment, opening my mouth to speak before one of them jumped on it and things got awkward. Again. "I think we can do that. " I reached into my back pocket and pulled out my drumsticks, twirling them as Ash sidled up to his bass to set her up. "It'll be nice to get it perfected"

Odd notes echoed around as I lowered myself onto the stool behind my kit, watching as Jonathan repeated the four-chord opening for the sixth track of what he often said would be our third album, waiting for Ash to jump in. The blonde cast a look back at me and his mouth twitched into the faintest hint of a smile as he struck his bass. I nodded, tapping my sticks together before crashing them against the drums as the music took shape, Alex's posture relaxing too as his fingers flew over the keys.

And then Jonathan closed his eyes, opened his mouth, and began to sing.

I felt the energy lift as the music flowed, my eyes scanning the backs of my friends as I looked for the tell-tale signs that all was not as it seemed, but as the music broke into a second of silence before the chorus kicked in, Ash and Jonathan high fived at finally nailing the bridge together and everything felt exactly as it had that first summer we'd played.

My head bowed, hands relaxed and arms tensed as I beat through the rhythm of the chorus, getting out of my head, my eyes closing as the beat ran away with me, my arms striking the drums from memory as my body acted instinctively.

I frowned as Jonathan hit a wrong note, the sharp intake of his breath echoing over the mic as he tried to shake it off, my eyes flying open to take in the three new faces watching us. Leaning by the wall were Matt and Brooke, his arm around her, his face buried in her neck as they spoke in whispers. She giggled, nodding to whatever he was saying as her eyes met mine, and then she smiled and slowly looked away. I followed her gaze to the other person who'd joined us, my cheeks straining with a smile as she stared right back. Rosie bit down on her lip, glancing anxiously to her brother and then back to me.

I shook my head. No, not yet.

She nodded, settling herself beside her best friend, the two of them whispering and giggling together. And if I wasn't sure before, I definitely was when Brooke looked at me again, her lips turning up as she grinned my way. Rosie had told her. Of course she had, girls didn't keep secrets from their closest friends. I glanced at Jonathan briefly, swallowing down the bile that crawled up my throat.

I looked back to Rosie, grinning like an idiot when she caught my eye. Although that wasn't a smart move. I didn't want to be caught out early for gazing adoringly at her, and I needed my head to be in the game. I couldn't let Rosie distract me. Instead I quickly glanced at the other happy couple in the room, watching as Matt leaned down and pressed a kiss to Brooke's exposed shoulder, his hand snaking tighter around her and grinning as she turned to kiss him back.

"Fuck." Jonathan pushed the mic away as he missed another note, dropping his guitar to the floor in betrayal. His shoulders slumped with defeat, the rest of us stopping to peer at him. His head lifted, and I knew from the way Brooke's cheeks burned that he was looking at her, but without so much as another word he disappeared from the room, the door slamming behind him.

"So..." I broke the tense silence, glancing between Ash and Alex. "All done?"

Alex sighed, shaking his head as he dropped himself down onto the sofa and kicked his feet up onto the table. "We canceled our plans for the sake of half a song?"

I ran a hand through my hair, still rooted behind my kit as Rosie looked my way, Ash joining his best friend and taking a seat. So much for getting Jonathan in a good mood. All I'd managed to accomplish was pissing everyone off.

"Well..." Matt cleared his throat, smiling awkwardly around at us. "We were thinking of going out for drinks if you guys want to join us?" Matt and I had never been in any classes together, and besides seeing him around school I'd barely spoken to him. But now he was dating our friend.

And from the expression on his face as he looked at her I could tell he wanted to integrate himself into the group. For her. You couldn't blame the guy for extending the offer.

Alex looked between me and Matt, shrugging before sitting up. "Count me in. Ash?"

Ash nodded, "Yeah, I'm game." All eyes in the room turned to me.

I nudged the toe of my converse against the leg of my stool. "Uhh...I should go and talk to Jonathan first."

A unanimous nod swept the room, no doubt they'd all assumed I was going to talk to him about his latest tantrum. Rosie knew better, breaking from the group as they talked amongst themselves, allowing us a brief moment. I took my chances as I stood, pulling her into me and hoping Brooke would keep Ash and Alex distracted long enough that I'd at least be able to kiss her.

I closed my eyes as I wrapped my arms around her slight frame, nuzzling into her soft blonde locks and breathing her in. It was surreal, finally holding her, and every time my arms wound around her I was unwilling to let go. I pecked a light kiss against her hair, grinning when her soft blue eyes met mine, her lips twitching into a smile before she anxiously glanced behind her. "Are you going to tell him?"

Sighing I nodded, stroking a flyaway strand of hair back into place. "Yeah. I was trying to get him into a good mood...kinda went the opposite way."

That was an understatement.

Actually I don't think it could've gone *any* worse. We all knew shit had gone down between Brooke and Jonathan, some of us more than others. I still remembered Jonathan sneaking back into our tent in the early hours at camping, trying to wipe the tint of Brookes lipstick from his mouth. But after that...I was in the dark. Jonathan wasn't the type to open up and share, and I wasn't gonna push it. After all, I understood. So I had absolutely no idea what the deal was.

Except Rachel had played a part.

Rosie reached out to stroke my jaw, smiling encouragingly. "He might be happy."

"He might also hit me."

"Nah," she grinned, "He likes you more than me."

I laughed, "Okay, then he might hit you."

"I hope not." She laughed with me, my arms reluctantly dropping as I stepped back, creating space as Alex shot us a curious look.

Time had run out.

I waited until our resident keyboardist had resumed conversation with the others, leaning down and pressing my lips to Rosie's earnestly, failing to hide the shallow groan that slipped from my mouth as she wound herself around me, returning the kiss. My heart was in my throat as I enjoyed her embrace, my tongue tasting her as my hands gripped the fabric of her hoodie like a lifeline. But all too soon I broke away, enjoying the pink flush in her cheeks.

"Let me go tell your brother so we don't have to sneak around. And then we can go out for drinks and celebrate."

Rosie's cheeks flushed further as she squeezed my hand, reluctantly moving to join our friends as I slipped from the room, taking a breath before I faced Jonathan.

I knew he'd be in a mood. No doubt mentally berating himself for dropping notes, missing cues, and fucking up another practice. And that wasn't even including Brooke. After camping I'd assumed the two of them would dance around each other a bit more, flirting and teasing in the way we'd all grown accustomed to. But maybe I'd got this wrong. Maybe Jonathan had just had too much to drink and Brooke was the only female available. But that didn't explain why he clammed up whenever she was around, or why he had an issue seeing her with Matt.

Was Jonathan gonna be the guy that didn't want Brooke, but didn't want anyone else to have her either? I sympathized, I'd thought about trying to sabotage Rosie's relationship with Zak for my own selfish reasons. But whatever was going on with Jonathan wasn't just affecting things with Brooke, it was seeping into band stuff.

Sighing I reluctantly opened the door to the kitchen and crossed the threshold to finally face him. He was sat on the kitchen counter, his back to me as he stared out of the window that stretched the length of the far wall, the door to the garden open as it filtered out the smoke from his cigarette. I closed the gap between us, his head turning a fraction as he heard my footsteps on the tile.

"Hey man..." I tried weakly, moving to lean on the counter beside him, pretending I didn't mind his second-hand smoke.

His lips pulled into a thin smile as he quickly assessed me, his shoulders dropping slightly. "Hey."

Had he been expecting someone else? Or maybe hoping...

"You okay?"

"Yeah..." He lifted the cigarette to his lips, taking a long, slow drag and closing his eyes. "Just distracted."

I nodded, looking out at the sky as the sun bled a deep orange across the horizon. "It's been a while since Rosie and Brooke joined us."

"It has."

This was more difficult than I assumed. I tried a different approach. "I think they might come around more often now."

He turned to look at me, the cigarette half raised to his lips before he frowned. "Why?"

"Just a hunch. Regarding recent...events."

"Oh." He dropped the remainder of the cigarette in the empty beer can beside him, resting his eyes on the floor. "You mean now Brooke is with Matt and Rosie ditched Zak?"

This was it. There wasn't going to be a more opportune time to get it out than right now. "And Rosie's new boyfriend."

There. Was that so hard?

But if I'd thought the weight would ease even slightly at finally getting the words out, I was wrong. In fact as Jonathan lifted his head to look at me they doubled, his eyes cold as they settled on me. "New boyfriend?" All I could do was nod, watching as he flicked his gaze to the door we'd just come through. And he definitely looked more pissed than I'd thought. "Who?"

My mouth was dry as I opened it, my fingers drumming against the wood paneling of the cupboard door beside me. Jonathan had never been overly protective of Rosie, but even he'd think we were on the rebound. It made sense since we'd become newly single, and it wouldn't be a bad assumption if it were another girl, but with Rosie I was only ever going to give her everything. I just had to make him see that too.

He cocked an eyebrow, clearing his throat to remind me I'd still not answered. "Who is it?"

I straightened up, smiling nervously, trying to maintain eye contact. "It's...me."

Disbelief flashed across his features, his jaw setting as he stared, completely dumbfounded. "What?"

I held my hands up, taking a step back just in case he decided I deserved five knuckles to the face. "I know how this must look, and if I were in your shoes I wouldn't be ecstatic about it either. But...she means the world to me, Jonathan. I'm completely crazy about her."

"What?"

I smiled weakly, trying again. "I...I like her. And she likes me too."

Jonathan jumped from the counter, running a hand through his hair before it dropped to his pocket, reacting instinctively to retrieve his lighter. "When did this happen?

"A couple of days ago. She came to tell me about Zak and Chloe and it seemed like a sign."

He paused, frowning at the floor. "It was Chloe..." He said it more to himself than me, before he began to trace the pattern he'd been walking on the floor again, his fingers idly flicking the lighter. Suddenly he stopped, looking at me. "Who else knows?"

"David." I saw him flinch slightly. Jonathan knew things with David were on a better road, but we were still on shaky ground. I couldn't blame Jonathan for being annoyed that he was second in line, but David *had* been the one to give me the push. "And Rosie just told Brooke."

Jonathan slipped his lighter back into his pocket and I relaxed slightly, that was a good sign. He fixed me with a curious stare instead, raising an eyebrow. "This isn't like with Chloe?"

A fair question. "Not a chance."

"And Rosie feels the same?"

"I..." I laughed nervously, "I hope so." We'd not really had a relationship talk since we'd shared our first kiss. We'd simply been happy with stealing more and agreeing on a date. Albeit even that was postponed until the Jonathan situation was handled.

His eyes shimmered, a lit cigarette appearing in his hand as he nodded, the moment obviously calling for one of his vices. "Okay."

I blinked. "Okay?"

He nodded, taking a drag on his cigarette as he watched me. His mouth pulled up into a grin as he let the smoke filter out slowly, satisfied with how anxious I was. "I'm happy for you. Well...her too." He added as an afterthought.

"You...are?" I'd planned for almost all responses, but Jonathan's blessing wasn't one of them. I imagined more glaring and at least one asshole comment. But maybe Zak had done me more of a favor than I cared to admit. He'd shown Jonathan the type of guy he didn't want around his baby sister, so anything else was a step up. It wasn't a comforting thought, but I'd take it.

"It's gonna take some adjusting. But...I couldn't wish for a better guy for her. " He locked eyes with me, his face relaxing, no grinning or bravado. "I trust you."

I stared at him, letting those three words echo around my head on a loop. We both knew what that meant to me, to hear him say it. But the expression on his face as he kept his eyes locked on mine didn't leave room for doubts. He really *did* trust me with her. "You don't know what that means to me...to us."

But of course he did. Because he knew me. Because despite the fact I struggled to let anyone close enough to try and figure me out, Jonathan was one of the few I didn't have to pretend with.

He cradled his cigarette, watching as it burned up. "I had no idea you saw her like that."

I shrugged half-heartedly, "I never thought it would happen. So I didn't see the point in sharing." Although David had figured me out.

"Hang on." he frowned at me, leaning against the counter he'd previously been using as a seat. "How long have you liked her?"

My cheeks burned as the heat of a blush swept rapidly up my face. "Oh, uh...a while." Try four years. Give or take. But I wasn't going to admit that as well.

"Shit." He laughed, shaking his head as he lifted his hand for another drag on his smoke. "Seriously?"

"Is that so hard to believe?"

"Not in a harsh way. I just... Congrats?"

I smiled as I leaned beside him, glad at the strange turn of events that I'd had no intentions to plan for. "Thanks man. We're all going out for drinks now if you wanna join? We're gonna break the news to the rest of the gang."

I didn't miss the look that clouded his features, his eyes looking past me at the garage door. "Everyone?"

He didn't need to drop names, I knew who he meant. I'd hoped that Rosie breaking up with Zak, and David and I patching things up, would help cement the group again but until Jonathan and Brooke put their differences aside it would still feel like we'd been split. Which meant everyone would still be picking sides. " Matt invited us out with him and Brooke..."

Jonathan nodded, crushing the cigarette in his hand as his powers disintegrated it in his grasp. "I'll pass."

I expected as much. I smiled weakly, skating over the issue as flippantly as I could, he wouldn't forgive me for pushing. And I still wanted to keep on his good side. "You gonna be writing more songs? Or perfecting the new stuff?"

"Probably a mix." He turned to face me, trying to block the garage door with my hulking frame. "Usually if I get inspired I jump on it."

I nodded, both of us jumping as the door behind me creaked open. We glanced over to see a crown of blonde hair appear, Rosie smiling bashfully as she took a nervous step into the room. "Are we okay?"

I couldn't hide my grin as I stepped towards her, "We are."

"Really?!" Her smile grew to match mine as she peered at her brother, positively beaming when he nodded.

She threw herself into my arms, wrapping herself tightly around me and pressing her lips against mine, just as relieved as I was that we'd got his blessing. We gave ourselves over to the other, my fingertips stroking her cheek as I forgot that we weren't alone. I grinned against her lips and held her tighter as we kissed, both ignoring the groan of annoyance from Jonathan as he turned away from the spectacle. But I couldn't help myself. I'd taken a chance on her, on myself. And it had all paid off. There was no grey cloud. And the only thing left to do was tell our friends and make it official.

And then I could kiss her like this forever.

Chapter 22

Brooke

I held my cell firmly, bubbles of excitement swelling as it vibrated with a notification, the corners of my mouth pulling up as his name flashed on the screen. Matt. Untangling my legs from beneath me I climbed from my seat by the bay window, grabbing my purse and making my way downstairs without even reading the message. It was second nature to us now. Matt always arrived ten minutes before he was due, and always gave me a five-minute warning...

My mouth twitched into a smile as my cell vibrated once more in my grip, my stomach fluttering with excited nerves. Things were progressing slowly with Matt, and while I was happy with where we were, I didn't feel the need to push for more. And hopefully neither did he. Holding hands as we traipsed between classed was a pleasure most teenagers overlooked. The soft kisses at the end of every day were never forceful or hungry. The gentle embraces were of comfort, not lust. But it was perfect, the right balance of chemistry and attraction, while still leaving us wanting. And we had all the time in the world to explore us.

Reaching the bottom of the staircase I heard James' familiar chuckle coming from the dining room, closely followed by Mom calling out his name disapprovingly before he laughed again. I headed towards the noise, smiling when I found them. It was a sight I'd once worried I'd never see again. Mom was sat in one of the high backed leather dining chairs, the books from the bar spread across the table. James was slouched back in a chair beside her, his hand tapping against the edge of the glass dining table. Daddy was stood behind Mom, looking over her shoulder at the pages of accounting while he massaged her back, kissing her hair occasionally.

All that was missing was Nathan sitting opposite, his nose buried in a book. It didn't take a genius to figure out where he'd be. Ever since he'd introduced himself to the new girl at school, the *nice* new girl, he'd been inseparable from her. Not that I blamed him, after all I was sneaking away to spend another afternoon snuggled up with Matt.

I headed into the room, ignoring the disapproving scowl from Mom as I passed up a chair and lifted myself onto the table, placing my cell down beside me and glancing at my family. James carried on whatever conversation he was having with Mom, leaning on the table as he flipped some of the papers around, his brow furrowing as he scanned the numbers.

Daddy looked over at me, smiling softly as my phone vibrated again, the noise louder against the table. "Matt?"

I glanced at it, frowning as his name lit up my screen once more and nodded at Daddy distractedly. It wasn't like Matt to text so much while driving. Swiping at the screen I brushed my thumb over the scanner, opening our conversation to read the three new messages.

I'm just about to set off gorgeous, I can't wait to see you! xxx

Brooke, I'm so sorry, Mom's car broke down and she's asked me to come pick her up. I won't be long, I promise xxx

Hey, I'm just running her to the ATM and then dropping her home. I'm sorry beautiful, I'll be half an hour. Tops xxx

"Everything okay Sweet-pea?"

I smiled at Daddy's pet name for me, quickly replying before I tucked my cell into my purse as I turned to face him. "Yeah," I nodded, "Matt just got held up."

Daddy's eyebrow rose a fraction, his smile thinning. "He's usually quite prompt"

I read between the lines, smiling weakly at his concern. "His Moms car broke down so he went to go help."

His posture relaxed, his smile softening slightly as he nodded. "He's proving himself."

"I don't think he was doing it for your approval, Daddy." I laughed, "He's just a nice guy."

"Is anyone nice enough for my baby girl?"

"No." I smirked, "But he's as close as you'll get."

Daddy laughed, shaking his head as his fingers went back to deftly working on the knot that had settled on Mom's shoulders. "Touché."

I looked at the two of them and smiled, watching how they interacted, knowing what the other needed without words. It was difficult to imagine the two of them in a world where the other didn't exist, to think of life before Daddy moved from Italy, or what could've happened if he never had. Not just because I was their daughter, or even that I wouldn't be here if things had been different. But because theirs was a love that enveloped you in their presence. It echoed through every room of the house, hidden in the smallest details, from the bone china vase that Nonna had gifted Mom, passed down through the family, to the framed movie poster that hung above the love seat in the lounge. The film Daddy had treated Mommy to on their first date.

Theirs was a love that most people could spend their whole lives searching for and only hope they ever caught a glimpse. Even I, the hopeless romantic I am, wasn't sure it would ever happen for me. I'd wondered if it could be Matt, if he was the one who'd make me smile like no-one else could. But I followed that by remembering I once thought it was Jonathan...

I'd taken my dose of reality when it came to love now. I was still a hopeless romantic, I still wanted the fairytale wedding with the happily ever after, but I also knew it didn't come easily. Not even for my parents. It took hard work and dedication. It meant apologizing when you're wrong and being graceful when you're right. It meant working as a team to overcome whatever was thrown at you, instead of giving up when it got tough and the hurdles got higher. It meant supporting someone else, and holding them when they felt like they couldn't do it alone, but also letting them spread their wings and better themselves, even if it meant you had to make sacrifices.

Because if it's real love, what the movies try to show us glimpses of with clever camera angles and soft music, if it's truly *meant to be*, that person would do all those things too.

I dared anyone to look at my parents and disagree, to watch Mom place her hand on top of Daddy's and give him an affectionate squeeze of thanks, to see the smile that crossed his face at the gesture. Or the way James rolled his eyes and looked away as Mom cracked a joke about the Italians invading, Daddy smirking as he kissed her ear.

Eww.

I caught James' eye, the two of us wearing matching expressions of resignation. That was always the downside of your parent's being madly in love. They never tired of showing it. "What *are* you talking about?!"

"I was just reminiscing about life before Tristan." Mom replied, the book forgotten as she leaned back into Daddy's grasp. "When me and Felix used to cause trouble, instead."

"Felix?" I racked my brain for the name, or the face. I had a faint memory of meeting a man who seemed to fit the bill, but the finer details were lost.

"You don't remember Felix?"

"Should I?"

James laughed, shaking his head with amusement. "Old friend of Moms?"

Nope, still drawing a blank.

"He moved to LA for work?"

Oh sure, I'd remember that.

"His parents live next door to our grandparents?"

Ohhhhh!

I smiled, finally placing him as James laughed. "Isn't he Ryder's dad?" Clearly I'd been more distracted with the handsome teenage boy he'd introduced me to at the time.

A fact that wasn't lost on my older brother. "You would remember *him*."

"Shut up!" I laughed, throwing him a playful scowl.

Daddy rolled his eyes, choosing to ignore the small infatuation I'd had on a boy I'd only ever known a few days. "When did you say he's coming over, Angel?"

"Wednesday." Mom smiled, scooping her papers together. "He said as soon as he's checked into his hotel he'll call."

Daddy nodded, "Is it just him?"

"For now. He's got a few viewings for houses but he's eager to move back."

I glanced at Daddy as he nodded again, the thin smile not reaching his eyes. "Yeah, he mentioned something when I saw him last. We should take him and Ally out for dinner when they're back home."

"That sounds lovely, Hunky." Mommy turned to kiss Daddy's hand on her shoulder, smiling up at him. "Between looking for a house and a studio too he's feeling the pressure. It'll be nice for him to have something to look forward to."

My brow furrowed as I looked between my parents, tilting my head. "A studio? Is he like a director?"

James laughed once more, tossing a ball of paper at me as he shook his head. "You really do live in your own little world, don't you?"

Scowling I swept the paper to the floor, "I can't help it if mundane life bores me."

"I'd say owning your own record label and traveling the world with rock stars was the exact opposite of mundane, little sister."

I paused, replaying James' words

He travels the world.

With rock stars.

Because he owns a record label...

"He's..." I looked at my parents, completely oblivious as they flirted. "Why...why did no-one mention this before?"

"What?" Mom turned to face me, Daddy's arms winding around her as he held her against him.

"That Felix had a record label. That we had connections!"

Daddy's forehead creased. "It wasn't a secret Sweet-pea."

"Half of my friends are in a band!"

"Well...yes. But we didn't realize that meant they had to meet Felix."

I almost groaned with frustration, but my parents didn't have a child in the band, a child that didn't want to go to college because they strived to play music to anyone who would listen. They didn't see the fire in Jonathan's eyes when he played, or the desperate need that swam through his veins, turning everything into a song. They wouldn't have made the connection I just did. Because they didn't know my friends like I did. And with Felix so far away and the band still at school, it wouldn't have worked.

But now...

Now school was almost over. Felix was moving back to Boston. And the band were falling apart because their futures were uncertain.

I hadn't meant to overhear their conversation after weekend practice. But maybe it had been fate. Because now I could do something about it. I could help.

"Do you..." I cleared my throat, turning to face them and smiling softly. "Do you think he'd listen to them play?"

I was asking a lot, Mom had literally just been saying how Felix was stressed, which could only mean he was coming back for a more relaxed lifestyle. And throwing The Plagiarists on his doorstep would be the opposite of that.

But I *had* to try.

For my friends...

"I don't know, Brooke." Mom frowned, glancing up at Daddy. "He's *really* busy."

"I know, but it doesn't have to be a *thing*." I pouted, looking at her pleadingly. "Please, Mom!"

I saw a brief flash of silent conversation pass between my parents, Daddy's eyebrow raising as Moms shoulders dropped with defeat. "Fine." She sighed, "I'll ask Felix to come to the bar on Friday for drinks and the band can play. But whatever happens, happens, Brooke."

I propelled myself from the table, throwing myself into the surprised arms of my parents and hugging them tightly, their arms wrapping around me while James smirked at me winning them over. As usual.

"Thank you!" I beamed, inching back to look up at them. "I've got to tell the band!"

I stepped back to the table, grabbing my purse and my cell as I felt in my pocket for my car keys, coming up short.

They were still in my room...

Because I wasn't taking my car.

Because I had a date with Matt.

And he was coming to pick me up in approximately twenty minutes.

My mouth stretched into an innocent smile as I turned to face my parents once again, fluttering my eyelashes. "Daddy?" I ignored the arched eyebrow of Mom as she looked my way, knowing exactly what it meant when my voice softened and I pouted at him.

"Yes Sweet-Pea?"

"You want to do your favorite child another favor?"

Daddy laughed, shaking his head in amusement. Either because he knew he'd do it, or that I'd had the cheek to call myself his favorite while James was in the room. Not that he objected either. "You ready?"

I nodded, taking a breath and gripping my purse tighter as I closed my eyes in preparation for the shift.

It wasn't the best way of traveling, the earth jumping beneath your feet instantly, taking you wherever you wanted in the blink of an eye. The first time I'd ever done it was with David. My arms locked around him as he shifted us to the middle of Times Square, the city that never sleeps buzzing around us. My hands had stayed locked on David's jacket once we'd stopped moving, my stomach lurching and my head spinning. It had been an uncomfortable experience as my body fought the transfer, but being a normal with a network of superhumans meant you handled it one of two ways. You dealt with it. Or you chose the long route.

I'd shifted with the guys several times since that first nauseating experience, and while it was easier every time, the first few seconds still made me feel like my stomach was trying to jump out of my mouth. Today was no different. My eyes remaining closed as I drew in a breath, tensing and relaxing the muscles in my legs where I stood before I tried taking that first step.

The playful banter of home had disappeared, replaced by the gentle thrum of a guitar hidden behind the walls of the house I was now standing before, the thudding of the drums meeting it. Letting out a breath I strode towards the front door, my heart settling back into its usual rhythm as a fear I hadn't anticipated was swept away by the drums. The keyboard. The low twang of the bass.

Jonathan wasn't alone.

It was weird knowing I was no longer privy to their scheduled rehearsals, but I hadn't made the effort to support them either. It had been selfish, but seeing him, being in close proximity, was difficult. The rest of the guys didn't blame me for keeping my distance, but how could I let my feelings for one of them get between the friendship I shared with the others? We were closer than that.

Now it was time to make amends. To bridge some of the cavernous gap that had built between us. All of us.

Steeling my nerves I reached out and knocked on the door, trying to drown out the voice in my head as it fought to be heard. I knew what it was saying, what it wanted me to acknowledge. But I wouldn't.

Luckily before I'd fully succumbed to arguing with myself there was movement behind the door, Jonathan and Rosie's mom, Liz, smiling brightly. Her hair was pulled into a loose bun at the nape of her neck, her eyes, the same ocean blue as her daughters, crinkling. "Hey Brooke."

"Hey Liz, how're you doing?" It felt weird trying to force small talk with my best friends mom, a woman who'd nurtured me almost as much as my own. Annoyance flared as I realized Jonathan had affected more than just my relationships with our friends. I couldn't remember the last time I'd turned up without an invitation and been treated to dinner by Liz, or curled up on the sofa with Rosie to watch the Red Sox with Cole. I was missing out on my second family.

"I'm good, thank you. I've got a few days away from the hospital so I'm just about to run a few errands." Her head turned a fraction as the noise in the garage picked up, her shoulders sagging. "I'm sure the entire street can hear that."

I smiled, trying to imagine a Jonathan that didn't need to be playing music with every scrap of time he had. "They'd miss it if it was quiet."

Liz smiled back at me, opening the door wider as she stepped aside. "Did you want to come in?"

I nodded, stepping into the house and glancing around. "I uh..." I cleared my throat, turning to face her as she closed the door behind me. "I've come to see Jonathan."

"Oh." She blinked at me. Trying to hide her surprise. I didn't know if she knew about me and Jonathan, whether Rosie had told her why I hadn't been around. Or maybe she'd seen the way I'd mooned over her only son. I'd always been too obvious about my feelings.

Liz smiled at me warmly, already over her initial shock as she nodded towards the door that was hiding the band. "Just follow the noise..." I nodded, watching as she strode back into the sitting room with a parting smile before I headed into the kitchen nervously.

I swallowed down my nerves, berating myself for being such a sap, and then immediately jumping when my phone buzzed from the clutches of my purse.

So much for controlling myself.

I dug around to find it, cursing at the fresh message.

Finally on my way. I can't wait to see you <3 xxx

Matt.

He'd be on his way to mine. Smiling anxiously I tapped out a quick reply, telling him about my change of plans. I anxiously read it back, hitting send and rationalizing why I'd kept Jonathan out of things. Matt wouldn't mind who I'd come to see, he knew I was close with Jonathan, but this felt too close to lying. Like I was trying to hide something.

I tried to forget about it, ignoring the voice in my head as it grew louder and slipping my cell away. Time wasn't on my side and I had to get the band to agree to playing Jays. I hadn't even considered the possibility the others might say no. I'd just assumed Jonathan would have the final say. My stomach flipped involuntarily as I headed for the door, thanking the heavens Jonathan wasn't alone

I slipped through the door, the utility room leading to the garage filled with the gentle melody Jonathan was playing. I closed myself in the space between the two rooms and took a moment to appreciate his talent, the song wrapping me in the moment as it weaved through the air.

Reaching out I nudged the door open further, taking the last nervous step towards him as the world rushed at me.

My hand dropped to my side as I let out an inaudible gasp, my eyes closing as I lost myself to the moment. To the music. To the storm.

Jonathan was alone. There was no band. He had his back to me as he sat on the sofa, his guitar cradled on his lap as the other instruments played by themselves. His fingers plucked the chords, expertly tugging on the strings of my heart as I was taken to a different place, my senses assaulted with his magic. I could taste beer and smores in the air. The hint of a long-forgotten campfire lingering as it burned to embers on the damp ground, the sound of thunder rolling above our heads. I could hear the gentle patter of rain as it hit the light walls of the tent, filling any silence that lingered between Jonathan's chords. My heart thudded in my chest rapidly as I thought back to the way his lips had felt on mine, the way my body fit into his so perfectly.

The memory slammed into me, bowling me over. Now I could taste his lips, his tongue, his skin. I could hear the way he groaned my name, breathless in my ear. I could feel his hand on my thigh, gripping me closer as his teeth nipped at my neck, the firm muscle of his chest pressed against mine as my own hands clawed at him desperately. The scent of fresh rain in the air.

The endless possibility of what could be hanging in the limited space between our writhing bodies.

And then I opened my eyes.

And I saw him.

He'd shifted forwards slightly, a pen held loosely in his hand as he bowed over the battered leather notebook I'd grown accustomed to seeing wherever he went. He leaned down, his pen scratching the page as he worked the words into the melody.

Then without warning he groaned, harshly blacking out the words before tossing the pen across the table and falling back into the comfort of the couch. He ran a hand through his hair, his shoulders slumping. "Jesus, Brooke..."

I flinched, heat spreading across my face. I hadn't even realized he knew I was there. "I'm sorry, I didn't mean to interrupt. Your mom let me in."

Jonathan jumped, turning to face me as he slammed the notebook closed, his face flushing. I stepped closer, watching the remnants of magic dying in his eyes as they returned to their usual shade, the instruments stalling and the music fading away. The smell of fire and rainfall in the forest being replaced by leather and oil. The air cleared, the humid tension of the storm waning and taking the sound of rolling thunder with it. There was no more clearing, no more camping. It was just Jonathan and I. Alone in the garage.

He cleared his throat as I stepped closer, sliding over on the couch and making space for me. He couldn't look at me as I joined him. "Don't worry about it."

"Do you do this a lot?" I asked.

He looked at me curiously.

"Play alone?"

"When I'm working on a new song." He shrugged nonchalantly, running a hand through his hair once more. "It's therapeutic."

"Does it help not having the guys around?"

He smiled weakly, finally looking in my direction but still not meeting my eyes. "In a way. I can just manipulate the instruments and play around. It's easier." He slumped back onto the couch, putting his feet up on the table. "Don't tell the guys. They already have one foot out of the door."

"I know." I smiled weakly, caught off guard as his eyes finally met mine, looking both surprised and wounded. "I overheard the other day. I'd just got here when I heard you talking, I was trying to sneak away again when Will saw me."

"Ah. I remember." He looked away again, his eyes burning into the songbook that lay closed between us on the table. "I'm just hoping we get some luck before they quit on me outright."

I smiled weakly, turning to face him. "I might be able to help." His body turned to mine in response, his brow furrowing as he considered my words. "A slot opened up at Jays on Friday. Mom's having a nightmare trying to cover it. I said I might know a band..."

I waited with bated breath as his eyebrow rose. Jays wasn't exactly known for hiring the local rock band, or any rock bands for that matter. The name my parents had associated with their bar attracted more family-friendly entertainment. Not four hormone fuelled teenage boys that would pull in half the girls within a ten-mile radius. And as much as The Plagiarists weren't the type of act Mom would hire, they weren't exactly used to that type of venue either. They frequented darkened bars with sticky floors, bodies pressed against each other tightly as fists pumped the air. The scent of sweat and alcohol clinging to every surface as people screamed for more.

"You...want us to play?" His eyes were glazed, his voice quiet.

"Yeah." I smiled softly, watching him.

His lips were pulled tight as he stared past me to where the drums were sat, I could almost hear him deliberating his options as his fingertips tapped against his jeans. Finally he spoke. "I have two questions."

"Shoot."

"Is it paid? And can we play our own material?"

"Yes." I grinned as his face finally broke into a smile, his eyebrows shooting up in surprise. "To both." My parents hadn't actually mentioned anything other than asking Felix to come, and I deliberately ignored the notion he might pass it up because he was busy, but the band playing their own music was a given. I'd negotiate with Daddy on the money if I had to.

Jonathan looked up at me cautiously, and I stared right back, my heart thumping in my throat as I gazed at him. I swallowed nervously, anticipating his move before he'd made it, but being surprised all the same when his body shifted into mine. His arms wrapped around me, his head against mine as he pulled me closer into his embrace. My body screamed out to react, my mind finally silencing as I slid into the comfort of his hold. I closed my eyes, nuzzling into his neck as my hands slid up the length of his back, breathing him in.

My head swam as his fingertips brushed the fabric of my jacket aside, my skin burning where his flesh met mine. "Thank you." His lips moved against my hair.

"It's okay..."

He pulled back a fraction, his eyes burning as they locked on mine. His hand reached out, brushing against the flush of my cheek as the other slid down my waist, eliciting a soft whimper of surprise to be wrenched from deep within me. His eyes searched mine, before falling on my lips as I licked them nervously.

"Brooke..." My name sounded like heaven as it slid off his tongue. "I..."

A horn blared from outside, the crunch of tires on gravel breaking us apart. The air between us cooled rapidly, the voice in my head screaming at deafening levels as I finally let it back in, my body scooting away from his. "Matt. I..." I grabbed my purse from where it had fallen to the floor in our clinch, my cheeks flaming, unable to look Jonathan in the eye.

He didn't speak, nodding as he hit the button to open the garage door. Sunlight spread across the floor and broke down the moment we'd shared, Matt's car coming into view, the engine still purring as his tanned arm hung from the window.

I didn't look back at Jonathan as I hurried away, trying to wipe away the guilt that would be written all over my face, hoping Matt wouldn't know I'd been so close to falling into Jonathan's web again. He was like a drug. He was bad for me, as skilled at playing women as he was the guitar, but I couldn't help myself.

The shame didn't creep up on me this time, it hit me full in the gut as Matt looked up from his cell and beamed.

What the hell are you doing, Brooke?

I smiled back, hoping my face wasn't betraying my cheating body. Matt was the guy that I so desperately wanted to want. He was good for me, and I enjoyed who I was when I was with him. He made me laugh. And he certainly didn't make me doubt myself like Jonathan did.

But as I opened the car door to join him I dared a glance back at the green-eyed boy who evoked reactions from me I was never consciously sure I was making, and the realization hit me like a freight train.

I could hide behind this stoic wall, I could force the lies to fit with the story I'd created for everyone else, and I could pretend the gap between us all was because he'd hurt me.

But I couldn't lie to myself.

I couldn't ignore the voice in my head anymore because I didn't like what she was saying. That I'd stayed away from him, not because I didn't trust him, but because I could never trust myself.

Because I was in love with Jonathan Taylor.

Chapter 23

Louise

Smile.

But not too much. You don't want them thinking you're psychotic. Or worse, not paying attention. Read the room. Note the conversation.

Make eye-contact.

Don't stare without blinking, but don't stare at the table either. And definitely don't hide behind your hair!

I paused, sweeping the dark curtain of hair from my face, tucking it behind my ear with a quick glance up at the rest of the party. Nathan had invited me to dinner with his family; a moderately smart affair in one of Boston's most exclusive restaurants. Which had given me a whole moment of excitement when I'd eagerly agreed, before turning into a writhing mass of nerves as the hour ticked nearer.

To say I was anxious would have been an understatement. To say I was nervous was even worse.

Growing up I hadn't had many friends, or even any. Not including the older sister I hadn't seen for three months. My parents both held demanding careers, meaning through my teenage years I'd grown accustomed to relocating before I'd got settled. Faces and names fading from memory before they'd even registered. It was a system, one I'd learned to adapt to from an early age. As a hopeful pre-teen I'd bounced into a new school and eagerly thrown myself into the fresh start. Class projects. Dance committees. Science fairs.

Only as the years slipped away, when I'd been pulled from one school to the next, I'd lost the thrill of even attempting to make friends.

What was the point when we'd relocate when the year was up? Promises to keep in touch dying as the car doors closed. Now, school was all I knew.

So why was Harrison different? Why had I agreed to coffee with Nathan? Late-night study sessions in the library? Slipping my hand into his as we walked from bookstore to bookstore, sharing our favorite stories and how we'd first stumbled across them.

The answer to that was easy.

Quite simply, I'd stopped hiding.

I dared a glance to where Nathan was sat, his hand resting on my knee as he spoke with his Mom. I'd felt the pull of Boston before I'd even got here. Before my parents told me they'd enrolled me in yet another school, while Dad went off to do field-work and Mom worked on whatever new breakthrough the medical world had stumbled on.

I'd known my school life was almost over, that college was calling. And was it a coincidence that the Ivy League university I strived to attend just so happened to be in Boston? Was it also coincidence that Nathan wanted to go to the same one? Was it fate that we met? When we had so much in common and our lives were heading down similar paths.

No. Probably not. But I wasn't going to pretend it wasn't happening either. I'd grabbed onto him with both hands and I wasn't letting go. Metaphorically speaking, of course. It was nice to finally have a friend, someone to confide in, and chat with. Someone who shared my love of academia. Who wanted to fill their spare time with knowledge, who wanted to reach their full potential and then keep pushing.

My parents encouraged it of course, my love of learning. More so than anything they'd ever encouraged with Annabelle. She often felt like the black sheep of the family, a free spirit in a house full of logical thinkers. Though looking around at the Danes I knew the siblings felt the same competitiveness, the strive for approval. Sure, Nathan was the brain, but from sharing classes with Brooke I knew she was more than just beauty. She was sharp. Her GPA almost as strong as her brother's. And James, though the brawn, seemed just as knowledgeable. But each of them had discovered their own niche and were determined to carve something from it.

I blushed, thinking how easily I could be part of this family. How much I wanted to be.

Everyone stopped talking to watch as a smartly dressed man slid into the enclosed space, smiling politely and waving his hand at Mr. and Mrs. Danes as they rose to greet him. "I'm sorry I'm late, traffic was a nightmare from the office." He smiled around at the group before claiming the empty seat beside James' girlfriend, Elle, leaning in to kiss her forehead as he sat down.

"It's okay, Dad." She placed a hand over his and gave the slightest squeeze, smiling up at him brightly. I glanced between the newcomer and the beautiful honey blonde sat beside him, and while his skin tone was several shades darker than hers, it was unmistakable that they were related. They shared the same alert brown eyes, the curve of their lips almost identical. "We've not been here long." Elle continued.

"Traffic was a nightmare for us too, Ed." Mr. Danes chuckled softly, glancing to his right where his wife shook her head slowly, grinning at her napkin. I picked up on the subtle hint of something not quite said, though the rest of the Danes understood. I made a note to ask Nathan later.

"That's a relief then." Ed laughed, nodding as the waiter reappeared from behind his partition and offered up a bottle of wine.

"It is." Mr. Danes smiled as the waiter dutifully refilled everyone's glasses, his eyes drifting around the table, settling on me for a moment before he glanced to his son. "And it'll be a nice opportunity to get to know everyone a little better."

I shuffled awkwardly, my hair falling back and hiding me from view once again. I'd spent years doing the 'getting to know you' routine. Only this was bigger, and so much scarier.

Nathan felt my reluctance, his hand sliding from my knee as he tucked my hair back. I met his eyes and he smiled, his fingertips lingering by my ear as my cheeks began to flush. "Everyone, this is Louise." Nathan's eyes never left me as he spoke, my cheeks flaming brighter as everyone looked in my direction. "My girlfriend."

Staring right back the surrounding noises faded into nothing, the faces of his family blurring into a mass of color. I'd felt the relationship we had was different, more than just friendship. I'd known from the moment I'd gotten that first book, before I'd known who Nathan was. When I was just crushing on the faceless person that was showing me their life through a medium we understood. Back when I had a crush on the smart boy in my classes who always knew the answer, and when he didn't he went to find it. Before I knew those two people were the same.

I leaned closer, trying to shield the moment from everyone else. "You mean that?"

"I do. If you'll have me?"

Nodding I lowered my head into his, no longer worried about his family watching as I brushed my lips delicately against his. "Definitely."

The smile that spread across his face was dazzling as he sat back into his chair, his hand sliding onto mine as he interlinked our fingers right there on the table for everyone to see. It felt nice. To want someone in that way and have them want you in return. And from the smile his parents shared I assumed they were happy too.

"Well this is Matt." Brooke shot me a smile as everyone's attention shifted to the opposite side of the table. "Matt...everyone."

Of course everyone had already met Matt, but they smiled regardless. I was thankful for the move. The air already less claustrophobic as we were no longer the center of attention. It was something the Danes had adapted to well, being the most popular kids in school and all. It came with the territory when your father was one of the most in-demand lawyers in America and you were stunningly attractive. And Brooke took to having all eyes on her like second nature.

Besides me Nathan shifted in his seat, leaning closer to his mom as she whispered to him. "Voi due siete una coppia perfetta." My ears pricked up at the hushed tones, speaking perfect Italian.

You two are a perfect couple.

I blushed, trying not to eavesdrop on their conversation, which they assumed I wasn't privy to.

"Thanks Mom," Nathan replied, casting me a quick smile as his Italian tongue took over, my arms breaking out in nervous goosebumps. "I really like her."

"She's very beautiful, too."

Nathan nodded, his cheeks flushing a deeper shade than even my own at his mother's words. "She's stunning."

"Grazie." I smiled shyly as they both turned to look at me in stunned silence, my eyes locking on Nathans as I built up the courage to continue. "Sono pazzo di te."

I'd barely registered the grin on Nathan's face before he cupped my chin, pulling me into his body and kissing me tenderly. My hands slid around his and I let out a shy giggle, enjoying the taste of red wine in his kiss. "You never told me you spoke Italian." He murmured, reluctant to break apart as he looked at me, reverting back to English with ease.

"We never got to that." I smiled softly, losing myself in his deep blue eyes. "I speak Korean, French. and Italian fluently. I know enough German to speak, but I'd not be able to hold conversation very well."

"Come ti ho trovato?"

How did I find you?

I interlinked our fingers once more, kissing the back of his hand. I'd wondered myself how I'd come to meet someone that matched myself so perfectly, but I still wasn't going to question it.

"Well if my brother and sister have finished introducing their dates, I'd like to introduce mine," James spoke up, his voice authoritative as everyone in the room broke from their conversations to look at the oldest Danes sibling, Nathan and I sliding apart as James' smile stretched across his face. He stood from his seat, looking down at the woman beside him. She rose to her feet elegantly as he offered her his hand, nuzzling into his side as he wrapped his arm around her.

Their eyes met, their grins spreading as everyone in the room looked upon them curiously. After all, Elle had been part of their family for long enough, the introduction James was about to make seemed superfluous. Matt and myself being the only people around the table who didn't truly know her.

But James carried on regardless. "This is Elle. My fiancée."

The room stilled.

Glasses paused on the way to mouths.

Eyes shining with surprise as Elle extended her hand, a beautiful white gold ring sitting pride of place on her ring finger, the diamond sparkling almost as brightly as her smile.

And then everyone moved at once, Elle's father jumping to his feet to shake the hand of his future son in law, Mrs. Danes moving to pull Elle into a firm hug as she wiped tears of happiness from the corners of her eyes. Brooke gushed about finally having a sister. Mr. Danes motioning for champagne as he went to join the happy couple. Nathan congratulating his brother and Elle on their celebration as he pulled me closer against him.

It felt strange to be on the outskirts of such a joyous occasion, but welcomed into sharing it as if I were a member of the family, my mouth tugging into a smile as I met Elle's stare and offered her a quiet congratulations among all the cheering and conversation.

She thanked me with a grin and a nod, turning to share the story of how James had proposed, recreating their first date and surprising her with the ring in the place they'd shared their first kiss. I listened as her father joined in and told how James had approached him before he'd gone to war, how he'd asked for Elle's hand before he'd been shipped out, with the promise that he'd return for her. I was moved when Mr. and Mrs. Danes recalled how Elle had turned up at Jays and asked for a job, because despite being overqualified, she wanted to be close to the family she considered her own. She wanted to feel close to James.

And now they were all reunited. And their families would be bound together.

I leaned into Nathan, smiling as his arm wrapped around me. "Your family are so close. And clearly very loving."

Nathan chuckled softly, his thumb tracing small circles on the bare skin of my shoulder. "It must be the Italian in us I guess." His head turned a fraction as he looked at me, his eyes burning with curiosity. "I'm looking forward to meeting yours..."

I smiled as I met his eyes. My parents had been pushing to meet Nathan for the better part of our...relationship? They'd found one of the books he'd left for me, splayed open with the message clear for all to see. Only at the time I didn't know how I'd even approach that with them. My parents weren't the overly protective type, they trusted my judgment. But even that would only go so far when faced with an anonymous admirer who bought me things.

I'd managed to keep them at bay by feeding them some line about it being the only copy they had left and how I needed it for English. I doubted either of them were fooled for long. Especially when the books kept coming. But they never pushed, they waited for me to approach them.

But the moment I did they'd jumped.

Originally Mom was from South Korea, she'd met Dad when he'd gone over for work, and the two of them had fallen in love, much to the chagrin of her family. They'd always dreamt she'd marry a 'nice Korean boy', so my very white, very Canadian father was a bit of a shortfall. Or at least he was at first.

They'd soon come to accept that they were in love, that their plans for the future included each other, and that meant Mom would leave her home and move to America. But they knew she'd do it regardless of their blessing.

So when I'd finally told my parents about Nathan they'd tried to avoid all the mistakes my grandparents made when they'd been introduced to my father. Ironically going in the opposite direction and making me just as terrified. Although they were probably just as excited that I'd made a friend, someone I shared common goals with, rather than looking at another year alone. I guess I had to cut them some slack. They'd obviously been worried about me.

"They'd love to meet you." I murmured, smiling at the handsome boy beside me. "They keep asking when they can."

"They do?"

I nodded, laughing at the shock all over Nathans adorably surprised face. "They keep asking me to invite you over for dinner."

"Then invite me!" He laughed.

"Okay...Nathan, would you like to come over for dinner and meet my parents?"

He smiled, leaning in to kiss the tip of my nose as he gazed into my eyes, my stomach jolting with the intimacy of such a minor show of romance. "I'd love to."

His arms wrapped around me, cradling me into his chest as I slowly took in the scene. James and Elle were seated once again, smiling lovingly at each other as James brushed his thumb over the rock on her hand. Nathans parents were deep in conversation with Elle's father, their bodies touching with subtle hints of love and passion. Mr. Danes hand resting on the base of his wife's spine, her body turned into his as her own hand stroked his shoulder. Brooke and Matt were sat laughing, Brooke tossing her hair as she smiled at her date, her fingers resting on his forearm as he leaned in to kiss her ear.

I smiled, relaxing into Nathan as I let myself be welcomed into the folds of the family. Not fighting the need to be alone or hide away from a world I might not be included in next year. I wanted to be in Boston. I wanted to be here.

With Nathan and his family.

With my boyfriend.

With my future?

Chapter 24

Jonathan

I tilted the small metal lighter, the warmth of it pulsing through my fingertips. The flame danced in response, flickering as it reached higher into the air. The colors swam, tendrils of purple coursing through the blue and pink. I watched them change again, my gaze steady as I took in a measured breath. Usually this parlor trick calmed my thoughts. Distracted them. But tonight was important. I could feel it with every tick of the clock as the hour crawled closer. So the nerves remained.

The guys had been relatively enthusiastic about the gig. Considering the recent low morale it was the best I could hope for, but I knew they were unconvinced. They no doubt figured it was a way to placate me against the inevitable. A way to soften the blow. I could almost picture it. Years from now we'd meet up for beers and reminisce about the days we used to play. We'd smile wistfully and talk about how naïve we'd been, how full of arrogance and hope. The thought was sobering. I didn't want to do that. To look back and wish I'd been more resilient. Tonight was perhaps just a gesture for them, but to me it meant so much more. It could be the last gig we played. I knew that. All too well.

So I'd make it count.

I'd play like I meant it. To feel the words I was singing, to have the music flow through me – not just *from* me. I needed to let it in. Easier said than done. But it was the only way. I had to play for her.

My gaze traveled from the flames licking the air to the monitors flanking the opposite wall. A sea of bodies migrated from one screen to the next, the sound muted as the crowd began to swell. It was the biggest one we'd seen for a long time. If ever. The word had spread about tonight and the teenagers had flocked obligingly. I only hoped they'd come for the right reasons – and not to witness the demise of The Plagiarists. The pressure began to surge beneath my bones, my fingers gripping the lighter as I took in the gathered bodies. If I messed up tonight it'd be a very public humiliation. The guys wouldn't forgive me. They'd barely be able to meet my gaze. They'd be embarrassed and ashamed. I shook my head to clear the thoughts, my eyes focusing on the faces in the crowd. To hell with pushing back those terrifying feelings that swarmed around me at the tug of a note. Tonight I'd embrace them and I'd embrace her.

Metaphorically speaking.

"Mom, I think F-"

I looked towards the door, my lighter extinguishing as I stared into Brooke's startled eyes. Her hand fell to her side as she paused, her cheeks warming.

"Oh, hey…I thought mom was up here."

I smiled weakly, offering a small shrug. "She said I could hide out up here."

Her dark eyes flickered to the screens on the wall, and then to the lighter in my hand. A soft smile tugged at her lips as she stepped into the room and closed the door. "Nervous?"

"Just a little." I smiled wryly, placing the lighter on the desk beside me.

"Wanna talk about it?"

I looked at her warily. "Really?"

"Yeah." She smiled, her gaze dropping to the floor as she closed the gap between us. Her dark hair fell like a curtain as she hoisted herself onto the desk, reaching up shyly to tuck the tendrils behind her ear. I watched her, my fingers itching to claim the task as my own.

Her eyes found mine again as the seconds slipped by, the silence stretching out. I smiled weakly, glancing back at the desk. I wasn't sure where to start. Or even that I should. Of all the people that didn't deserve me whining to them, Brooke topped the list. And yet, here she was. After everything that'd happened – or nearly happened – between us, she still cared.

I let out a low sigh, drawing my gaze up to meet hers. "I'm afraid I'm gonna mess up."

She stared at me quietly, her expression somber as my words resonated."You won't." Her hand came out to rest against mine, trembling as she hesitantly brushed her thumb along the edge of my wrist. "Just be yourself. Enjoy playing. Like you used to."

I turned my hand from beneath hers, extending my palm to interlink our fingers. "I want to."

"Then what's stopping you?"

I smiled bitterly, relishing each fresh volt of adrenaline that sped through me as my skin grazed hers. "It's complicated."

She didn't speak. Her dark eyes followed mine and a smile warmed her lips, her hand giving a gentle squeeze. I grinned at the gesture, trying in vain to keep the blush from crawling along my neck.

"I'll be there." She murmured quietly, drawing her eyes to mine.

I held her gaze a moment longer, our hands remaining locked. "Thank you, Brooke."

Her cheeks tinged pink as she shrugged, a smile playing on her lips. "Everyone needs a little encouragement now and again. Even you."

I smirked at that, raising an eyebrow. "You sound surprised."

She chuckled, tilting her head at me. "You always seem so sure of yourself."

"For the most part I am."

"Then just channel that part of you." Her eyes lowered to our clasped hands. "He always delivers."

I followed her gaze, feeling every jolt as it shot from her skin to mine, my mouth tugging into a curious smile. It was bizarre how such a simple gesture affected me. These weren't butterflies dancing around at her touch…It was an entire stampede. My smile dropped as I considered whether she was feeling those same sparks. Deep down the answer was likely a resounding no. Perhaps once she had. But now? Now she got her butterflies from another guy. A guy who was waiting downstairs, ready to witness the humiliation of Jonathan Taylor.

"I should probably…"

I blinked as the reverie broke. She smiled at me shyly as she slowly withdrew her hand from mine, the cold air hitting it like a slap. I nodded weakly and averted my gaze.

"I'll see you down there?" Brooke peered at me, slipping from the desk.

I nodded dumbly as my mind swam. Although her touch had sent electricity shooting through my body, it had also cleared the fog. Now her hand had left mine, the doubts were back. My fingers twitched towards her as she stepped past me, her movements slow as she walked towards the door. I frowned as she opened it an inch, the low hum from downstairs rising to greet us.

Her hand cradled the wood as she paused, her expression unreadable as she turned back. "Not that you need it, but good luck."

I smiled, nodding as I watched her. "Thanks."

She hesitated a moment longer, a sad smile tugging at her lips as she slipped through the gap, the door closing softly behind her. The sound died, cloaking the room in thick silence as the hour drew closer. I shook my head, running a hand through my hair. She'd be there. Listening. Just as she'd done for years. Except now she knew what the lyrics meant. Who they were for. I frowned at the door. She did know, didn't she? She had to. I was hardly discreet. Confusing, sure. But discreet? Not my style.

I let out a sigh as I stood, pocketing my lighter. I'd run out of time to delay the inevitable. I wanted to enjoy this gig. I wanted to feel like I belonged on that stage, that I deserved to play those songs and they deserved to be heard. Hiding away up here afraid of missing a note wouldn't achieve that. She had faith in me to do this and do it well. So I would.

My eyes fixed on the door she'd gone through, my gaze set as I avoided another glance at the monitors. I steeled myself, taking in a deep breath and shaking it through my limbs. My feet led me towards the door before my head could stop them. The low hum greeted me once more, the excited chatter growing louder with each step I took along the corridor that led back down to the bar. I descended the stairs, my jaw setting in determination. This would be euphoric, and it would hurt. But it was necessary.

I stepped into the room, looking around uneasily at the throng of bodies blocking my way to the stage. The rest of the guys were up there already, equipment primed and ready to go. The lights were beginning to dim on cue, a quiet hush sweeping the crowd as they waited with anticipation. I peered past the wall of teenagers in my path and closed my eyes, conjuring a cordless mic as I finally allowed the bricks around my heart to crumble.

The first image summoned came easily enough. The ghost of her touch was still on my hand as I held the mic to my lips, my mouth parting to quietly sing into the abyss. My voice rose a fraction as I recalled how soft her skin felt, the current of electricity that pulsed as she'd stroked my wrist. With my eyes still closed I thought up the scent of her perfume. The way it would wrap itself around me when she entered a room, the floral scents dancing with something more...exotic. I could never place it, and lately I'd tried to block it out altogether, but the aroma trapped me. It was her all over. A measure of sweetness mixed with something tantalizing and dangerous.

I opened my eyes as the words fell from my lips, a smile tugging at my mouth as those before me stared back in stunned silence. I became aware of the entire room listening as I sang, the gentle rapping of drums filling the space. My smile grew as Alex played some notes on his keyboard, the bass echoing his effort. My voice rose above them as I took a step further into the crowd, their bodies parting wordlessly.

The lyrics poured from my mouth as I moved through the crowd slowly, my voice growing more confident as the walls finally came down. I thought about what it'd been like to kiss her. To feel her wanting me back. The tremble in her lips, the soft whimper as she'd urged her body closer to mine. My heart ached at that memory, but my voice had risen above it, the anguish escaping my mouth. The music picked up as I gripped the shoulder of a bystander, using them to hoist myself onto one of the tables. Teenagers grabbed their drinks with startled laughs, their grins widening as I turned to serenade the entire room.

I closed my eyes, sure that if I were to spot her I'd stumble and fall. The chorus rolled up to greet me and I arched back to really sing the words to them, my free hand outstretching. The sound of their approval rose, the drums thundering as Will drove the song into full force. With the loud orchestra of instruments pulsing around me I pictured the taste of her lips, the beautiful onyx of her eyes, and the smile I'd once upon a time been responsible for. In that brief moment in that tent, I'd made her happy.

Me.

The heat from that night cloaked my skin as I sang, the soft texture of her hair coursing through my outstretched fingers. I smiled and opened my eyes to the ceiling above me, the scattered lights amidst the darkness imitating the glorious night sky I'd stared at before sneaking in to find her. I tore my jacket off, flinging it aside as the humidity warmed my skin. The crowd yelled out gleefully as they threw their hands up to seize the prize, one I wasn't likely to get back. I peered towards the stage and the lights that swam across it in an arc of colors, glimpses of the guys playing reflected in bursts. Two more tables stood between us.

I smirked as I launched myself across to the second, the table leaning with me in the motion. It settled back onto its haunches, not a single beat missed as I repeated the motion to get to the next. As I neared the stage I turned to finally look around at the people who'd come to hear us, taking in the wide grins and nodding heads. They looked happy. Entertained. I crouched to serenade those nearest to me, picturing her shy smile and sweet laughter. As my eyes scanned the crowd, the instruments reaching their peak, I saw her.

She smiled at me through the throng of bodies, the light dancing across her hair and turning it a thousand shades of blue and purple. I smiled back, our gazes locked as I held the mic inches from my lips. Her mouth began to move slowly, her dark eyebrow arching as she sang. The sound was lost in the din, but I grinned and sang back to her, standing to my full height. She beamed back at me, her lips still echoing the lyrics.

I took a step back from the table, outstretched hands guiding me to the stage as I kept my gaze on hers. The grin still played on my lips as I replaced the mic on its stand and drew my guitar around my shoulder, looking to the guy for their attention.

I held my hand up, signaling silence.

The music all dropped at once, a stillness cloaking the entire room.

I heard my own breathing as I stared out at the expectant crowd, glee on their faces as they watched for their next treat.

I waited another beat, allowing the anticipation to build before throwing my hand down to my guitar, my fingers teasing the chords from their slumber. The music thundered around me at the cue, the sheer power of it humbling as I inched towards the mic and sang again. The lights flared to mirror our effort, the smiling faces of each individual reflected back at us. I grinned at them, watching as they tried to move their lips in time to words they'd never heard before. I beckoned them to continue.

To try.

As the song ended, the lights dulled and an odd sense of satisfied silence engulfed us. They brought their hands together to applaud, but before they could get very far I'd begun to play into the next song. The drums held the beat behind me, the bass providing the backbone. I gripped the mic and glanced behind me to see Will straining to get it all exactly right, concentration etched on his face as a sheen of sweat cloaked his arms, soaking through his shirt. My gaze traveled to Ash as he stared down at his bass, his head bowed in thought. He was trying his best not to mess up too, and normally I'd be right there with them. But for the first time in a long time, I wasn't afraid of that. I felt each word and note and I loved them.

Because she was there in all of it.

I could taste it on my lips and feel it in my fingers as I played. It would sound beautiful, because it was her. I looked across at Alex and grinned as he caught my eye, his hands moving deftly across the keyboard. He smiled back, exhilaration evident on his face.

I searched for her again, smiling as I heard the soft crackle of a fire in a campsite. The distant smell of beer and smoke as we locked gazes over a colorful flame. The warmth of her blush as my gaze had lingered on her lips, the ecstasy of her fingertips grazing my jaw. I held her there in my mind, the stars blinking back at us from a clear sky. For each song we played I went back there. To that night where I had her. For a few hours, she was mine and I was hers. The outside world hadn't interrupted us and nothing had been destroyed. There were no rumors, no crossed wires, and no broken hearts.

Just us.

I heard the rasp in my voice as I sang about her, to her. Knowing she was gone. That I'd lost her.

I gripped the mic and moved around the stage, embracing the darkness as the lights escaped me. The music swallowed me as I performed, the melodies coursing through me and commanding me. To sing. To play. To be heard. I'd beckoned the nameless faces to sing along, extending the mic to the ones I could reach. They'd laughed and shaken their heads, cheeks flooding with color as they looked around them in humility. I'd leaned to them and sang with them. I'd shared the words until they were singing them right back, their smiles wide.

And as our final song was coming to its climax, I'd looked around at them all in wonder. I'd felt the heat on my skin, the echo of their voices, and the faint smell of the smoke machines as they plumed across the room. I'd tried to take it all in and savor it. To make it last. My words ceased as the last beats of the song played out, the crowd chanting lines back to me. I cradled the mic and found her again, smiling as I saw her dark eyes glinting proudly, her own lips moving in time.

As the music dulled to a hush, the chanting still breaking through the quiet, I closed my eyes and pulled off a maneuver I hadn't exactly cleared with Brooke's mom. A thunderous noise bellowed out as a sea of metallic confetti drifted down to shower us all.

I watched Brooke grinning up at the ceiling and back at me, the dark silver settling on her like drifts of snow.

I leaned into the mic and waited for the excited chatter to die down a fraction, a smirk playing on my mouth. "We're the Plagiarists."

They screamed and yelled their approval, applause mingling with excited laughter. I stepped back from the mic and lowered my guitar to the ground. The lights dimmed as I moved in a daze from the stage, my body a polar mix of exhausted and exhilarated. I reached the bar and, gripping the edge as I fought to wipe the smile from my lips. The lights in the room returned to normal, revealing the swarm of sweaty teenagers as they stood rooted in place, a scattering of confetti coating every surface. I looked around at them in silence, grinning as they began to talk to their friends with rasping voices, their expressions animated.

"That's the best we've ever played!" Will yelled to me, his hands gripping my shoulders.

I laughed, raising an eyebrow as Alex shook his head in disbelief. "That was incredible. Every second."

"Why can't all our gigs be like that?" Ash echoed, grinning as he clapped me on the back.

"Who says they can't?"

We turned in unison to face the guy I'd been stood beside at the bar. He smiled wryly, taking a casual sip of his beer. I frowned at him, tilting my head a little. He looked familiar, but I was sure I hadn't seen him around Boston. He didn't look like he was in any band I'd seen, but…there was something.

"Felix Young." He chuckled, outstretching his hand. "Pleased to meet you."

Shit.

No way.

"I do know you!" I exclaimed, shaking my head as he let out a laugh. "I mean. I'm a big fan."

He smiled quizzically, raising an eyebrow. "I don't think anyone's ever said that to me before."

I realized his hand was still hovering before me and reached out to shake it, grinning as I shook my head again in disbelief. "I've read about you. You have great taste in music."

"Thanks." He smiled, offering a small shrug. "It helps with the job."

Will frowned between us, "You play?"

"Not well." He admitted, "But music has always been my passion, so I found another path to take."

I looked around at the guys with a grin, "This guy represents The Expensive Regrets." They were one of my favorite bands. They'd been around a few years, but their stuff was genius. Each song held a different story. I'd heard the lead singer wrote them all and that was…Well, inspirational. I turned back to him, raising an eyebrow, "You have to let me buy you a drink."

Felix laughed, shaking his head. "I'm pretty sure Leigh wouldn't serve you, but thanks."

I frowned, "You know Leigh?"

He nodded, sipping his beer. "We grew up together."

"Wow…"

He raised an eyebrow at me, glancing to the others.

I exchanged a knowing look with Will before turning back to him. "I have to ask. What'd you think?"

Felix chuckled and gave a small nod as he looked out at the crowd, still chattering excitedly. "I've not seen talent like that in years. You guys have the full package."

"Can I quote you on that?"

Ash arched an eyebrow, "Say yes or he won't stop bugging you."

He let out a laugh. "I don't say things I don't mean."

"Thanks." I beamed, following his gaze. "It'll definitely help with the flyers."

And hopefully keeping the band together another few months.

"Flyers?"

I smiled weakly at him, nodding. "Our gigs haven't exactly had this response so far."

He frowned, turning to face me fully. "What do you think I'm here for?"

"To see Leigh?"

Felix laughed, shrugging. "She is a nice bonus. But no, Brooke asked me if I'd come and listen to you guys. Did she not tell you?"

"No." I shook my head dumbly, "She didn't."

Ash frowned between us. "Brooke set this up?"

"She asked me to listen." Felix clarified, his eyebrow raised. "But no way am I letting you go. So, if you wanna talk business, I'm all ears."

I looked at him, dazed. "You…You wanna sign us?"

"I'd be stupid not to."

The guys stared at me expectantly, before Will stepped forward with a laugh. "Yes. We say yes."

Felix beamed, reaching into his wallet to produce a business card. I smiled shakily as he placed it in my hand. This was actually happening. Unless, I'd fallen asleep in the office and dreamt the whole gig. I became aware of Felix talking and frowned as I tried to pick up on what he'd said.

"I'm moving back to Boston, so I don't have much to work with. But come around to mine one day next week and we'll get the paperwork signed. Start planning your debut."

"Dude!" Alex laughed beside me, clapping me on the shoulder. "You did it."

"We did it." I corrected, looking up at them all with a grin.

Will edged around me to shake Felix's hand, beaming. "You have no idea how much this means to us."

"We have to celebrate!" Ash grinned, leaning across the bar to gesture for service.

I stared back at the card in my hand, my heartbeat quickening as I realized what this meant. Not only that the band was saved, that we could play together and be paid for it, that people would want to hear *our* songs. But that I could keep writing about her. That I could go on picturing her as I sang to crowds. I could feel the way I had tonight over and over. Only…I frowned as I placed the card in my pocket, drawing my gaze to the throngs on the dance floor before the stage. There was something missing. A pretty huge factor, actually. I moved past the guys, staring ahead dumbly. I'd tuned out everything tonight but my heart. And it was still behind the wheel, because it was all I could hear as I edged around excited teenagers to reach the spot I'd last seen her. The electricity began to pulse in my veins as I neared her, gently ushering the others out of my path. Her brown locks came into view, her laughter ringing out.

I reached out to touch her. She glanced back at me with a smile, her dark eyes glistened as she turned to face me. My heart pounded dangerously as her perfume filled my senses, a smile playing on my lips. I inched closer, drawing her into me as I thought of the memory I'd trapped away. The one that brought everything to a head.

I brushed my lips against hers softly, holding her waist to mine as I pictured the way her lips had moved in time to my songs that day too. How sweet they'd sounded on her lips. She froze as she brought her hand to rest against my chest. The kiss was gentle at first, but as her hand relaxed against my muscles I held her closer and urged my mouth against hers. She let out a soft whimper as she returned the kiss, her fingertips gently tracing the contours of my collarbone.

I thought of the first few droplets that had fled the sky, the clouds pushing their way through the clear air above the bandstand. I could feel the chill on my skin as they scattered down. I could see the smile in her eyes as she peered up at the heavens and welcomed the storm. But most of all I could feel her lips on mine as the thunder rolled, the longing unspoken in our kiss. In that moment, it was just us. It was every song I'd written. Every note I'd played.

It was all for that kiss.

She moaned against my lips and drew me closer, gripping the back of my head to hold me to her. I could taste the urgency in the kiss, my hands holding her to me as her fingers coursed through my hair. I wanted to lose myself in her, to only know this moment where she was kissing me with as much desire as I knew I felt for her. It was perfect. It was-

Her hand pushed back against my chest gently, cold air meeting my lips as she pulled away. Her dark eyes were searching, her cheeks flushed as she stared back. I gazed at her silently, lost for words. The soft sound of music rose around us as we returned to the room, bodies coming into focus one by one. Brooke glanced from my eyes to my lips, closing her mouth as she took a step back. Her hands trailed from me slowly, her eyes widening as she looked to the side. I frowned and followed her gaze, my insides becoming lead.

Matt.

Thank You

Dear reader...

I could simply say thank you for buying this book – but I won't.

What I will say is thank you for reading (and hopefully loving) it.

For enduring the more mundane elements (Ash and Alex - I'm

looking at you) and for not just skipping ahead to my chapters.

Although I can understand the temptation.

Seriously though, a lot of hours and passion went into this and I

appreciate you taking the time to lose yourself in it.

You won't regret that decision.

This book begins the story of The Plagiarists, our loves and our

downfalls.

And it is just that – the beginning.

You're in for a hell of a ride.

Jonathan Taylor

P.S. I'd take good care of this – that autograph will be worth
something someday.

About The Author

Casey and Bridget met at college when they were both fresh faced teenagers with a shared love of all things nerdy. Their friendship was automatic due to their combined love of similar books, movies, TV shows and bands.

Over the years these things have been imperative to their friendship, and their love of storytelling, with the pair travelling across cities to catch their favourite musicians, as well as heading 'across the pond' to visit the city they fell in love with and set their story in.

The pair live in England. Casey with her two young children, and Bridget with her fiancé and new baby.

This is their debut novel in the Starstruck series.

They're currently working on the second instalment.

You can follow them at Starstruckbooks on Facebook and Instagram

Printed by Amazon Italia Logistica S.r.l.
Torrazza Piemonte (TO), Italy

13662837R00195